Afternoon Tea at the Sunflower Café

Milly Johnson

W F HOWES LTD

This large print edition published in 2016 by
W F Howes Ltd
Unit 5, St George's House, Rearsby Business Park,
Gaddesby Lane, Rearsby, Leicester LE7 4YH

1 3 5 7 9 10 8 6 4 2

First published in the United Kingdom in 2015
by Simon & Schuster UK Ltd

A CIP catalogue record for this book is available
from the British Library

ISBN 978 1 51003 449 5

Typeset by Palimpsest Book Production Limited,
Falkirk, Stirlingshire

Printed and bound in Great Britain
by TJ International Ltd, Padstow, Cornwall

MIX
Paper from
responsible sources
FSC
www.fsc.org FSC® C013056

For my nanna Hubbard.
A woman who loved her cakes and
was the best cleaner in Christendom.
I miss you.

A smart girl leaves before she is left.

MARILYN MONROE

PROLOGUE

The awning that hangs over the window is a tired yellow and white stripe and much of the paint has flaked off the sign above the door announcing that this is The Sunflower Café. On a quiet lane in the village of Pogley Top, it barely registers as a place of interest. But should your eye venture past the unspectacular façade and you push open the door and walk in, you would find yellow walls as cheerful as sunshine, pretty sky-blue curtains dotted with sunflowers and a long window affording the village's prettiest view of the adjacent stream. You would find a warmth as if the café has a spirit that welcomes you and is happiest when filled with laughter and chatter. Of the women who visit here to partake of the owner's delicious and generous afternoon teas, many of them are like the café – you would never guess what beauty and strength sit beneath the ordinary outside.

Hung up are many pictures of sunflowers but one, near the door, in particular catches the eye. Underneath the smiling giant petalled head is written a poem:

Be Like the Sunflower
Brave, bright
bold, cheery
Be golden and shine
Keep your roots strong
Your head held high
Your face to the sun
And the shadows will fall behind you

This is the story of three women who never realised they had the capacity to be the tallest, boldest, brightest flowers in the field.

CHAPTER 1

When Jimmy Diamond told Della on Thursday morning that she would have to cancel her day off on Friday, he could not have known what wheels he had started in motion.

When Della protested and said that she'd had it booked for weeks; it was her old boss's retirement party, Jimmy still insisted that she couldn't take it.

He said no.

In the fifteen years she had worked for him, he had never said no before. He might have man-grumbled a bit under his breath when she asked for a favour, but he knew what side his bread was buttered where Della was concerned. He would never have found anyone else who worked over and above the call of duty as she did, watching his back, doing his dirty work, covering his tracks more than Della did and if she had to take a rare afternoon off for a dental appointment or if there was a panic on with her elderly mother, it had never been a problem before.

Had he said yes, this story would never have

been told and life would have trundled on in much the same way as it had for years. One woman would have continued to exist unhappily on the begging end of a non-relationship and one woman would have eaten the equivalent weight of a small emergent country in truffles. But Jimmy Diamond had said no.

The office junior Ivanka had turned up to work that Thursday morning acting limp and tearful with a sickness and diarrhoea bug, obviously unfit to work, so Della had sent her back home again. Ivanka had protested a little before relenting and saying that she would be in after the weekend. Then Jimmy breezed in and announced that he was off that afternoon to schmooze on a golf course and wouldn't be back until Tuesday. When Della reminded him that she had booked Friday off, Jimmy had thrown up his hands and said that someone was needed in the office and as he couldn't be there and she had sent Ivanka home, who did that leave? Nope, there was nothing for it: as office manageress, it was Della's duty to be there, especially in such a busy period. Once upon a time, cleaners had been ten a penny, now demand outstripped supply and they were like gold dust. Della's attendance was needed more in manning the phones than it was in Whitby, eating vol au vents and drinking warm white wine out of a plastic tumbler at the party of a bloke who probably wouldn't even remember who she was, said Jimmy firmly.

4

'Of course he'll remember who I am,' said Della, her mouth a defiant thin line. 'I worked for him longer than I've worked for you.'

Della saw the features of his face soften and she guessed he was about to change tactic.

'Oh, Dells,' he sighed and held out his hands in a gesture of apologetic surrender. 'Of *course* he'd remember you. But he won't *need* you like I do. I *have* to go on this golfing weekend with Pookie Barnes. I owe him after he's shifted all his business to us from Cleancheap and he's making noises about recommending our girls to clean the offices of his contacts. I have to keep him on side. I hear that Roy Frog is hopping about it.'

Jimmy laughed at his own joke. He and Roy Frog's firm Cleancheap had a long-standing rivalry. Della knew that it was thanks to Jimmy's schmoozing that Pookie Barnes, Cleancheap's biggest customer, had jumped ship faster than a rat on the *Titanic* wearing a lifejacket.

Still Della tried to reason with him. 'Jimmy . . .'

'You shouldn't have let that Ivanka go home.' He wagged his finger at her, intimating that this situation was of her own doing. He always referred to the office junior as *that Ivanka* as if she still wasn't part of the Diamond Shine crew despite working there for six months.

'I couldn't exactly chain her to the desk, could I?' replied Della. 'Besides which, she wouldn't have been much use in her state.'

'I've worked through worse.'

'Well good for you, but the lass wasn't putting it on. Any idiot could have seen that. Bed was the best place for her.'

'Aye, I suppose you're right. She should spend the day in bed.' He grinned. 'Send your old inferior boss a present instead with apologies for your absence.'

'It might not arrive in time.'

'Send him a bottle of champagne. On me. Overnight delivery.'

If Della's eyes had opened any further they would have burst out of their orbits and dropped onto the desk. Jimmy Diamond was as tight as a duck's stitched-up arse. He would sooner have cut his own balls off than paid next day delivery on anything, never mind champagne for a bloke he didn't even know. He must be desperate for her to cover the office if he was offering to go to those lengths.

'I can tell what you're thinking,' said Jimmy, guessing correctly. 'I'm not exactly famous for charging champagne to the company account for people I don't know, but I *really* need you here, we're too busy for you to be off at the moment. Come on, Dells, don't be mad with me.'

He gave her his best round puppy-dog eyes.

'Okay, Della, what do I have to do for us not to fall out about this? Do you want me to beg? Look, I'm begging,' and Jimmy got down on his knees and clenched his hands together as if praying to her.

'Oh get up, you fool,' said Della, trying her best to remain annoyed.

'I love you, Della. You know I do.'

Oh, if only, thought Della.

'And you love me, which is why you're going to send that bloke some champagne instead of going to his crap party.'

He was right.

'Please please please, Dells. Be my friend and tell me that you agree with me,' Jimmy insisted until her face broke into a resigned smile and she knew that he had won her over. Again. He always could because with the tiniest bit of flirting, a little bodily contact, the mere hint of appeal in his voice, she was putty in his hands and had been for fifteen years.

'Don't go mad though. No frigging Dom Perignon. Bubbles is bubbles.'

That sounded more like him. He hasn't gone totally mad after all, thought Della.

'Oh, and order some chocs for the missus will you, love. Top notch, big box.'

Della sighed. 'Okay. If I must.'

She had really wanted to go to Whitby, but Jimmy needed her. And Jimmy was the number one man in her life, as she was his number one woman. Despite what Connie, his Lady Muck of a wife, might have thought.

CHAPTER 2

In one single hour, Cheryl Parker's whole existence had tipped upside down and her insides had been scooped out. At least that's what it felt like as she stood in her tiny kitchen, hand shaking as she gripped the piece of paper which had ended her life as she knew it.

She wished life were like TV. She wished she could press the rewind button back to just before she had opened the envelope. She wished she had put it on one side until she returned from work so that Gary could have found it first and had time to think up an excuse which she might have swallowed and life would have carried on as normal. But she *had* opened it and what she had found could not be unread. An hour ago she had been making breakfast toast and tea for two whilst Gary was taking a shower and it was just a normal Thursday morning; two more days at work to get out of the way and then the familiar joy of the weekend to look forward to: fish and chips from Cod's Gift with Gary for Saturday lunch as usual, a bottle of wine and some beers in front of *Ant and Dec* on the TV. Now she was

8

alone – single – and couldn't think past the moment. And her heart had been ripped out and stamped all over.

The postman hardly ever came first thing in the morning, but today he had. And he had delivered three envelopes: one containing a catalogue full of rubbishy gadgets, a dental reminder for Cheryl and *that* one from the building society. A quarterly statement. And Cheryl had opened it and found that the account which should have had four thousand seven hundred and twenty pounds in it, had a nil balance.

She didn't know how long she stood there, unable to move, listening to Gary mooching about upstairs. She imagined him towel-drying his thick light-brown hair, spraying a cloud of Lynx over himself, getting dressed, blissfully unaware of what trauma his long-term girlfriend was going through. Cheryl heard his feet on the stairs, watched the door into the kitchen open. She saw his eyes lock on to the paper she was holding, then flick up to her face and from the expression she was wearing, he knew instantly what she had discovered.

The words came out in a croak. 'Where's it gone, Gary? Where's the money?' It was a rhetorical question because she knew. She would have bet her life savings – *oh, the irony* – that the money was in the till of William Hill.

Gary's eyes began to flicker, which they did when he was anxious. She knew that his brain would be scrabbling around for something viable to tell her.

'You won't believe me . . .' he began eventually. No, she wouldn't. Because she had wanted to believe him every single time and every single time he had let her down.

'Try me,' she said. Deep down she wished he would say those words which would make it all right. But also, deeper down, she knew he wouldn't.

'You weren't supposed to know. I was hoping to have it back in the account before you noticed,' he said. His hands were in his hair. 'Oh God, Chez, I am so sorry. I thought I could do it. One last time. For us. For the ba—'

'No!' The loudness in her own voice surprised her. 'Don't you dare say it. Don't you DARE.'

He had used those same words eighteen months ago. He had taken the money she had scrimped and squirrelled away for IVF treatment in the hope of doubling it, trebling it even, he said. He'd been given a tip – a sure thing from someone in the know. She would never forget the name of the horse as long as she lived – *Babyface*. He had put every penny on its nose and it had come in second. And he had cried and she had comforted him and told him that she forgave him but this was the last chance – no more gambling. And he had given her his word that he would never bet on another horse or dog ever. And she had started saving all over again and had been stupid enough to give him the benefit of the doubt and keep

10

their joint account going as a sign of her trust in his ability to change.

But he would never change, she knew that now. They'd reached the end of the road. Actually they'd done that eighteen months ago and now they were well off the beaten track, stumbling over increasingly rough terrain until they had arrived at this point and could go no further. For ten years she had listened to his Del-boy Trotter promises that 'this time next year they would be millionaires' and yet they were still living in the same tiny two-up, two-down rented house with no garden and damp patches on the walls because Gary had been convinced he could win his fortune. For ten years she had been trapped in a vicious circle of her saving a bit of money in a teapot, him gambling his wage away, her having to borrow back from the teapot, him promising to alter his ways and doing it for a couple of months, him gambling his wage away . . . This time her heart would not be penetrated by the sight of the tears slipping down his face.

When she looked back later, she couldn't remember in detail what words had been said that day. She told him it was over and he knew somehow that she meant it this time. He asked her if he should leave and she said yes. He packed a few things in a suitcase and wiped his eyes, telling her that he was sorry and he loved her and he'd put the money back whatever happened. He promised. She hadn't believed him. She hadn't attached any faith to his words, she'd seen them for the bullshit they were. Then he had walked out with his head bent low to the same battered car they'd had for the past eight years. And it hadn't been new when they'd bought it.

Cheryl listened to the car starting, heard the engine chugging: the hole in the exhaust was getting worse. Her ear followed the rattle until it was no longer discernible and she hiccupped a single sob, as she felt whatever it was that had held them together finally stretch to its limit and then snap.

Don't you dare, she said to herself. *Don't you dare cry one more tear over that man. Haven't you shed enough?*

Enough to fill five mop buckets over the years. And she had enough tears inside her now to fill another. She daren't let a single one drop out because it would be quickly joined by thousands more. Something inside her groaned, probably her stomach, but it sounded as if her heart had cracked. And she felt as if it had, too.

She threw the building society statement down on the work surface and picked up her bag full of cleaning stuff. She was doing her monthly blitz on Mr Ackworth's house this morning, which she hated because he barked orders at her as if she were a dog, then a four-hander at her favourite client's with lazy Ruth Fallis, then a one-off clean in an office. It was going to be a long, hard day.

She needed to get to work, keep busy and not think about anything but the jobs in hand. *If only life could be spruced up and made perfect with a J-cloth and a spray of Mr Sheen*, she thought as she realised that if today wasn't bad enough already, she'd have to get the bus to work from now on.

CHAPTER 3

'And I don't touch bleach; brings me out in blisters, even through gloves. I . . . don't climb ladders to do windows and I don't scrub floors by hand. It's mop, Hoover or nowt. And I can't bend to do skirting boards because I've got a problem with a disc. And I've got a bad knee so I don't do kneeling either.' Lesley Clamp dictated the last of her non-negotiable working terms and sat back in the chair.

Della clung on to her patience as well as a strained rictus smile after hearing the long list of 'won't dos'. This was all she needed today. How Lesley Clamp had managed to clock up twenty years as a self-professed highly praised cleaner when she was either allergic to or refused to touch most of the contents of a house was beyond her. The good news was that Lesley could work quite happily with lemon juice, vinegar, salt and newspaper. Della was tempted to tell her that she'd be better off getting a job in a chip shop, then. Della had a thick rejection file in her drawer of people that she wouldn't employ in a million years. Lesley Clamp's name would be joining it shortly.

'If we take you on, we will supply you with your cleaning equipment,' began Della. Not that Lesley Clamp would need to know that, because Diamond Shine would not be taking her on. The woman smelt of trouble. She was the type who'd complain about everyone and everything and Jimmy wouldn't fork out for fripperies like non-latex specialist gloves and branded goods like Cillit Bang. Although Des's Discount Warehouse did an import version called 'Fillit Bong,' which once burst into flame and burnt off Ruth Fallis's eyebrow when she squirted it on a work surface whilst smoking a fag.

'We pay the minimum wage per hour . . .'

'Is that all?' humphed Lesley. 'You must be creaming the profits, then?'

Della so wanted this miserable sow out of her office. She should be planning a jolly trip to Whitby, not staring at the hairy mole on Lesley Clamp's sneering top lip.

'We supply a guaranteed wage, insurance, cleaning supplies and back-up service when clients are difficult. Those are the things you get in return for paying administration costs, Mrs Clamp.'

Lesley huffed again. 'I had a pound an hour above minimum wage at Dreamclean.'

And Dreamclean were unorganised and chucked money away and went down the pan, which is why you're here asking me for a job, thought Della to herself. *And no way did they offer a pound above minimum wage either, but nice try, Lesley.* No, she decided. Desperate as they were for more cleaners, there was no way she could employ this awful woman.

'I'm afraid that's the standard rate for everyone. I'm so sorry that we aren't suitable for your requireme—'

'I didn't say that,' replied Lesley with an impatient snap in her voice. 'It's just less than I'm used to.'

Della had had enough for this afternoon. She'd ordered chocolates for Jimmy's fat wife and had interviewed three badly needed potential cleaners so far today and not one was up to the standard she expected. Her reject file was as full as her potential file was empty. She stood up to indicate this meeting was at a close.

'I'll be contacting the successful applicants by the end of next week,' she said. 'I have your number, Mrs Clamp, and I'll be in touch.' God help Mr Clamp.

Lesley Clamp rose to her fat little feet. She looked so much older than the forty-five years she purported to be in her Miss Marple shoes and her thick tweed coat straining across her swollen bosom and stomach.

'Oh and I can't do Wednesdays or after three on Fridays,' she said at the door, turning to deliver a parting shot.

Della dropped onto the chair and blew out two relieved cheekfuls of air. She should have known that the chances were anyone with 'Clamp' as a surname would be a no-go, but she didn't think

16

it fair to tar everyone with the same brush, since Josie Clamp had been one of their star workers until her death two years ago. The Clamps were one of the town's most notorious families, along with the Crookes, the Bellfields and the O'Gowans; but the Clamps were by far the biggest. For decades past, there hadn't been a month when the Clamp name wasn't mentioned in either the *Barnsley Chronicle* or the *Daily Trumpet* for some misdemeanour or other, from the days of that notorious old confidence trickster 'Velvet' Vernon Clamp, right down to the present generation. Only last week, one of the younger lot – the inaptly named 'Chiffon' Clamp, had been given two hundred hours community service for shoplifting booze from Morrisons. And the papers had reported – God forbid – her cousin Mandy's marriage to one of the Crooke boys. They'd already started to push out a brood of hybrid villains into the world with twins Sinitta-Paris and Brooklyn-Jaiden.

Della wished that Ivanka had been there to put the kettle on for her because she could murder a rest and a cup of tea. She thought back to how pale the poor girl had been that morning. Della had grown quite fond of Ivanka in the time they'd worked together and hoped she'd be all right, as she lived alone.

Admittedly Della hadn't been best pleased six months ago when Jimmy had suggested they employ an office junior. She wasn't comfortable

17

with having another female around, even if she really did need some help with her workload. Jimmy had insisted, though.

'Get one of those East European girls,' he had told her. 'They work for peanuts.'

Typical Jimmy. Not one to splash the cash and when he did, it was more than likely because he was up to something, as Della knew too well. So Ivanka joined them. Nineteen years old, tall, curvy and leggy, with tumbles of bottle-blonde hair which by rights should have sealed Della's disapproval, because Jimmy Diamond had a sweet tooth for eye candy and there was no way that Della would have employed a rival for her idol's affections. But whilst Della had noticed Jimmy's eyes sweep over the legs of the brunette and over the bum of the redhead who came to be interviewed for the post, they barely acknowledged the existence of Miss Ivanka Szczepanska. In fact the only two comments he made after seeing her were, one: *She's got a lot of spots, hasn't she?* And two: *Her name must sweep up the points on a Scrabble board.*

Ivanka fitted in surprisingly well. She was quiet, with a terrible phone manner, but she seemed to want to learn everything that running an office entailed, albeit at a very relaxed pace. Still, it was a relief for Della to be able to hand over a chunk of her workload, even if Ivanka didn't seem very keen on doing the more mundane office junior jobs such as filing and making the tea. Ivanka would take an age to boil a kettle and strung out her trips to the post office, but Della found that she liked having another presence in the office and Ivanka's surly ways amused her more than they annoyed her. Della got the impression, from the snippets that Ivanka supplied, that her home life in Poland hadn't been up to much. She didn't seem very close to her parents, which Della could relate to, and Della had to admire such a young girl moving over to a strange country in the hope of making something of herself. Though her parents remained in Krakow, Ivanka did have a few relatives who had moved to the area and she saw them quite often, which Della thought must be nice for her. In short, Della was grateful for Ivanka's company and extra pair of hands, especially as those hands seemed to be as invisible to Jimmy as the rest of her was.

Della went into the small office kitchen and made herself a cup of strong tea. She even allowed herself a consoling Oreo from the tin today, even though she didn't usually partake of biscuits or chocolate, unlike Jimmy's wife who most certainly did. Connie Diamond, according to how Della pictured her, must be a chocolate-filled, pampered whale with a blood group of gat-O positive by now. Even Jimmy had said before that Cadbury's would be out of business if it wasn't for his wife. Della had never been one for snacking, except on the odd banana, which is why she still tipped the scales at no more than eight stone – the same weight she had been thirty years ago when she was twenty-one.

'Hello, only me,' said a voice from the front office, just as Della had finished off the last of her biscuit. 'Anyone in?'

Della stepped back through to find the enormous square bulk of Pookie Barnes. He always looked as if he had shoplifted a forty-two inch TV and was smuggling it inside his clothes.

'Thought I'd walked onto the *Marie Celeste* for a moment there.' Pookie's lips wore their usual broad smile, but it was one that should never be trusted – a crocodile-fake arc of teeth. Della always imagined that he would have the same expression whether he won the lottery or was waterboarding a business rival.

'Thought I'd drag him out for an hour. You can spare him, can't you? Where is he?' wheezed Pookie, still breathless from climbing the stairs.

'He's on a golf course in Hampshire with you,' said Della, her calm collected exterior masking the grip of the horrible confusion which had suddenly seized her whole body.

'Oh shit.' Pookie's ever-present grin momentarily dropped from his face as he realised his faux pas, but he was as slippery as a greased eel and would wriggle hard to get himself out of any situation. He raised his finger to indicate a recall of memory. 'Ah, I forgot he was going on ahead. I had a bit of unexpected business to do. Cropped up last minute.' That plastic smile was back sitting comfortably once again on his lips. 'I might as well set off down to Evertrees in Hampshire sooner rather than later then if he's waiting for me.'

He's emphasising the destination so that I know where he was supposed to be going, thought Della. He must think I'm daft.

Pookie's fleshy neck was growing more purple-crimson around his collar. He might have been able to hang on to his composure, but he didn't have much control over his blood pressure, or the vein in his forehead that looked as if it might pop at any minute.

'No need to mention I dropped by,' he said, tapping the side of his bulbous nose. 'Don't want old Jim thinking I was dragging my feet going down there. I said I'd meet him in the nineteeth hole at four. I better ring him and tell him that I'm stuck in traffic.'

'Have a good time,' Della said with as much sweetness as she could muster. 'And don't worry, your secret is safe with me.' She tapped her considerably slimmer nose twice and smiled.

Pookie turned on his heel and was out of the door as fast as his stubby little legs could carry him. Della locked the door behind him and sank onto the nearest chair before she fell, because she felt as if someone had taken all the bones out of her legs and replaced them with jelly. She wasn't fooled by Pookie's attempted patching of the situation. He was no more meeting with Jimmy that afternoon than she could audition to be a Playboy bunny.

Jimmy had lied to her.

Why, why would he start to lie to her after all these years of trusting her with all his dodgiest secrets?

In the fifteen years she had worked for Jimmy Diamond, she had never known him to keep things from her before – and Della thought she could smell a fib from three hundred paces. But he had today – and why, because he had no reason to. She knew about his tax fiddles and his double-dealings and his many short-lived dalliances. She'd even lied for him to his wife when Jimmy was cosying up to some fancy piece and Connie rang up asking to speak to him. She even booked the hotels for Jimmy to do his cosying up in. She didn't feel a jot of guilt about doing it either; in fact – were she to admit it – she felt a hit of glee that he disrespected his wife so much. It convinced her that there was no connection between them, that their marriage was hanging on by a thread and one day that thread would finally break and he would come to her, his soul-mate, the woman who knew everything about him and accepted him and adored him.

She never felt threatened by Jimmy's flings. He didn't go into detail about them, but from the little hints he dropped, Della knew that they were 'a scratch to an itch' because he wasn't 'getting it' at home, which Della was glad about because she was wildly jealous of Connie Diamond's position as the woman who had his name.

So why hadn't Jimmy told Della where he was really going? All she knew was that whatever the reason, it had to be something significant.

Della flew to her desk and ripped off the key which was stuck to the back of the drawer with brown sticky tape. Jimmy didn't know she had access to the locked bottom drawer in his own desk. She couldn't remember when she had last snooped but it was certainly over a year and a half ago and she'd never found anything in it that she didn't know about already.

This time was different.

This time she found a large brown envelope and it was stuffed full of receipts. A receipt for a silver heart-shaped locket from Tiffany. Receipts for overnight stays and dinner for two in five-star hotels in the centre of London and theatre tickets. Receipts for flowers, a teddy bear, a bracelet, earrings, clothes. A CAR – Della gasped, an Audi TT and brand new at that. Thank goodness Jimmy was so tight he had hung on to them all. He might not have been able to put these through the office books, but he was holding them in case he could find some other way of getting some tax relief.

Ivanka wore a heart-shaped silver locket. And she drove an Audi TT. She had saved up years for it, she'd told Della four months ago when she proudly first drove it into their car park. Her cousin, a garage mechanic, had got her a terrific deal on it.

And, if the next receipt which Della picked up was anything to go by, Jimmy Diamond wasn't waiting for Pookie Barnes in a golf club bar in Hampshire, he was on a last-minute-booked, long weekend break in a very swanky hotel in the Costa Blanca with a certain Miss Ivanka Szczepanska.

CHAPTER 4

When Cheryl got to Mr Ackworth's house, she found a note on the kitchen table to say that he was out. Normally that would have cheered her but her heart felt too physically weighed down with sadness and she cried as she vacuumed and mopped and dusted, periodically having to stop and clear her eyes of the tears obscuring her vision.

She wished there'd been someone she could have rung up and poured everything out to, a close friend who would be there on her doorstep after work with cake and a bottle of wine, but there was no one. She had a sister, but she was a wrong 'un and they didn't talk and her mother had always put bingo, blokes and booze before her daughters. The friends she had had at school and college had all moved upwards and onwards to good jobs and other friendship groups. She and Gary occasionally went out in couples with his mates and their partners, but the girls were already in a clique which she didn't belong to and wouldn't have wanted to, either. Her only friends were her fellow cleaners with whom she met up once a month for a joint moan over tea, sandwiches and scones at the Sunflower Café. She was fond of them, but she had her pride and wouldn't have wanted them to know how much – and how many times – she'd been duped by the same man. There was no one whose shoulder she could cry on. She was alone.

She wished she didn't have to work at Edith's with Ruth Fallis today. She usually loved her afternoons at Brambles Cottage but Ruth Fallis was a horrible woman and why Della had chosen her of all people to share the shift with was anyone's guess. Ruth Fallis was the laziest cow walking so it was no surprise to Cheryl that Ruth hadn't arrived by the time she got to Edith Gardiner's house, and she was fifteen minutes late herself because of roadworks holding up the bus.

Cheryl walked up the path to Brambles and, as always, a wistful sigh escaped her as she came to the bright green front door. It was such a pretty place, biscuit-tin beautiful with lots of little windows and white stone walls. It was the sort of house that the other Cheryl Parker, in a parallel universe, lived in. That Cheryl Parker wasn't pushing down on her heartbreak in order to get through the day. That Cheryl was solvent and happily single and tended to the garden of Brambles with all the zeal that Edith did.

Ernest Gardiner had built the cottage for his new bride and they had lived happily together there until his death thirty-three years ago. Brambles itself wasn't huge, but the garden which

26

surrounded it on all four sides was, and until eight years ago, when she was eighty-five, Edith had maintained it alone. Now she employed the services of a local gardener: something which Lance, Edith's nephew, had been less than happy about when he arrived on the scene a few months ago. He obviously didn't want to see any of his inheritance frittered away on 'domestics'. Despite only living a few miles away in Wakefield, he hadn't ever visited his aunt before last August. There had been a huge falling out in Edith's family years ago and it was only when Lance's parents died that he made contact with his aunt again via a Christmas card promising to come and see her when he wasn't so busy. Ten years passed and he had never done so, although he rang to enquire after her health every few months. Then Edith had let it slip in a conversation with him that she was considering increasing her bequest to 'those kind people from the Maud Haworth home for cats' and suddenly Lance could find the time to drive over – and quite often too, always with a pack of cheap biscuits by way of a sweetener. They weren't even branded biscuits: they were Pricechopper's own. Cheryl didn't like Lance, he was spiv-smarmy with greased dyed black hair and a lot of sly activity going on behind his little piggy eyes. It wasn't her place to say anything but whenever she happened to be in the house when he was there, she kept her eyes peeled. She was very fond of Edith and felt fiercely protective towards her.

'Only me,' said Cheryl, knocking twice on the door before opening it and walking in. Oh, how she wished Brambles was hers. It had such a lovely feel to it, as if all the people who had ever visited had left a smile behind.

'Good morning, dear Cheryl, I'm in here,' Edith called from the light-filled kitchen which doubled up as her garden room. She was taking bulbs out of pots and wrapping them up in newspaper.

'I shall repot these before Christmas so they flower again and brighten next January. Such a dull and depressing month,' she said. 'I do love hyacinths. Now, let me put that kettle on for us.'

'No, don't worry,' said Cheryl. 'I won't have time for a cuppa today. Sorry I was late. There were roadworks. But don't you worry: I'll be here for the full one and a half hours. You do remember I'm only here for half the time today?'

'Sorry, dear, remind me again what's happening,' said Edith, nudging a stray lock of snow-white hair back in place. 'Why is the other lady coming?'

'Because I've got another job booked in straight after this one,' Cheryl explained clearly and patiently again. 'Someone wants their offices spruced up because they're having a visit from some top brass tomorrow so rather than me do a three-hour clean by myself, there will be two of us doing an hour and a half.'

'Ah yes, I remember now. The other lady hasn't turned up yet. I imagine she's been caught up in the roadworks too,' said Edith.

'Probably,' Cheryl nodded, though she doubted it. Ruth was notorious for always arriving at jobs late and leaving them early. Jimmy had employed Ruth Fallis, she wouldn't have got past an interview with Della.

'Everything all right, dear? You don't look yourself,' Despite her age and rheumy eyes and foggy memory, Edith could spot that Cheryl wasn't on top form.

'Bit tired,' said Cheryl, pushing out a smile. 'I'm ready for a rest at the weekend.'

She noticed two cups by the sink and an open packet of Pricechopper ginger nuts on the work surface.

'You've just missed Lance,' said Edith, following her line of vision. 'He brought me some biscuits. I asked him to try and find me some Gypsy Creams but I don't think they make them any more. I like them better with cream in the middle. These are a bit hard for my teeth.'

Cheryl tried to stop her lip from curling at the thought of him smarming around Edith. As she went over to wash the cups, she noticed Edith's chequebook was wedged in the runner of the odds and sods drawer, preventing it from closing. Cheryl had to manipulate it back and forth to free it.

'What is it, Cheryl?' asked Edith.

'It's your chequebook. It's jammed and I don't want to tear any of the pages.'

'Oh it doesn't matter,' said Edith. 'I don't write cheques anyway.'

When Cheryl managed to release it, she made a pretence of examining it for rips, but noticed five cheques had been taken out and no details had been recorded. They weren't in sequence, either, as if they had been removed in order not to arouse suspicion. It didn't take a genius to work out what was happening. What she could do about it was another matter.

'You should check your bank accounts from time to time, Edith. Just to make sure you know where you are with them,' said Cheryl, not wanting to distress Edith, but trying at the same time to put her on her guard.

Edith flapped her hand. 'I can't be doing with all those figures. Oh, by the way, you'll notice that I've moved the Renoir. I thought it might look better in the lounge than in the hallway.'

Cheryl turned around sharply. 'Edith. How the heck did you get it off the wall, never mind back up on another one?'

'Step ladder of course,' replied Edith. 'Don't you tell me off; I took it slowly.'

'You should have waited for me.' Cheryl shook her head. The old lady was incorrigible. 'Or asked your Lance to do it.' Then again, it would probably suit Lance if his aunt fell off the ladder and snuffed it. He wouldn't have to sneak around stealing blank cheques. 'Please tell me that you don't take that ladder upstairs and change the paintings around.'

'No, silly.' Edith dismissed such a ridiculous

suggestion with a roll of her eyes. 'Only the down-stairs ones. All my artists upstairs are happy where they are and I think the downstairs lot are too now, so there will be no more changing. I feel Mr Renoir will be much happier in the lounge with Mr Monet. They were great friends in person, you know.'

Bless her, thought Cheryl. Edith was, like the ginger nuts, a few biscuits short of the packet. She truly believed that all the paintings in her house were originals: the Monet and the Renoir, now in the lounge, and a Mona Lisa hanging in the spare bedroom, amongst others. Edith's grand-father Percy Lake, so she said, was a painter himself who'd been friends with Van Gogh.

'My *Sunflowers* are the most precious of all the works here, you remember that,' Edith once confided quietly in her. *If that were true then Van Gogh must have done them in his blind drunk phase,* thought Cheryl, because the painting was terrible. A five-year-old kid with a blindfold on could have done better.

Cheryl felt Edith's small bony hand on hers. 'Cheryl, I have something to tell you. Something you're going to like. Guess what I'm going to do . . .'

Then there was a knock on the door and the moment was broken, and Cheryl didn't find out what Edith was about to say. Ruth had arrived. Edith went to let her in.

'Freezing in here,' she shuddered as she walked into the kitchen. She nodded at Cheryl. 'Alreight?'

31

'Fine. Are you?' replied Cheryl, catching a whiff of Ruth's smoky aroma.

'Aye, not bad.'

'Lance is always cold here too, but I never am,' said Edith, shaking her head. 'I can't understand it.'

If anyone was going to feel the cold, it would be Edith, who was tiny, with paper-thin skin. Cheryl never felt it either. Maybe the house only saved its inviting warmth for nice people, she thought. And Lance was not nice. *He looks like a Lance* had been her first thought when she'd found him a few months ago ensconced in the lounge drinking tea. He was tall, straight and skinny, with an angular face and a beaky nose which had a precise black line of moustache running underneath it. He had long thin fingers, a mean mouth and sharp little bird eyes, He had looked Cheryl up and down with disdain and suspicion, and she'd heard him say to his aunt, when she was barely out of earshot, 'Can you trust that woman in your house?'

The bloody cheek of it, even more so from seeing Edith's plundered cheque book that morning. She would make sure when their paths next crossed that she let him know that she'd asked Edith to check her bank account for fraudulent withdrawals.

Ruth had a cup of tea and five ginger nuts before unzipping her cleaning bag, by which time Cheryl had already done Edith's bedroom. They met on the landing. Ruth shivered as she squirted some polish onto a duster and tackled all the surfaces she could find at waist height. Trust her not to get down on her hands and knees and wipe down the skirting boards, thought Cheryl.

'Creepy, this house, innit?' said Ruth when they had moved downstairs. 'I heard this whole area was built on an old Red Indian burial ground.'

Cheryl fought the urge to laugh out loud. 'Really?' she said, thinking that Ruth Fallis had about as many brain cells as she did work cells. Norma Know-it-All, the others called her.

'Not that it bothers me. There's no house creepier than Mr Savant's. Eh, she's got a bob or two, 'asn't she?' said Ruth, in a loud stage whisper. 'Jock would love to have a look around here.'

Her husband Jock Fallis was a local antiques dealer. At least that's what he imagined himself to be. His shop was a mucky little hole full of junk down by the Carlton village scrapyards. Jock Fallis was the type who would rip off his own granny for a penny; Cheryl hoped he wouldn't come sniffing around here asking if Edith had anything to sell, and so she tried to put Ruth off the scent.

'Naw, it's all car boot rubbish,' she said. 'She's only got her pension. House is falling to bits.' As if to validate her story, at that very moment a chunk of plaster fell onto the floor from the side of the window. *Now would you believe that,* thought Cheryl with a secret grin. The house seemed to be on her side.

Cheryl rinsed out her cloth and washed down some fingerprints on the walls. She needed to keep busy, keep her mind from second-guessing what Gary would be doing now, what would be going through his head. Where would he sleep tonight? Cheryl assumed at his mother's or his sister's – either way she'd feel her ears burning because Gary's account of the split would be twisted to make her the villain of the piece. However much she tried to firewall them though, questions she didn't want to answer broke through: How would she manage to pay all the rent by herself? How would she cope without having use of the car? What would it be like to sit in the house by herself night after night?

She hadn't planned her life to be like this and it scared her that she couldn't see past this present depression. Material things had never been top of her wish-list, but a family was. She wanted a child to love so much, a child to bring up in the sort of family she had always wanted for herself: mum and dad, a strong unit, a warm house – not necessarily big – but clean and comfortable with plenty of food in the cupboards and lots of love in it. She and Gary had been given two chances at IVF on the NHS but both had failed and now it was down to them to fund it. She did cash-in-hand work cleaning the local pub when their regular woman let them down to bring in some extra money, and put away as much as she could in the building society. The joke wasn't lost on her that she'd lectured Edith on keeping an eye on her savings when she hadn't done so with her own. But Gary hadn't just emptied their account; he had emptied her trust. He had emptied her heart. He had emptied her womb.

The text alert on her phone went off and she dived out into the hallway to see if it was Gary. She pulled the phone out of her coat pocket, heart springing with anticipation, then felt the heavy plunge of disappointment to find it was Dominos Pizzas informing her that there was a special offer on. As she was returning to the lounge, she was aware that something wasn't quite right. She took a few steps back and swept her eyes around the hallway but couldn't put her finger on what was bothering her. Odd, she thought. But then, this whole day had been odd.

Five minutes passed, then Ruth appeared in the doorway with her coat on.

'There, that's me done. I'm off.'

Cheryl looked across to the clock on the wall. 'Er, I don't think so. You've half an hour to go. You were twenty minutes late, remember.'

Ruth pulled a face. 'Hark at you, the cleaning police.'

'No I'm not, but I do the hours I'm paid for.' Cheryl jiggled the rocking chair back into place and caught her ankle on the edge. The pain that flared up made her want to kick something. Or someone. But she couldn't stop Ruth going home, could she? The most she could do was look annoyed and huff a bit.

'Have you any spare window cleaner?' asked Cheryl. 'I've run out.'

'Loads. I'll get it for you,' said Ruth. It was probably the same bottle she'd started out with two years ago, thought Cheryl.

She followed Ruth back into the hallway and again that odd feeling visited her. As Ruth foraged in her bag for the window cleaner, Cheryl's eyes roved slowly up and down and along the walls, determined to discover what was bugging her. It was when they came to the console table in front of the radiator that she realised what it was: a small oval porcelain trinket box with a pink rose on the lid wasn't there. She had been cleaning for Edith for five years and it had always stood between the pot of artificial violets and the carved lucky imp. And the big giveaway that something was amiss was that Ruth, being Ruth, had done a slap-dash polish, and there was a tell-tale perfect oval of clean wood on the table, where the box had sat, surrounded by dust.

A prickle of unpleasantness stabbed Cheryl in the back of the head.

'Here you go. See you later,' said Ruth, handing over a half-empty bottle of 'Kristalglaz'. Then she picked up her bags and bobbed her head into the kitchen. 'Bye, love. It's been nice meeting you,' she said in a voice that intimated Edith was both daft and deaf.

As soon as the door shut behind her, Cheryl called to Edith.

'Edith? Have you moved that little box off the table in the hallway?'

Edith was still busy with her gardening pots. 'No, Cheryl. Why?'

The thieving cow. First Lance and now Ruth trampling over Edith's vulnerability. Today was not a good day to get on Cheryl's bad side. She threw open the front door, and marched down the path to catch up with Ruth Fallis.

'Oy.'

Ruth turned. 'What's up?'

'Give it back,' snarled Cheryl, beckoning the item's return with a flutter of her fingers.

'Give what back? What you on about? Oy, gerroff,' Ruth protested as Cheryl grabbed her bag and rasped the zip down.

'Don't come it with me. You frigging know what.'

'I said gerroff, you mad—' But Ruth's words died in her throat as Cheryl's hand touched on something hard secreted in a nest of dusters. She pulled it out, it was the missing box.

'I were only tekking it to show to our Jock. I'd have brought it back,' Ruth huffed.

'When would that have been then?' Cheryl growled. 'Edith isn't one of your ladies, this job is a one-off for you. I'm not an idiot – you nicked this and meant to keep it.' She opened up the box. There was a gold ring inside with a diamond cluster sitting proud. 'Gonna bring this back an' all, were you?'

'I didn't know it were in,' stuttered Ruth, her chins wobbling.

'Bollocks.'

'Oh fuck you, you self-righteous bitch,' Ruth came back at her.

Cheryl stuffed the trinket box in her pocket and grabbed Ruth's coat at the collar, pulling her face close.

'I'm telling Della. You shouldn't be in anyone's house, especially not old people's.'

'You better not,' said Ruth, struggling to free herself, but years of frustration and hurt and anger were concentrated in Cheryl's hands which remained locked on Ruth's tatty work coat.

'Or what? What you going to do? Send Fat Jock around to sit on me? You're a lazy, heartless bitch, Ruth Fallis, and you're lucky I'm not going to tell Edith because she or her nephew would have the coppers round at yours before you had chance to catch your breath. Now fuck off.'

Cheryl released her hands, pushing the red-faced Ruth backwards.

'You mad bitch,' she snarled, rubbing at her neck. 'You'll be sorry when I tell our Jock.'

Cheryl took a step in her direction and Ruth snatched up her bag and toddled away sharply, looking over her shoulder every few steps to make sure Cheryl was at a safe distance.

Cheryl put the dish back on the table so that Edith would be none the wiser. She didn't want Lance to get to know about this incident because it would give him all the excuse he needed to tar all cleaners with the same brush.

Cheryl hoped that the answering machine would pick up her message to Della rather than have to speak to her directly. She really couldn't face any more drama today.

CHAPTER 5

Revenge is a dish best served cold, so the saying went. Well, bollocks to that, thought Della. Her whole body was taken over by the desire to avenge herself on that lying bastard of a man she worked for. How dare he treat her with such disdain after all she had done for him? And not just Jimmy, but Ivanka. Even though she had known the girl for only six months, the deception hit hard. She had bent over backwards to make her feel at home in the office. She wouldn't have given anyone else as much leeway. Della was shaking with shock and hurt at the realisation she had been made a complete fool of, but mostly she felt rage.

Calm yourself, she said, hearing her heart race dangerously in her chest. She didn't want to die of a heart attack before she had made James Arthur Diamond sit up and notice. She took a long deep breath in and let a long deep breath go; she had to think. She needed to backtrack over several months; the last six to be exact. When had his affair with Ivanka started? And how had that little madam been able to dupe her so easily – Della hadn't even had a sniff that something was going on between them under her very nose. The earliest receipt was for the car – four months ago. But had it been going on for longer?

Think, Della, think. Go right back to the beginning. She herded her thoughts in order.

It was last July when Jimmy suggested they get an office junior. *An East European girl,* he had definitely specified. Had Jimmy deliberately ensured that Della saw him salivating over the other two applicants? Had she thought at the time that it was odd he hadn't been in the slightest bit interested in the young, leggy blonde? Jimmy would have eyed up anyone and yet he had remained impervious to Ivanka – why hadn't that sounded a warning bell in her? Because she was too pleased to see that Ivanka obviously hadn't floated his boat, that's why. In the end it had been she who had insisted on choosing Ivanka without realising she had been expertly manipulated into her choice. Jimmy Diamond had done her up like a kipper.

In the six months since she had been there, Jimmy and Ivanka had been nothing but polite and professional with each other, veering on the side of frosty. Jimmy hadn't joked around with her, although he had excused that by whispering to Della, 'She's a cold fish, that one.'

Della reached for the office diary and found the entries where Ivanka had been either off ill or on holiday. There was a Friday in November when

Ivanka had rung in sick with a stomach bug – Jimmy was supposedly in Nottingham that day at a meeting. Or was he? Della rifled through the receipts in the brown envelope and found that Jimmy had actually been in a swanky London hotel on that night – in a double room, of course. And he and A. N. Other had been to the theatre, because there were two ticket stubs for *Les Misérables*. The Tuesday in January when Ivanka was off, apparently in the grip of period pains, tied up with a receipt for one night in a five-star suite in York, plus dinner (lobster and chateaubriand) plus his and hers massages in the hotel spa. There was more.

It had been going on since before Ivanka had joined Diamond Shine, Della knew. That's why she came to work here. Jimmy didn't take women to the theatre. He didn't even take his wife there. He took women for meals and to cheap hotels. And he was careful to do it with females who wanted the same no-strings-attached flings. But strangely, Della hadn't been asked to book him any rendezvous for about ten or eleven months now. She'd taken that as a sign that he had finished sowing his wild oats and was finally settling. That he might want a relationship that was deep and meaningful and monogamous. That he might turn to her for it.

There was a wad of bank statements going back two years pertaining to a high interest account and a current account. Exactly seven months ago, the latter started showing an amount of one thousand seven hundred pounds leaving on the first of every month to go to Ivan Szcz. *Ivanka.* He was either topping her wage up on the sly or paying for services rendered – probably both.

Then, folded with last month's statement, Della found it. A receipt for a diamond ring.

An engagement ring.

Her hand flew to her mouth, stifling the cry of shock. There was no mistaking who it was for, either, because there was an instruction to engrave it with the words: J & I TRUE LOVE.

The awful truth dawned on her that Jimmy and Ivanka were in a committed relationship; well, as much as you could be when you were married to someone else. Jimmy wouldn't have employed someone he wanted to shag and leave; he was serious about her. A hot column of fury coursed through Della's centre and she wanted to hit something hard and release the pressure of it. How could he do this to her? How could he have used her like this? She was virtually running his company whilst he was bonking the office junior. So what was the long-term plan? Oh, it really didn't take that much working out: he was paving the path for Ivanka to replace her. What a blind, gullible idiot she had been.

Ivanka. For a nineteen year old, she was a crafty one, thought Della. She had slipped under her radar as if she were a buttered stealth bomber. Della flicked away the single rogue tear which

43

rolled down her cheek. *How dare they?* A sudden picture shot into her head of Ivanka and Jimmy laughing at her behind her back. That skinny, frumpy woman nearly three times the age of Ivanka, totally oblivious to the goings on under her long pointy nose. She imagined them planning the scene they'd acted out so faultlessly that morning. Oh how they must have enjoyed it; otherwise why didn't Ivanka just ring in sick rather than go to all the pretence of playacting the poor vomiting victim? There was no other explanation than they wanted to see themselves get away with their deception first-hand, pull the wool over her eyes, make a fool of her, show each other how clever they were. Well, they wouldn't be laughing for much longer. Della was going to put a very big bomb underneath Jimmy Diamond's secret little world and she'd start by telling his stupid wife exactly what he was up to.

CHAPTER 6

Della in angry mode was a frightening spectacle. By the end of the afternoon, she had ripped the office apart looking for further proof of Jimmy's deception, but all the damning evidence had been concentrated in his locked drawer. Oh, she couldn't wait to see the look on his wife's face. That stuck-up madam had it coming to her. On the few occasions when Della had to ring Jimmy at home and Connie had picked up the phone, Della could feel her disdain dripping down the line in her direction that one of Jimmy's minions had dared to ring their mansion. Likewise, whenever Connie had to ring the office to get hold of Jimmy, Della couldn't help playing delaying tactical games, taking ages to find Jimmy and put him through or saying that he was busy and asking who was calling, when she knew all along that it was his wife. Alas these exchanges happened more often than not, because Jimmy refused to have a mobile phone. He said that he would never be a slave to a lump of metal. That was obviously an excuse to keep himself elusive because in the envelope of receipts was one for a pay-as-you-go phone and the number, which Della noted down. Oh my, Della was looking forward to seeing Mrs Constance Diamond's perfect little bubble of superiority well and truly popped.

When Della was satisfied that everything was back in place, except the envelope of evidence which was in her bag, she picked up her keys and took one last look behind her. She wouldn't be in tomorrow, or ever again. And she wouldn't answer Jimmy's calls – she'd just leave him to work out why she had left. He would be in a total mess without her at the helm. Good.

Just as Della opened the door to go, the phone rang. Della made an instinctive movement to pick it up, then stopped herself and let the answering machine handle it.

'Hi, it's Cheryl. I've just had a fight with Ruth Fallis because I caught her nicking stuff out of Edith Gardiner's house . . .'

Hearing enough, Della closed the door. Let Jimmy and Ivanka deal with that. It would be a nice welcome home for them on Tuesday morning.

CHAPTER 7

'Jimmy, darlink. Put some oil on my back,' Ivanka drawled lazily from her face-down position on the sunbed as she tilted her left hand from side to side so the sun glinted on the substantial solitaire diamond ring she wore on the third finger.

'Of course, my angel,' said Jimmy, jumping to attention and squirting some coconut-scented liquid into his hand to warm it slightly before it hit Ivanka's soft, young skin.

She purred as he rubbed in the oil and copped a crafty feel of the side of her boobs.

'I can't believe we're here,' said Jimmy, lifting his head to look at the sun which was freakishly hot for the end of February. Was it really only that morning that he'd been standing in his office putting his foot down with Della?

'I can't believe that we are here as an engaged couple.'

'Well, we are, honeybuns,' said Jimmy. In the throes of passion, he had stupidly agreed to buy her a ring to prove that his intentions towards her were honourable. Well, as honourable as they could be, becoming engaged to a nineteen year old whilst still married to his wife of twenty-four years.

'It's beautiful diamond. I love it,' crooned Ivanka.

'Only wear it when we are out, don't go and forget and put it on in the office.'

'Of course,' said Ivanka impatiently, clicking her tongue. 'I am not idiot, Jimmy. And I will say proper thank you when we go back to the hotel.' She twisted her head and licked her lips and he felt a stirring in his groin.

'This is the life,' he said, wanting to scream it from the nearest rooftop. He knew how Shirley Valentine felt now. He'd been forced to watch that tripe with Ivanka one evening in a London hotel and had thought it unbelievable that anyone could refuse to go home after her holiday had ended, but today – for the first time – he really got it.

He weighed up the possibility of doing exactly that on Tuesday as his hand glided over Ivanka's back. Della could run his office quite easily without him. He'd have to pay her a bit extra, but she'd do anything for him. Della Frostick was a dried-up twig of a woman starving for affection and all he'd had to do was throw her the odd compliment or stare at her for what was longer than necessary to make her fall in love with him. She would move the world for him if she could, or fetch his slippers in her mouth because she was as loyal as a dog. The image of Della on all fours with his stinky moccasins between her teeth made him giggle to himself. He trusted her with everything; well, that wasn't strictly true, because though she saw most of the company bank statements, she didn't see all of them and she didn't know that he was shagging the office junior. Or that he had proposed to her a month ago, mid blow-job.

Oh, he wished he could split himself in two because though he relished the thought of sharing his bed every night with Ivanka and her golden body, Connie was a nice, simple, warm, good-hearted, uncomplicated and undemanding wife. He could have his cake and eat it with Connie. She never questioned his comings and goings and, bless her, was too thick to realise that he'd had more extra-marital affairs than Ken Barlow. Divorcing her wasn't an option he had really considered until he got carried away and opened his big trap and asked another woman to marry him.

He was fond of Connie, really he was. She was good to him and she kept a clean, comfortable house. He didn't know if it was love. They'd been together since they were teenagers and stuck with each other but he'd never felt that he wanted to bonk her continually, which was how he thought about Ivanka.

His hand smoothed Hawaiian Tropic over Ivanka's yielding buttocks. It was all starting to become a problem. Ivanka was a pleasure model and he couldn't picture her washing his smalls and becoming the new 'Connie'. But he needed a Connie in the background. He frowned . . . he had juggled them all quite adequately for almost a year without anyone finding out; there was no reason not to think they couldn't carry on as they were. Except they couldn't really now, because Jimmy had bought Ivanka an engagement ring and had stupidly thought she would be pacified by that and not expect a marriage to follow soon after. Why could she not be happy with their snatched moments in the office when Della was out shopping in her lunch hour, their nights in swanky hotels, the presents he bought her . . . not making their relationship public had kept it edgy and exciting, couldn't she see that? Anyway, sod it, there was no point in being here and worrying about the future so Jimmy did what he was expert at doing: ignoring the fact that his actions might have consequences. At least until he was forced into facing up to them.

'I'm going for a dip, darling,' he said, snapping the top back on the oil. He stood up and sucked in his stomach which was hanging a little too much over his budgie smugglers these days for his liking – but that was contentment for you. Too many five-course meals and champagne. It was a good job he was so energetic in the sack and some calories at least were burned off in the process.

Jimmy swaggered down to the beach, knowing that he still cut a good figure at forty-four, bare-chested and in a pair of short shorts: tall and handsome with twinkling eyes and a smile that could disarm a shark with a cocked machine gun. Jimmy Diamond had 'likeability' by the bucketload and boy, did he know it and use it. He'd learned the art of seduction from watching his dad sell second-hand cars. Stan Diamond had Cary Grant looks and a silver tongue that could have sold condoms to nuns.

And, as he got older, Jimmy, like his father, was acquiring those crinkles around the eyes that only added to his attractiveness, unlike what was happening to the eyes of Pookie Barnes who had grown bags so big you could have carried your shopping home in them. Pookie's hair was thinning by the day as well, unlike Jimmy's which remained thick and brown with no hint of a monk's patch at the crown and only the merest hint of white at the temples. And Jimmy didn't need Viagra as Pookie did. But then Pookie's missus was twice the size of Connie and had a face like a squashed bat, so no wonder Pookie needed some medical intervention in that department.

Jimmy stood in the deliciously cool sea as the sun shone down on him and thought of that George Best story: there he was in a hotel room with Miss World and a bed covered in thousands of pounds that he had just won on the horses and the waiter who brought them in champagne to celebrate with had asked him, 'So where did it all go wrong then, George?' Jimmy Diamond felt like that at this moment. He laughed to himself. A wife who washed his clothes, a woman who ran his office like an oiled premium machine and was madly in love with him, a teenage sex-goddess for a mistress, a successful business, a stashed bank account, a nice car . . . where did it all go wrong, Jimmy?

Life at the moment was the best.

CHAPTER 8

Jimmy's house was detached but incredibly modest compared to what he could have afforded according to the profits on the company accounts, never mind the secret accounts she had just discovered, thought Della as her car nosed up his drive. And it was looking a bit shabby to her. The windows needed replacing, for one thing.

He was always pleading poverty with the girls whenever any of them asked for a pay rise, and Della had loyally kept schtum because he gave her a generous, at least by his standards, annual pay increase to make sure she did so. There was a car in the drive which she presumed must belong to Connie. A small, red Ford with a dented bumper and a fair bit of rust on the wheel arches, a far cry from Jimmy's swanky motor. Della wondered what Connie would say when she found out Ivanka was driving around in a brand new sports car and chuckled to herself.

Jimmy's daughter Jane was grown up and living with a man in Holland so it wouldn't be as if she were smashing up a family unit. As for hurting

Connie Diamond with what she was about to do, well stuff her. Connie Diamond was the woman whom Della tried not to think about, the woman who was the mother of his child. Despite his misdemeanours, she was still the woman he went to bed with every night and woke up with every morning, and the woman he spent Christmas Day with and to whom he signed anniversary cards (even if Della bought them for him). Della nearly turned green every time she thought about Connie Diamond but somehow it made it easier to think of her as cold, lazy, ugly and snooty. Everything that was undesirable in a wife, Della projected onto Connie.

Della had only seen Connie a handful of times, the last being over thirteen years ago, when the money really started rolling in big-time for Jimmy. Della had chosen to interpret her quiet, shy demeanour as stand-offish, her refusal of refreshment as snobbish. In her mind's eye Della imagined the woman who was going to open the front door to her in a few moments: coiffeured and regal with shellaced nails, looking every inch the fat queen bee. She would be chilly and frigid and would bore Jimmy senseless, which is why he couldn't keep it in his trousers and sought his pleasures in other beds. Well, however much Botox Connie's forehead was pumped full of, what Della had to say to her would force her frozen face to react.

Della pressed her finger hard into the doorbell

button and heard rich Westminster chimes coming from inside the house. Then she saw a hint of movement behind the blurred glass in the door and a figure approaching, a lock being turned. Then the door opened and a frumpy, plump woman in a shapeless dress opened it.

'Could I speak to . . .' At first Della didn't recognise her and wondered for a second if she had the right house. She had been about to ask if Mrs Diamond was in, then she noticed the woman's soft grey eyes and she knew this was Connie.

Blimey moses, thought Della, *surely not.*

'Connie?'

'Yes, I'm Connie,' came the reply. 'Della?'

Connie recognised her immediately because Della had barely changed in the years since they had last met. Her brown hair was flecked with grey now, but she was still wearing it in the same style, scraped back from her thin angular face into a small immaculate bun above the nape of her neck. Della's eyes were still as bright and dark and all-knowing. It had been her eyes that Connie remembered about her most – like a bird of prey, missing nothing.

The air that stood between these two women almost crackled with the wariness that each had for the other. Connie knew that Jimmy was an expert in making a woman feel special. Even her own mother had been enchanted by his 'Jimmy charm'. Connie suspected that Della might have read too much into any flirting; she could tell from the way Della answered the phone that she was never pleased to have to put a call from his wife through to Jimmy.

'Can I please come in? I have something important to say,' said Della, her voice clipped and spiky. She didn't expect Connie to nod and move aside so easily, but Connie was intrigued if nothing else.

'Yes, please do,' she said.

Della followed her boss's wife down the hallway and into the small, square kitchen which gleamed with cleanliness. Then again, Lady Muck here had plenty of time to clean, being a lady of leisure, thought Della. Some people had to work for a living. Jimmy's rich wife didn't.

'Won't you sit down?' Connie asked her, pulling out a chair from under the dining table. Della noticed it wasn't exactly high end. She'd imagined Jimmy to have better taste; then again, it was probably his wife who picked the furniture. And she'd made a crap job of it. The shine on the wood couldn't mask the cheap quality. Della's eyes roamed around the kitchen, falling on the large double-layered box of truffles which was on the table. She recognised it.

'I'll stand, thanks,' said Della stiffly. 'What I have to say won't take long. I can't stay,' she sniffed, shifting her attention back to Connie. 'I'm just dropping the office keys off. You can tell Jimmy for me that I won't be working for him any more.'

Della waited for Connie to react. When she had played this scene out in her head on the drive over here, she had imagined a slow smile spreading across Connie's face which she would then proceed to wipe off. But Connie gave no reaction, other than to say a very surprised 'Oh.'

'I suppose you want to know why so I'll tell you.' Della was determined to have her moment with or without Connie's participation. She looked directly into Connie's grey eyes. Her eyes were what Della had remembered most about her, big and shiny and beautiful, fringed with thick, black lashes.

This was it. The moment she had been waiting for.

'You see, I won't lie for him any more. Jimmy is in a five-star hotel in Spain with his mistress, Ivanka. The office junior. It's been going on for months. She's driving around in the brand new car he's just bought her. An Audi TT.'

Della crossed her arms and waited for Connie's mouth to fall open with shock or for her to start shouting or screaming for her to get out – anything to show that she had scored a bullseye, but, other than a small swallow, there was nothing. Della shook her head in disbelief and couldn't help a small incredulous laugh escaping.

This was surreal. 'Did you hear what I just said?'

'Yes,' replied Connie, her voice quiet and slightly wavering. 'I heard.'

'No, I don't think you did hear me properly,' Della barked. 'Your husband is bonking a nineteen year old, and has been for at least six months.'

'I think you should leave now,' Connie replied, trying to control the shake in her voice. Inside her head she was attempting to rationalise the situation. For some reason Della was really annoyed with Jimmy and hitting out. It was preposterous to think that Jimmy and a nineteen year old were having an affair. She refused to give this woman the satisfaction of even entertaining such a ridiculous suggestion.

'Good grief.' Della shook her head from side to side at Connie's non-reaction. Connie was even more pathetic than she had given her credit for. 'Don't you care?'

'My husband loves me,' said Connie calmly.

'Yeah, he loves you so much that he has me running around buying boxes of chocolates for you because he can't even be bothered doing that.'

And then Connie Diamond gave Della the open-mouthed wounded expression that she had been waiting for. Not at the revelation that her husband was shagging around, but because he didn't buy her the boxes of chocolates she scoffed.

'Those rose creams on the table, for instance,' Della went on. 'Think he brought them home from a business trip in Devon last week, did you? Wrong. I ordered them from a shop in Exeter. And when he went to Bruges last month, could he be arsed bringing you anything back? No. I purchased them online for him and they were delivered to the office.'

'*You* buy them?' Connie said, her voice barely louder than her breath.

'I have done ever since I started working for him. Christmas, birthday, even the heart-shaped boxes on Valentine's Day,' said Della. 'Oh, and the one you'll be getting on Tuesday when he gets back home will be especially impressive. I've noticed that the bigger the box of chocolates he asks for, the more guilt it's been bought with. But then again he is totally smitten by Ivanka. Enough to get engaged to her as a matter of fact.'

Della was really sticking the boot in and it felt so totally cathartic to smash up the heart of the woman whose husband had smashed *her* heart up.

Connie's brain was awash with Della's disclosures now. Saturated with them. They flooded her whole being and whipped her strength away. 'Please leave . . . g . . . go,' Connie said, her voice now a full-on wobble. She was holding onto the back of a chair as if it was the only thing stopping her from falling to the ground.

'No point in you getting this upset if you've put up with it for at least fifteen years,' said Della.

Connie's head snapped up and her eyes widened with shock.

'Fifteen years? What do you mean at least fifteen years?'

Della's eyebrows raised. Surely she knew?

'I've been working for Diamond Shine for fifteen years and on my first day Jimmy left me to familiarise myself with the office because he was "having a liaison". It obviously wasn't his first.'

Connie blanched before Della's eyes.

'I must say,' sniffed Della, looking round, 'with all that money in his business and with what he spends on hotels and champagne, I'd have thought he could have at least spent some on the house.'

'Get out,' said Connie, some steel in her voice at last.

'Oh, don't worry, Lady Muck, I'm off. Here are the keys and here's some night-time reading for you. It's better than a Thomas Harris novel.' Della slammed both the keys and the envelope full of receipts down onto the table. 'He can get someone else to do his dirty work and buy your bloody chocolates from now on.'

And she turned and flounced out, wishing she had done it a second sooner because then she wouldn't have seen Connie Diamond crumple and the tears start to drop heavily down her face.

CHAPTER 9

When Connie heard the front door slam in its frame, she sank onto the chair, put her head in her hands and sobbed hard. The noise she made was horrible, more as if it came from an injured animal than a human being. Jimmy couldn't be having an affair. Could he? He wouldn't do that to her. Not again. He wasn't the type. No, no, no, no, no, she would have known. They had been together twenty-four years – she knew him inside out.

The year after their marriage she had discovered that he had been having a fling with her so-called friend, Jessie Mountjoy. She had confronted him and screamed at him and driven him out of the house. He had come back, of course, because it was a crazy time, an awful, terrible part of their lives. But they had managed to put it behind them. 'Trust me,' he'd pleaded with her. 'I promise I'll never do that to you again. You are my best girl, always remember that.'

And so she had trusted him, because what was a marriage without trust, and they had built a life together and had a daughter. Della was wrong.

Jimmy would never be that cruel. He didn't have time, anyway – he was always working, always chasing the money. They had an okay-ish house and when the money came rolling in, Jimmy had promised her they would do it up from top to bottom. But, though trade had increased over the years, they hadn't exactly drowned in the profits. This was the truth she had been led to believe. Jimmy might have worked hard in the foreground, but Connie had worked harder in the background. She had brought up their child more or less single-handed, she had cared for Jimmy's unwell parents and her own mother, not that she minded because families pulled together and looked after each other as best they could. And whenever he worked away, he always brought her beautiful chocolates and over the years those truffles had become a symbol of his devotion to her. They were his way of saying, 'I love you and I appreciate you,' because he never said the actual words.

Except that he hadn't bought those chocolates, which changed everything.

With her fingers trembling, she reached for the envelope which Della had brought and tipped the contents out onto the table. She was immediately relieved that there were no photographs of him *in flagrante delicto* with other women, only sheets with writing and numbers on them: receipts, statements.

There was a hotel bill for the Waldorf in London. Theatre tickets at one hundred and fifty pounds each. A bar bill for two three-hundred-pound bottles of champagne. A receipt for a pair of Jimmy Choo shoes, size eight. Bouquets of flowers. A gold bracelet, a Tiffany necklace . . . every receipt was a proof of sheer indulgence. But, looking at the bank statements that were also in the envelope, what Jimmy had spent on himself and 'Ms Szczepanksa' could be easily afforded.

She didn't know he even had an account with the Northumbria Bank. Well, two as it happens – a high interest account and a current account and he'd had them both for twenty years, or so it seemed from the letter accompanying one of the statements, congratulating him on being a customer for so long and informing him that they were enclosing a thank-you key ring. She most certainly didn't know he was keeping that amount of money secret from her. There was only one reason why he must be doing that, and that was because of how he was spending it. *No, no, no, he wouldn't*, she whispered over and over again, but she felt like Canute inside herself, trying to stem the tide of evidence as it rolled towards her like a great wave and threatened to engulf her.

Della's words came thudding into her head again. *Jimmy is in a five-star hotel in Spain with his mistress. She's driving around in the brand new car he's just bought her. An Audi TT.* And: *He loves you so much that he has me running around buying boxes of chocolates for you because he can't even be bothered doing that.* But according to the receipts, he had bought chocolates online from Le Mansion de Cocoa. Connie had never had chocolates from there. He had bothered to buy them for his mistress but not his wife. Connie squeezed at her temples with her fingertips. It was as if a lorry had tipped its whole massive load of crap into her head. Hundreds of lies rose up like animated corpses in the memory banks of her brain from all her years with Jimmy. Connie's tears plopped onto the table but they didn't carry any of the hurt away from her which stayed resolutely inside her as a solid cold stone block.

She needed to hold them back. She needed the medicine that would take all the pain away. Connie plunged into the box of chocolates on the table and grabbed a handful, stuffing them into her mouth and chewing hard, chomping, trying to concentrate on nothing but the sweet mix of rose cream and chocolate, fending off everything that tried to seize her brain's attention. The chocolate could do that for her. *The taste, just think of the taste and nothing else.* Chocolate had made her feel loved, cherished. Chocolate had made her think she was still his best girl. *More chocolates, you need more.* She bit down on as many of them as she could get in her mouth as the questions in her head became louder and more insistent that she take notice of them, crashing through the protective chocolate wall she had built up around herself.

Connie lifted her head and caught sight of herself in the long mirror which hung at the side of the door. She looked disgusting. Her eyes were swollen and red, her cheeks were pudgy and extended hamster-like full of chocolate; and what must the neat and smart Della have thought of her in that comfy loose pale-grey pinafore that made her seem twice the size she was.

Connie pushed the last of the chocolates in the box into her mouth to divert the primary receptors in her brain from thought activity to taste. *We'll make everything better*, they seemed to call when they were sitting brown and glossy in the box. But as soon as her teeth released the flavours, their voices changed. *Fooled you. We'll make it WORSE. A moment on the lips, a lifetime on the hips. Swallow. There's a good girl. Fatty fatty fatty fatty.* The voices were right; she was fat, ugly and revolting. No wonder her husband preferred to bonk outside his marital bed rather than in it. And in that one moment those years of betrayal, which ran far deeper than a few flings, and a besotted young Polish girl, became fused with the taste, the smell, the texture, the colour, everything about chocolate. The boxes he gave her didn't demonstrate how much he loved her but how little he cared. She'd been a fool and a far bigger one than even Della could possibly have imagined.

There were no friends she could call to pour all this out to. She hadn't had friends for years, not since Jane was little and she'd met some nice women at the school gates, but they'd drifted away when Jane went to big school and then out into the world. Her mum had been her best friend and she was gone now too. There was the woman in the newsagent who always passed the time of day with her and the chatty girl at the petrol station – but they weren't 'friends'. She suddenly felt very aware of her social isolation. How had she become such a friendless, dull, stupid, *trusting* lump? *Get a grip, get a grip* said a calming voice that came from deep inside her, as if it were a secret store of sense for use only in emergencies and her despair had broken the glass that encased it and let it free. *You need to think.*

She took a deep breath, and another in an attempt to chase away the shock that brought with it so many exaggerated emotions. *What do you feel, Connie Diamond?* she asked herself. *Not what you think you should feel, what do you* actually *feel?* And she surprised herself with the answer. Yes, she felt hurt, humiliated, fear at finding herself in an alien marital landscape, but more than anything she felt anger like a heat in every part of her.

She wiped a tear away as a steely voice in her head growled: *By God, Jimmy Diamond, I'll make you pay for this.* Rage felt vitalising as it boiled inside her. It drove her tears back to their waiting place; it put iron in her heart and steel in her limbs. The medicine of anger would allow her to function.

She could either cave in to the tears or think up a plan for how she was going to leave her husband on a chariot of fire rather than let him unceremoniously dump her like an old boot for his 'fiancée'. At least, by ripping her out of her bubble of false security, Della had allowed her the chance to claw back some dignity.

She didn't know whether to thank the woman or curse her.

CHAPTER 10

Della did not sleep very well that night. Guilt kept her awake; Connie's sad pale moon face kept drifting across her brain. Della had accomplished what she set out to, wound Connie, kick-start Jimmy's demise, and she had done it very successfully – so why did she feel such a cow? However much she tried to shake off the vision of Connie's tears streaming down her face, she couldn't. She'd been cruel to a woman who really didn't deserve it.

Defeated by her insomnia, she got out of bed at six and had some coffee and toast, then tried to read the newly delivered newspaper, but the words weren't sinking in. There was only one thing which would appease her troubled spirit and that was to go back to Connie and apologise. She set off at half-past ten, calling in at Dodley Co-op en route to buy a tin of Celebrations as a peace offering – a gift of chocolate surely would stop Connie slamming the door in her face.

She rang the bell and Connie opened her front door, carrying a mop and wearing past-their-best-by-a-long-time black leggings and a voluminous smock-top. Her face was drawn and her eyes puffy and sore-looking and Della guessed that it had been a rough night for her too. Della mentally swatted at the mosquito of guilt that was attempting yet again to sting her. She held out the tin as she said, 'I came to apologise.'

Connie's eyes dipped to the tin and as she did so she made a small hiccup, or a retch – Della couldn't tell which. Then her bright grey eyes flicked back up to Della's face. 'Come in. I'm glad you're here,' she said, her voice hard but polite.

Della was confused. Why on earth would Connie be glad that she'd come back? Nevertheless, she followed her inside.

'Coffee or tea?' asked Connie, when they reached the kitchen. She pulled out two mugs from a cupboard. 'Please sit down.'

Della felt a bony hand of trepidation reach into her chest and squeeze her heart. This was getting odder. Maybe Connie had invited her in to poison her. She was very cool and collected, almost artificially so.

'Whatever you're having. I take it black no sugar whether it's tea or coffee, thank you.'

'Coffee. I'm having coffee,' said Connie.

Della watched as Connie tipped water over instant granules and stirred and wondered what was going through her mind.

'These are for you. Peace offering,' said Della, setting the tin on the table.

'Thank you,' said Connie. 'That's very kind, but I don't eat chocolate any more so I won't be offended if you take them back.'

Don't eat chocolate? thought Della. Who the hell was she trying to kid. She didn't get a backside like that through scoffing broccoli.

'Starting Lent early?'

'What?'

'It's not Lent until next Wednesday.'

'Oh, is it?' Connie replied.

Obviously that wasn't it; she wasn't giving up chocolate for Lent then, thought Della.

Connie took the chair opposite her. Della noticed there was a light in her eyes that hadn't been there yesterday. She felt quite uncomfortable under the intense grey gaze but she deserved the disapproval. She took a deep breath and began a formal and very genuinely meant apology.

'I shouldn't have come storming over here yesterday. I was totally out of order. I was angry, that isn't any excuse, but—' Connie interrupted her.

'Let me say something before you go on any further. I've been turning over in my head what you told me yesterday and I've gone through everything in the envelope you brought.'

'I shouldn't have—'

Connie interrupted her again. 'Just answer me this, would you: why are you really leaving, Della? Sour grapes?'

Della's back stiffened in the chair.

'Look, I know how Jimmy is,' continued Connie. 'He's a terrible flirt.'

'If you're insinuating that I've had an affair with your husband as well, let me just put you right on that.' She and Jimmy had never even had as much as a snog. Physically she was guilt-free; emotionally she was less whiter than white. Jimmy had given her fifteen years of mental foreplay which he never meant to escalate to the physical, she knew that now. Sour grapes? Oh yes, her grapes were so sour she could have bottled them and sold them as chip shop vinegar.

'So why, then?'

'Because I can see what is going to happen.' Connie wasn't the only one who had been thinking in the last hours, going over past events, clawing and raking through months of interchanges for proof of her suspicions. 'Jimmy will replace me with Ivanka. My years of loyalty to him obviously mean nothing.'

She had recalled lots of small instances which she hadn't flagged up as anything dangerous at the time, yet she had remembered them all the same. For instance, how Ivanka had started to flex her bossy muscles, asking Della if she would just file this whilst she was over by the cabinet, or take a bag of rubbish down to the bins as she was going out of the door on her lunch break. Ivanka was on a quest to squeeze Della out and Jimmy had to be condoning it, she could see that now. They were both treating her like trash. How else could the events of the previous day be explained? They had booked a last-minute holiday and then played out a ridiculous drama to sneak off on it so that no one would suspect, for which Della had had to cancel an event she had been looking forward to for weeks.

'Della, I've been up all night, thinking. I don't want you to leave Diamond Shine,' said Connie, after taking a long drink of her coffee.

Della froze mid-swallow, her head scrabbling around for why that would be, although it wasn't hard to stab at a guess. Connie wanted to use her to get rid of Ivanka. And when Ivanka was gone, Connie would then get rid of Della.

'Sorry, but my mind is made up. End of,' replied Della, moving her head decisively from side to side. 'Nothing will make me stay, I can assure you of that. I can't work with Jimmy any more.'

'Will you work against him then?'

The words dropped like a stone into a still pool of water, sending shock ripples out to the four corners of the room.

'I beg your pardon?' said Della eventually, doubting her ears were working properly.

'I have a proposition for you,' said Connie, holding her cup as if she were pulling the warmth from it. She'd had the idea at exactly ten past three this morning. It had popped into her brain and woken her and she'd got out of bed, opened up a pad and started to plot. It was an insane, ridiculous, idea. So nuts that it might just work. Connie took in two huge lungfuls of air before her next words. 'What would you think about going into business with me?'

Della's eyebrows rose and she pulled her chin back into her neck. Was she hearing this correctly?

'Into business with you?' She repeated the words slowly to make sure.

'Yes,' said Connie, nodding. 'With me.'

Della tried not to let a sarcastic smile warp her mouth. 'What sort of business?' She couldn't imagine.

'Cleaning, of course,' replied Connie, as if the answer was obvious.

'Cleaning?'

'Let me explain.' Connie tucked a stray strand of her dull-blonde hair behind her ear. Her voice was calm and controlled as she spoke, even though inside she had started to shake. Once the words were out, they couldn't be taken back. 'I've been thinking about the situation I now find myself in. My years of loyalty to my husband obviously mean nothing to him either. Now, I could sit back and wait for Jimmy to tell me that he's divorcing me and let him give me the scraps from his table as a divorce settlement or I can walk out of my marriage with some dignity, some pride and something of what he owes. I don't see that I have any other option but to show him that I'm not taking what he has done to me lying down.'

Connie released a deep sigh and she waited to

see what Della's reaction was. She knew she had taken a massive risk in telling Della what she intended to do. She was gladdened to find she had Della's full attention.

'Go on,' Della prompted eventually.

'I thought of a plan. I am going to open up a rival cleaning firm. You stay in your job in Diamond Shine and dismantle it from the inside. You filter all the best clients to me and all the best cleaners. I undercut Diamond Shine's prices at every turn. I don't need to make a profit; I can run the business at a loss if I have to, at least for a while. I searched the net and found an office in Maltstone which the business can operate from. It's a room above a place that used to be a bridal shop. I was on the phone this morning first thing to them and I've fixed up an appointment to have a look at it this afternoon.'

'You don't let the grass grow under your feet, do you?' said Della, with some admiration.

I didn't want to give myself the chance to back out, Connie didn't tell her.

'Let me just ask: what, pray, do I get out of it all? And what's to stop you telling your husband that I'd be causing chaos from within?' Della wasn't born yesterday and she wouldn't be used by another of the Diamond family. After all, Connie owed her no loyalty.

Connie had been prepared for this question, which was a fair one. 'Okay then, let me turn that question around on you: what's to stop you telling

74

Jimmy what I plan to do? I'm trusting you with this information, aren't I?'

Della crossed her arms over her small flat breasts. 'And why *are* you trusting me after what I told you?'

'Because I have nothing to lose,' replied Connie, a croak claiming her throat on the last word. 'Look at me, Della,' she spread her arms out to her sides. 'Tell me that you didn't see me yesterday and think "what a mess". And you're right. For more than half of my life I've looked after everyone but myself and I'm going to be thrown on the dung-heap for it. Well, it's time for things to change.' Her strength was gathering now.

Della dropped her head, unable to meet Connie's eyes. She had enabled Jimmy's many infidelities and relished his disrespect for his wife because it made her feel close to him, closer to him than the woman he was married to because she was privy to his secrets. She'd judged him to be a lovable rogue rather than the total bastard she could now see that he was, stamping all over everyone in pursuit of his own pleasure.

'Cast your eyes around my house, Della,' Connie went on. 'My bedroom window has had a plastic bag blocking up a crack in it for eighteen months. My clothes are cheap, my car is held together with rust – and I've put up with all of it because I *knew* that most of the little profit Jimmy made was ploughed back into the company. *Hard times,* he said. *We're lucky to be riding the recession; once we get to the other side, we can splash out a bit.* He's been saying that for years and I've been so proud of him for trying. Huh.'

Her voice was loud now; spittle was flying off her lips in small energetic drops. She could have gone on and told Della so much more about why she was so angry, but bit back the words. She had told Della all she needed to know.

'As for what you'd get out of it, well, you'd still get your salary from Jimmy and I'd match what he pays you – cash in hand.'

Della studied the offer for a moment. There was a fatal flaw in the plan.

'How will you be able to afford to do that?' If Connie had any money, surely she would have bought some windows herself. 'And you say you'd run the business at a loss?'

'I don't intend to run it at a loss for ever,' Connie came back. 'I'm prepared to run it at a loss until Jimmy is removed as a rival. My mother died last year. She had an insurance policy. Not a fortune, but enough to spend on this. I didn't want to touch it. Jimmy asked me if I'd invest it into the business and I felt so guilty when I said no because I put it away for my daughter. But I think my mother would approve of what I'm going to do with it. You won't lose out, whatever happens, Della. I'll make sure you're properly financially compensated.' She turned to face the tall, spiky woman head on. 'If I'm going to do this, I will have to throw myself headfirst into it.

I want to close down Diamond Shine and end my marriage by May the first.' Mayday sounded appropriate.

Della coughed in shock. 'May the first? That's not very long.'

'It's long enough.'

'You're very calm,' said Della, her eyes narrow as she studied Connie's stone-face.

'Maybe on the outside. I can assure you I am not on the inside. Well?'

Della felt as if she was on the top of a very high diving board and if she took the leap, there was no guarantee of a safe landing. Then she thought of Jimmy and the way he looked at her, forcing her to believe that there was a connection between them. He had used her. He had slipped under all her defence barriers and made her fall in love with him when he had no intention of opening his heart to her. *The bastard.*

She caught sight of the calendar on Connie's kitchen wall. There were just short of nine weeks to May.

'You won't lose money,' she said. 'You can undercut Jimmy's prices considerably and still make a good profit. If nothing's happened by Mayday, we part company and never admit that we spoke about this, all right?'

'So that means you're in, then?' asked Connie, her chest thudding with palpitations.

'It looks like it, doesn't it?' replied Della.

Connie held out her hand and Della's came out

tentatively to reach it, but her handshake was firm and sure. The unlikeliest pairing in history had just been formed: a union of hate against a joint object of love.

CHAPTER 11

Connie parked her car on Wheatfield Lane, down the side of the old empty bridal shop in Maltstone. Standing outside and waiting was a man with a clipboard who she presumed was the estate agent. She reckoned he would have been in his early twenties, a man blossoming from a boy. He had a slim frame, long arms, long legs and was sporting a sharp suit in bright blue with a pink shirt – brave colours for the fearless young with their whole lives ahead of them. The sight of him made her smile. Max would have been his age now. *Her boy.* With any luck he would have inherited his father's wide cheeky smile and tall, handsome physique but have her sensitivity and less selfish heart. Sometimes she imagined him in uniform as a pilot, sometimes in a wig and gown breezing into court but if he'd been a road sweeper and happy it wouldn't have mattered. He had been beautiful when he was born, ten tiny fingers with a dot of nail on them, dark eyelashes, a pink bud of a mouth . . .

Connie snapped her thoughts back into the here and now, as she'd had to do so many times over the years to survive, and just remembered to slip her wedding ring off her finger and into the side pocket of her handbag before getting out of the car.

The man came towards her with his hand outstretched in greeting.

'Miss Smith, Tom Stamp,' he said confidently. Connie had given the estate agency her aunt's name. 'How do you do.' His handshake was warm and energetic. 'Lovely day. Bit nippy, but nice and bright.'

'Thanks for seeing me at such short notice,' Connie replied.

'No worries. I like someone who knows what they want. It makes my job a lot easier,' said Tom Stamp, taking a key out of his pocket. 'Let's see what you think of it.'

The entrance to the upper office was at the back of the property. Nice and private, Connie thought. The smell of fresh paint greeted them. The staircase was wide, the carpet on it looked new.

'It's all been done out recently,' said Tom. 'To be honest, it was a bit of a mess when it first came on our books. The roof had leaked. We couldn't have rented it out as it was so the owner had to put his hands in his pockets. Looks good, doesn't it?'

The room at the top of the stairs was much more light and airy than Connie could have imagined. The front windows were small; at the back they were much bigger and south-facing. The room was long and narrow with white painted walls and an entirely respectable, neutral-coloured carpet. Lines of pine shelving filled an alcove, which would come in handy, thought Connie.

'There's a toilet and a sink and a small kitchen,' said Tom, beckoning Connie over to see them. The kitchen was smaller than the loo, but it wasn't really needed at all. A plug point for a kettle would have sufficed, and there seemed to be lots of plug points around.

'Phone line needs connecting, obviously,' said Tom, pointing to the phone socket on the wall with a flourish worthy of an air stewardess indicating an emergency exit.

'That's fine,' replied Connie. She would get on to that as soon as possible but for now, she and Della would be able to speak via two mobile pay-as-you-go phones which she had just picked up from Asda.

'Our client would prefer a six-month rental agreement,' said Tom, dropping his voice to a whisper. 'I think he was bitten by the last client. He's asked for a five hundred pound bond and two months' rent up front.'

He winced a little, probably expecting Connie to back out at that point. But instead she said, 'Understandable.'

Anyone who had been cheated tended to lose their trust. That was one thing to which she could testify first-hand.

Connie imagined sitting at a desk by the window.

She wouldn't need half the space offered, but it was in a perfect out-of-the-way location without being too far a drive from home. She had made another appointment to view a property in Penistone after this, but she decided she would cancel it. This was perfect for her needs. 'And if I went ahead, how soon could I move in?' she asked.

'A few days, I should imagine,' replied Tom, who from the expression on his face hadn't been expecting that easy a deal.

Connie liked it. It felt a good fresh space. Now she had to ask an awkward question which she knew was going to sound ridiculous.

'And how private would my details be? Let me clarify,' she went on, seeing Tom Stamp's eyebrow rise like Roger Moore's. Although she wasn't sure she was going to be able to convince him now that she wasn't a crime-lord. Maybe the best way forward was honesty? Then again, she had always respected honesty and where had that got her?

'I must be totally frank with you, I have a stalker,' she blurted out. Even her own brain was thinking, *what the frigging hell are you saying?* 'It's a police matter and the situation is being monitored, but I have to be careful, which is why I am moving out of my present offices. I would have to insist that you keep my details strictly to yourselves. It's a very distressing situation so you'll understand my concern. The police may be in touch with you to make sure that steps are taken to protect my identity.'

Tom Stamp's eyes were wide as dinner-plates. He hadn't come across this scenario in his short career to date but his answer was slick and professional.

'That's awful. It's my dad's estate agency so don't worry, I will make personally sure that all your details are kept off the main filing systems and secure in Mum's office – she takes care of all the money.'

'I will, of course, supply you with my real details and my present financial and personal credentials, which you will need.'

'Brilliant, brilliant.' Tom nodded enthusiastically as if all this was very exciting to him.

'You could endanger my life if protocol isn't followed,' added Connie, just in case he was dying to brag to his mates down the pub what had happened today.

'You don't have to worry at all, Miss *Smith*.' Tom gave her a conspiratorial wink. 'You're safe as houses with the "Stamp of Approval" agency.'

And Tom Stamp once again held out his hand, this time for Miss Smith to shake on the deal.

CHAPTER 12

Sitting on the balcony, bathed in sunlight, Ivanka looked at the sparkly diamond on the third finger of her left hand and smiled. It really was beautiful – and so big. If Jimmy ever dumped her, at least she could sell it for a tidy sum, not that she wanted to. That was the problem. She had thought she would feel more secure when Jimmy bought her a ring of commitment but it had had the opposite effect. If a man could get engaged to a girl when he was married to his wife, how worthless was that arrangement really?

Jimmy had introduced her to fine dining and hotel suites, spas and foreign travel, jewellery and fast cars. She couldn't – and wouldn't – give it up now for anyone. She had pushed and nagged for an engagement ring and got it – so she needed to push and nag for a wedding. Only as Mrs Ivanka Diamond would she have that security of never being without money again. She looked over at him lying supine on the sunbed, mouth open, snoring gently. She loved him. Or at least she thought she did. She liked the excitement of their relationship; pretending there was nothing between them in the office even when Della wasn't around. Very rarely, when Della was out at lunch, he might draw his finger once across the back of her neck or she might trace the line of Jimmy's trouser fly, sit across from his desk and cross her legs Sharon-Stone style and it drove them both crazy that they were forbidden to touch each other until later. She enjoyed going to the theatre and drinking the champagne he bought and opening the presents he gave her, and going to bed with him was no hardship because Jimmy was generous and attentive to her body and she loved sex and he obviously adored her and she relished the power her youth and confidence had over him. That was love, wasn't it?

They had managed to keep their relationship boiling for almost a year thanks to the intrigue and surprises and sex, but Ivanka wasn't stupid enough to think that the momentum would last for ever: a drop in temperature was imminent and so she needed to establish her place on a joint cheque book before that happened.

It would be Lent on Wednesday and Ivanka Szczepanska decided there and then what she was going to give up for it: sex until she and Jimmy could carry on their relationship in the open. If denying him the delights of her body didn't rush him to a solicitor for his divorce papers, very little else would.

CHAPTER 13

On Sunday morning, Cheryl shuffled across the mattress to snuggle up to Gary's warm back and jerked fully awake when she nearly fell out of bed. She had been dreaming when she'd heard him say, 'Cuddle up, Chez.' Gary wasn't there. This was the third morning she had woken up alone and once again, the pain was waiting for her eyes to open so it could pounce on her. She pressed her face into the pillow where her partner used to lay his head and as she breathed in his fading scent, she began to sob noisily.

He hadn't phoned or texted; she'd thought he might have. If he had, she would have caved in and told him to come back, given him yet another last chance just to plug up this hole of agony that his absence was inflicting upon her. But she had done too much of a good job on Thursday morning convincing him that it was over and she was beginning to hate herself for that.

Cheryl's whole body ached with flu-like stiffness. She felt as if tears had been dragged from every part of her body and dried her out until she was so brittle she could have snapped and shattered into small pieces. The weekend had been a torturous long one in which everything around her was flavoured with Gary. Even when she put on the TV, it was to find the opening scene of *The A Team* – his favourite film. She drank a full bottle of wine on the Friday evening to try and numb her, but it had the opposite effect. She was sick through the night and Gary appeared to her in technicolour dreams, soothing her brow, promising that he would go downstairs and fetch a glass of water for her and a couple of paracetamol – but he never came.

Usually on Sundays, Cheryl did her laundry, but today she sat huddled in her dressing gown on the sofa and watched the hands of the clock crawl forwards. Instead of a cosy home-made Sunday lunch with Gary, she ate half of a Pot Noodle and let depression squeeze her until she felt ill.

She was glad when Monday came and she had to get up and go off to work, even if it was to a new client that wasn't one of her favourites. Six months ago her first call of the week had been to two wonderful old gentlemen, brothers Maurice and Wensley Herbert, and their ancient Pekinese, Gerald. But Wensley died just before Christmas, then Gerald had to be put down and after that Maurice lost the will to live. Cheryl was convinced he had died of a broken heart. He had left Cheryl a very sweet note thanking her for looking after them all, which made her think that he had run to death with his arms outstretched in welcome. Monday mornings were a lot less bright for not seeing the Herberts. This one was especially dull and as she left the house to catch the bus, the weather reflected her mood perfectly: cold and miserable and full of dark clouds.

There was no one in the client's house and the central heating had been turned off, so it was freezing and there wasn't any hot water either. She earned every penny of her money at this place as it was little better than a pigsty every week and she always wondered how a single person could make such a mess. She rolled up her sleeves, put on her Marigolds and got out her Fillit Bong, but cleaning in that empty house gave her too much time to think and Gary took over her whole head.

She made a ridiculous promise to herself that if she hadn't heard from him by half-past ten then she would give him a quick call. She knew she shouldn't, but she also knew that she wouldn't be able to stop herself because her resolve was at a low ebb. At ten-thirty exactly she got out her mobile and pressed speed-dial number one.

Her mouth was watering with nervous anxiety as the dialling tone burred. She should ring off, but what would it matter because even if he didn't answer, he would see that he had missed a call from her. With a sinking heart she heard his chirpy-as-ever voicemail kick in, asking the caller to leave a message. She listened to the end, drinking him in and then clicked off before the beep. She wanted to speak to him so much, she *had* to. Maybe his phone was on silent. She'd try his mum's house. She brought up her contact list. Ann Gladstone – Gary's mother – was the first name she came to. Cheryl pressed the small telephone icon and the call was answered almost immediately.

'Hell-ow and who's calling?' Ann answered in her familiar, friendly voice.

'Hello Ann, it's Cheryl.'

There was a pause. 'Oh, it's you is it?' There was no warmth at all in Ann's words and Cheryl was hurt by her tone. Ann had always been so welcoming to her. Cheryl supposed now that loyalties of blood had been called upon, she was out in the cold.

'I . . . I just wondered if Gary was there.'

'No, he isn't,' came the blunt response.

'Oh. Is he doing okay?' Cheryl asked, feeling an ache in her eyes as though tears were threatening.

'Huh. Apart from the fact that you chucked him out of his home, yes,' snapped Ann.

Cheryl's mouth opened in a half-gasp. That wasn't really fair. She wondered how much Gary had told his mother.

'Ann, it wasn't as simple as that . . .'

'Look, it's none of my business. I don't want to get involved,' clipped Ann, even though it sounded as if she was very much involved.

'He's all right, though?'

Ann huffed. 'Well if you mean by "all right" that

he hasn't slashed his wrists then yes, he's "all right". Sorry if that disappoints you.'

Cheryl quickly protested. 'I didn't mean—'

'Fancy ringing up to check on the effect you're having on him!' Ann's usually quiet voice rose in volume. 'Well know this, lady, he's more than all right, he's well rid. Don't ring this house again and embarrass yourself.'

She was still chuntering to herself about the cheek of it all when she disconnected the call, leaving Cheryl in a pool of tears that she thought would never dry up. She wished she hadn't rung. Now she would be waiting all day for him to ring her back. And if he didn't return her call it would really hurt.

CHAPTER 14

Della walked into the office and though everything looked the same as she had left it on Thursday when she'd shut the door intending never to return, it felt very different now. All the furniture was in the same position, the carpet was the same colour, the light was the same wattage, but the ambience had been stripped and replaced with one that fizzed and spat and felt like a living entity. There were no messages on the answer machine, no one would ever have known that the office was unmanned on Friday. She could have gone to Whitby after all, which was another reason to snarl in the general direction of Jimmy Diamond and Ivanka.

She so wanted to just carry on, business as normal at Diamond Shine, putting her heart and soul into finding new cleaners and matching them up with clients for Jimmy, pretending that the last few days hadn't happened, but the knowledge that she was being betrayed by two people in the world of whom she was most fond could not be unknown.

It felt as if the whole weekend had been taken up with brain activity about the situation and the more she thought about it, the more ridiculous it sounded. She had gone into work that morning having decided that the best way forward would be to ring Connie and tell her that she had made a mistake in saying she would join forces with her. She needed to speak to Connie anyway because she still had the envelope of receipts which needed to be put back in Jimmy's drawer. She presumed that Connie had calmed down too. They'd had their tantrum, and in the cold light of day had put their temporary angry insanity to bed.

Now Della was armed with the knowledge of Jimmy's relationship with Ivanka, she would be able to watch out, take notes, engineer events to give her ammunition should she have to take him to court for constructive dismissal. That path would be so much easier to tread. She was about to pick up the phone and punch in Connie's number, but it rang before her hand touched the buttons. Pookie's PA, Paula was on the end of the line. Or Princess Paula, as Della thought of her. She suspected Paula had been knocking Pookie off for years behind his wife's back and was full of her own importance because of it. She batted away the irony that she understood that mindset a little too well.

'Hi. Can you put me through to Jimmy? I've got Pookie on the line for him,' Paula said in her faux-plummy voice.

'He's not in until tomorrow,' Della replied. At

least that's what Jimmy had told her, but she couldn't rely on anything that came out of his mouth, it seemed.

'Oh. Er . . . Pookie had to return early from his golfing weekend. Jimmy said he might do the same. Oh well, never mind then. Pookie, no doubt, will be in touch tomorrow.'

Della chose her next words carefully and tried not to let them sound like a snarl.

'You can't keep Jimmy off a golf course once he's on there. Hope they've had a nice time.'

'Sounds like they did. Pookie arrived a bit late but he got there in the end so whatever you do, don't drop him in it and say that he popped by your office.' Paula laughed, but it was too jolly and clearly fake. 'Thanks anyway,' she said.

'Pleasure,' said Della dryly as she slowly replaced the phone upon the receiver. Pookie must have been cacking his pants all weekend thinking that he had dropped Jimmy in the dung. So it wasn't just Jimmy, Ivanka and Pookie who thought she was an idiot, it appeared that Paula was privy to Jimmy's deception as well. Something dark and nasty started to swirl inside her, then it rose up and swallowed any ideas she'd had about pulling out of Connie's plans.

Della settled into her seat. The first job of the day was to sack Ruth Fallis. Someone was going to bear the brunt of her annoyance this morning; it might as well be that thieving old bag.

★   ★   ★

Gary hadn't rung by the end of Cheryl's shift. She sat on the bus and tried to imagine what the conversation between Gary and his mother would be. How much of a twist would Ann put on what had passed between them earlier? Would she say that Cheryl had phoned her to make sure Gary hadn't been missing her so much that he had decided to hang himself? Thinking back, Ann had been deliciously scathing to Cheryl about Gary's ex, weighting her with the qualities of a she-devil. Maybe it was her turn now to be the evil one. The thought of the once-friendly Ann, who always gave her a hug when she saw her, turning against her and slagging her off gave her a physical pain in her gut.

Cheryl shifted her attention to the view through the window so that no one would see her eyes filling up. Was this all life had intended for her? To live by herself in a tiny little rented house cleaning other people's bogs? It was a terrifying thing to be given a peep into a future that appeared to have no hope in it.

The phone call to Ruth Fallis wasn't a pleasant one. Della could usually deal with the Ruth Fallises of the world all day every day, but there was something about the woman that made her want not to be professional but to squash her like a fly. Stealing from old ladies was deplorable and wouldn't be tolerated. The call stretched Della's patience to the limit, especially when Ruth's argument sank to the depths of a lot of swearing and slagging off everyone and everything to do with Diamond Shine. Ruth was always more comfortable arguing on a fish-wife level though and couldn't deal with Della's controlled and non-negotiable half of the conversation. She ended up telling Della to 'piss off, you frozen-faced bitch' and slammed down the phone. It was water off a duck's back to Della, who was relieved she had an excuse to get rid of the woman.

Ruth didn't need the money; Jock Fallis wasn't without a bob or two, in fact the only reason that Della could think of why Ruth worked at all for the pittance Diamond Shine paid was to sniff out possible leads for Jock to pursue, and obviously to line her own pocket when she thought she could get away with it. Della had just replaced the handset on the receiver when there was a courtesy knock on the door and in walked Connie with the envelope of evidence which Della had left with her on Friday.

Connie was wearing a bulky blue swing coat which made her look like Demis Roussos on steroids. The woman knew nothing about style, thought Della, and then realised, to her own surprise, that the thought was more sympathetic than scathing. Connie's cheeks seemed to have sunk since Friday and paled by five shades.

'I brought you these back,' said Connie, handing over the receipts.

'Thanks,' said Della, waiting for Connie to carry

on speaking: *Let's just forget this, shall we. I'll pretend you didn't say anything and you can pretend I was never here.* But she didn't. Instead she peeped into Jimmy's office and the kitchen and stood in front of Ivanka's desk, staring at the empty chair as if trying to visualise the girl sitting there.

'I haven't been here since he moved into the place,' said Connie, looking around at Jimmy's Kingdom. 'I thought it was much smaller.'

'He had the kitchen wall moved to make this part of the office bigger,' Della answered. 'And had the windows enlarged.'

'New windows?' asked Connie.

'Yes.'

Connie gave a small humourless laugh.

Then the phone rang and Della recognised the number on the caller display.

'It's Ivanka,' she said.

'Pick it up,' said Connie, sitting down on the seat at the other side of Della's desk.

Della placed her finger up against her lips, warning Connie to be quiet, then pressed the speaker-phone button.

'Hello Ivanka, my dear,' began Della, sounding very un-Della like in the syrupy tones of sympathetic warmth. 'How are you?'

Cough, cough, sniff. 'I am much better, thank you, Della.' *Sniff.* 'I will be in work tomorrow.'

'Don't you rush back if you are still poorly,' said Della, looking directly at Connie, who was hearing the voice of her husband's mistress for the first time. 'I would rather you stayed off until you are fully recovered.'

'I am sure I will be fine tomorrow,' *sniff, cough.* 'I have had plenty of time in bed over weekend.'

I bet you have, mouthed Connie at Della.

'Well, if you are sure. You take care and rest today.'

Sniff, cough, sniff. 'Thank you, I will.'

And the line went dead.

'She sounds so young,' said Connie.

'She is. But not up here,' said Della, tapping her temple with her finger. 'Have you heard from Jimmy?'

'No,' replied Connie. 'He never rings when he's away "on business".' She gave the words a hefty weight.

'You could ring him on the mobile you now know he has,' said Della.

'I've been very tempted to do that this weekend,' replied Connie.

'He'll be bringing you some chocolates,' Della said. 'They're from a shop in Hampshire called Simone le Bon. They're being delivered here this afternoon. Very expensive rose creams – your favourite, I do believe.'

Connie felt something in her stomach rise up and not in a pleasant way at the thought of one of those chocolates passing her lips.

'I shan't be eating them,' replied Connie, her mood visibly dropping now. Della could see her shoulders slump and heard the sigh leave her and prepared herself for what Connie had to say, that she was going to roll over and let Jimmy kick her. She was such a different creature to the one Della had fashioned of her over the years. Not that Della wanted to feel anything for her that wasn't on a purely business level. She had to keep in her sights that Connie had information about her now that she could use against her with Jimmy. They were as dangerous as each other to each other.

'Can I get you a drink?' asked Della.

'No thanks,' replied Connie. 'I've got things I need to do today.' Della saw her throat rise and drop with a gulp before she continued. 'Have you had any more thoughts over the weekend?'

'I've done nothing but have thoughts over the weekend,' huffed Della.

'I'll be honest,' said Connie. 'I expected you to have changed your mind.' Della opened her mouth to speak but Connie wouldn't let her. 'If you have, I won't blame you. And I won't say anything, you can rely on me for that.'

Della doubted it, but she didn't contradict her on it.

'I changed mine,' Connie went on.

I knew it, thought Della. *So, to plan B then. Proceed to collecting evidence against possible future constructive dismissal court case.*

'. . . but only for a minute. There is no way back for me,' Connie said with a steely determination in her voice that seemed out of place for the sad-looking, frumpy, soft woman sitting across from

Della. 'I've secured the base in Maltstone and I'm just off to the retail park in Batley to buy office equipment.'

'Really?' said Della.

'So please pretend we never had a meeting—'

'Whoa there, I'm still in,' blurted Della. 'There's no way back for me either.'

'Wow,' said Connie, with delighted surprise in her voice. 'Well, I'm glad.'

'Today I'll get you a list of all the women waiting for an interview and all the ones we already employ. Jimmy has some good workers on his books. I happen to know that a few of them would respond very well to the carrot-dangle of a pay increase if you were considering poaching a few from us. Off the top of my head: Cheryl, Astrid, Hilda, Gemma, Val, Ava, Wenda Marie and Sandra are his best. I'll round up all the companies who I think might be possible future customers and those who have approached us – you can contact them with a lower quote. I'll drop off the information by the end of the day. You'll have as much as I can give you to blast Diamond Shine to kingdom come if you work at it from the outside.'

'And you work at it from the inside,' added Connie.

'Precisely.'

'Oh, I nearly forgot.' Connie unzipped her cavernous handbag and started rooting around in it until she had found the mobile phone. 'This is for you. I've put in the number of my new mobile next to our company name.'

Della raised an impressed duet of eyebrows.

'New company name? You've thought of one then. So what are we going to be called?' asked Della.

Connie allowed herself a wry smile as she answered, 'Lady Muck.'

CHAPTER 15

Connie had a wonderful day wandering around Staples and Ikea and filled up her car with everything the small office might need, from a desk to a waste paper bin and everything in between. She had also ordered a sign to be placed next to the door of the office in Maltstone: F. U. J. Financial Holdings. It was anonymous enough, if a little tongue in cheek.

Connie called into the estate agency, paid the bond and the advance rent and Tom Stamp handed over the key. The owner was apparently happy to let her move in immediately. So a delighted Connie drove over to Maltstone, parked up on Wheatfield Lane and tugged all the contents of her shopping haul up the stairs.

Armed with a small toolbox and the allen keys supplied in the Ikea boxes, Connie set about erecting her new desk. Connie's father had never been on the scene when she was growing up so her mother had acted both parental roles and been the one who mended plugs, put up pictures and fixed the leaky taps because workmen cost money that they didn't have. Connie had put her first set of shelves up in her bedroom before her fifteenth birthday.

Next Connie unwrapped the filing cabinet and put that together and the new flat-packed office chair. She filled the desk drawers with the reams of paper and stationery items which she had bought from Staples and took out the new printer from the box, ready to hook up to her new laptop, then she set some empty files on the resident shelves. Everything was fresh and new in this office from the furniture to the pens.

Standing back to admire her handiwork before she locked up, she was suddenly gripped by a fierce panic. What on earth was she doing? What the hell was she starting? A stern voice was stabbing its index finger into her brain, causing her to doubt her own sanity. If she carried on with this, she wouldn't be able to stop, it warned her. Was she really sure she could take all this on? People's livelihoods were going to be at stake. What if she poached staff promising them the world and then her business failed?

Connie shook her head as if to jiggle some sense to the forefront. She couldn't allow herself to prioritise the welfare of the cleaners above all else. What she hadn't said to Della was that she hadn't thought any further forward than destroying Jimmy's business. Della and the cleaning women of Diamond Shine were merely a bunch of strangers to her and, though it went against her usual caring personality, she *wouldn't* give precedence to their needs over what she had to do. Connie had to keep her goal firmly in her mind. Her jaw hardened in determination as she pictured herself delivering a speech of victory over the destroyed form of her soon-to-be-ex-husband. For once, Connie was going to put her own interests first.

Afterwards she drove across town, past the sprawling Ketherwood estate, through Elsecar and then onto the industrial estate where the office of Diamond Shine was situated. It was exactly five o'clock when she arrived and Della was switching off the lights. Usually she stayed until at least half-past, but not any more. Her goodwill days were over.

'I was just about to ring you,' said Della. 'I didn't know whether to drop this off at your house or not.' She held up a blue cardboard file. 'There's all the information in there that you'll need to start crippling Diamond Shine.'

Connie noticed the slight reticence in handing it over.

'Thank you,' she said. 'I appreciate it. I'll make a start ringing around in the morning. I've been setting up the new office.'

Della was impressed. 'You've moved in already?'

'I've paid the bond and the rent so the estate agent handed over the key.'

Della blew out her cheeks. Things *were* moving fast. 'So, how do you think you'll react when you see Jimmy tonight?'

Connie gave a humourless laugh. 'I don't have a clue.'

She knew that Della thought she would crumble and so she added, 'But don't think I'll collapse into a useless heap, if that's what you mean. I have no idea what I'll be like when I see him again, but I can assure you that I won't be falling into his arms and begging him not to leave me.'

Della looked at the frumpy woman in front of her in the awful coat and tried to reconcile her with the Boudicca-type fighting talk and found it impossible. Connie didn't strike her as the strong type and though her initial anger might hold her up for a few hours, she would more than likely crack up in no time and this was all going to end horribly, she knew it. What the hell had she been thinking of agreeing to this mad plan? She wanted to grab that file back and destroy it. She wanted to lock up the doors to Diamond Shine and run off away from anyone who had a connection with the place. Oh God!

Connie noticed the box of chocolates on Della's desk.

'Are those for me?'

'Yes. No doubt Jimmy will pick them up from here on his way home. That's what he usually does.'

The ribbon around them was the colour of bile.

'I'll be in touch,' said Connie, turning to go. 'Good luck in the morning. Let me know how it goes and I'll let you know how tonight goes, though I can tell you now really. Jimmy will come in, present me with the box of chocolates, sit at the table and eat the meal I have prepared for him, then he will yawn, say he is very tired and we will go to bed. He will stay on his side and I will stay on mine until the alarm goes off at seven, when I will get up, make him poached eggs on toast and he will drive here. Sometimes he even remembers to say goodbye to me, but not always.' She was smiling as she was talking, but her tone was one of sadness.

The two women walked out to their cars together and drove off in opposite directions. Seeing Jimmy again face to face was something neither of them was looking forward to, although there was a tiny rebellious part of them that couldn't wait and was beckoning, 'bring it on.'

CHAPTER 16

Connie checked the clock on the oven to see that it was exactly nine thirty p.m. Just after she turned the oven heat down before the home-made shepherd's pie was cremated, she saw the gleam of headlamps slice through the Venetian blinds at the kitchen window and she felt a kick of adrenaline. This is where it all really begins, she thought: the pretence, the deception, the game-playing – all things that were alien to her, but she'd have to learn to master the art of them fast if she were to survive. She shook the sudden attack of anxiety pins and needles out of her hands and pasted on a welcoming smile in readiness for the appearance of her lying, cheating git of a husband. Within the minute he had appeared at the back door, dragging his suitcase with one hand and carrying the large box of chocolates with the sickly green ribbon in the other.

'I'm home,' he called, full-beam grin plastered over his face. 'Bloody traffic. Articulated lorry jack-knifed and there was only one lane open on the motorway out of Hampshire.'

Hearing his lies made it easier to be strong and keep hold of that fortifying anger and, ironically at this moment, she was grateful for them.

'So, how's my best girl then?' Jimmy said, dumping his suitcase on the floor, then he pulled Connie close with his free arm and stamped a kiss on the top of her head. 'I brought you these. Hampshire's finest. I had to drive all over the place to find them, but I know how you love your chocolate. Rose creams, your favourite as well. I couldn't have come home without them.'

He handed over the box which Connie took from his hands with a fake delighted smile.

'These look pricey.'

Jimmy waved the expense away with a flap of his hand. 'So what,' he said. 'Only the best for you. That smells good. Shepherd's pie, is it?'

Connie tilted her head to one side and made sure that Jimmy noticed she was studying him. 'Yep. You're nice and tanned, Jimmy. Was it sunny?'

'Naw. Pissed it down on Saturday so Pookie and I hit the spa and had a spray tan. I think they used too dark a shade,' smiled Jimmy, his teeth looking artificially white against the brown of his skin.

He was so smooth with his lies, thought Connie. He had probably been practising that line on the plane. She wondered if Ivanka would be sun-kissed too.

'I'm going to go up to change into my trackies. Be a love and pour me a beer, Con. I didn't stop at any motorway services and I'm parched.'

'Course I will,' Connie said. 'Dinner will be served up by the time you come down.'

Jimmy smiled. 'That sounds perfect.' He stretched out his arms and yawned. 'It's surprisingly tiring playing golf and talking business,' he said, lifting up his suitcase and walking wearily across the kitchen towards the staircase. 'But I think we covered a lot of ground. We have got plans.'

'Well done you,' said Connie, her smile dropping as he turned his back. She had plans too. He didn't know what they were yet, but he soon would. She threw the chocolates down onto the table with disgust and opened the oven door.

CHAPTER 17

'You're very brown,' said Della the next morning, studying Ivanka in much the same way that Connie had looked at her husband the night before.

'My cousin has sun-bed,' said Ivanka, flicking a shank of long blonde hair behind her shoulder. 'She said it would do me good. It makes vitamin D in the body.'

'I'll have to get one myself.' Della let loose a light trill of laughter as she picked up the empty water bottle from Ivanka's desk. 'You look as if you've been abroad.'

'I wish,' said Ivanka, with a small sniff. Della had to admire her composure. Ivanka didn't even flinch when she hovered near to the truth.

'Some more water?' asked Della. Ivanka never drank tea or coffee, only bottles of sparkling water which took up most of the small kitchen fridge. She had been at work an hour so far but hadn't offered to make tea for Della. Any other time and Della would have nudged her with a request, but not today. There was mischief in her heart.

'Yes,' said Ivanka, whilst stapling two sheets of paper together.

If she thinks I'm setting a precedent by turning into the drinks-lady she can think again, thought Della. But now in the light of all sorts of new information, Della could see why Ivanka had been acting more and more imperiously every day.

As Della was bringing in the mug of tea and a bottle of water, Jimmy was just arriving.

'Morning girls,' he said, his white smile bright against his David Dickinson tan.

'Morning,' replied Della, plastic smile pulled out of the bag. She watched Ivanka giving him one of her nods and the usual mumbled greeting. And to think that Della had interpreted that as a sign that Ivanka had no liking for the man. Oh they'd been clever; they both could have won Oscars for their acting.

'Another one with a tan,' Della remarked.

'Well, I don't know about Ivanka's, but mine came out of a bottle,' said Jimmy, turning to her and asking, 'Are you feeling better now?'

'Yes, thank you,' she said. No emotion, no hint they were anything more than boss and office junior.

'You should get out more,' he said. 'I feel marvellous playing golf for a few days and filling my lungs up to the top with fresh air.'

Ivanka flashed him a polite smile and returned to her stapling. God they were good. No wonder that Della had never guessed what was going on under her nose.

110

'I'll bring you a cup of coffee through, Jimmy,' Della said, returning to the kitchen and slyly peering through the viewing slit between door and jamb. She waited for a single telling glance to pass between them, but nothing. They clearly weren't risking the slightest chance that they could be caught. She had worked in offices since she was sixteen and knew that the tiniest gesture could set tongues wagging. Those careless little faux pas were always the undoing of couples who were having affairs.

Ivanka had gone to the loo and Jimmy was in his office when Della breezed back with a mug of coffee and a small plate of biscuits for the boss.

'So, you enjoyed your weekend away, did you? Did Connie like her chocolates?' said Della.

'Oh yes. I expect there won't be any left by the time I get home,' said Jimmy. 'She does like her sweet stuff does old Connie. Mind you, how could you not like chocolates at that price? Brownie points for those, Del. Oh, I'll possibly be going to Edinburgh next month. Do a bit of research into any chocolate shops up there will you, my love.'

'Of course, Jimmy.'

'And when Ivana, sorry Ivanka, silly bloody name, comes back from whatever she's doing, can you send her in here. I want to dictate a couple of letters.'

'Certainly,' said Della, smiling her sweetest, as she shut the door behind her.

*   *   *

111

Connie paid over the odds for her new business cards, but they were ready in record time and she was very, very pleased with them when she picked them up from Clough & Sons printers on the outskirts of town. They were printed on thick card, solid black no-nonsense font on gold, with rounded corners: they smacked of quality without being tacky.

Lady Muck
Reliable, Trustworthy Staff
Any price beaten, any job bettered.
You'll wonder how you lived without us!
Tel: 07965 320941

She was keen to get straight down to work then. Not that she was sure where to start – did she set cleaners on first or ring the existing clients of Diamond Shine and present an altogether superior service? She tried to remember back years ago to when she and Jimmy had first set up Diamond Shine. They hadn't had a computer then; Connie and her mother had trudged for hours dropping leaflets through letterboxes trying to round up both clients and cleaners. In those days there had been far more cleaners out there than clients. She had interviewed the girls in their homes so she could be certain of their standards and left the schmoozing of the clients to Jimmy. She had enjoyed working at Diamond Shine when every client gained was a massive cause for celebration. She remembered how she and Jimmy had danced around the room when he landed a contract for a large office block which would need four cleaners once a week for four hours. Then Connie fell pregnant and Jane came along and Jimmy's mum was ill so Connie had to juggle lots of balls in the air until it became impossible and she'd had to pass her job on to a series of assistants, none of whom Jimmy seemed to gel with until Della came along. The thing was that Connie could never have realised how good Della was at her job because she had been led to believe that they were hanging on to their business by the fingernails, not rich enough to bathe in asses' milk.

'Why are you setting someone else on if things are so bad?' she'd asked, when Jimmy hired Ivanka.

'Because a bit of fresh blood might help rev things up,' he'd explained. 'You know when you have an old dog and it's flagging? Well, you get a young pup in and the old dog starts to perk up; so, I thought I'd give that a try.'

'And what if the "old dog" doesn't perk up?' Connie had asked.

'Well, you shoot it,' Jimmy had replied.

'You're not going to shoot Della, are you?'

'Don't be daft,' he'd laughed. 'If she doesn't perk up, I'll let her go. But she has been with me for fifteen years. What sort of bastard would I be if I didn't give her the chance to redeem herself? She was shit-hot in her prime and there is such a thing as loyalty.'

And Connie had swallowed it hook, line and sinker.

She decided she would open Della's secret file and then plunge into the waters head first and see where the tides took her.

Della picked up the phone and dialled the number on the notepad in front of her.

'Hello,' came a coarse voice down the receiver. Della shuddered. She couldn't actually believe what she was about to do. It went against every grain she had.

'Is that Lesley Clamp? This is Della Frostick from Diamond Shine.'

'Oh aye.'

'I'm just ringing to say that we would like to offer you a job if you are still interested.'

'Reight. When do I start?'

'Maybe in a couple of weeks. I'll ring you back when I have clients in place for you. Is that okay?'

'S'pose.'

I'm offering you a job, woman, not trying to take out your liver, thought Della at the woman's monosyllabic miserable response.

'I'll be in touch.'

'As tha' got any more jobs going? Me nieces Alaska and Nepal want one.'

Della raised her eyes heavenward. Alaska and Nepal Clamp on the payroll along with Auntie Lesley would be totally unthinkable. Absolutely preposterous. At least it would be unthinkable if

114

she had to deal with them on a weekly basis, but by then she'd be long gone.

'Yes. If you give me their telephone numbers, I'm sure there will soon be vacancies for them too.'

Della took down the numbers and fought the urge to growl. It stuck in her craw to set people on such as anyone with Clamp in their name, because she knew they'd be total nightmares from the off. Just as Ruth Fallis was.

Della took the file out of her drawer labelled 'Rejections', removed all the contents and put them back in a new file, along with Alaska and Nepal Clamp's telephone numbers. Then she wrote on it in very large black letters which couldn't be missed, 'Priority list of potential cleaners.' If ever a firm deserved cleaners such as Ruth Fallis and the Clampettes, it was Diamond Shine, thought Della, trying not to smirk.

CHAPTER 18

Connie sat at her new desk with a coffee and Della's file under a heavy, black cloud of self-doubt. Women whose husbands were shagging their staff went to the solicitors and started divorce proceedings; they didn't throw away an inheritance on setting up a rival company. What the hell was she doing? Was she totally crackers? She reached down for her purse to retrieve Tom Stamp's business card. She'd ring him and make a hypothetical enquiry about what would happen if she decided that she didn't want the office after all. It was in the pocket at the back with her credit cards and a couple of small photos she always kept with her: Jane's school photo, a grainy black and white one of herself and Jimmy as teenage sweethearts, and the one she was holding now – Jane as a baby being held by Connie's mum, Janet, and standing next to them was her formidable auntie Marilyn with her hourglass figure and her bleach-blonde hair. Connie picked it up and stared hard at it. She knew the feisty pair would be willing her to stop being a wet lettuce and get her shoulder to the bloody grindstone. She propped the photo up against a stapler just as she knew their image would prop her up in turn in her weaker moments. Next she wriggled off her wedding ring because here, at work, she wasn't Mrs Connie Diamond, she was either Lady Muck or Marilyn Smith and neither of them was weighed down by a useless marriage.

Right, let's do it.

She filled up her lungs to capacity with a deep breath and stabbed the first number on Della's 'potential list' into her mobile phone. It was answered almost immediately by a youthful female voice.

'Hello, Dartley Carpets, how can we help you?'

Connie's mouth froze in a long O. She pressed end call and growled at herself. *Come on, Con,* she geed herself up. *This isn't going to knit the baby a bonnet.* She thought of her auntie Marilyn and the confidence she oozed. Even when she was very ill and no doubt frightened and depressed, the face Marilyn showed to the world was a bright and beautiful one full of strength. Connie hit redial. The same voice answered.

'Hello, Dartley Carpets, how can we help you?'

'Hello there. I'm so sorry, I've just rung but I was cut off.'

'Oh, it's always doing that. Our phones are rubbish, sorry about that.'

The girl believed her. That's what a confident delivery did for you.

'I hear that your company is looking for office cleaners. I may be able to help you on that.'

'Really?' The girl on the phone sounded as if Connie had just offered her front row tickets to see the Chippendales. 'I'll put you through to the manager, Jeff Froom.'

Connie barely had time to take in a breath before a gruff voice answered.

'Hello. Jeff Froom, Dartley Carpets, who is it?'

Connie straightened her spine and became the auntie who was sassy and sexy with a great figure and a fluff of Marilyn Monroe hair and who had died, much too young, of womb cancer. As Marilyn Smith incarnated, Connie answered him with confidence. 'Good morning, Mr Froom. My name is Marilyn Smith. I hear that you are looking for cleaners for your factory.'

'Oh aye. And who have you heard that off?'

'Industry gossip, Mr Froom. I'm ringing on behalf of Lady Muck cleaners. Can we step in to help?'

Jeff Froom gave a throaty laugh. 'Lady Muck? Like it. Not heard of you before though. Are you Barnsley based?'

'Indeed.' Connie was amazed by how confident she sounded. Or rather how confident *Marilyn* sounded. 'And we are new. The present firms can't cope but we know we can. And our standards and prices are better.'

'Really?'

The tone of his voice told Connie that she definitely had Jeff Froom's full attention now. He was a Yorkshireman, after all – and they loved a bargain.

'Yes, really.'

Five minutes later, Lady Muck had its first customer on its books. Connie smiled with relief – if she could hook one person, she could hook more. She rang the second name on Della's list to find an automated message saying the firm was no longer trading. Then she rang a third number which was picked up just as Connie was about to put down the phone presuming no one was going to answer.

'Hello, hello, sorry about that,' said a breathy male voice.

'Mr Brandon Locke?'

'That's my name,' he answered cheerfully and continued in the same vein. 'Now please, I'm in the middle of something quite important so if you're someone about to ask me to help you with a survey or ask me if I've had an accident recently which wasn't my fault, I'm going to have to tell you that I can't talk to you.'

Connie grinned. He was far more polite than she would have been if she'd been interrupted by a nuisance caller.

'No, I have no interest in asking you lots of questions about your current mortgage or possible cuts and bruises,' she answered.

'Good. So, how can I help you then?'

'My name is Marilyn Smith and I'm calling from Lady Muck, a firm of house and office cleaners—'

Mr Locke cut her off.

'Please tell me you have a lovely lady who has space in her diary for me.'

'I was just about to.'

'Oh, deep joy.' Mr Locke sounded even more delighted than Dartley Carpets had. 'What a well-timed call. What firm are you again?'

'Lady Muck. We're new, although all of my staff have been cleaners for many years.' Connie instinctively touched her nose to see if it had grown.

'Lady Muck?' Mr Locke rolled the name around. 'Have I rung you? I'm sure I would have remembered the name.'

'No. We have links with other firms. Occasionally we share client lists and help each other out.' Connie was amazed how easily the lie slipped off her tongue and how equally easily it was believed.

'How kind,' said Mr Locke. 'Well, I would be delighted if you could give me a cleaner. And the sooner the better.'

'I need to come out and make an assessment, initially,' replied Connie. 'Is tomorrow too soon?'

'It's not soon enough, but I'll survive,' said Mr Locke. 'Do you have my address?'

Connie looked down at the file. 'Yes. Box House, Outer Hoodley.'

'Ah, well officially it is Outer Hoodley, but it's actually "outa" Outer Hoodley. As you turn off the Barnsley-Wentworth Road it's on your left before you get into the hamlet. If you've passed the Dick Turpin's Arms, you've gone too far. There is a sign but it's been overgrown by a tree. I haven't been in here very long and it's number four hundred and seventy-six on my list of jobs to sort out.'

'Half past ten okay?' asked Connie, liking the sound of Mr Locke and wondering what he looked like. She was going into Dartley Carpets to assess their cleaning needs just after nine.

'Just perfect,' said Mr Locke. 'Thank you so much. See you then.'

Connie was grinning as she put the phone down. 'This is going to be easier than I thought,' she said to herself, even though Lady Muck had no bank of cleaners yet. Not that it mattered at the moment because Connie would do the houses and offices herself if she had to. There were proper cleaners and those who pushed the dust around from one place to another and Connie's mother and granny before her were *proper* proper cleaners. These days, good cleaners were needed everywhere and Lady Muck was going to supply that demand.

By end of business that day, Connie was ready to eat her own words in a big fat sandwich with disappointment-flavoured mayonnaise. After her initial luck with Dartley Carpets and Mr Locke, there had been no other clients for Lady Muck. Despite the 'beat any price' and quality of service guarantee, most of the people she had rung today seemed reticent to trust a brand new company. Connie went home and put on the kettle to make a commiseratory cup of tea and, without thinking, opened the box of chocolates which Jimmy had brought for her.

Then the smell drifted up to her nose and she came to her senses. But oh, they were so pretty with their pink piped icing toppings. Every one a poisoned apple. Every one a fusion of cream, sugar, lies and deceit. She had always loved the chocolates he brought her, always hand-made. They made her feel that however hard Jimmy worked, or whatever was going on in his head, that her presence in his life and in his heart was both needed and wanted. That act of buying them for her kept them attached to each other with an unbreakable bond. Or so she had thought before she had come to realise that chocolate had been the thing which ripped them apart.

She lifted one out with careful pincered fingers and touched it to her lips. Her teeth bit through the double-dipped shell through to a soft sweet scented truffle and her brain sighed with old familiar pleasure. Chocolate had comforted her for so many years. Chocolate had reassured her and given her pleasure whenever she needed it. Chocolate had been a friend. No – chocolate had been an enemy. Chocolate had lied to her and laughed at her behind her back. Chocolate had made her into an idiot.

She spat the chocolate into the sink and then took eight more out of the box and squashed them between two squares of kitchen roll. The sickly perfume of rose filled the air around her, the odour of so much hurt, the scent of the end of her marriage. She buried them in the bottom of the bin and replaced the lid back on the Hampshire Simone le Bon box. Never again would chocolate pass her lips.

CHAPTER 19

Connie studied Jimmy as he stuffed the pancakes into his mouth whilst reading the newspaper. Butter had dribbled down his chin and made it glossy.

She was fascinated by her own feelings as she watched him. It was as if she were viewing a stranger, even though this man had shared her marriage bed for twenty-four years. Did Ivanka know that they still slept in the same bed, she wondered. Mind you, all they did in it was sleep. She couldn't remember the last time she and Jimmy had made love. Not had sex, because she could remember that – last Easter. They'd both had a bit too much to drink and he'd been booze-horny. There was no foreplay, no kissing, just an in-and-out bonk that he couldn't finish off because he'd had too much alcohol. He was snoring seconds after falling off her and, tipsy as she was, she'd had a moment of total clarity that she might as well have been a hole in the wall. She couldn't remember when he had last cared enough to bring her to the heights of ecstasy. She couldn't even remember when he had last kissed her on the mouth.

Did he 'make love' to Ivanka? she thought watching him lick the gloopy home-made chocolate sauce from his fork. He had been capable of great tenderness in their youth. He liked sex and Connie had enjoyed it too. He couldn't have gone to someone else because she denied him his conjugal rights, because she never had. Well, maybe a couple of times when she had been pregnant, which was to be expected. When had the fabric of their marriage started to unravel? When had she begun to find the missing part of her marriage in chocolate? Did she get plump and that's what turned him to other women or did he turn to other women which made try and feed her starved heart as she would feed a hungry stomach?

'What's up with you not having any pancakes on Pancake Day?' asked Jimmy, turning from his newspaper and catching her staring at him.

'I just feel a bit off,' replied Connie, patting her tummy.

'You must be if you aren't having anything with chocolate on it,' he laughed.

'Yes I must, mustn't I?' Connie tried to laugh too but the sound that came out was hollow and false. Luckily for her, Jimmy didn't notice. He was too busy eating and reading.

Connie tried not to retch as a fresh wave of chocolate scent overcame her. It was as if she had suddenly become hypersensitive to it. It seemed to stick to the inside of her nostrils and pump its strong sweet aroma into her lungs. She had hated making the sauces earlier on, but she wanted life for Jimmy to appear as normal as possible and he always had pancakes with a trio of chocolate sauces on this day. She didn't want him to have any inkling that he was about to be toppled from his throne before it happened.

Connie sat at the table nursing a coffee in her hands as Jimmy shovelled forkfuls of pancake into his mouth and cooed with pleasure, like a pigeon on happy pills.

'This is my favourite dessert of all time,' he said through the contents. 'We should have Pancake Day every day.' He pointed to the pink box on the work surface with his fork. 'You eaten all your chocolates yet?'

'I've had quite a few but I've got some left which I've decided to save for Easter because I'm . . . I'm going to give up chocolate for Lent.' She hadn't planned on saying that, but it fitted. He didn't need to know that she would never eat it again for now. She didn't want to arouse even the slightest suspicion that things were about to change.

Jimmy grinned

'You, give up chocolate? I've heard everything now.'

'I am,' she said decisively. 'Just for Lent though.'

'What for? What good will it do anyone?'

'I want to prove to myself that I can.'

'I'll bet you a tenner that you can't.'

Connie held out her hand. 'Check the box now,

and then check it again on the seventeenth of April. There won't be any more gone.'

Jimmy grinned and put down his fork so he could shake his wife's hand.

'You could no more give up eating chocolate for Lent than I could give up breathing,' he said, his tone more mocking than joking, she thought.

'You're probably right.' She nodded, but knew that he was very, very wrong.

CHAPTER 20

When Cheryl came home she found an egg splattered on her front window. Today had been awful from start to finish. She had been sent to do an all-day clean on a ridiculously scruffy house belonging to a recently deceased old man, whose relatives wanted it blitzing before they put it on the market. Usually that would have been a two-woman job but there was no one else available. It had been more of a task for environmental health services and if Della had known how bad it was, she would never have agreed to taking the job on. It had upset Cheryl to see how the old man had lived. It was a part of the job she hated, encountering old people who had no hope left and who sat all day, every day with no company and nothing to do. She had cried whilst she had vacuumed up months of crumbs from the carpet and scrubbed at the grime and filth which covered everything he had owned.

Della had rung to say that she'd had to carve up Ruth Fallis's rota and had given Cheryl Mr Morgan on Wednesdays, starting tomorrow. 'Morgan the Organ' as he was known locally, had been the organist for the local church in Maltstone for over thirty years and appeared sometimes in the *Barnsley Chronicle* or the *Daily Trumpet* standing next to the giant Wurlitzer which he had in his house. A fine upstanding citizen. Mr Morgan was just around the corner from Cheryl's two-hour slot with fussy Mrs Hopkinson. Cheryl was grateful for the extra hours because she needed all the money she could get. Gary still hadn't returned her call and she supposed he wouldn't now. Over and over she had imagined Ann Gladstone telling her son what a nightmare he had escaped from. Cheryl didn't want him to think that and wished more than anything he would ring just so that she could hear in his voice that he still cared about her.

'I've told him you'll do everything Ruth did,' said Della. 'His upstairs, his downstairs, and convinced him, I hope, that his Wurlitzer was in good hands with you. He's obviously one of those types who likes things done a certain way so just make sure you do what she did . . .' *Which probably means eat all his biscuits and nick from his house,* thought Della. 'He might be a bit awkward because unfortunately some types would rather keep an old familiar bad cleaner than have a new strange good one. He'll give you a key when you go tomorrow.'

As Cheryl looked at the mess on the front of her house, she wondered if this was a message from the Fallis family because Ruth knew that

129

she'd been the one who had reported her to Della. It was unlikely to be a drive past random egg-throw because she lived in a quiet cul-de-sac. Jock Fallis was a nasty beggar and so was their son Jock Junior. Then again, Jock Fallis's M.O. was more horse's head in the bed than yolk dripping down her glass. Still, it niggled her that the two might be connected.

She scrubbed the mess off her window then put on some beans on toast for her tea; not that she was in the slightest bit hungry but she was shaking from not eating. Her appetite had been zero since Gary had gone. She felt as if she were treading water, surviving rather than living, and she didn't think she'd ever laugh again. God knows, life with Gary was hardly high octane, but she believed they had sorted out all their problems and she had been content in her little world. Now, she felt as if the top layer of her skin had been peeled back and she was sensitive to everything. Even when a thought of him brushed against her brain, it made it ache.

They'd been so close to affording a cycle of IVF and this time she was convinced that it would work, because she had been doing yoga to de-stress, eating healthily, abstaining from alcohol, following every faddy tip – however daft – that the internet had to offer to give her body the best chance of growing the baby. She had imagined spending the summer with a swelling belly and shopping for tiny baby outfits – the dream had been so near she could have touched it. But as with even the most vivid dreams, it was all gone in the blink of an eye.

She switched on the TV to divert her attention but it was a thriller about a man who gambled away all his fortune and then killed his wife to claim on the insurance. Cheryl switched it off and went to bed. She came down the next morning to find six broken eggs all over her window and front door.

CHAPTER 21

'How's my best girl this morning?' Jimmy said, swaggering into the office the next day with his magic grin on full beam. Della's heart still quickened slightly, betraying the more measured and sensible activity going on in her brain. She had adored Jimmy Diamond. She would have done anything for him, but her feelings had been exposed as one-way traffic. How had she fooled herself into thinking that a man who rode so rough-shod over his family would genuinely treasure her? It was the first day of Lent today and Della was going to give up being a mug.

'I'm fine, as always,' said Della – her standard response. She switched on a smile, but it took an effort today.

As she put the kettle on she noticed that Ivanka walked in five minutes after Jimmy had and it came to her that that was the standard pattern of every morning. She hadn't noticed it before, because she hadn't been on the look-out for any suspicious activity, but Ivanka *always* turned into the office five minutes after her boss. They must meet before work, Della realised, and Ivanka waited around the corner so they didn't arrive together. A huge technicolour high-definition picture of them both passionately clawing at each other in Jimmy's car rose up in her brain and a sharp ache spread underneath her ribs. She felt as betrayed as Connie did.

'I'm going out for a long business lunch today,' Jimmy announced as she handed him his coffee in the World's Best Boss mug she had bought him for his birthday.

'There's nothing in the diary,' huffed Della.

'Sorry,' he slapped his forehead with the palm of his hand. 'Forgot to tell you.'

He was always forgetting to tell her about last-minute meetings recently, which made her life awkward sometimes, but she had forgiven him anything until now.

'Naughty,' she said, as usual in this situation, but she couldn't manage to sustain her smile.

'Is it okay if I take hour and half for lunch today? I have cousin's present to buy for birthday tomorrow,' Ivanka asked Della as she was taking her coat off.

'Yes, of course.' It came out as a hiss that a king cobra would have been proud of. It had just struck her how many cousins Ivanka claimed to have: a cousin whose birthday was tomorrow, a cousin who dealt in cars, a cousin who had a sunbed, a cousin who was a model and gave her cast-off designer clothes, a cousin who bought her a silver Tiffany necklace for Christmas. So very many of them.

'An hour and a half?' Jimmy didn't sound very pleased.

'An hour is not enough. Sometimes it takes me ages to find parking space and I must buy the present today.'

Della watched the interchange between them with fascination. There was absolutely no clue at all that they were in a relationship. Jimmy turned to Della then and winked. 'I suppose so in that case. If Della is okay with it.'

'Try not to be any later though, Ivanka,' said Della, in her best accommodating voice.

Then Val Turner, the oldest cleaner on their books, turned up to replenish her bag of supplies and life in the office carried on as normal, at least on the surface.

It was the morning from hell for Della as it seemed that the phone didn't stop ringing and Ivanka was taking even longer than usual to do the simplest tasks as if her head was anywhere but on the job. It took her half an hour to fetch a packet of biscuits from the shop around the corner for which she blamed a long queue at the till. Under normal circumstances Della would have taken her to task about her dawdling, but she bit her lip because the more Ivanka thought she was getting away with things, the more cocky and careless she would become. But still, Della earned her wage that morning fielding calls for Jimmy (mostly golf buddies) and dealing with pernickety clients, reps trying to sell her cheap cloths and wonder-aids, and cleaners moaning about their wages being wrong. Della had trusted Ivanka to calculate the girls' hours last week and she had managed to totally balls it up. Della had been planning to teach the girl all she knew about running the office, but that would have to stop now seeing as it was the equivalent of digging her own grave.

Della had just started on her lunchtime sandwich when Wenda Sykes rang up with the crème of the crème call of the morning. She was refusing to clean Mr Savant's house again because she said it was haunted.

'Don't be bloody silly, Wenda,' said Della, none too patiently.

'I tell you, I'm not going there again. No, sorry, Della you'll have to find someone else and there's no point asking any of the others either because I've told them all about it.'

'Oh well, that's just marvellous.'

Wenda was not budging on the decision either.

Della could do with this like a hole in the head today.

'The dead can't hurt you, Wenda,' she snapped.

'Well, they already did. I heard a noise and fell backwards over a nest of tables. I've got a bruise the size of Africa on my arse.'

'Look, Wenda, I've carved up Ruth's clients fair and square and you got Mr Savant. Cheryl got Mr Morgan and Gemma, Sandra and Astrid got the rest.'

But Wenda was adamant. 'I'm telling you, Della, those noises I heard were as real as the nose on my face. Banging, banging. As if someone had been bricked up in a wall.'

'It's an old building. It'll be the pipes making a noise.'

'Pipes don't say, "Hello, is there anybody there," though, do they?'

'You've been watching too much *Britain's Most Haunted*, Wenda.'

'He was playing this horrible loud opera music and then the record finished and it went all quiet. That's when I heard it: "Hello, is there anybody there" it said in a woman's voice.'

'Maybe, just maybe, Wenda, the music didn't go off. Maybe that voice was part of the opera. Maybe you heard Madame Butterfly herself, or Carmen or Barbara of Seville.'

'You can laugh all you like, Della, but I'll pull my own bowel out with a crochet needle before I'll go back there again.'

There was an image Della didn't want to think about when she was half-way through a potted meat sandwich.

'Ruth never said anything about any strange noises.'

'Ruth's earholes are as lazy as the rest of her.'

Della was about to battle some more and employ her usual 'you can't pick and choose' speech, then her brain caught up with her mouth.

If there was no one who would clean his house at Diamond Shine, then Lady Muck could soak up his business.

'Okay, okay,' said Della. 'I'll ring him.'

'You will?' Wenda's gasp was audible. She was almost winded by Della's conceding defeat. She had been expecting Della to use the line she was famous for: 'If you think you can pick and choose your own clients, you can go and pick and choose another firm to work for.'

'Yes, I said I will.'

Della heard Wenda say 'Blimey' as she put down the phone and fought off the smile that threatened to push up the corners of her mouth.

'What is wrong?' asked Ivanka, as Della put down the phone.

'Wenda won't clean Mr Savant's house again,' replied Della.

'Why? What is up with the house?'

'It used to be an undertaker's business and because of that, it's got the reputation of being haunted. Wenda's heard banging. She thinks Mr Savant has bricked someone up in the wall.' Della swept her eyes upwards in exasperation.

'You should make her,' said Ivanka. 'You should say, I will sack you if you don't clean the house.'

Della tried not to resort to a sarcastic thank you to Ivanka for telling her how to do her job. She shrugged her shoulders.

'I can't physically drag her in to clean it though,

can I? I'll have to make up some excuse to tell him because she's scared everyone else off from going there as well.'

'So it looks as if we are going to lose his business then?' Ivanka shook her head slowly from side to side with disgust.

'Yep,' nodded Della.

'Maybe you should do the job for a while until we find cleaner who will go in, Della?'

Ivanka chuckled, but Della knew she was testing how far she could push her. Something had happened in Spain to make Ivanka believe her status had changed and the bets were on it being to do with that engagement ring.

'Do you know, Ivanka, that same thought has crossed my mind too,' said Della. 'I might have to leave the office in your capable hands and take up a mop myself.' She had to let Ivanka think she was getting the upper hand but it went against every bit of grain her soul possessed. Out of the corner of her eye, she saw Ivanka's jaw momentarily drop open. The silly girl actually thought Della meant it. Della had to turn away and bite her lip when she saw the delighted smirk on Ivanka's face.

'Would you like a drink, dear?' asked Della, playing the office junior card to full effect.

CHAPTER 22

Cheryl knocked on the door to Mr Morgan's large detached house and was glad that he didn't take long to answer it because it was freezing.

'Hello, Mr Morgan. I'm Cheryl from Diamond Shine, your new Ruth,' Cheryl introduced herself with a nervous laugh.

'Wonderful, come in, new Ruth,' said Mr Morgan, standing aside to let her in. The rush of hot air in the house nearly knocked Cheryl off her feet. Talk about moving from one extreme to another.

'Please, let me take your coat,' he said, nearly dragging Cheryl backwards with the action. She hoped that his hands had brushed against the sides of her breasts by accident, because she'd had a couple of touchy-feely customers before. She'd had to report them both to Della in the end, who rang them up, gave them a mouthful and said that they wouldn't be sending any more of their ladies to work for them. Della might be a grumpy old stick, but she was on the girls' side when it counted.

'So,' Mr Morgan clapped his hands together. 'You're going to do everything Ruth did for me.'

'Yes, that's right. Obviously, I'll be more in the swing of things next week.'

'Oh that's good, that's very good to hear,' Mr Morgan said, looking strangely relieved. 'I pulled my back and can't bend properly, you see.'

'Oh dear,' Cheryl sympathised, wondering what that had to do with anything. But then she had learned that the older end of her clients often had a loose grip on relevance in conversations. Their minds flitted from one subject to another like butterflies who'd had too much espresso.

'I'm going to my chiropractor this afternoon.'

'Well, you just sit and rest and I'll clean.' Looking around, the place looked as if it hadn't had a good going-over for weeks – but that was no surprise with slack Ruth Fallis as his domestic.

She started upstairs. There were months-old cobwebs hanging from the curtains and Cheryl was at a loss to understand why Mr Morgan hadn't reported Ruth. Rather disconcertingly he followed her from room to room, sitting on a chair in order to watch her work.

'You don't mind me being here, do you?' he asked.

'No, not at all,' she fibbed. She'd rather he weren't, but presumed he must be lonely.

'You clean very well, very thoroughly.'

'Thank you, Mr Morgan.'

'I bet you'll do a wonderful job on my organ.'

'I shall do my best. I know how important it is to you that your er . . . instrument is treated with care.'

'Well, obviously you can do my downstairs next week, all being well.'

'That's right. I think it's going to take me all my time today to clean up here, Mr Morgan.'

'Precisely.' Mr Morgan shrugged his shoulders. 'I must say that I heartily approve of you, Cheryl. I didn't think I'd find another Ruth.'

Well, that was hardly a compliment, thought Cheryl. But clients often grew attached to cleaners and if Mr Morgan was a lonely soul, then it was perfectly credible that he had formed an attachment to the thieving, idle old bat.

'You're much smaller than Ruth though,' he went on with a chuckle.

Who wasn't, thought Cheryl. Moby Dick was smaller than Ruth. Cheryl wiped the perspiration from her brow. It was boiling in this house.

'Should I turn the heating down?' he asked.

'It is very hot in here,' replied Cheryl.

'I'll do it now,' he said and rose slowly from the chair, holding on to his aching back. 'There was no point in having it so high today, was there?'

'Er no,' replied Cheryl, though she hadn't a clue what he meant.

By the time she had cleaned three bedrooms, a bathroom, the hall and stairs there was no time left to do anything else.

Mr Morgan had left a hundred pounds out for her on the hall table. No wonder Ruth enjoyed coming here, thought Cheryl. Here was another

141

old person she was fleecing. Cheryl lifted only the money she was due and left the rest.

'Oh you must take it,' Mr Morgan insisted, pressing it into her hand. 'Go and buy yourself something for next week.'

'No, really Mr Morgan, I can't.' She'd accepted the odd fiver tip from a client, but this was a bit much. When he turned his back to take her coat from the hallstand, she opened a drawer in the hall table and quickly slipped the excess money into it. She didn't know how anyone slept at night robbing from old folk.

Mr Morgan held out the coat for Cheryl to slip her arms into. Again, his fingers skimmed her edges of her breasts and this time she was sure it was more deliberate than clumsy.

Cheryl lifted up her bag and walked quickly out. Next week she wouldn't give him the slightest opportunity to touch her inappropriately.

'Jimmy's gone out. So has Ivanka,' said Della, talking to Connie via her new mobile phone just after half-past twelve. 'How are you getting on?'

'Not brilliantly,' sighed Connie. 'I've managed to find one more client but it's only for two hours every fortnight and a couple of people haven't committed, but said they'd ring back. People seem to be wary of a brand new firm with no website, no land-line number yet and no testimonials to offer. I can't remember it being this hard to drum up business when we first set up Diamond Shine.'

It was too early for Connie to start panicking, but she was panicking.

'Think of it like a huge snowball at the top of a mountain,' said Della. 'It might take a bit of huffing and puffing to budge it at first, but once it starts to roll . . .'

'Knowing my luck, I'll do my back in pushing it and we'll be stuck at the top of the mountain for ever and I'll die of frostbite.'

'That kind of defeatist attitude won't get you anywhere,' Della admonished her. 'Now, I have an idea. What you need, Connie, is a good, strong curry . . .'

CHAPTER 23

Cheryl came downstairs the next morning to find more eggs all over her windowsill and door. She knew now that her house was being deliberately targeted and it could only be someone from the Fallis family. She had entertained the idea for no more than seconds that it could be Gary's mother. Ann Gladstone would never have stooped so low as to be involved in anything as sly and undignified as that.

Gary still had lots of things in the house – his passport in the drawer, some clothes, a watch, a book, trainers, a guitar that he had bought but never even plucked. She had initially taken that as a sign that he had 'wedged the door open'. That he knew he would be coming back. Of course she still loved him; she might not have wanted to, but she missed him terribly. They had been together for a decade of dreadful lows but some lovely highs too. The house was so quiet without him and much tidier. She'd always reprimanded him for leaving crumbs on the work surface or not hanging his coat up but she would have given anything to have him back with his irritating little ways. *But you can't,* said the calm but definitive voice of reason in her head. *You would never trust him again.* One more chance, just ring him and tell him you'll give him one more chance, her heart argued. *No,* said her head. *You gave him one more chance twice before. Let him go. Bag up his stuff and take it round to his mum's house. You have to.*

Cheryl cleaned up the eggy mess outside. Her neighbour spent the winter months in Benidorm and wasn't back until Easter so Cheryl couldn't ask her if she'd seen anyone suspicious hanging around. The neighbours further up were old and she didn't want to frighten them so she would just have to hope that Jock or Jock Junior Fallis got bored very quickly.

At least on Thursday afternoon Cheryl had her dear Edith to clean for in the afternoon and though the old lady was the favourite of her clients, she had some others she was very fond of too. There was her Friday morning gentleman Mr Fairbanks, who was a retired lecturer and had a beautiful house full of exquisite treasures, and her Friday afternoon lady, eighty-year-old Miss Potter, an ex-business manager who had never been fully able to retire and was always wheeling and dealing on the internet. Then there was her Monday afternoon lady, the glamorous Miss Molloy, who was kind and clever and rich and had her own private school for educating adults. Cheryl wished she had been blessed with brains and could have run her own business but she knew that people like her were put on this earth to be the servers of others. Still, as jobs went, she liked hers most of the time and was good at it.

The postman called just after lunch as she was setting off to Edith's house and delivered a letter. It was rare for Cheryl to get anything other than junk mail so the textured white envelope with the words 'Cripwell, Oliver and Clapham – Solicitors' in the top corner, made her slightly nervous. Why would a solicitor be writing to her? She slipped an apprehensive finger under the flap and slit it open. A piece of paper fluttered to the ground and Cheryl picked it up to find it was a cheque. For five thousand pounds.

Dear Miss Parker

Re: Our client: The Executors of the late Maurice William Herbert

We are instructed by the Executors of the late Mr Herbert to distribute certain bequests from his estate. Mr Herbert left instructions that you be given the sum of £5,000 for your kindnesses to him, his brother and their dog Gerald.

We therefore enclose a cheque in respect of that bequest.

Yours sincerely,
David Oliver

Cheryl's eyes flicked between the letter and the cheque. *Five thousand pounds.* She couldn't believe it. Oh, dear Mr Herbert. Her eyes clouded over with emotion. If only he was standing there in front of her now, she would throw her arms around him. This money would allow her to pay her gas bill without having to wait for the red reminder. Or she could buy herself a little car for work. And she badly needed a new coat.

NO.

The word sounded so loudly in her head it was as if it had been shouted into her ear. Just one word, but its meaning was clear as Dartington crystal. Mr Herbert had left her that money to do something special with it – and paying her gas bill wasn't it. It was a massive amount of money for her and she didn't want to fritter it away. How ironic was it that she could have afforded a cycle of IVF with it and here she was – single. She would know what to do with the money when the time was right, but that time wasn't now.

She blew a kiss up to heaven where it was sure to find the Herbert brothers and bobble-eyed Gerald with the wobbly arthritic legs. 'Thank you,' she said. 'I'll spend it wisely, boys. I promise.'

CHAPTER 24

The offices of Dartley Carpets would need two cleaners twice a week, which was great news if Connie had any on her books. For now, she would have to do it on her own, which would be really hard work. The smile trembled on her mouth as Jeff Froom signed the agreement form which she had printed off for potential clients. Then, when she went back to her car, she sank her head into her hands and wondered, yet again, what the hell she had got herself into. She had a thrumming stress headache by the time she left Dartley and had to divert to a petrol station to buy some paracetamol and a bottle of water. There were shelves full of chocolate in the garage and Connie couldn't remember the last time she had been in a shop and not bought any. It made her feel sick to even look at it. Giving it up for Lent and beyond would be no challenge at all.

Next stop was her appointment with Brandon Locke. Connie drove on to Box House but when she reached the Dick Turpin's Arms she knew she must have passed it and turned back. She almost missed the opening to the drive again but managed to brake in time. The drive from the main road down to Box House was very overgrown with big ugly hedges and skeletal branches of trees, but what a pretty house lay at the end of it: Victorian double-fronted with two huge bay windows and the biggest front door that Connie had ever seen. There was an old-fashioned brass bell pull at the side of it which was incredibly stiff and needed a generous squirt of WD40 in her opinion. As she stood on the doorstep and waited, she imagined, from the sound of his voice on the telephone, that Brandon Locke would be a sedate older gentleman, slightly built, smartly dressed, with short-cropped hair, if any, looking like a retired solicitor. When the door eventually opened, she could see how wrong she had been. He was much younger, taller and broader than she'd pictured, with mad wavy hair falling to his shoulders in natural stripes of black, white and grey. His eyes were twinkling and dark brown – *happy eyes*, her mum would have called them. His nose had a bump in it, as if he'd had it broken playing rugby, but it was a nose that suited him and sat in harmony with his other features. She hoped her pupils weren't dilating so much that he could see.

'Hello,' he said, his voice brimming with welcome and his hand extended towards hers.

'Hello,' echoed Connie.

'Am I glad to see you, Miss Smith. Do come in.'

'Marilyn, please.'

'Come in then, *Marilyn*. I'm Brandon Locke, nice to meet you.'

The smell of chocolate hit her as soon as she had crossed the threshold. It flooded her brain so much that she could not appreciate what a beautiful space she had just stepped into because she was trying to concentrate on breathing in as little of it as possible.

'I've not been in here very long, as I think I explained,' said Brandon, clapping his hands before beginning to talk. 'This is my post-divorce purchase. It was a bit of a tip and the builders have just finished all the essential work like rewiring and new skirting boards, and as you can see there is plaster dust everywhere. It's an impossible task to keep on top of it. It's driving me insane,' and he sneezed loudly.

'It does tend to outstay its welcome,' agreed Connie. Not that she would know first-hand. She would have killed for some after-renovation plaster dust in her house.

She walked behind him into the front room and the smell of chocolate followed her. He must have been baking buns or muffins, she presumed. Sunlight poured through the bay window and highlighted hundreds of motes of plaster dust drifting aimlessly.

'This is the lounge, obviously,' said Brandon.

'What a beautiful big room,' said Connie, still trying to breathe in a way that stopped her smelling the chocolatey air.

'I'm pleased with it, I have to admit. This is the only room that's finished so far, though. The carpet is new and super-bouncy but it's moulting.' He bent down and picked up a handful of loose fibres. 'I'm always clogging up the vacuum.'

'The peril of a new carpet,' smiled Connie, not that she'd experienced the feel of a new lounge carpet in many years either. And even when it was freshly laid it wasn't that bouncy because Jimmy had insisted on saving some money by choosing a cheap, thin underlay.

Brandon led her into a huge kitchen which took up the total back length of the house. It was tidy except for one long work surface which had bowls and spoons spread all over it and a chrome machine that was whirring with motion. Here the smell of chocolate was at its strongest, heavy and cloying. With the scent came a wave of memories from so many years with Jimmy. Years that had been full of hard work, laughter, tears, love – or so she had thought. Tears jerked to her eyes as her stomach bucked.

'Are you all right?' asked Brandon Locke as Connie's hand shot up to her mouth.

'Er, yes, fine,' she said, nodding vigorously.

'I've never had anyone retch in here before,' he sighed, but appeared amused. 'I'm very worried now.'

Connie was embarrassed. 'Please, don't be. It's just that I don't . . . don't like chocolate.'

Brandon laughed at that and it was a very merry

sound. 'A woman who doesn't like chocolate? I didn't know you existed. I hope it isn't catching, you'll put me out of business.'

'Business?' That ruled the baking a cake or tray of muffins theory out then.

'I make chocolates,' he explained. 'I have a small factory in Oxworth which produces them, but this is my man-cave for product development. Chox – have you heard of me?'

There was barely a brand of chocolate that Connie wasn't familiar with and yes – she had heard of them, and eaten quite a few boxes of Chox in her time, and very nice they had been too, though Jimmy hadn't bought her any of them.

'Yes, I have,' she replied, sweeping her eyes slowly around the kitchen and marvelling at how large it was, yet it still managed to feel homely. She turned back to Brandon and found him studying her.

'Sorry,' he said. 'I thought . . . No, doesn't matter,' he waved away whatever had been in his head. 'Let me show you upstairs.'

Up the very grand oak staircase were five bedrooms and two bathrooms and another stair-case led to two attic rooms. It was a huge house for one man – at least she presumed he was single after the comment about the divorce. There was certainly no evidence of anyone else living here, as only one of the bedrooms showed signs of being occupied and only one toothbrush was standing to attention in a glass tumbler in his ensuite.

'I could really do with someone hanging curtains

too, if you offer that service. I'm waiting for some to be delivered. I can do it, I'm not useless,' he added quickly, 'but it would help. Do you change beds? Putting my quilt cover on is something I hate even more. I end up inside it; it's as if the thing is trying to eat me.'

'Yes, we can do that all for you,' nodded Connie, smiling. Brandon Locke was incredibly charming and very likeable. He wouldn't be single for long, she thought. Someone who looked like that with his own chocolate firm? He'd have them queuing up in no time. 'I can come next week for three hours and see how we get on at that, if you're happy with our price and terms.' She handed him an envelope containing the Lady Muck paperwork.

'Where do I sign?' he asked, taking it quickly from her hand. 'I absolutely agree to every term and condition you can throw at me.'

CHAPTER 25

Cheryl knocked on the door to Brambles, tried the handle and walked in with a frustrated sigh.

'Edith? Edith, are you in?'

'Yes dear, I'm in the study,' came the old lady's voice.

'What have I told you about keeping that front door locked,' Cheryl admonished her old client gently. 'I could have been anyone walking in off the street.'

'I'm expecting Lance at three o'clock, dear, that's why I unlocked it.'

'That's hours away.'

'Oh, is it?'

Cheryl found herself shuddering. She didn't trust Edith's prodigal nephew Lance Nettleton as far as she could throw him. It was none of her business, of course, but she couldn't shake off the feeling that Lance's motives were sinister more than they were sly. He made the hairs on the back of her neck rise whenever he was near her.

'Would you like a cup of tea?' called Cheryl.

'Not yet,' called Edith. 'I'll have one when I've found what I'm looking for.'

'Can I help?'

Edith's head popped around the door and she smiled her adorable old lady smile.

'Nope,' she said. 'It's in here, I know it. I put it in a safe place but I can't remember where that was, but I do know that it is definitely in here somewhere.'

Cheryl got straight down to work then and left her to it. It was the turn of the lounge and the dining-room curtains to be washed this week. Cheryl climbed up the stepladder and unhooked them, then put them on a delicate wash in the machine. Then she sponged down the sofa and all the cushions and they looked like new when she had finished. She gave Edith's pretty pale pink bedroom a spruce and changed her sheets, dusted and vacuumed all around and then rehung the curtains when they were still a little damp, knowing they'd soon dry and the weight would pull out any creases. She always ended up staying at Edith's longer than she was paid for because she wanted to. Edith was a pleasure to work for and in summer she always insisted Cheryl sit in the stunning garden and have afternoon tea with her. She still made her own scones and jams from the wild strawberries which she grew in pots and the raspberries which rambled over the back fence and everything was delicious – Sunflower Café standard. Cheryl was folding up the stepladders when Edith trotted into the hallway holding an envelope.

'I knew it was in there somewhere. I'd put it inside a book to keep it safe.' She frothed with excitement. 'Come into the kitchen, dear Cheryl, and let's have that tea. I want to tell you something. I've meant to show you before but it slipped my mind.'

'Let me put the steps away first, Edith. I don't want anyone tripping over them.' Except Lance, she added to herself. Then, when she had done that, she went through into the kitchen where Edith was spooning loose tea into a large brown teapot. She refused to use teabags because she said they never tasted as good.

'Shall I take over?' asked Cheryl.

'No, you sit there and wait,' Edith replied firmly.

Cheryl watched the old lady setting cups and saucers out on a tray with hands that shook a little more with every passing week. The duchess hump on her back was becoming more pronounced too, and yet Cheryl had never once heard Edith complain about any aches and pains she might have – and she must have had them. Her knuckles were large knots of arthritis and her gait was unsteady because of a worn-out hip.

'Sit,' Edith commanded, as Cheryl rose to her feet to take the tray from her. Cheryl obeyed, but at least she won the battle over who should pour out the tea.

'You look tired, dear. Are you all right?' asked

Edith. She placed her thin hand over Cheryl's and that small, sympathetic act was enough to bring tears flooding to Cheryl's eyes.

Cheryl searched her pockets for tissues, but there were none. 'Sorry, Edith,' she apologised, wiping her eyes on the back of her hand until Edith produced a cotton handkerchief from up her sleeve.

'It's not been used,' she said.

It was pressed and soft with many years of washing and had a pink E embroidered on it. It smelt faintly of violets, the scent of Edith.

'Sorry,' Cheryl apologised again. 'It's been a very mixed week. One of those ones I wouldn't want to repeat in a long time.'

'I could see you were sad when you came in today,' said Edith. 'You were smiling, but not in your eyes. That gave the game away. Here.' Edith nudged the cup of tea towards Cheryl. It was her best china, with the tiny yellow daisies painted on it.

Cheryl took a sip and wished her eyes would stop leaking, but they wouldn't.

'I'm guessing it's a man who is making you upset,' said Edith, peering over the top of her glasses.

Cheryl nodded. 'I had to end my relationship with Gary last week.'

'Oh dear,' said Edith. 'You'd been together quite a long time, hadn't you?'

'Just over ten years,' sniffed Cheryl. 'We met on my twenty-first birthday.'

'And you finished it? If someone like you does that, it tells me that you'd reached a limit and there's no turning back.'

Cheryl couldn't believe how astute Edith could be sometimes. Most of the time she was away with the fairies, but when she was in the room, she was almost psychic.

'We . . . well, I had been saving up for IVF. We haven't had any luck conceiving naturally, even though there's nothing wrong with either of us, because we've had all the tests. *Unexplained infertility*, is all they can come up with. I made sure that we both wanted to go ahead with having a baby. I know it can put a lot of strain on a relationship, but we were okay.'

Cheryl paused to wipe her nose.

'But?' prompted Edith.

'He spent all my savings, Edith. He gambled them on a horse.'

'And it wasn't the first time?' Edith asked softly.

Cheryl shook her head, unable to speak.

'Oh dear.' Edith topped up Cheryl's cup with tea. 'And your heart wishes that you'd never found that out because you still love him.'

Cheryl nodded, tears coursing down her face.

'But your head is telling you that you can't have a relationship with a man who could do that to you, especially when it's far more than money that he's taken from you.'

Cheryl threw her arms around Edith – she couldn't stop herself – and sobbed on the old lady's shoulder. She could smell Edith's sweet floral perfume and she realised that she loved her more than she did any woman she had ever known.

'I miss him so much, Edith. My whole life feels as if it's been emptied of hope.'

Edith pulled Cheryl away from her, held her arms firmly and stared hard into her eyes.

'Now you listen here, young lady, you are worth far more than to settle for second-best in life. A relationship can't survive on love alone, whatever tosh some people try to tell you. There has to be trust and respect. Both ways. If there isn't, then . . .' She left the sentence hanging, but Cheryl understood. The old lady wasn't telling her anything she didn't know already.

'You know, before I met Ernest, I was very much in love with an older man,' said Edith. 'I was innocent and he was worldly to the extent that he ran rings around my heart. He would break up with me and then come thundering back into my life until abandonment and reconciliation dictated our whole relationship. I wanted to trust that I was safe with him, but I never could. I was constantly being tossed between despair and ridiculous joy of having him return to me. It was exhausting, and not in a good way. It took every bit of strength I had to break away from him, and I cried for a long time, but I knew deep down that it wasn't the sort of love I was destined for. I was meant for a man who cared for me and put my feelings before his own, a man whom I could care for and put his feelings before mine. I found that man in Ernest. Do you understand what I'm telling you?'

Cheryl nodded. She was tired of forgiving Gary, tired of the fights, the confrontations, the disappointments and the apologies. Love wasn't about having a battalion of soldiers stationed around her heart in case of emergency. She needed to do what Edith had done and be strong. There was an Ernest out there waiting for her but he wouldn't get near her if her heart was full of Gary.

Edith's hand came out to cup Cheryl's face.

'I want to see that chin lifted from now on. Sometimes you have to accept that the cards you are dealt can't be changed. I couldn't have children and yes, I cried a lot about that, so Ernest and I had to have a different life to the one we would have chosen.' The old lady leaned forward and placed a kiss on Cheryl's cheek.

'If I'd had a daughter, I would have wished she were just like you. You'd have made me very proud.'

Cheryl started sobbing again and Edith chuckled.

'I wish my mum had been like you,' said Cheryl. 'She shouldn't have had kids and you should have. Life isn't fair, is it?'

'No, and the sooner that's an accepted universal fact, the happier everyone would be,' said Edith. 'Now, whilst I seem to be in control of my faculties, which is a rare enough occurrence these days, let me show you this.' Edith got out of the chair and crossed to the work surface to retrieve the envelope she had placed there.

'It's my will,' she announced.

'Oh, do you want me to witness something for you?'

'Shhh, Cheryl,' Edith gently slapped Cheryl's hand with her knobbly wrinkled fingers. 'I want you to listen. Lance, as you know, is my nephew . . .'

Cheryl tried not to sneer. The thought of him being in Edith's life for five minutes and inheriting all she had would make her feel sick if she let it. He wouldn't treasure Brambles, he'd sell it for a quick buck.

'. . . my elder sister Ivy's child. And I can't say that having him come back into my life hasn't stirred up some memories of when Ivy and I were younger. We did have some happy times. Before she married Bill Nettleton and the pair of them cheated me and Ernest out of thousands of pounds, which was an awful lot of money back then.'

Cheryl's eyebrows sprang up. She wasn't expecting that.

'It's an awful lot of money these days too, Edith,' she said.

'My own sister and that . . . that man. The pair of them together were a proper *folie à deux*, I can tell you. It broke my heart at the time. And Ernest's. Bless him, he was always so ready to think the best of people.'

'Don't upset yourself, love.'

161

'It was all very long ago.' Edith smiled sadly. 'But I'd be lying if I said it didn't still pain me to think of it. I missed my sister so much. Despite what she did to us, I missed her. It was as if my head were sensible but my heart was stupid.'

'I know what you mean,' nodded Cheryl.

'And I missed seeing Lance. He was such a sweet baby.'

Cheryl tried to imagine Lance as a sweet baby but couldn't. She supposed that Edith's contact with him must have been cut off very early on. She conjured up a picture of Lance in a pram, with an adult head and that horrible black spiv moustache, pulling wings off butterflies.

'You never made it up with Ivy, then?' Cheryl asked.

'No.' Edith's tone was hard. 'The stress of it all contributed to Ernest's heart attack. He was taken from me too soon and I am convinced I would have had him for years more had they not done what they did, so no. How could I? They're both in the ground now but I still can't forgive them. I could stand the loss of the money, but never the loss of trust.'

'I'm so sorry to hear that,' said Cheryl, though it came as little surprise to learn that Lance hailed from dodgy stock.

'It's been very interesting having him back in my life,' said Edith. 'He's told me so much about how Ivy and Bill fared over the years, what they did and what they became. I would never have known, otherwise.'

Edith used the word 'interesting', thought Cheryl. Not wonderful or exciting or lovely, but *interesting*.

'I rather think that fate paid them back for their duplicity,' Edith went on. 'Bill stole money from us to put into a business which turned out to be a dismal failure. He milked funds from it and bought a flash sports car, crashed it and ended up a paraplegic. Alas, he became very bitter about his fate and Ivy left him on numerous occasions. I think young Lance grew up in a very unhappy household.'

'Oh, that's a shame,' said Cheryl and she meant that. Lance might have been a creep, but no child deserved to be brought up with warring parents. Cheryl knew only too well what that was like.

'It was always my intention to leave my money to the Maud Haworth Home for Cats and Brambles to Lance,' said Edith.

Noooo, Edith. Leave the lot to the kitties, Cheryl wished inside.

'I have no children. I thought the cottage should go to someone in the family. But, I'm afraid, having got to know him, Brambles will fall to hell before I leave it to Lance.'

A pin-drop silence ensued. Cheryl had NOT been expecting that.

'No, I might be in my nineties but I'm not entirely daft,' Edith went on with a little laugh. 'I know that Lance wouldn't cherish my beloved Brambles. The house doesn't like him. I can tell that because he always feels cold in it.'

163

Just like Ruth Fallis did, thought Cheryl. Brambles was an excellent judge of character.

'Ironically, had I not met him again, I would have left things as they were.' Edith sighed and shook her head as if trying to rid it of a nasty thought. 'He came into my life to ensure his inheritance and he's ended up losing it. Oh, it's been fascinating finding out about all those missing years, but I'm afraid I've discovered that Lance is more than a chip off the old block and I shan't be fooled by a Nettleton again. I don't want to see him any more after today.'

Edith shivered. The little old lady who thought she lived in the Louvre still had some razor-sharp faculties.

'Thank God,' sighed Cheryl. She wouldn't have to worry about Lance stealing from Edith again.

'So I've decided to leave Brambles to you.'

Cheryl froze, not sure if Edith was joking or not. It wouldn't have been typical of Edith's humour to make such a statement if she didn't mean it, but then again, she couldn't be serious, could she?

As if suspecting what was running through Cheryl's mind, Edith attempted to convince her she *was* serious.

'I mean it, Cheryl. I've written a new will. I'm going to take it to the solicitor's office in the morning. Look.' Edith took the wad of papers out of the long envelope and handed them over to Cheryl. 'When I die, Brambles will be all yours.'

Cheryl took the papers and unfolded them with fingers that had started to tingle. Her eyes flittered over the words until they locked onto her own name.

I revoke all previous wills and codicils . . . I Edith Mary Gardiner . . . savings to Maud Haworth home for cats . . . Brambles and all of its contents to my cleaner and friend Cheryl Parker . . .

Cheryl now had trouble reading the document because her hands were shaking so much. She tried to talk but her mouth was so dry that her words came out as a hoarse whisper.

'Edith . . . I can't . . . I can't . . .'

'Who else can I leave it to who would love it? I know you care for Brambles and Brambles cares for you. I have decided it will be yours and there's an end to it.'

Cheryl shook her head slowly in amazement. The words were starting to distort on the page. Her eyes were reading but her brain couldn't absorb the information. It was too big for her grey cells to take in. She wasn't the sort of person to inherit a house. It was so huge and generous a bequest that it felt wrong.

'I . . . can't . . .'

'Yes you can and you will.'

'I don't know what to say, Edith. I really don't.'

'Don't say anything. You don't need to. I just wanted to tell you so you were prepared. This is our little secret of course. Lance won't like it, but by then I'll be gone and he won't be able to do

165

anything about it. Now go, on your way. I'll see you next week.' Edith lifted the will from Cheryl's hands and tucked it back in the envelope.

'Edith, I don't know what to say.'

'You've said that already,' chuckled Edith. 'You don't have to say anything, my dear girl. This is what I want and so it will happen. Brambles will be in the hands of the best person I know and I shall lie very happily in my grave knowing that.'

Cheryl didn't want to think about Edith's passing. She put her arms around Edith as if wanting to protect her.

'I'll look after it for you. I promise.'

'I know.' Edith put her small hand on Cheryl's cheek. 'I know you will.'

Half-dazed, Cheryl walked through into the hallway, colliding with Lance who appeared to be eavesdropping behind the door. The shock brought Cheryl immediately to her senses. How on earth had he managed to enter the house without either herself or Edith hearing the front door crack open? The man moved like a cat on a hoverboard.

'Careful where you go,' said Lance, holding out his hands to steady her whilst smiling like someone from the war days who sold silk stockings on the black market.

'Oh hello, Lance. You're early,' said Edith, appearing behind Cheryl.

'Well, I know you haven't been too well recently, Auntie Edith. I was worried about you.'

'Don't talk rot. I'm right as rain,' humphed Edith

indignantly. 'Have a nice weekend, Cheryl. I will see you next Thursday, as usual.'

Edith turned and walked stiffly into the kitchen. Cheryl stood and watched her go, having a strange sense that she shouldn't leave her. What if Lance had overheard their conversation? That might put Edith in danger.

'On your way,' whispered Lance with an oily smirk as he passed her.

Cheryl dawdled in the hallway, taking a long time to put on her coat, ear cocked towards the conversation happening in the kitchen.

'Here, let me lift that tin of biscuits down for you, Auntie. You shouldn't be stretching that high,' she heard Lance's obsequious voice.

'I reached to put them up there, Lance. I'm sure I can reach to bring them down again.' Edith's voice was full of snap.

'Are you all right, Auntie? You seem a little out of sorts? I'll put the kettle on. We'll have a nice pot of tea.'

Cheryl couldn't linger behind any longer. Her bus was due in less than five minutes and the next one wasn't for another half-hour. She closed the door as Edith said, 'I don't want you to stay for long, Lance. I want to read my book in peace.'

They were the last words Cheryl ever heard Edith Gardiner speak.

CHAPTER 26

Hilda Curry was exactly where Della had said she would be when she last spoke to Connie on their secret mobile phones – at the corner table in the Sunflower Café. The reason that Della knew this was because Hilda suffered obsessive compulsive disorder and her timetable was as unbending as a steel rod. Although 'suffer' was the wrong word where Hilda was concerned because she enjoyed the order that the condition brought to her life and the reputation it brought to her cleaning. She had been 'a domestic operator' for over forty years and was the Queen Bee at Diamond Shine. Where she led, the others followed.

The Sunflower Café was on a quiet lane in the village of Pogley Top, a mile away from the town centre. Sandwiched between a post office and a tile shop, it didn't look much from the outside with its shabby facade, but when Connie pushed open the door, she found a bright and cheery bustling café with walls the colour of sunshine and sunflowers everywhere she looked. As she waited for someone to come and show her to a seat, as a sign on a small table requested, a picture of a giant yellow flower head hanging up caught her eye. There was a poem underneath about being bright and bold like a sunflower. If only. Connie knew she was more of a wallflower, or one of those weeds that people didn't have any compunction about treading on. No one stood on sunflowers. They were the kick-asses of the flower world.

The tables by the window were all occupied by pairs of old ladies partaking of afternoon tea, if the three-tiered cake stands of finger sandwiches, sweet-filled pastries and scones were anything to go by. Hilda was always assured of securing the corner table because her younger sister Patricia owned the café. At three-thirty every Thursday, Hilda Curry had a pot of tea and a cream scone here and as luck would have it, Connie noticed that the only vacant table was right next to Hilda's.

Patricia appeared from the kitchen at the back apologising for keeping Connie waiting. She had the same red hair and ruddy complexion as her sister but didn't share her much older sister's dainty build. Connie bumbled towards the vacant table with a huge bag of cleaning products and her mop and bucket props, making sure that Hilda couldn't fail to notice her.

Connie dumped all her stuff and took off her coat and sat down. She could feel Hilda's sideways glance on her as she studied the menu. When Patricia came to take her order, Connie asked for tea and a cream scone too, as if it were some sort of staple snack for cleaners. Anything was worth a go to strike up a conversation with Hilda.

'What a bonny place,' commented Connie, turning to talk. 'I never knew this cafe existed.'

Hilda smiled politely but didn't engage.

'Bit nippy out today,' Connie tried.

'Yes it is.'

Connie was just thinking what to do next when Patricia arrived with a tray holding a generously-sized teapot and a jug of milk, a scone almost bigger than the plate it sat on, butter curls and two dishes of jam and cream, plus cutlery.

'Oh, I'm ready for this,' Connie said over-loudly to Patricia. 'There's nothing better than a tea and a scone after scrubbing someone's house.'

'Get it down you and hope you enjoy it, love,' said Patricia with a smoky chuckle.

Connie was aware that Hilda was still studying her. She turned quickly to catch her and smiled. 'The scones look delicious, don't they?'

'Yes, they are very good,' replied Hilda. 'The jam is home-made and the clotted cream comes from Yorkshire, not Devon. And you get butter as well. In a lot of places that serve afternoon teas, you don't, you know.'

'I know,' replied Connie, relieved that the conversation was now flowing two ways. 'Cream scones served with no butter, it's unthinkable, isn't it? Come here a lot, do you?'

'Every week. My sister owns it. She's the best baker of scones in Yorkshire,' Hilda bragged proudly, then she leaned over to impart a confidentiality. 'Well, my half-sister, I should say. Her mother, my step-mother, is younger than me.'

'Funny you should say that because I'm actually older than my auntie,' lied Connie, but she was sure that God would forgive her in the circumstances. Connie inclined her head towards Hilda's mop and bucket resting against the wall in the corner. 'You been out cleaning as well?'

'Yes, I'm a professional,' Hilda nodded. 'Have been for forty years.'

'Forty years? Never.' Connie spread the jam on her scone and didn't have to act that she was impressed by either on the information or the quality of the baking, because she was in both cases. 'You don't work for Lady Muck, I take it?'

'Pardon?'

'Lady Muck. I tell you, if you don't, you should.' Connie took a bite from her scone and poured herself a cup of tea from the pot.

'What's Lady Muck?' asked Hilda, showing interest.

'It's a cleaning firm. New one.' Connie leant forwards towards Hilda as if divulging a great secret. 'I've never been on so much money per hour. Two pounds above minimum wage.'

'Really?' Hilda twisted in her seat to fully face Connie.

'And they'll recompense you if any clients cancel. And they give you an allowance so you can buy your own cleaning stuff,' Connie went on.

She was reeling Hilda in now. Della had told her how much she hated using the substandard products which Diamond Shine supplied and always substituted her own for them, paid for by herself.

'And they do an Employee of the Month award and the winner gets fifty pounds.'

Connie had thought of that on the spot.

'And they give you some money towards travelling expenses.'

Whoa, slow down, said a voice in Connie's head. She'd be saying that they made up a packed lunch for everyone in a minute.

'And you get a Christmas bonus. And a bit of sick pay, cash in hand.'

Now that really is it! the voice said. Hilda had been fully hooked out of the water after the Employee of the Month, there had been no need for more bait.

'You're joking?'

'I'm not.'

Connie knew that Diamond Shine offered their workers very little in the way of benefits. Jimmy only employed each girl for a limited amount of hours each week so he wouldn't have to pay out sick or maternity pay; any extra hours were paid cash in hand. He had learned many lessons from Dick Gibson who used to own a rival firm, Victoria's Sponges. Dick employed full-time workers with sick pay, overtime, maternity and redundancy money. Victoria's Sponges had ended up folding because, in Jimmy's words, 'half of

Dick's cleaners got pregnant and he'd ended up paying for them just to sit on their arses lactating.' Jimmy preferred to concentrate on extolling the basic virtues of working for an agency when they were recruiting: that the company found them their work, and he paid insurance in case one of them knocked over a precious vase. A cleaner who worked for Diamond Shine didn't have to fanny about with all the essential business stuff: all they had to concern themselves with was their cleaning. And if any client started being funny about handing over their money, Della would be straight on the case. No one messed with Diamond Shine.

The cleaners often developed attachments to their clients and vice versa. Della had told Connie that if Hilda moved firms, her entire client list would move with her and when Hilda moved, the other girls wouldn't be far behind. What Connie hadn't taken into account was that the girls themselves might still feel some loyalty towards Jimmy.

'Lady Muck, you say?' Hilda took a pencil out of her pocket and scribbled the name on a serviette.

'I've got a card somewhere,' said Connie, digging in her own pocket and pulling out a handful of them. 'She's looking for new cleaners and she told me to give them out. You should give her a ring.'

'Where's she based?'

'Penistone way, but I don't need to go to the office.'

'How do you get the money to them then?'

'The ones that don't pay by direct debit give me

cash and I hand it in to a financial agent in Maltstone once a fortnight,' she replied.

'Hmm.' Hilda studied the card whilst she sipped her tea.

'I can tell you this though: she's had so many cleaners ringing her that you ought to get in fast if you want to get on the books.' She raised her hand and looked at her watch. 'Oh flaming hell, my bus will be here in a minute. I knew I didn't really have time to come in here. Plus I didn't think the scones would be this big. I'll have to come here again.'

Connie grabbed her mop and bucket and took another quick bite of scone for dramatic effect. 'See you again probably,' she said to Hilda.

'Yes, yes, see you,' said Hilda, although she didn't raise her head to say goodbye as she was too busy staring at the business card with Lady Muck's details on it.

CHAPTER 27

Astrid and Wenda were just about to do a bomb on a house that Friday morning, which was the recognised term for an intensive and usually multi-handed clean, and the pair of them had called in to the office to replenish their cleaning stocks from the store cupboard. The two women were the physical opposites of each other: Astrid, long golden hair, a six-foot-four German Amazon who used to be a loose-head prop rugby-player with a beard and balls. Wenda, a tiny, skinny little woman with short dyed fluorescent tangerine hair; and yet they were best friends and preferred to go on jobs together. They were the bomb queens of the firm.

'I've had another complaint about you,' said Della to Wenda's back, which was protruding from the store cupboard. 'Mrs Forrester says you were late again yesterday.'

'Mrs Forrester can fuck right off,' said Wenda with a sniff. 'I was half an hour late and I stayed three-quarters of an hour extra to make up for it.'

'That's not the point. She wants you to be on time.'

'You tell her why you vere late, Venda,' said the formidable Astrid in her odd half very-broad-Yorkshire, half German accent. 'She could do nowt else, Della.'

'What do you mean?' said Della. 'You could do nothing else about what?'

'Mr Vilson. Und his bluddy family,' put in Astrid before Wenda could speak. 'Ze bastards.'

'I go to Mr Wilson before Mrs Forrester, don't I? I couldn't leave the old guy in the state he was in,' said Wenda, zipping up her bag. 'His lot pay for a cleaner because they can't be bothered going over and helping him themselves. He'd shit the bed and it was days old. I had to hammer the muck off his sheets before they went in the machine. He shouldn't be by himself.'

'Tell her abart ze dog.' Astrid nudged Wenda, nearly knocking her over.

'Dog hadn't been fed or watered. I hated myself for it but I had to ring the RSPCA last week. He can't look after it. I thought the little thing were dead when I walked in. It were just sat at side of him on t'sofa.' Wenda wiped her eye with the back of her hand. 'He loved that dog but he had to let them take it away.'

'He should be in a hom,' added Astrid. 'An old peoples hom.'

'He should,' nodded Wenda. 'Nobody goes to see that old lad. Only me. He sits staring at the TV all day every day and you can tell he's not really taking owt in. I opened his fridge to make him a sandwich and everything in it was blue wi' mould.'

'Venda vent shopping.' Astrid clarified to Della.

'Just a few bits. Can't you ring his family, Della? It's wrong.'

'Ze bastards,' added Astrid, flicking her long hair extensions behind her powerful shoulders. 'Zay don't give a flying chuff.'

'You're a cleaner not a bloody social worker,' said Della. 'It's none of our business so no, I won't ring.'

Wenda grabbed the handles of her bag and jerked them upwards.

'Sometimes you have to make it your business, Della. Go and see the state of him and tell me you can walk off and not think about him.'

'Venda and I are taking him a pie oop later,' added Astrid.

'Well you shouldn't get involved,' sniffed Della.

'Jesus, Della. I wish I were as cold as you. I might get more sleep at night. Come on, Astrid.' Wenda flounced across the office towards the door.

'How can you be so bluddy hard, Della?' Astrid's nose was wrinkled up in disgust as she passed by her desk in Wenda's wake.

How indeed, thought Della, as the door slammed shut behind them. Hard, cold. Yes, she fitted both of those words. And she had done for many years. And at the moment, she felt colder and harder than ever, as if her whole insides had been scooped out and replaced with huge solid blocks of ice which ground together and caused her pain. Jimmy Diamond was the man who had begun to thaw her cold heart after years of abuse by men, and he had turned out to be the biggest dick of them all.

Her father had left on her sixth birthday. She was eating a slice of her birthday cake at the time, when there was an almighty commotion. Her mother was screaming at her father, trying to stop him getting to the door with his suitcase in his hand but he was a powerfully built man and her mother was as thin as a twig. Pleas turned to vitriol. As her father stepped out of the door, her mother picked up Della's beautiful cake all covered in chocolate buttons and launched it at his back. And when he had gone her mother had sobbed and howled and blamed her little daughter for her stretch marks during a pregnancy that hadn't been planned or wanted, and had led eventually to the end of her marriage. The smell of chocolate cake had always had the power to drag Della back to that unhappy day when she last saw her father. She hadn't touched it since. And she had never cried in front of anyone since either. Even at that young age, she had made up her mind never to let anyone see how much they could wound her.

Her first love, Charlie Decker, had only gone out with her for a bet. She had been devastated to discover how many people had been laughing behind her back at the very idea that she – Della

Frostick – could ever really pull a dish as gorgeous as Charlie. He humiliated her, crushed her, but she never let Charlie and his gang see that. In fact her peers were impressed by how little she let it affect her. Or so they thought. Inside, her heart was shredded by his cruelty. It took years to piece back together, yet a shadow always remained.

It took Richard Grindle two persistent years to worm his way into her heart and bed when she was twenty-two. Within three months of their marriage, he had run off with the neighbour's daughter and Della's savings. She had made up her mind never again to let a man even near the perimeter of her heart. She parked barbed wire and Alsatians around it, but somehow the cheeky, handsome head of a cleaning firm with a hearty line in chatter and a big grin had dodged all her defences: Jimmy Diamond. Despite the fact that Jimmy Diamond's lips had never strayed beyond her cheek, despite the fact that Jimmy Diamond's hands had never touched her intimately, despite the fact that Jimmy Diamond had a wife and daughter and promised her nothing, she had fallen in love with him and stayed in love with him for fifteen years. Nothing had ever tipped over into actually happening so the intimacy remained pure, intact and perfect in Della's head. Jimmy's kisses would never have satisfied in real life as they did in her imagination, nor would his love-making. That he sometimes looked at Della as if he wanted to rip her knickers off there and then had fuelled her fantasies and coloured her dreams. But it had all been a lie – and it felt like the biggest lie of all. One deception too far. All the past hurts and lies had accumulated and Jimmy Diamond was going to take the blame for them all.

Hard and cold – oh yes, Della was frozen solid. Everyone she had ever liked or loved had stabbed her either in the back or the front and she would never allow anyone near her again. She wouldn't blink an eyelid whilst she destroyed Jimmy Diamond's business knowing that she would destroy him too. In fact, she was looking forward to it.

CHAPTER 28

At lunch time when Jimmy was supposedly having a business lunch in Wakefield and Ivanka was supposedly out shopping, Della rang Connie on the secret mobile phone.

'How are you getting on? Has Hilda phoned you yet?'

'No,' replied Connie with a heavy sigh.

'Give it time,' said Della. 'She might want the weekend to think about things.'

'That's what I was hoping.' Although Connie didn't have a good feeling about it, if she was honest. After telling Hilda that cleaning places were limited at Lady Muck, she would have thought she might have made an initial enquiry at least.

'I'm going to ring a client of ours now – a Mr Savant – to tell him that we can't clean for him any more. I had to sack the woman who did him – Ruth Fallis. If by any chance she gets hold of your number and asks for a job, stay well clear. Anyway, the girls say his house is haunted, which is a load of old codswallop. It used to be an undertaker's place. It's a big creepy house and no doubt creaks a lot but if you're like me, you'll know that ghosts don't exist.'

'Well, I've never seen one,' smiled Connie. 'So . . .'

'I'll text you his number. As soon as I've spoken to him I'll text you so you can get in touch with him right away and offer him your services. I'll keep trying if I can't get him straight off, okay?'

'Thanks, Della.' Another customer would be good. She'd had a bit of luck that morning as an old lady from Della's files had rung back and said she would like a cleaner for two hours per week. Then again, Connie didn't want to take on too many customers before she had the cleaners to work for them. She had started dreaming about chickens and eggs.

Mr Savant wasn't in when Della rang. She left a message asking if he would please call her then she made herself a coffee and sat back in her chair wondering what else she could do to drive business from Diamond Shine to Lady Muck.

The windows were totally steamed up on Jimmy's BMW as he and Ivanka writhed around snogging on the back seat whilst they were parked up a country lane. Jimmy slipped his hand up Ivanka's skirt and hooked his fingers around the side of her knickers, and was gobsmacked when she firmly pushed him back and extricated herself from his arms.

'No, Jimmy, I can't.'

'You can't what?' said Jimmy, wiping the sweat

from his brow with one hand and adjusting the tightness in his trousers with the other.

'I can't have sex.'

'What's up? Are you on? We can do other things then. Come here.'

She jerked backwards as his arms came out and his eyebrows dipped in confusion.

'What's up?' She was usually gagging for it. There was something about sex in the car that really got her going.

'It's Lent,' she said coolly, inspecting her fingernails for chips.

'What?'

'It's Lent,' Ivanka repeated. 'I have given up sex for Lent.'

Jimmy stared at her for a few moments, then his face cracked into a grin. 'You little tease,' he said. 'You had me going there.'

'No, I mean it, Jimmy.' Ivanka's hand came out to stop him coming forwards. 'We can kiss but that's all.'

'Kiss?' Jimmy exclaimed, as if she had just said they could roll around in pig manure.

'Yes. Just kissing. Until Easter.'

'Easter? That's . . .' Jimmy tried to calculate when that was.

'I think Lent is just a little bit longer than forty days and forty nights. It started on Wednesday.'

'I know when Lent started,' Jimmy huffed. 'Connie said she'd given up chocolate for it.'

Ivanka jerked squarely back in her seat and

folded her arms. She hated when Jimmy mentioned his wife, which wasn't often, to be fair.

'What's up now?' Jimmy said, seeing the sour look on her face.

'You mention your wife. I don't like it when you do that.'

'Oh come on, love.' Jimmy reached out to tenderly touch her plump cheek and she pulled back from him.

'I want to be Mrs Diamond,' she pouted.

'And you will, my angel.'

Ivanka spun her head towards him sharply. 'When? You have given me no date. We are engaged but you have no intention of marrying me.'

'I have,' Jimmy protested, but not very forcibly. In truth he had pushed the next stage of his relationship out of his mind, hoping it would all go away. So far it had all been pretty plain sailing but what was to come would be very sticky and messy.

'When? When are you going to tell your wife that you are divorcing?'

'Soon,' said Jimmy, raking his fingers back through his thick brown hair.

'Well soon is not good enough any more, Jimmy.' Ivanka raised her two perfect tadpoles of eyebrows. 'I will give up sex for Lent and you will give up trying to be married.'

'What?' said Jimmy, his heart starting to increase in pace.

'You will tell your wife you want divorce at the end of Lent or we are finished. I mean it. I will wait no longer. Now I am going to drive back to the office.' And she got out of his car and into her own which was parked next to it.

Jimmy knew she was serious and he couldn't really blame her for being annoyed. He shouldn't have given her that bloody engagement ring until he was free to do so. Now she had got ideas in her head – hadn't she made him drive slowly past a bridal shop last week so she should see the frocks in the window? The idea of being married to Ivanka was fabulous but the thought of having to end things with Connie made him feel sick. He'd always seen himself as a Tom Jones sort of bloke: a man who married early but had the audacity to become more attractive to the female eye with age. The temptations were too great to ignore, but his wife was his best girl and one day – when it was all out of his system – he would settle down properly with her. Then he met golden Ivanka and she was one turn-on too far.

He lifted his eyes to the rear-view mirror and saw Ivanka's Audi screech off. He set off himself then and paused at the T-junction whilst deciding whether to turn left and follow her straight back to the office, or go right and call in the pub for a quiet half-pint away from everyone. One thing was sure, whatever direction he drove the car in, he was inevitably heading for shit creek without a paddle.

Della noticed that Ivanka was in a very grumpy mood when she came back from lunch. Fifteen minutes later, Jimmy walked in and also had a face like a slapped backside. It was clear they'd had a row, especially as Jimmy went straight back out again with his briefcase, mumbling about going to see Pookie, and Ivanka didn't even lift her head to acknowledge his 'see you later, girls.'

'Oh dear, someone's not happy,' said Della as she looked out of the window and watched his car driving away. 'Wonder what's up with him.'

Ivanka lifted her shoulders and dropped them again. 'Who knows? This is why I don't get involved with men. They are moody and sulky.'

'I think sometimes this business gets him down,' said Della with a gentle sigh. She had decided in her lunch hour to plant some nice fat seeds in Ivanka's brain that would grow and flourish into killer triffids. 'Some of the clients think they're buying his soul when they rent a cleaner; they need taking down a peg or two. I mean, who do some of them think they are? Half the time they're just lazy people who like to lord it above others. They think they're living in the Victorian age with servants. And as for the girls? I say "girls",' and she laughed lightly, 'they want their cake and to eat it. They don't know how lucky they are working for Jimmy. They wouldn't get treated as well anywhere else and they know that. They might rattle their fists sometimes to get their own way, but Jimmy has always stood firm against the unreasonable demands they occasionally try to make and none of them have left to go to another firm. So what does that tell you, eh?'

'That they don't know how good they have it here?' suggested Ivanka.

'Precisely,' nodded Della. 'I'll put the kettle on. Shall I bring you a bottle of sparkling water through?'

'Yes, that would be good.'

She went into the kitchen pod and put on the kettle for herself and pulled out a bottle of water from the fridge for Ivanka, whose manners were atrocious. She had to bite back on her lip and not say 'a please would be nice occasionally.' She stood over the kettle waiting for it to boil and heard the phone ring in the office. Della couldn't have timed her tea-making interlude any more perfectly.

'Hello, Diamon' Shined,' Ivanka said in her usual way as she picked up the phone. 'Oh hello, Mr Savant . . . so you are returning call . . . okay, could you please wait a moment.'

Ivanka put Mr Savant on hold and called out to Della.

Della popped her head out of the kitchen. 'It's about not being able to supply a cleaner to him any more. Just tell him we haven't got anyone. Don't mention it's because the girls think his house is haunted, whatever you do. I don't know what the legal repercussions would be for Jimmy.'

She congratulated herself with that ridiculous statement and listened from behind the door.

Ivanka's bad mood, mixed with nuggets from her recent conversation with Della plus a misplaced confidence in her ability to step into Della's shoes combined to make a fire in her veins. *Listen and learn,* she mouthed silently at Della through the wall. As the future Mrs Diamond she was going to start asserting her position. She pressed the button that took Mr Savant off hold.

'Hello Mr Savant, this is Ivanka speaking. I am sorry, but we have bad news, we can no longer supply a cleaner to you.'

'You can't supply a cleaner?' said Mr Savant at the other end of the line with dignified disbelief. 'Have I just heard right? Are you turning down my business?

'That is correct.'

'But what about the girl who came this week?'

'She does not want to work for you.'

'And why not?' Mr Savant's polite tone was being strangled now by mounting annoyance.

'Because . . . because . . .' Warned not to mention the house, Ivanka was forced to think of a reason on her feet, and she wasn't very good at doing that. '. . . Because she doesn't, okay? We do not have to give you reasons but if you want one, we do not like you here at Diamond Shine.'

Behind the door, Della winced.

'I beg your pardon, young lady?'

Young lady? thought Ivanka. He wasn't taking her seriously. Well, he might in a moment.

'Yes, that is correct. No one wants to work for you from here so you will have to find other cleaner.'

'Oh don't you worry, I w—' but his words were lost as Ivanka cut him off.

'Creep,' she yelled at the phone. 'We do not need weirdy customers like you with your haunted houses. Go to hell.'

In the kitchen, Della slipped the mobile out of her pocket and texted Connie RING SAVANT. Within five minutes, Connie had added another customer to the client list of Lady Muck.

CHAPTER 29

What Della didn't know was that once a month on a Friday, as many Diamond Shine girls as possible congregated for afternoon tea at the Sunflower Café at four p.m. and they had been doing so for a year and a half now. It had been Astrid's idea. She had been a big man in a welding factory before she became a big woman in a cleaner's uniform. As the girls didn't belong to an official guild, it could only help if any of them needed some advice, she said. No one was particularly disgruntled about anything, so, so far, it had been more of an informal get-together over pots of Darjeeling and Patricia's excellent afternoon teas. A few of the women preferred to keep themselves to themselves and didn't participate, but plenty did. They enjoyed the secret meetings and finding that they weren't alone in some of their mini-moans.

Patricia closed the café to the public at three-thirty on these days as a courtesy to her big sister. It was commercially worth it to her because of all the afternoon teas she sold to the women, even at mates' rates. Three-tiered plates were dotted around the room, holding Patricia's famous clotted cream scones on top, her sweet and savoury pastries on the middle and finger sandwiches on the bottom. Today the choice was Wensleydale cheese and apple savoury, egg mayonnaise and red onion, chicken and celery crunch, ham and pea-shoots and mustard chutney. Patricia liked to test out new flavours on them knowing that none of the Diamond Shine women were renowned for holding back on their true opinions. Hilda, as the longest serving cleaner, had assumed the role of group leader and officiated from her seat in the corner.

She banged a salt cellar down on the table to start off proceedings.

'Ladies, let us begin,' she said. 'Before I forget, the next meeting is the second Friday of the month because it's our anniversary on the first Friday and we're off out for a swanky meal. Everyone all right with that?'

There was a mix of 'yeses', nods, 'oohs' and thumbs up by way of response. Hilda went on, 'Right, has anyone got anything they wish to share with the group?'

'Yes, a bloody big cheer that Norma Know-it-All has gone,' said Val Turner. A sentiment that was echoed by them all, if the applause that followed was anything to go by.

'Norma? Who's she?' asked Gemma Robinson, sitting at the far table. She was cleaning in her gap year to earn some money, then she was off to university to do Film and Media studies. She spoke with a very plummy accent, but was a friendly, down-to-earth girl. Everyone was very fond of Gemma.

'Ruth bloody Fallis,' said Hilda. 'But we call her Norma Know-it-All. You're a lucky lass if you haven't come across her.'

'She once swore me blind that Lionel Blair was in *The Exorcist*,' said Sandra Batty through a mouthful of sandwich. 'She wouldn't have it that he wasn't.'

'Thick as pig shit,' someone shouted.

That reminded Cheryl. 'Does anyone know if Ruth lives on a farm?'

'That's a funny question,' replied Ava Preston. 'What made you ask that?'

'Oh, just something someone said.' Cheryl underplayed it. Much as she didn't like Ruth Fallis, she wouldn't have falsely accused her.

'No, she lives on Ketherwood Avenue, the Wombwell end. Her house is at the side of Jock's scrapyard but their son used to work at Hedges battery farm, I'm sure,' said Hilda. 'Not sure if he still does.'

'Cheers,' said Cheryl.

'Did you know she'd shagged a Grumbleweed?' said Ava. 'She once told me that. Hinted that she wasn't sure if he or Jock was her son's dad.'

'I'd have thought that little twat would be in prison by now,' Marie Blackstock spat. 'He was always trouble. Mind you, with Ruth and Jock as your parents, what would you expect?'

'Or a Grumbleweed,' Ava put in.

'No chance of that,' said Hilda. 'Jock junior is the spit of Jock senior. God help them both.'

'Will they replace her?' asked Gemma.

'I heard that Lesley Clamp's been in for an interview,' said Ava and everyone hissed as if they were in a pantomime and the villain had just walked on stage.

'If any of the Clamps come in, I can assure you I'm straight out of the door,' snarled Hilda. 'Josie Clamp was a good lass, God rest her soul, but she's the only one out of the whole brood who knew how a duster worked.'

'I heard that Nepal Clamp—' started Marie, but Hilda cut her off.

'Don't mention that little tart's name in my presence, Marie.'

'These cheese and apple sandwiches are nice,' said Meg Thompson, who was always far more interested in the food than any politics. She held a thumb up to Patricia who was wiping down her counter at the front of the café.

'Sorry, Hilda,' said Marie, putting her hand over her mouth because she'd just remembered why she shouldn't mention Nepal Clamp in particular to Hilda.

'She's had more balls in her mouth than a Hungry Hippo that one,' Wenda said. 'You wouldn't recognise her without a cock stuck down her throat.'

Wenda always caused a lot of giggling with

her inability to mince her words. And some gagging noises.

'I've got a question,' said Val, changing the subject quickly because Hilda wasn't joining in any laughter. On the contrary, her expression was darkening more with every passing second. 'If I thump that spotty cow Ivanka in the office, will I get sacked?'

'Yes, you will,' said Hilda, after sipping some tea. 'Why, what's up?'

'She looks right down her nose at me whenever I go in there. At least miserable Della doesn't do that, even if she barely acknowledges you're there. I'd rather be ignored than have some little snot think I don't belong to the same species.'

'Astrid reckons there's something going on with her and Jimmy,' said Wenda, through a mouthful of scone.

This was met with a ripple of amused disbelief.

'It's true,' said Astrid. 'Jimmy flirts with every woman in the world except her. Vat does that tell you?'

But no one could follow Astrid's 'logic'. She obviously didn't think like a woman yet, they thought collectively. Women spotted other women having affairs.

'I'm getting fed up with those Des's Discount products,' said Gemma. 'They're absolutely rubbish, aren't they?'

'I won't use that Fillit Bong,' huffed Hilda. 'I'll make a note of that and we'll have a word with

Della. Again. That window and glass cleaner should be relabelled "feck all" because then it would do exactly what it said on the tin. I'm sure it's just water with some green food colouring in it.'

There was a bee-like mumble of *hmms* in agreement.

'I've told Della that I'm not doing Mr Savant's house again,' said Wenda then, as she poured herself another cup of tea. 'And I've told her none of us are doing it either. She said she was going to ring him and let him go.'

Everyone froze in position.

'She said what?' said Hilda, eventually.

'You heard.'

'Della said she would turn away his custom?' asked Sandra, as open-mouthed as the others.

'Yep.' Wenda was proud of the impact her words had had on them all.

'She must be going through the change,' said Astrid. 'Or she has been doppelgängered.'

'Anyway, moving on . . .' coughed Hilda.

Cheryl's hand slowly rose to signify she had another point. Hilda smiled. 'You've got summat to say, love?'

Hilda felt sorry for Cheryl. She knew she must have split up with her partner because she lived around the corner from Ann Gladstone and saw that her son had moved back in with her. She'd never thought much of the Gladstones and was inclined to think that Cheryl was well rid, but the lass was pale and a fair bit thinner than the last time she had seen her and she deduced from that that she must be suffering from a dose of heartbreak.

'It's Mr Morgan. I've inherited him from Ruth Fallis's workload. Has anyone else here cleaned for him?'

It was clear from the reaction of mumbled 'nos' that no one had.

'Why, what's up?' asked Hilda.

'I can't work out if he's a dirty old man or not. I'm sure he had a feel at my boobs as he was helping me off and on with my coat.'

'Then he's a dirty old man,' Meg spluttered through her sixth cheese finger.

'You put him in his place if he is,' said Hilda firmly. 'We don't have to stand for any of that in our job.'

'Kick him in the bollocks if he does it again,' said Wenda, as she sank her teeth into a mini cherry cheesecake. 'If being a filthy old bastard was an Olympic event, some blokes wouldn't be able to stand up for the weight of gold around their bloody necks.'

Meg was almost choking on pastry now.

'Remember Friddle the Fiddle?' Wenda said to everyone, resulting in a wave of head-nods, yes-noises and shudders. 'Some pervs only understand the international language of knee-in-the-cobblers, which Josie Clamp was only too happy to give him.'

'I vill teach you some Kung Fu moves after this tea just in case,' Astrid called over.

'Hark at Mr Miyage over there,' said Marie and set them all off laughing.

'Thanks, Astrid,' smiled Cheryl, knowing that whatever Astrid taught her in ten minutes was hardly going to help. Mr Morgan was stout and at least six foot tall. And who was to say he didn't know any self-defence moves himself?

'Now we come to my big news,' said Hilda, clapping her hands to restore order again because she was impatient to deliver it. 'I was in here yesterday and this woman came in with a mop and bucket. And we got talking, like you do, and I found out that there's a new cleaning company in town.'

All eyes were fixed on her, waiting to hear the significance of the mystery woman with the cleaning tools.

'Anyone heard of Lady Muck?' she carried on, facing a sea of shaking heads and mumbled 'nos'. 'Well apparently this woman works for a new firm called Lady Muck.' Hilda reached in her pocket and got out the handful of business cards which Connie had given to her the previous day and passed them around. 'She said this Lady Muck woman pays two pounds an hour above the minimum wage and every month someone gets fifty pounds for being Employee of the Month. And they give you an allowance towards buying your own cleaning stuff and they even give you a bit of sick pay cash in hand. And some money towards your travelling expenses. And a Christmas bonus.'

'You're joking,' was the response, muttered in various different ways. Even Meg Thompson had stopped scoffing and had joined in a sub-group of chatter.

'Have you rung them, Hilda?' asked Gemma.

Hilda called them to order. 'No, I haven't called them. You know what they say about things that look too good to be true, they usually are too good to be true. I've looked them up on the internet and couldn't find anything about them—'

'If it's a new firm, they might not have set one up yet though,' said Marie.

'I shan't move anywhere if I can't take my clients with me,' said Hilda, resolutely.

'They'd go where you go, surely?' said Cheryl.

'Of course they will,' said Hilda, nudging her small bosom up with her folded arms, Les Dawson style.

'We could go to Della and tell her what other firms are offering. Might make her sit up and take notice,' said Gemma.

'Well, there's no point in going to Cleancheap because my cousin works for them and Roy Frog pays worse than Jimmy does. Plus the word is that it's going down the pan,' said Irene.

Hilda nodded. She'd heard that rumour too and was inclined to believe it. 'Thing is, I've worked for Jimmy Diamond a lot of years. He might be tighter than a gnat's chuff but there's such a thing as loyalty.'

'Bugger loyalty,' said Marie.

'Yeah but if this Lady Muck can give out all that, I'm sure as hell he could,' Hilda argued. Everyone nodded a vigorous agreement.

'We all know he's creaming off us,' Meg said, stuffing a scone in her chops.

'If we went en masse to Jimmy and pressured him, he just might give us what we want: more money per hour, better cleaning products et cetera.' This from Gemma.

Hilda picked up one of the business cards, looked at it again then cast it disdainfully back down on the table. 'I think this woman might be a flash in the pan. I will have a word with Della and see what she says but I'll stay put for now.'

'Better the devil you know,' someone shouted from the back, making them all laugh.

They knew that Hilda didn't like change. She liked order and familiarity above all. They also knew that, despite being ruled by her condition, she was a wise old bird and had their best interests at heart. They trusted her judgement implicitly.

It was decided that Hilda would go in to the office on Monday and talk to Della. When the afternoon teas were finished and doggy bags filled, although Meg had hoovered up a lot of what was left as usual, Astrid gave Cheryl a lift home and in her tiny front room attempted to show her a couple of self-defence moves, which was very kind of her, but Cheryl knew in a million years that she wouldn't be brave enough to attempt them.

Astrid's hands landed on her hips and she shook her head.

'I'm vasting my time, aren't I?'

'Oh Astrid, I do appreciate you doing this but I'm not going to be able to put all this into practice,' Cheryl sighed in response.

'I can't believe you could tackle Ruth Fallis and yet you are afraid to kick zis Mr Morgan in ze knackers if he tries to feel you up.'

Maybe if she had found Mr Morgan feeling up Edith, she would have stormed in there like Uma Thurman, but Cheryl knew she had more courage when standing up for others than she had standing up for herself.

'Look, I'll be all right. I might have got it wrong; after all he is a church organist. He could have just been clumsy with his hands rather than gropey.'

Astrid smiled sympathetically.

'Okay, here is vat we will do. Next week, you go to my Mr Price on Wednesday and I vill go to Mr Morgan. Mr Price is a nice bloke. He keeps out of your way doing ze *Times* crossword in his conservatory. I vill make sure zat Mr Morgan is very clear where his boundaries are.' Cheryl opened her mouth to protest but Astrid was having none of it. 'T''is settled. I inzist.'

'That's so kind of you, Astrid,' said Cheryl. 'I bet I've got it wrong though and he didn't mean to touch me.'

'I hope so,' replied Astrid. 'Mr Morgan would never be the same man afterwards if he tried it on vith me.'

Cheryl was only glad that Astrid was on her side.

CHAPTER 30

Everyone in South Yorkshire woke up to a vista of white the next morning as heavy snow had fallen through the night, even though the weather forecast had only warned of light flurries and the council had heeded that and not sent any gritting lorries out. In the kitchen, Connie stood and stared out onto her garden. She could feel a draught through the shoddy windows and was forced to move back into the warm inner body of the room.

Jimmy was like a cat on hot bricks, frustrated because he said he was supposed to be having a round of golf with Pookie Barnes and a potential new client, one of Pookie's cronies. Connie didn't believe him. He wouldn't have been that agitated to miss a game of golf with a man he schmoozed with but in reality didn't like that much. Jimmy stomped around a bit, huffing at the clouds, then put on his coat and said he was going out to the hut where the fire-bin was to burn a load of rubbish.

Connie remembered back to the first year of their marriage when they had been snowed in.

They didn't have a great deal of money and had been living with her mum who was the most wonderful baker. They'd sat on the huge furry rug in front of the fire and scoffed a whole apple pie and cream between them. Connie had been six months pregnant and glowing and felt as sexy as hell. She'd loved and fancied Jimmy so much. Okay, so they had married too young, but their dreams had fitted together like a perfect two-piece jigsaw puzzle then. Connie would raise a family and Jimmy would go out to work, just like they did in the old days. That's what Connie wanted most of all because her dad had never been around and her mum, though she hated having to do it, had to leave a key so that Connie could let herself into their chilly, empty house from school. She used to pray sometimes that her mum would fall ever so slightly ill so she couldn't work and would be there cooking her tea when she came home.

They'd both played their parts – Jimmy had been the breadwinner, Connie had kept house. So why did it all go wrong?

That night in bed, Connie felt Jimmy hunch over to her side of the bed until he was spooning her and she stiffened, trying to work out whether he was asleep or not.

Then he clarified that by speaking. 'You awake, Con?'

'Er, yes,' she replied.

'What's the weather forecast for tomorrow?'

'More of the same.'

'Oh for fuck's sake.' She felt his breathy sigh of annoyance on the back of her neck.

'Is it so bad being cooped up in the house with me?' Connie asked, trying to stop her heart from quickening in anticipation of his answer.

'No, no. It's just that I've got things to do, places to go.'

'People to see?' She ended the phrase for him.

'If you count Pookie as a person,' he came straight back at her. 'If he doesn't stop slapping weight on, he'll soon be able to body-double for Jabba the Hut.'

Connie lay in the dark listening to the clock's baritone tick-tock downstairs in the hallway, aware of her husband's close proximity. Was it her imagination or was he inching closer to her? Then she felt his lips on her neck and his hand on her waist, pulling her over to face him.

'My best girl,' he said. He had always called her that and only now did she realise the underlying meaning of the words. Was she the one he saved for best? The one that he stuffed away in a cupboard and only took out occasionally when he wanted to use her? In that case she wasn't so much 'best' as a 'standby'.

Connie unexpectedly felt like crying. She had been clinging to anger to drive her on, but she suddenly wanted to let it go, let the softness and vulnerability flow back into her.

'Am I, Jimmy? Am I really?'

'Yes.' He kissed her and she kissed him back, fervently, desperately. His hands touched her and her hands touched him.

'I love you,' she said, unable to stop the words from leaving her. It had been so long since they made love that it almost physically hurt. Tears rolled from the corner of her eye onto the pillow as his breathing quickened and he held her. She loved him and she hated him, she wanted him miles away from her and she wanted his body to stay next to hers for ever. She wanted *her* Jimmy back again, the man who bought 'his best girl' fancy chocolates because he didn't want her to forget that even though he might not give her as much attention as he should, he loved her. But that Jimmy had existed only as a shiny veneer on a cunning tosspot of a husband. Connie felt as if the husband she loved had died an age ago but she had just found out about it. Her grief was no less for the years in between, in fact it was more, for the waste of emotion and time and opportunities she could have had. This impostor, now inside her, shared his shape, his smell, his voice and her body wanted to believe he was still *her* Jimmy. But her head was denying her that ability to self-deceive.

Sated, Jimmy pressed his lips to Connie's forehead.

'I love you,' he said, before rolling over and settling his head on his pillow. It didn't take him long to fall into sleep but Connie lay staring into space, knowing that he had lied to her. Yet again.

CHAPTER 31

It was a different Connie who woke up to the one who had let her husband use her the previous night. She had dreamt of her mum handing her a small present wrapped roughly in brown paper.

'Connie Elizabeth Clarke, you can do anything you put your mind to and don't you forget it. Don't let anyone laugh at you, unless it's on the other side of their faces.'

She'd been looking up at her lovely black-haired mum as if she were a small child again as her hand came out for the present. And she opened it as she had in real life all those years ago and saw the magic.

Cheryl had gone through the whole house and filled a carrier bag full of Gary's detritus, plus the guitar. She didn't know what to do with it: should she just dump it on Ann Gladstone's doorstep or should she ring Gary to come and collect it? But she couldn't bring herself to phone him. How could it be that they had been together for ten years, how could they have shared so much for so long and overnight have turned into strangers?

Cheryl stared out of the window at the white bumps of snow-covered cars in the street. There was no let-up in the weather and the forecasters were now saying that it could go on for a week. At least she might have a few days respite from the phantom egg thrower.

She thought of how beautiful Edith's garden would look today – like a frozen fairyland. Was the old lady okay? Did she have enough food in? Was she warm enough? Cheryl picked her notebook out of her bag and found Edith's number. She shouldn't ring really, but she did.

Lance answered.

For an initial second, Cheryl was relieved that someone was there with the old lady. She wasn't alone, she had someone on hand who would watch out for her. Then sense kicked in: *this was Lance. This was the nephew she had been about to disinherit.*

'It's Cheryl. The cleaner,' she gulped. 'I'm just ringing to see if Edith is okay in this weather.'

'Thank you, she's fine,' came the clipped but polite reply.

Cheryl very badly wanted to hear Edith's voice. 'Can I speak to her?'

'She's having a lie down. I'm happy to pass a message on for you.'

Edith very rarely took naps during the day. She might have been ninety-three but she always fought against them, so she could sleep properly at night, she said.

'She's not ill, is she?'

She heard Lance's breath of impatience before he answered her. 'Look, I'm sure you mean well but I'm here so she isn't alone. Oh and whilst you're on the phone, let me just say that there will be no need for your services this week as my aunt has a hospital appointment.'

'I can reschedule,' Cheryl answered quickly, which seemed to annoy Lance considerably. His voice dropped all politeness and acquired a nasty hiss. Cheryl had a sudden vision of him as a giant snake, coiled around the phone.

'Oh for goodness sake, you annoying bitch. I'd appreciate you keeping your nose out of our business. Isn't this slightly above and beyond the call of your duties? If you ring again, I'll ensure my aunt sacks you and moves to another cleaning firm. Now piss off.' And with that he put the phone down.

His words hit Cheryl like a thump. She would be heartbroken if he persuaded Edith to sack her or fixed it so that she didn't see the old lady again, and she had no doubt that he would carry out that threat if he had to. She shouldn't have rung. But then again, she wouldn't have been able to rest thinking that Edith might be alone. Lance might have given her an earful but it was worth it to know that her old friend had company. She was being overdramatic thinking that Lance might do her some harm and should chill out a bit. She'd been watching too many thrillers on the TV. Even

Lance's slimy presence was better than none, she decided, if it meant he would keep Edith safe.

Della's call was answered by the familiar voice of Joyce, the manageress at Sunset Park.

'Morning, it's Della Frostick, Moira Frostick's daughter. I won't be able to get up there today to see Mum.'

'Morning, Miss Frostick. Isn't the weather terrible,' replied Joyce. 'I'm just glad I live on the premises. But don't you worry, there's no change. She was calling out for Gillian again quite a bit through the night.'

She always calls for Gillian, said Della to herself. *Never me.*

'She's having her lunch at the table by the window, watching the snow come down. She's very calm. I'll tell her you rang.'

Her eyes won't even flicker, thought Della, putting the phone back down. She thinks Gillian is her daughter because she always wanted Gillian to be her daughter. Not Della. Not Della who grew in her belly like a poisoned seed and then emerged with the sole purpose of ruining her life.

CHAPTER 32

The snow didn't stop falling until that night, then the rain started. Then the temperature plunged to Siberian-type numbers in the early hours of Monday morning and South Yorkshire was gripped by a plague of treacherous black ice. Even the council gritting lorries had some hairy moments on the roads. One skidded into a Barnsley footballer's Ferrari, which would make the front cover of the *Chronicle* that week. No buses were running, nor taxis and everyone wished they had a pound for every time they heard the words quoted: 'Well, in all my born days, I've never seen the weather as bad as this.'

The cleaners knew they wouldn't get paid for the work they had missed, which was doubling the attraction of taking the risk and working for Lady Muck, as much of an unknown quantity as she was. Now they had been introduced to a company that seemed to have workers' interests more at heart, their discontent with their present situation started to bubble and foam.

Jimmy was like a caged tiger at home. When the girls weren't able to earn, it was as if he could visualise money slipping through his fingers and he hated that. And Ivanka was being very teasing on the phone and driving him half-mad with lust. He hadn't had sex with her since they were in Spain and he was due a fix. He hoped she wouldn't find out what he and Connie had done on Saturday night. He'd been so horny – and she'd been there and warm and willing and familiar. He knew he had used her and he felt slightly bad for that. Oh, the irony – that he had been unfaithful to his mistress with his wife. It was all so screwed up.

Connie had been due at the bank on Tuesday morning to open up an account in the name of Lady Muck but had rescheduled it for Thursday out of earshot of Jimmy. She was as frustrated by the weather as he was. She had limited time to implement her plan and didn't want to let any of her customers down by not turning up to clean. More snow came down in the afternoon, soft white flakes of innocence that everyone was sick of the sight of now.

It was with joyous relief, then, that on Tuesday night the temperatures rose, a melting rain fell all night and all that was left of the snow and ice were a few stubborn hillocks of white on the pavements. It was business as usual on Wednesday, thank God. Jimmy hoped that Ivanka had thawed as well and got that stupid Lent business out of her head. He would take her to that posh French place in Wakefield after work for an early dinner which might loosen her knicker elastic.

Connie watched her husband shoot off towards his car like a cheetah on performance-enhancing drugs. Being trapped at home with him for so long had aptly demonstrated how much her marriage was dead in the water. His body had been grumping around the house but his head had been with his mistress, she knew that. And yes, it hurt that she might as well have been invisible for all the notice he took of her, apart from Saturday night, when a blow-up doll would have served the same purpose.

At least with her not even showing up as a blip on his radar, it had given her the opportunity to do some research on her laptop on the kitchen table whilst she was cooped up in the house. She read stories of how businesses had sabotaged their competitors and realised how many evil – yet inventive – people there were out there. Releasing bags of mice and cockroaches in rival restaurants, making fake bookings, computer hacking . . . there were lots of stories to rake over. There were some tactics that she wouldn't have sunk to in a million years, but a little computer hacking was well within the remits. In the secret A4 file which Della had given her she found the access information for the Diamond Shine website, which Jimmy thought only he had.

Jimmy presumed his wife was playing Candy Crush on her laptop, which was understandable, as she did drop the odd exclamation about how evil chocolate was as she made a little secret tweak here and there to his company website.

CHAPTER 33

Connie hadn't needed to do an assessment on Mr Savant's house. He had requested a three-hour clean once a week which, he said, was the adequate arrangement he had with his last firm. He sounded like a man with exacting standards who knew what he wanted.

From the outside, his house Crow Edge was an imposing, tall, gothic revival building with its arched windows and steeply pitched roof. It reminded Connie of a creepy gingerbread house. Mr Savant fitted the house perfectly, with his long pale face and smart black attire, but he was scrupulously polite as he herded Connie quickly into the warmth of his house and out of the cold.

Connie found herself in a huge square hallway with a heavily carved magnificent staircase winding upwards to the next floor. Tapestries and old portraits hung on the red-painted walls and there was even a suit of armour standing to attention in the corner. The furniture was ornate, baroque in style with deep rich colours. Connie thought it was beautiful, even if it did remind her of a set on a Hammer Horror film. She could see why some of the girls had imagined it could be haunted.

Music was playing, an orchestra with a string-heavy base and a man's voice talking. Connie was knowledgeable about classical music but she couldn't place this. Mr Savant must have sensed the workings in her brain because he offered the title.

'*Pygmalion.*'

'Oh. I haven't heard of that one.'

'Better seen than listened to, as two of the characters have silent roles,' Mr Savant smiled. 'But I have seen it so many times that I can imagine it all. Anyway, let me not waste any more of your precious time. Once I begin to talk about opera, I'm afraid you'll not be able to stop me. Please come through to the sitting room.'

The room echoed the style of the hallway, with dark oak panels and two huge wooden bookcases filled with hardback books, and Connie presumed, rightly, that the grandeur would be repeated throughout the house. The music was coming from a vintage gramophone with a highly polished horn on a table in the corner.

'This room will only need minimal attention. Never use a mop on this floor,' Mr Savant warned. 'Only a floor duster. I don't want the oak boards to warp.'

Connie made a note in the small pad she had taken out of her bag. She followed Mr Savant from room to room recording his instructions, noting how very tidy and clean everything was. She couldn't understand why none of the Diamond Shine girls wanted this job because it would be far easier than some of the houses she knew they must have to do. And Mr Savant was quiet and looked every inch the caricature of a retired undertaker, but he was very courteous. He invited Connie to make herself a cup of tea if she ever wanted one and to help herself to 'anything she desired from the refrigerator'. Connie thanked him but said she preferred to just get on and clean.

She started upstairs. As with Brandon Locke's house, only one of the bedrooms seemed to be occupied but she had three hours to fill so she vacuumed and dusted all of the bedrooms then started on the bathroom, putting out fresh towels and mopping a floor that was shining already. She vacuumed the staircase and polished the beautiful dark wooden rail until it shone. Next she wiped down the surfaces of the kitchen and the fronts of the units. She opened the fridge door to get right into the grooves of the seal and was surprised at the stocks of food inside. On the lower shelves were vegetables, butter, milk – standard 'fridge fare' but the top two shelves were crammed full of cakes: éclairs, meringues, scones oozing clotted cream. There was a fat Victoria Sponge and a cheesecake covered in crushed chocolate. Connie averted her eyes as she wiped.

Pygmalion was starting to grate on her by the time her hours were up. There was no singing, just

215

music and that man's voice talking, informing the audience in whatever tongue he was speaking how he had fallen in love with a statue he had created and was begging the Gods to make her come to life and return his affection.

Mr Savant paid Connie cash and she left wondering how anyone could think that the warm beautiful house might be haunted. She didn't believe in ghosts. She wanted to but if there had been such things, her mother would have been in contact by now, as she had assured her she would. 'When I've gone, I'll let you know I've found him,' she said. 'I'll find a way, I promise.' But she never had.

CHAPTER 34

There was a delegation of cleaners led by Hilda waiting for Della when she came back from her lunch break. *Oh goody*, she thought, because she knew what this would be about, but she tried to look serious and impatient.

'Have you got five minutes, Della?' Hilda asked. 'We've got summat to say.'

'I suppose so,' replied Della with a weary sigh, as if expecting trouble. She took off her coat and hung it up, aware that Ivanka might have slunk into the kitchen out of the way but would be listening to every word.

'We think it's time Jimmy gave us a pay rise,' began Hilda, sitting down in the chair at the other side of Della's desk, the others spread behind her like a peacock's fantail.

'Good luck with that one,' huffed Della.

'Some firms out there are paying two pounds an hour above minimum wage.'

'And giving bonuses,' added Wenda.

'And another thing, that Des's Warehouse stuff is crap. I've got more disinfectant in my bleeding spit than there is in that "Bugzoff". It couldn't kill a bloody germ with a rocket launcher at point blank range.'

'Well, I can only ask Jimmy for you,' replied Della. 'I can't sanction anything, personally.'

''Ve haven't had a pay rise in a long time,' replied Astrid, towering over everyone at the back.

'Like I said, I can only put what you tell me to Jimmy.'

'When will he be back? Shall we wait?' asked Hilda.

'He's out all day at a sales conference, so there's not really much point,' Della said, knowing that there was no such conference because she had rung up and checked, so God only knew where he was, but she would bet her life that Ivanka would ask for an extended lunch break so she could meet up with him. 'I promise you, I'll tell him what you've told me.'

'We've got a list of demands,' said Hilda firmly, sounding like someone out of *Die Hard*. She slapped a folded sheet of A4 paper down on the desk. 'Tell him from us that we're not happy, Della. If he doesn't want a mass walk-out, then he needs to do a bit of thinking and digging in his pocket. We don't want to leave Jimmy in the lurch so we're asking for some compromising.'

Jeez, who'd have thought that the girls had so much loyalty for Jimmy. At this moment they had far more of it than she had, thought Della.

'I said I'd tell him and I will.'

The Diamond Shine girls might have been on

the edge of a cliff, ready to fall into Lady Muck's safety blanket waiting below; but they were clinging on to it with all their might, it seemed.

'Oh, and we've lost two days' work. What are the chances of some compensation?' Wenda shouted aggressively over Hilda's shoulder.

'I think you know the answer to that one already,' said Della.

'Aye, thought as much,' grumbled Hilda, rising abruptly to her feet. 'Come on, girls. We've done what we came to do.'

The six women trailed out of the door, shutting it behind them. 'And a fat lot of bleedin' good it'll have done.' Wenda's voice rang out deliberately loud enough to be heard.

Ivanka came out of the kitchen and walked over to the coat stand. She was shaking her head and tutting like Skippy the kangaroo.

'They are not really knowing how much jam they have on their teacakes, are they?'

'You sound like Jimmy,' Della laughed – she couldn't resist pointing it out to see if Ivanka reacted. But Ivanka was a cool customer, she merely shrugged her shoulders once.

'I hear it from him so much in the office, I must have picked it up. Okay, now I go for lunch. I am very hungry. Ees it okay if I take extra half-hour? My cousin is over for short break from Krakow. He will have news of my parents.'

'Take two. You go and treat yourself to a nice roll.' Della smiled sweetly. The smile dropped as soon as Ivanka made her exit. Della sat back in her chair and puffed out her cheeks. How far was all this going to go, she asked herself. What was next?

She found the answer to that one within the next ten minutes, when she made a cursory trip to the Diamond Shine website.

CHAPTER 35

A woman wearing a wedding ring answered Brandon Locke's door. A tall, slim woman with long dark hair, wearing a beautifully tailored blue coat and a puzzled, disdainful expression at finding another female on the doorstep who was obviously awaiting admittance.

'I'm the cleaner,' Connie explained, as if it wasn't entirely clear why she was standing there with a mop and bucket in her hand. Then again, she supposed, she could have been a very fastidious burglar who liked to tidy up after herself.

The woman swept her eyes once over Connie then called over her shoulder.

'Brandon. You've got company.'

She left Connie standing outside until Brandon came.

'Sorry, sorry, I was on the phone. Do come in, Marilyn. Here, let me help you.'

He insisted on taking the bucket from her as Connie walked into the chocolate-scented hallway. There was so much cocoa in the air that Connie could feel it sticking to the insides of her lungs. Every breath she took was probably fifty calories.

Once upon a time she would have been in heaven at the thought. Now, it just made her want to block off her nasal receptors.

'Bran, I'm going. I'll leave you to it. And remember what I said, give yourself a break.' The woman claimed his attention as she leaned forwards and kissed him on the cheek; very near to his mouth, too. Then she breezed past Connie as if she were non-existent.

'Sorry about that,' said Brandon after he had closed the door on her. 'Helena. The ex-wife. Comes around to lecture me occasionally.' He dropped a sigh, which hinted that he wasn't altogether pleased that she did so.

They must have made a striking couple once with their good looks and beautiful flowing hair, thought Connie, although her first impressions of Helena's other attributes weren't that favourable.

'Nice you can stay friends with your ex-wife,' she said, whilst thinking: *even if she is a snobby sod up her own designer backside.*

'Well, we had to work at it,' replied Brandon. 'We went to Relate to help us break up civilly. I didn't want to be one of those hateful, bitter people who are obsessed with getting even and resort to things like sewing prawns into curtains.'

Connie nodded politely but didn't fess up that she was one of those people. She and Brandon were clearly very different types, because there was no intermediary on earth or elsewhere who could convince her to be reasonable in the break-up of her marriage. The first chance she got, she would sew prawns into Jimmy's testicles, never mind his curtains.

'Apparently I live to work, not work to live,' Brandon said as Connie followed him into the kitchen. 'I was building the business up and Chox was my mistress. Helena is happily married to the guy she left me for and I live in sin with a kitchen full of ingredients.'

Connie smiled. This would be her destiny soon – married to a business filled with cloths and bleach, though, rather than cocoa butter and icing bags.

'If you don't mind, I'll be working in the kitchen whilst you're here, but I'll keep to this small corner and promise not to get in your way.'

'It's your house, Mr Locke, I'll work around you,'

'Brandon, please. Or sir,' Brandon replied with a twinkle in his nice shiny eyes.

'I always start from the top and work down,' said Connie.

'Oh, well, that's nice to know.' Brandon raised his eyebrows.

Connie felt a blush spread over her cheeks and she grabbed her bucket and mop and headed for upstairs. She heard a text alert from her secret phone, and had to stop and search for it in her bag. Della had sent her a message: WHAT ON EARTH HAVE YOU DONE TO THE WEBSITE ;) ???

As she vacuumed around his bedroom she

wondered why the haughty Helena was coming around to lecture him. Was it possible she still felt some ownership of her ex-husband? She wouldn't have been surprised, from the way Helena had bristled when she found a strange female on the doorstep, even if it was a dumpy woman with her hair dragged back in a ponytail carrying a carrier bag full of cleaning substances.

'Can I get you a coffee, Marilyn?' asked Brandon when Connie started on the kitchen.

'No, I'm fine, honestly.'

'Want to sample some chocs? Can I tempt you to a burnt sugar caramel?' He proffered a tray of glossy chocolate ovals.

Even the word 'caramel' was enough to conjure up a vision of Jimmy standing in their kitchen, proudly holding out a blue box filled with hand-made caramel truffles which he had found in a small shop in Truro, he said. He'd gone into detail about the shop: an idyllic cottage with roses around the door. The chocolatier-owner was Italian and was training his son to take over. Oh, the arrogance of his lies. Funnily enough, she had looked it up at the weekend to find that there was no 'shop' – the industry was run from a 1960s bungalow and did mail-order only. The choco-latier was from Dartmoor, like his father and grandfather before him. And he was childless.

'No thanks.' Connie declined them, turning her head from them. 'Honestly.'

'Sure?'

Her brain plucked out image of her biting into a caramel, heavy and syrupy, sugar crystals scratching against her teeth and she covered her mouth as her stomach bucked.

Brandon was watching her and Connie was stricken with embarrassment.

'You really do have it bad, don't you?' he said, with a heavy hint of amusement in his voice, as he moved the chocolates away from her immediate space.

'I'm afraid so.'

'Okay, if I can't lure you over to the dark side, then I'll leave you to it.' He had a nice smile, lazy and open, thought Connie. Not like Jimmy's, which might as well have been tattooed on. You could never tell if Jimmy was genuinely pleased about something or putting on an act. He had a first class honours degree in insincerity.

Brandon returned to his chocolate laboratory on the other side of the kitchen. But despite his resolution to leave 'Marilyn' to get on with the cleaning, it wasn't long before he started up another conversation.

'So who is Lady Muck?' he asked, as he roughly chopped up some candied orange peel.

'Don't know her real name,' replied Connie as she scrubbed down the pine dining table.

'Where are the offices based? Sorry – am I disturbing you? I'm not used to having anyone here during the day.'

'Not at all,' replied Connie, hoping that if she

answered the second question he might forget about the first. 'I'm not used to being with people during the day either.'

'I don't mind it really. Luckily I'm used to my own company.'

'Are you an only child like me?' asked Connie, suspecting he was. Children with no siblings were good at surviving without anyone to talk to.

'God no,' replied Brandon, which surprised her. 'I'm the eldest of four. They've all got very serious and sensible jobs: solicitor, financier, gym manager . . . and then there's me – the Yorkshire Willy Wonka, which is how one newspaper referred to me.'

Connie smiled. 'That's very sweet.'

'Hey, good pun.' Brandon clicked his fingers. 'Sorry, I'm off again.'

'It's fine,' said Connie. 'I don't mind.' Nor did she. She'd chatted more to Brandon Locke since entering his house today than she had done to her own husband throughout the long, snowy weekend. They used to talk a long time ago – together. Then it turned into Connie talking to Jimmy as he fiddled on his laptop and only half-heard her. Then he didn't hear her at all, so she stopped trying to get his attention.

'I always loved that book – *Charlie and the Chocolate Factory*,' she said. 'I used to read it to my daughter and we'd make our own chocolates. Not quite up to the standard of yours, I hasten to add.' The memory of Jane's hands covered in chocolate visited her in glorious technicolour.

'I loved it too,' said Brandon enthusiastically. 'That book changed my life. As soon as I read it, I knew that's what I wanted to be when I grew up.'

'And you did.'

'Well, I did *eventually*,' Brandon amended. 'It was a bit of a long and winding road to get to where I am now, but touch wood . . .' he put his hand on the top of his head '. . . I'm going onwards and upwards on a nice manageable gradient.'

Connie was curious and asked, 'Weren't you frightened about setting up in business yourself, Mr Locke?'

'Erm, yes, of course I was, but I wanted to do it very much as well. I love being at the wheel of my own business. And if I'm brutally honest,' he said, checking in an exaggerated fashion to either side of himself as if he might be overheard, 'there were a few people I wanted to prove wrong. Our careers advisor at school, for instance. When I told him I wanted to be a chocolatier, he asked me if I was a homosexual.'

'No,' said Connie with open-mouthed disbelief.

'Yup.' Brandon threw back his head and laughed. 'If I'd been a girl, it would have been okay to go into catering, but not a big strapping lad like me. I was meant to be an engineer, because I got an A in my physics A-level.'

'Thank God things have changed,' laughed Connie. Her eyes flicked to the clock and she saw that her three hours were over five minutes ago. 'Good for you for sticking to your guns.'

'Do you know why I did?' asked Brandon, putting down his knife and folding his arms. 'When I was in primary school, I was in the playground one day with my friends and we were laughing at this little girl trying to do a handstand against the wall. Kids can be sods, can't they? I make no apologies for myself. Anyway, all the slim, pretty girls could do it effortlessly, but this one podgy little girl just couldn't kick her legs high enough. But there she was, every day, still trying to do that handstand and refusing to let her friend help her by pushing her legs up: she was determined to do it by herself. I stopped laughing at her and I started willing her to do it and show everyone that she could. And then one day . . .'

'She did it?' asked Connie.

'No, she fell over and broke her neck.'

'Oh no.'

'Joking,' said Brandon. 'Sorry, couldn't resist; you were hanging on to my every word. Yeah, she did it. There she was, in a whole line of upside-down girls. And I clapped and I think she saw me because she beamed. A big upside-down smile, which showed her front tooth missing. I've never forgotten her. She was so brave, and though ergonomically she wasn't designed to do handstands, shall we say, she did it and that shut everyone up.'

Connie swallowed nervously. She'd been a girl like that. There was one in every class in every primary school, someone chubbier than the rest, not as pretty, a bit more useless at gymnastics.

Brandon caught sight of the time. 'Sorry, sorry. I'm making you late. Big apologies. Here, let me pay you. Cash okay, until I can sort out a direct debit?'

'That's fine.'

He pulled a wallet from his back pocket and extracted the money. 'And I'll see you next week, Marilyn. I promise, I'll be very quiet and not put you off your work.'

Connie laughed. 'I don't mind at all. It's nice to talk to you,' she said. And she meant it.

Connie looked into his lovely chocolatey brown smiling eyes as she took the money from his hand and wished she had assessed him as needing an extra hour at least.

Della's hand was over her mouth as she read the reworded blurb on the website yet again and wondered how long it would take Jimmy to notice it.

DIRE SHITE CLEANING SERVICES

Want affordable domestic services tailor made to your budget and lifestyle? Need a dependable laundry service on a weekly, fortnightly clean or a famous intensive spring clean 'Bomb'?

Well, look no further than DIRE SHITE! We are based in Barnsley and we provide a load of lazy tarts who will take your money from you, raid your fridge, drink your vodka supplies and thieve your valuables.

We are DIRE SHITE and that's exactly what we supply to all our valued customers.

Della coughed down the nervous giggle that was tickling her throat, closed the page and deleted her search history for super safety. Connie Diamond had surprised her. Every day since they started this whole thing, she had been expecting Connie to panic and call things off. Now, after reading this, Della believed for the first time that she would actually take this right to the bitter end.

CHAPTER 36

Mr Morgan wasn't expecting his substitute cleaner to be a six foot four wall of beauty with long tumbling blonde locks of hair and eyelashes longer than his thumb. Cheryl, apparently, was ill but someone with a foreign accent from Diamond Shine had phoned to tell him that they would be sending another lady – Astrid.

'Hello, Mr Morgan. I am Astrid,' she said in a breathy, deep voice. He was so taken aback that he didn't realise her accent was remarkably similar to that of the woman who phoned him less than an hour ago.

'Come in, Astrid,' said Mr Morgan. 'Can I help you off with your coat?'

'Thank you,' said Astrid, turning to let him. She felt Mr Morgan's hands brush her neck as he reached up to her collar, and was that his outstretched fingers on the side of her boobs? It could very well have been, but she wasn't one hundred per cent sure so she would allow him the benefit of the doubt on that one. 'Isn't it cold today, Mr Morgan?' She turned around and Mr

Morgan was greeted by the sight of Astrid's erect nipples pushing at her clothes.

'Very,' he agreed, wriggling a little, as if adjusting some movement in his trousers.

'Okay. Where would you like me to start? Shall I do the top first?' Astrid gave him her best slow, seductive smile followed by a discreet, yet very discernible, lick of her lips.

'Just to clarify, the agency hasn't sent you as my new Ruth?' said Mr Morgan.

'If you mean that I am your permanent girl, then no,' replied Astrid. 'I am just here to take zee place of poor ill Cheryl.'

'I see.' Mr Morgan sighed heavily. 'I was hoping to return to stability.'

'I vill do whatever you ask,' smiled Astrid, determined to give him every encouragement to reveal his true colours and protect Cheryl from any further unwanted attention.

'Well, just a general clean around I suppose,' said Mr Morgan. 'Can I make you a drink at all?'

'Thank you, but no.' She fanned her face. It was ridiculously warm in Mr Morgan's house.

'I'll go and turn the central heating down, if you're not my new Ruth,' said Mr Morgan.

Now what on earth does that mean? thought Astrid, picking up her Fillit Bong. But then again, they all knew that Ruth Fallis was cold-blooded.

Astrid cleaned around, totally unbothered by Mr Morgan. It would seem that Cheryl had got it wrong; but Astrid was a creature of intuition and something was niggling her about the church organist that she couldn't put her finger on. Maybe it was that Mr Morgan wouldn't have dared be inappropriate towards the Amazonian Astrid, but – like a typical bully – might pick on a much smaller, softer woman like Cheryl. It worried Astrid that in their last meeting in the Sunflower Café, Cheryl had been quite sure that she had been touched up, but then had done what a lot of women tended to do when they lacked confidence in themselves: they doubted their own judgement, rationalised their correct conclusions until they crumbled into dust and blew them conveniently away. So, just to be on the safe side, Astrid thought she would make it very clear to Mr Morgan that if he did have any intentions of unseemly behaviour towards her friend, then she would nip his proclivities in the bud. Literally.

'Okay, I am almost finished now, Mr Morgan.' Astrid bobbed her head into his music room where he was sitting at his organ playing something that belonged on an *Abominable Dr Phibes* film.

Mr Morgan stopped playing and got up from the stool.

'And Ruth . . . I mean, Cheryl will definitely be back next week?' he asked, nodding vigorously as if willing Astrid to confirm that she would be.

'I think you like Cheryl, Herr Morgan.'

'I do. I think she's going to be a very suitable substitute for my dear Ruth.'

The smile he was wearing turned immediately sour when Astrid reached forward, closed her fingers around his genitals and pinched.

'Jesus Christ, what are you doing?' he groaned when he found some breath. His lungs felt as crushed as his conkers.

'Now, I'm just giving you some advice, Mr Morgan. If you are ze sort of man who likes to invade a woman's personal space, I am telling you not to do that. Do you understand?' Astrid's voice couldn't have been calmer, sweeter or more threatening.

Mr Morgan didn't immediately answer, so Astrid was forced to exert a pound of extra pressure to prompt a response.

'Yes yes yes yes yes. I wouldn't.' A fat drop of sweat from his forehead landed on Astrid's hand.

'Good. I would hate to come back here and have this talk again.'

'Yes yes yes yes yes. Aaargh. I mean no no no. Or is it yes? Please . . . just let . . . go.'

She snatched her hand away and Mr Morgan doubled up, cradling his privates and feeling four times his sixty-two years.

Astrid put on her coat and picked up her bag 'Now, I just need my payment and I'll be out of your life for good. Unless . . .' She left the threat hanging. Mr Morgan stumbled out of the room and behind him Astrid tried not to giggle at his zombie-like gait as he crossed towards the table in the hallway where his wallet was lying.

'Thank you,' he said, hitting a top C of continuing pain.

'Goodbye, Mr Morgan. I do hope you remember zis conversation,' said Astrid, taking the money from his outstretched quivering hand. She sashayed out of the house and back to her car, sure in the knowledge that Cheryl would be perfectly safe the next time she came to clean for Mr Morgan. She didn't anticipate that when he got his breath back the first thing he would do was to ring Diamond Shine to ask why they were employing massive German psychopaths and demanding that Astrid be sacked or he would report her to the police.

CHAPTER 37

Della couldn't help but feel a quivery thrill as she put the phone down. Mr Morgan had sounded as if he had been practising a soprano solo and his voice had got stuck in the range. She was just about to ring Astrid and find out what had been going on when Jimmy walked in. He was the colour of an old weathered teak sideboard.

'Just been to the health club salon for a top up on my fake tan,' he said, anticipating Della's response to his bronzed appearance. 'They're a bit heavier handed with the spray gun than they were in the Hampshire spa.'

Was he still throwing out the lie about him being on a golf course when he was actually in the Costa Blanca? thought Della, with an inward sigh of disgust. She threw him back a lie of her own.

'It makes you look healthy and glowing.'

'Does it?' Jimmy checked his reflection in the glass door of the bookcase to his side. He smiled at himself like a cat that not only had the cream, but had found that it was clotted cream from Harrods.

'You had the cleaners here yesterday in uprising,' said Ivanka, obviously hoping to score some brownie points by having her finger on the pulse of the office action.

'Eh?' Jimmy's attention broke away from himself. 'Uprising? What uprising?' He glared at Della with an *I employ you to handle this shit* message obvious in his eyes.

'Hilda and a few others want a pay rise,' Della began, trying not to let any of the amusement she felt within turn into a giggle that he could see.

'Eh?'

'And better cleaning products than the rubbishy ones from the Des shop,' threw in Ivanka.

'Oh. Anything else whilst we're at it? Galvanised handles on their buckets? Sheepskin sponges? Gold-leaf sprinkles in their bleach?' Jimmy's lip was curled so far back over his teeth that he looked like a wolf at full moon.

'They have a list of demands,' said Ivanka, like a slimy teacher's pet. She got up from her desk and snatched up the list from Della's filing tray. Under other circumstances, Della would have snapped at her to get on with her work, thank you, but she reckoned it was much better that Ivanka should be the messenger who might hopefully get shot.

Jimmy took the sheet of paper from her and unfolded it.

'That's the trouble with that lot, they don't realise how much jam they've got on their teacakes,' he said and Della seized her chance to stir up some mischief.

'You've got Ivanka saying that now.'

'What?' he snapped.

'Ivanka's picking up all your phrases.' Della smiled sweetly. 'She's started saying that some people don't realise how much jam they've got on their teacakes.'

Jimmy said nothing but his neck was mottling red, which it did when he got angry. Della knew his brain was whirring as he pinned his eyes to the paper in his hand.

'Bonus . . . Employee of the Month . . . *fifty pounds* . . .What have they been frigging drinking?' He laughed as he disdainfully smacked the sheet with the back of his hand. 'Are they having a laugh? Thick bleach? String mops? Travelling allowances? Have they got me mixed up with Richard fucking Branson?'

'Please don't swear, Jimmy,' said Ivanka. Jimmy's head span around to her; Della's flipped up and then travelled back and forth between him and Ivanka as if she was watching a high speed tennis match, as Ivanka realised she had carelessly spoken to him as an intimate and not as a boss.

Jimmy looked furious. His face had grown red under his tan and the colouring on his neck gave it the appearance of corned beef.

'Della, tell them all to piss off with their bloody demands,' he said, defiantly stressing the swear words. 'I'm going out in ten minutes. I think I might have a sandwich in the Green Man.' He strode into his office and slammed the door behind him. He had spoken to Della, but she knew the emphasis was for the benefit of Ivanka, who she suspected might be in big trouble.

'I will have an early lunch and go into the centre of town,' said Ivanka, five minutes later. 'The atmosphere in here is giving me a headache and I need fresh air.'

'Yes, you get yourself off,' said Della. 'I shan't bother going out anywhere today. I've brought a sandwich with me and I ought to try and defuse this situation with the girls and their demands. I don't know where it's suddenly come from. And God knows what is happening with Astrid and Cheryl because I can't get either of them on the phone.'

The door to Jimmy's office swung open and he stood there in his beautifully smart Crombie, his expression still one of deep displeasure.

'Would you be a dear and fetch me some ibuprofen?' Della asked Ivanka. She had the stirrings of a headache herself.

'Jesus Christ, don't you be getting ill and taking time off,' said Jimmy. 'The whole office will fall to bits.'

Now there was an idea, thought Della. She had never taken a day off sick in all the time she had worked for Jimmy. Maybe it was about time she did.

'If I go near a chemist, I will,' said Ivanka, somewhat begrudgingly.

'I thought you were going into the town centre?' Della couldn't resist pointing out her little error. She really was starting to become wonderfully careless.

Jimmy marched out of the office, but not before Della saw him flash another quick but deadly glance at Ivanka.

Oh dear, thought Della as her office junior left, a few minutes afterwards. How she wished she could be a fly on the wall of the Green Man for the next hour; because if Ivanka was going into the town centre for some fresh air, she was Princess Anne.

CHAPTER 38

Mr Price was as nice a gentleman as Astrid had said he was, thank goodness. Astrid rang Cheryl on her mobile just after twelve o'clock to tell her that Mr Morgan wouldn't be giving her any more trouble if he knew what was good for him. Then Della's number showed on the screen, but she didn't dare pick up the phone. Della left her an annoyed voicemail message asking why Astrid had been to Mr Morgan's to clean and why Mr Morgan had rung the office talking like Orville the duck and calling Astrid a psycho. Cheryl didn't ring back.

She had a free afternoon because Mrs Hopkinson had visitors and didn't want a clean that week, which meant her money would be down considerably, especially as she wasn't going to Edith's the next day either. Cheryl wanted to ring her again to check on her but was afraid that Lance would answer and complain about her to Della and she was already in trouble with the Mr Morgan thing. She decided to kill two birds with one stone that afternoon – take Gary's things over to his mum's house and ask the taxi driver if he'd make a detour past Brambles to check that all looked well, at least from the outside. She cared about Edith so much and was still in shock that one day that wonderful little cottage would be all hers. She would make sure that the garden stayed every bit as looked after. Living there she'd always feel close to Edith; it was just sad that when she inherited it, it would mean that the old lady had died.

Jimmy was waiting for Ivanka in the car park of the Green Man. He didn't look at her when she climbed into the passenger seat of his car, but continued to stare straight ahead at two kids playing on the outdoor climbing frame. His annoyance was almost tangible.

'Jimmy, I'm sorry, okay. I made mistake,' said Ivanka. 'It's not that big a deal, though. Della didn't notice.'

'Della didn't notice, are you kidding?' Jimmy shifted in his seat to face her. 'Did you see the way she looked at me and then at you? She's sniffed out a connection. Don't give her anything that could link us together. She's an intelligent woman is Della. Nothing gets past her.'

'What?' Ivanka gave a loud humourless *huh*. 'We have "got past her" for six whole months, Jimmy.'

'Because we've been careful,' he parried. 'Today you weren't bloody careful. One minute you say you're going into the town centre, the next you might not be going anywhere near a chemist. Then . . . then, you say to me in front of Della.

"Please don't swear Jimmy",' he parodied her voice. 'You sounded like my wife, not my office junior.'

'I am going to be your wife,' spat Ivanka. 'Have you forgotten this? So what does it matter? You are going to tell everyone after Lent. You promised.'

'Did I? When did I say the words "I promise"?'

'And why did you say that the office would fall to bits if Della was ill?' Ivanka had a full-on pout now. 'Why do you care so much what she thinks? Who is she to you?'

'Oh come on, Ivanka, you know she means nothing to me. It's called bullshit. I had to try and flirt a bit and distract her after you nearly gave the game away.'

'You are sacking Della, aren't you, like you promised? I won't work for her, you know. And she will definitely not work for me.'

Jimmy's head sank in his hands. In truth, he couldn't remember what he had promised Ivanka any more. Did he really say he'd get rid of Della? He couldn't remember being that stupid. That would be the equivalent of throwing the captain of his ship overboard. He wouldn't be able to skive off and play golf and go to the gym for whole afternoons if Della wasn't there holding the fort. He really really hadn't thought all this through. But that's what happened when a willy was in charge of planning and not a brain.

He batted back, attacking defensively. 'And what

was that comment Della made about you sounding like me? Talking about jam on teacakes? I tell you, she knows there is something going on.'

'She does not know, Jimmy. You say this jam and teacake phrase all the time in the office. Of course I am going to repeat things. You are being paralysed.'

'Paralytic . . . I mean paranoid.' Jesus, he felt as if he was losing it.

'Whatever.'

'I might be in a better mood if I had some sex,' said Jimmy. 'My balls are the size of watermelons. I can't think straight when I'm frustrated.'

'You can have sex with your hand until Lent is over,' said Ivanka, throwing open the car door. 'I have waited long enough, Jimmy. Now you can know how it feels to have denied to you something you want.'

And with that, Ivanka exited the car and did not turn around to watch Jimmy squeal out of the car park, which was exactly the same way that he had entered it.

The taxi drove past Edith's house and Cheryl spotted Lance's car down the drive. Everything looked normal. Cheryl should have been relieved but she couldn't shake off her concern. She had tried to think of a way she could turn up un-announced and see Edith. Maybe to say she was just passing and had she left her watch or her key or her scarf there, but Lance would know she was snooping. She would just have to sit it out until next Thursday, when nothing would stop her going to Edith's to clean. If, by any chance, a message came from the office to say she hadn't to go there again, she would pretend that she never received it.

For the full length of the taxi journey to the Gladstone residence Cheryl was trying to second-guess what she would feel when she saw Gary's car outside the house, knowing that it meant the chances were he would be inside. She felt sick with anxiety at the thought of it; yet when the taxi pulled near to the neat little terrace house and the car wasn't there, she felt hollowed out by disappointment. She asked the driver to wait around the corner whilst she delivered the black bin liners and the guitar to their rightful owner. Her hand was shaking as it reached out to the doorbell.

Ann Gladstone answered it almost immediately and any smile she had intended to give the visitor sank back inside her when she found who was standing by her hydrangea. Her arms made a slow fold over her chest and her lips pushed out a moue of annoyance.

'Oh, I thought you'd show up in person eventually.'

'I've just brought Gary's things back. From the house. He left them behind,' said Cheryl, her voice as shaky as the rest of her.

'I'll take them.' Ann lifted them up and dumped them behind her in her immaculate hallway.

'Is he all right?' She didn't want to ask after him; he didn't deserve her concern, but she couldn't help herself.

'Of course he's all right. He's better than ever,' barked Ann.

It was hard being on the receiving end of Ann's narrowed eyes and barbed voice, especially as they'd been friends.

'I never . . . I didn't want . . .' Cheryl floundered on. She didn't want to bad-mouth Ann's son to her face, but it didn't matter anyway because Ann wouldn't let her say any more.

'As sure as water is wet you were bad luck for my lad, Cheryl Parker, we know that now. It's over, so stop making yourself look daft trying to bother him.'

'I'm not trying to bother him, honestly.' Unwanted tears started springing to Cheryl's eyes at the unfairness of it all. How come she was the object of such vitriol when it had been Gary who made it impossible for them to stay together? 'I still care about him, I'm in bits.' She couldn't hold the sobs back, they burbled and hiccupped out of her and the force of them set her shoulders shaking.

'Oh Cheryl, get a grip of yourself. You're being pathetic,' snapped Ann Gladstone without a shred of sympathy as she pushed the door shut in Cheryl's face.

'You all right, love?' asked the taxi driver, appearing

from round the corner to check what the shouting was about.

'Yeah.' Cheryl sniffed and nodded. 'Can you drop me back home again, please. I've done all I can for today.'

CHAPTER 39

'He touched my titty so I squeezed his bollocks. It's as simple as zat, Della. He won't be doing it again, I can assure you,' said Astrid, who had eventually returned Della's calls.

'You're right there, because he's threatened to have a restraining order put out on you. And how come you were cleaning his house and not Cheryl?' Della was genuinely annoyed about this. She had always run a tight ship and it was against her nature for standards to slip, unless she was implementing those slipping standards for her own ends.

'Look, Cheryl felt that he was being touchy-feely, so ve swapped for one week so I could teach the old dirty man a lesson. Is that the end of the matter? Can I get on viz my life now?'

There was a question, thought Della. It was on the tip of her tongue to administer a warning and that would be the end of it, because Astrid was one of their star cleaners. But here was a perfect opportunity to drive her into the arms of Lady Muck.

'I'll have to refer it to Jimmy,' said Della. 'He won't be happy.'

'*You'll have to refer what to Jimmy?*' asked the man himself, striding in and looking in the foulest of moods already. 'And why won't he be happy?'

Della covered up the mouthpiece of the phone as she whispered to Jimmy, making sure the balance of the story was suitably as twisted as Mr Morgan's genitalia. 'Astrid has assaulted Mr Morgan. She's mangled his privates. I managed to get him to agree not to press charges but he wants her sacked. He was talking about going to the newspapers unless we do something.'

Jimmy closed his eyes to shut out everything in his sight and only wished he could shut off everything in his brain as well. 'This is all I frigging need,' he said, exhaling a long, laboured breath.

Della could see that Jimmy was under pressure about something and likely to make a hasty decision he would later regret. With any luck. She poked the fire a little more for good measure. 'He's very well connected. If he decides to make trouble, we'll lose more than just his business. What do you want me to do?'

'What do you think I want you to do? Get shot of him . . . her I mean,' he said. Della had removed her hand away from the mouthpiece so that Astrid could hear him rant.

Is that all that women do – squeeze men's nuts, literally and metaphorically? Jimmy thought.

'How dare you call me *him*,' Astrid's voice screamed out of the phone.

'You can't go around squeezing clients' gonads.' Jimmy snatched the phone from Della's hand and shouted down the mouthpiece. 'That is gross misconduct. You'll have to work notice till the end of next week if you want your money.'

'Bastard!' yelled Astrid and cut him off.

Della wanted to argue Astrid's case for her and knew she could have got round Jimmy and smoothed things over; but more than that she wanted Astrid to work for Lady Muck, so she shrugged her shoulders and said, 'Of course you're right to do that, Jimmy. She went too far. You couldn't have done anything else. Mr Morgan could have sullied your name everywhere. This way he will keep quiet. He gave me his word.'

The trouble was that Astrid was a fabulously hard worker, and Della knew that Jimmy would calm down and give her her job back before the end of Astrid's notice period. She just hoped that Lady Muck had snapped her up by then.

Astrid was red-faced with fury as she foraged in her cavernous handbag for the business card which she had picked up from the table in the Sunflower Cafe during their last staff meeting. When she located it, she stabbed in the mobile number and waited impatiently for it to be picked up, which it was after five rings.

'Hello, Lady Muck speaking,' said Connie, with

silky rounded vowels, as her auntie Marilyn would have said it.

'Hello, my name is Astrid Kirschbaum and I was a cleaner at Diamond Shine. I am looking for a new job.'

Connie recognised the name immediately. One of Jimmy's star cleaners.

'I know your reputation very well, Miss Kirschbaum,' said Connie.

'And I will bring all my clients with me. I finish next Friday so please, ven can I start working for you?'

CHAPTER 40

On Saturday morning Della's mother was having one of her better days, which was good for her, but unfortunately those were the ones which wounded Della more than the times when she was totally confused. On her 'hazy days', as Joyce the manageress euphemistically called them, Moira Frostick sometimes mistook her daughter for one of the physiotherapists and would joke with her and smile and say she was a bonny lass. But the more lucid she was, the more Moira's mouth locked in a disapproving slit whenever her daughter was near.

As Della bent over to give her mother a kiss on her dry cheek, she felt her flinch and once again it was as if her heart had been slapped. It had happened so many times and still she had never got used to the pain.

'Hello Mum. How are you today? They said we'd have a bit more snow but, thank goodness, the weather forecasters got it wrong again.'

'What are you doing here? You haven't been in ages, so why bother now,' snapped Moira, giving

Della the sort of steely glare that most people saved for a traffic warden.

'I come twice a week, Mum, sometimes more. You've just forgotten,' said Della. The staff at Diamond Shine would have been mesmerised by her tenderness if they could see her now. Not even Jimmy had ever witnessed her being so patient and soft.

Moira didn't answer but continued to sit with her hands clenched together in her lap, staring straight ahead.

'Tea shouldn't be long,' said Della, as brightly as she could. 'I can hear the trolley. I've brought you some of those biscuits you like. They stopped making them for a while; then I found them in Asda last night so I bought a few packets.' She'd been delighted, too. Even at fifty-one she was still hoping to reach that elusive pot of gold at the end of the rainbow: her mother's approval.

'I don't want tea,' said Moira, as the trolley trundled down the corridor. 'I like coffee.'

'Well, the girl always asks what you want so you can have a coffee instead.' That was one of the things Della liked about Sunset Park, that the staff never presumed that what the residents preferred one day was a standard set. But then Sunset Park was one of the most reputable residential care homes around, bettered only by Rose Manor, the most recent to be opened in the area.

Della took a packet of biscuits out of her bag.

'No point in you opening them, I don't like them,' said Moira. 'I've never liked them.'

You said they were your favourites last time you had them. You ate nearly half a packet in one sitting, thought Della, but she put them back in her bag and said, 'Oh. All right then. We'll just see what they bring. There's always such a nice selection so they're bound to have something you do like.'

When the trolley came, Moira picked three Rich Tea biscuits from the plate and dipped each delicately into her coffee before lifting it to her mouth.

Della wanted to reach out and enclose her mother's hand in hers and hold it against her cheek. She tried it once before but her mother snatched her hand away as if she was revolted by Della's touch.

Another visitor walked into the lounge holding the hand of a toddler with shoulder-length blonde hair. Moira's mouth curved upwards into a happy smile, which was echoed in the light that suddenly brightened her faded blue eyes.

'It's Gillian. I knew she'd come. Gillian, Gillian,' she called to the little girl who looked up at her mother with confusion.

'It's not Gillian, Mum. Gillian's family moved away to Spain when she was fourteen, can you remember?'

Moira's eyes were fixed on the little girl who was now sitting on a chair next to her grandmother. 'Such a pretty girl. I used to brush her hair and plait it when she came to play with you.'

Gillian Goodchild had lived next door to them and was in the year below Della at school. Gillian had long shiny golden hair and a sweet round face but was all too aware that 'Auntie Moira' preferred her to her own daughter, and used to taunt Della with that fact at every opportunity. If ever there was a misnomer, 'Goodchild' was it: Gillian Goodchild made Damien Thorn look like Shirley Temple. Moira had made Della have her hair cut short in case she caught nits, but would sit and brush Gillian's hair and plait it and pin it up whenever she came round to play. One Christmas Moira had bought Gillian a toy shop till, the same as she'd bought Della, except Gillian's was the deluxe model with the till roll, the one that Della had been desperate for. The Goodchilds had emigrated to Spain when Gillian was a teenager and Della could remember how inconsolable her mother had been when they left.

'Gillian's over there, look. She's my daughter.'

'Gillian isn't your daughter, Mum. I am,' Della said gently.

Moira slowly turned her head from the little girl to Della and when she spoke, the words were spat out with bitterness.

'Cry, cry, cry, that's all you did for the first months after you came out. It drove him mad. I couldn't shut you up.'

'I couldn't help it, Mum. I was only a baby.'

'We were all right until you came. You hid inside

me so that I didn't know about you until it was too late.'

Too late to do anything about it. Too late to abort you is what she meant, Della knew, because she had said it to her so many times over the years.

'He left me because of you.' Moira was getting upset now. Della reached for her cup before she spilt her tea over herself and as she came close, Moira's hand shot out and clawed her face.

A nurse rushed over from the other side of the room and settled Moira back in her chair, at the same time asking Della if she was all right. Della nodded, but she was gulping back a throatful of shocked tears. There had been real hate in her mother's action.

'Here, you look at this magazine, Moira,' said the nurse, opening up a *Hello* and placing it on the old lady's lap. 'She likes the pictures,' she explained quietly to Della. 'Let me get you some antiseptic, you're bleeding.'

'I'm okay,' said Della, feeling something warm and liquid slide down her cheek and patting it with a tissue from her pocket.

'No, I insist.'

Della waited until the nurse returned and stood there like a child whilst she dabbed antiseptic on the scratch with cotton wool. A picture rose up of her mother doing the same once, with yellow stuff, when she had grazed her cheek jumping off the wall. She could be lovely sometimes, her mum, in between the outbursts and accusations. Moira's moods swung from pole to pole and somehow that was always harder to deal with than if she had been consistently hostile.

On her way out, Della bumped into Joyce in the corridor and the friendly manageress gave her arm a comforting squeeze: no words, just that soft touch that said *I know what you're going through and I feel for you.* Della barely made it to the exit before the tears coursed down her cheeks, darkening the material of her plum-coloured suit.

Jimmy and Ivanka were sitting in a dark corner of a pub just outside Castleton, although Jimmy had told Connie he was going to the garage in Sheffield to have new brake pads fitted. He wasn't in the best of moods because he had driven through the Peak District hoping to have his pork pulled in a layby and Ivanka had refused point blank. So here they were having pulled pork on hot brown baguettes instead.

'I meant it, Jimmy,' said Ivanka, as she caught sight of him scowling at her. 'I won't have sex until you have told your wife you are divorcing her.'

Her resolve had been strengthened on this point after watching a documentary about Anne Boleyn on the TV that week. She had refused to be the king's mistress and had demanded the status of queen. The story paralleled theirs in another way: Jimmy and Connie had been married for twenty-four years, just like Henry VIII and his first wife Catherine of Aragon. *Jimmy was getting off lightly,*

Ivanka had thought as she watched it. She wasn't asking him to change religion or risk international war; she just wanted to be called Mrs Diamond, and to have secure legal access to his assets in exchange for conjugal duties.

'You ought to be careful, young lady,' said Jimmy with a sneer. 'I might just go and resume matrimonial duties with my wife.' He tried not to look smug when he heard Ivanka gasp at that.

Then she said, in a barely managed stage whisper, 'You promised you would not do that, Jimmy. Have you done this to me already? You have, haven't you?'

'Don't be bloody daft,' said Jimmy, dipping his eyes in case she could read the lie in them. 'But I might if you keep withholding sex. I have needs, you know. I have a lot on my mind and sex relieves pressure,' he added, knowing that he was so smooth he could have passed a Jeremy Kyle lie detector if he'd been wired up to one just then.

Ivanka foraged in her bag and slapped an envelope down on the table.

'What's that?' he asked.

'Eez a one-way ticket to Krakow dated twenty April,' said Ivanka, with one confident eyebrow raised. 'Easter Sunday. The first Sunday after Lent. If you don't tell your wife that you are getting married to me by then, I will be using it. If you do, then I will rip it up.' Anne Boleyn had been prepared to walk away to get what she wanted, she'd learned from watching the programme.

Now it was Jimmy's turn to gulp. He thought of Ivanka getting on a plane and never giving him one of her fantastic blow-jobs ever again.

'Okay, okay, I said I'd tell her and I meant it,' he replied, placing his tanned hand on her knee. 'Jesus Christ, I gave you my word, didn't I? I can't give you any more solid assurance than that, can I?'

'At the end of Lent? Not one day more.'

Jimmy gave a concessionary sigh. 'At the end of Lent.'

Ivanka let loose a breath of relief and smiled. 'I am looking forward to having sex again, Jimmy.'

'Me too,' said Jimmy but for once sex was situated far behind all the worries in his mind. Even if Ivanka had stripped off and laid down on the pub table in front of him now, he could no more have rogered her than run a marathon on a bellyful of pies.

CHAPTER 41

Cheryl was awoken at six o'clock on the Sunday morning by a sharp blip on a car horn outside, as if someone had nudged it by mistake. She was just about to drift back to sleep again when she heard a crack and then another, and she knew that whoever was throwing eggs at her house was doing it now, at this moment.

Cheryl flung herself across the room to the window and jerked the curtains open.

She saw a man dive into a grotty old 4 × 4 and do a mad three point turn before zooming off, but she had seen part of the number plate and she could make an educated guess at whom it belonged to. *F4 LL.*

Connie delivered a full English breakfast to the table for her husband. As a rule he ate very healthily because he liked to keep his weight down, but he had always allowed himself a Sunday fry-up. Until recently she had joined him, but her appetite had waned so much recently that she had made do with a slice of toast. She had lost over a stone already. She hadn't given Jimmy the opportunity to see that because she had kept on wearing her loose-fitting frumpy frocks around the house.

'I think I need a new car,' she said, as casually as she could. 'Mine is ancient now.'

Jimmy looked up from his newspaper as if she had just asked for a mink coat from Rodeo Drive.

'It's not about the age, it's about the mileage. And seeing as you don't go anywhere except to the supermarket, it's virtually brand new, that car.'

'The heater's broken. It's freezing inside.'

'Get it fixed then. It'll be a damned sight cheaper than buying another car,' Jimmy humphed. 'You can't just go out and replace a vehicle every time something goes wrong with it.'

'That's easy for you to say when you're driving around in a brand new BMW,' said Connie.

'Con,' Jimmy sighed. 'You know how these things work, I've got to make myself look like a man of means. Anyway, as I've told you before, my Beemer is the bottom of the range. You can get Mondeos which are more expensive than that but a Beemer has the reputation, and business these days is all about image.'

He was lying of course, again. Out of interest, she had recently looked up his car to find it was the executive model.

'Can't we get one through the business? A Mini Countryman – they're nice.'

Jimmy nearly spat out his sausage. 'Have you seen how much one of those things costs?'

A lot less than your mistress's sports car, she was desperate to say to him.

'And no, we can't. These are rough economic times if you haven't noticed, Con. I'm struggling to keep our heads above water.'

Connie couldn't resist. 'We've been struggling for so many years, though, Jim. Isn't it time to pack it in if it's so hard to make a buck?'

But Jimmy volleyed an answer straight back.

'And do what? I can't retire on fresh air, can I? Now is the time when I need to lay my hands on as much spare cash as I can. Roy Frog and his crappy Cleancheap are on the way out and I'm going to mop up all his clientele when he eventually swallows his pride and asks me to strike a bargain. Bloody Mini Countryman, ha!'

Jimmy carried on chewing.

'Okay,' said Connie, smiling at him. 'I'll get my heater fixed and stick with my old banger.'

'We're a team, Connie,' said Jimmy, nodding at her. 'We have to work together. We've done okay so far, haven't we, love? Things will change for the better soon.' At least he wasn't lying when he said that last part, they both secretly thought.

CHAPTER 42

'What the frigging 'ell?'

Jimmy's eyeballs were the size of dinner plates as he scrolled down the screen. 'Dire Shite? "We are DIRE SHITE and that's exactly what we supply to all our valued customers." What the fucking hell is going on?'

Della got up from her seat and went into Jimmy's office, from where she could hear him ranting.

'What's the matter?' she asked.

'Look at this.' He gestured angrily towards the PC screen.

Della made a pretence of reading the sabotaged home page for the first time.

'Dear God,' she said, sounding as horrified as she could. 'Who's done that?'

'I wish I knew,' growled Jimmy. 'I'm the only one with the password to this website so I've obviously been hacked.' He laid a finger thoughtfully on his lip. 'Hang on, why would I be a target? Do you think it's random, Del?'

Della stroked her chin in contemplation. 'Could it be a rival?'

Jimmy sat in silence, his thoughts almost

whirring with activity, until he slammed his hands down on his desk as enlightenment dawned on him.

'It's Roy Frog, who else?' he said, thrusting himself out of his chair and striding up and down as he spoke. 'Hang on, it's starting to add up. Hasn't he got a son doing computers at uni?'

Actually he'd graduated last year with a masters in biochemistry, Della remembered from an article in the *Barnsley Chronicle*. But she wasn't going to let the facts get in the way of a good opportunity.

'I think so. A master's degree as well.'

'The f—' Jimmy was so livid that he couldn't get the f-word out. 'It's Frog, I can feel it. How long has the website been like that? How much business have I lost? Well, he won't get away with it.'

Della couldn't recall Jimmy being as enraged as this for a long time. The serious look on his face made her want to laugh very badly. She pointed through to the outer office where Ivanka was sitting and mouthed at Jimmy, 'She doesn't know anything about it, does she?'

'I doubt it,' he mouthed back. 'She has difficulty breaking into a bag of crisps, never mind a secure website.'

Della nodded in agreement. 'Well then, it seems you might be right.'

'It's definitely Roy Frog. I'm telling you, when he comes sniffing around me wanting me to buy

264

him out, he'll pay for doing this to me.' Jimmy laughed humourlessly.

'Yes, you should make him, Jimmy,' agreed Della, impishly. 'How dare he? Roy Frog has always been above himself. Remember when he snubbed you at the Mop and Bucket Award ceremony a couple of years ago?'

Jimmy had clearly forgotten that until Della hooked the unwelcome memory out of the water and threw it at him.

'Yes, yes, he did didn't he, the twat?'

'It must be killing him that you're so successful now and he's a few inches away from biting the commercial dust.' Della couldn't have stirred things up any further if she'd had a six-foot-wide spoon.

Jimmy's eyes narrowed. 'Bitter little baldy bleeder. I'm going to ring him, Del, and have it out with him.'

'No, don't be daft,' replied Della quickly, putting her hand over the phone to prevent him from making the call. 'Think, Jimmy. Change the wording back, reset your passwords and bide your time. He'll lose out in the end. If he wants you to buy him out, he's playing a very stupid short game. Biting the hand that's going to feed you is such an idiotic thing to do.'

Jimmy's hand fell on top of Della's. It was so warm and big. He smiled at her, the smile that she had visualised so many times mirroring hers in bed seconds before he kissed her to initiate their

265

love-making, and her heart seemed to kick against her ribcage.

'Thank God I have you, Del. You're my best girl and you always will be.'

Still, after all he had done to her, Della so wanted to believe him.

CHAPTER 43

By Tuesday night Cheryl still hadn't worked out the best way to tackle the Fallises about the egg throwing. They weren't people you messed with, but at the same time, now that Cheryl was ninety-nine point-nine-nine per cent recurring convinced that they were behind the vandalism, she knew she couldn't sit back any longer and do nothing.

Della woke her with a phone call at seven the next morning to ask if there was any chance she could cover Sandra's eight o'clock clean as she was having a menopausal turn. Apparently she'd been sweating so much during the night that she'd had to get up and put on a snorkel and was fit for nothing this morning. It was only a two-hour job, but Cheryl needed the money. She'd been tempted more than once to dip into that five thousand pounds, but a loud 'No' had annoyingly stopped her every time.

Sandra's client was around the corner from Mrs Hopkinson so Della made a couple of calls and arranged that Cheryl go to her next then onto Mr Morgan in the afternoon. Mrs Hopkinson grumbled a bit, but then she was never happier than when she was moaning about something.

Cheryl sat on the bus journeying to the first of her three jobs of the day and wished that something would come along and help her be brave enough to march up to the front door of the Fallis family and confront them head-on.

Sometimes the Gods were listening.

Connie had a spring in her step as she set off to Mr Savant's house that morning. Another one of Jimmy's cleaners – Gemma Robinson – had defected to Lady Muck and Jimmy was still utterly convinced that Roy Frog had doctored the website. He had remained in a deliciously foul mood for two days since discovering the sabotage. Lady Muck had also managed to secure a one-off bomb clean next Monday in a house that was going up for sale. Connie would tackle that together with Astrid on her first day working for Lady Muck, then she would set Astrid and Gemma on the Dartley Carpets job which would free up her time to work in the office. Small steps, but sure ones and all in the right direction.

The weather was awful that morning, the sky dark and filled with grumpy clouds which threatened lots of rain. Crow Edge looked particularly creepy in the low light, not unlike the house in *The Addams Family*. Connie knocked on the door and Mr Savant opened it almost immediately, ushering her inside out of the cold. Gallantly he took her coat and hung it up for her on an ornate heavy coat stand. The same music was playing that had greeted her last week – *Pygmalion*. She wished she'd brought some ear-plugs.

'Marilyn, do help yourself to a cup of tea to warm you up,' said Mr Savant.

'Thank you,' said Connie, wondering why none of the girls liked working here. The house was beautiful and easy to clean because Mr Savant must have dusted and vacuumed in between her visits and he was quiet and genteel with impeccable manners. She could only put it down to them being suckered in to Crow Edge's history as a funeral parlour.

Connie decided that she would make herself a hot drink today. She went into the fridge to get milk and found it stocked to the gills again with cakes: fresh cream chocolate profiteroles – chocolate on every shelf, even bottles of chocolate milk shakes. She took the carton of milk from the shelf and tried to shut out the sweet sickly smell. Whilst the kettle was boiling, she held her hands against the old cast-iron radiator and her mother's voice sounded in her head: 'You'll get chilblains and then you'll know about it.'

Connie would risk it this morning though, as the radiator was cosy-warm and was hitting the spot. Her mother would have loved this house, she knew. The inside reminded her of Sunset Park, the premium residential home that she had gone to look around some years ago. She'd thought

269

then, *My mum would be happy here, because it's full of all the things she likes.* Putting her mother in a home had been heartbreaking, but she had needed specialist care that only a home could give her, or a private nurse, which they couldn't afford.

A small noise broke Connie out of her reverie: a gentle knocking against the wall. No doubt the radiator pipes battling with airpockets. Or someone bricked up in the cavity, as one of the Diamond Shine women had believed; so Della had told her with a chuckle.

Connie drank her tea quickly because she wasn't the type to stand around doing nothing for long. She took out her window cleaner and a chamois and climbed up onto the work surface so she could get to the glass. It was like the early days of Diamond Shine all over again, except she couldn't chat to her mother any more whilst they were scrubbing and wiping. Ghosts. Connie hoped Mr Savant's house *was* haunted, for then it would give her hope that her mother was looking out for her, watching her tackle the smears on the glass, telling her that she'd missed a bit.

Mrs Hopkinson was in an unreasonably picky mood, which stretched Cheryl's patience to its limit. She had decided to dock Cheryl an hour's pay for not cleaning her bath properly the last time she came. There was a definite ring around it, she insisted, which Cheryl knew was a complete lie, but she hadn't got the strength to argue and would let Della sort that out. The advantage of working with an agency was that when things went wrong, there was back-up and Cheryl knew that however frosty Della might have been, she had complete confidence in the abilities of her workers, at least the ones she had employed, and would back them to the hilt.

Cheryl had a thump of a headache which was building to a crescendo and she wished she didn't have to do Mr Morgan's house today. She was not only tired from not sleeping well but nervous about what he might say to her after Astrid's visit. She called in at the newsagent at the end of Mr Morgan's street for some paracetamol which she hoped would rid her of the annoying pulse in her temple and a can of Red Bull to give her an energy boost.

She was relieved to find that Mr Morgan greeted her as if nothing had happened. In fact he was most effusive in welcoming her inside. Again the house was so warm that Mr Morgan's dark brown toupee appeared to be sweating. He wiped the sides of his face with a large handkerchief and asked if she was better and, in turn, she asked him if his backache was cured. He seemed delighted that she had asked that.

'So,' he clapped his hands together, when she had taken off her own coat. 'You know exactly what you are doing here this week then?'

'Yes, yes, I'm sure I do,' nodded Cheryl.

'Excellent, excellent . . . Right then, I'll go in

271

my music room and let you . . . prepare upstairs. Then you can . . . do my downstairs at . . . let's say quarter to two.' He gestured towards the large grandfather clock in his hallway which, on cue, rang out a small jingle to mark that it was quarter past one.

'Oh, that doesn't give me a lot of time to do upstairs,' replied Cheryl.

'It doesn't matter,' said Mr Morgan. 'I'd rather you concentrated on my downstairs and my organ. It hasn't been tended to since Ruth left.'

'Ah, I see,' nodded Cheryl. Della had said he was insistent that his pride and joy should be the main focus of her attention. Well, he was paying the wage so she'd do as he asked. It did account for why his upstairs had been neglected though. Half an hour to do a whole top floor was no good.

Cheryl cleaned the bathroom and dusted around and at exactly quarter to two, as he requested, she picked up her bag of cleaning products and headed for his music room, thinking to herself that it was obviously National Finicky Day.

Connie was just about to let herself into Brandon's house as she had rung the bell and left it a respectable minute, but no one came. Then the door suddenly swung open and luckily, it was no swishy-haired Helena who was standing there, but Brandon himself.

'Come in, come in, into the warm,' he said, beckoning her over the threshold, just as Mr

Savant had done, except Mr Savant hadn't made her feel quite as smiley when he helped her off with her coat as Brandon Locke did.

The smell of chocolate weighed down the air but at least it didn't make her retch this time. It was as if her nose had detected it and diverted it to a part of the brain where the unimportant stuff was, rather than the place which dealt with the high-alert concerns.

'You'll have to excuse me,' said Brandon. 'I've got some cream and honey on the boil and if I don't get back to stirring it, it'll caramelise and the world will end as we know it.'

Connie chuckled. 'It's fine. You go ahead, I know my way around.'

'Help yourself to a tea or a coffee whenever you want,' he called behind him and Connie allowed herself to watch him stride back into the kitchen. He didn't look like a chocolatier. From behind he looked more like a builder with his big back and wide shoulders. And his hands looked far too large to pipe the delicate shapes which decorated his creations.

Plaster dust from all the renovation work Brandon had had done to the house was still circulating in the air, settling on any surface it could find only to float back into the air at the fearful sight of a cloth. As much as Connie cleaned, she knew it would be the same the following week. Plaster dust was the Ronnie Biggs of the cleaning world – unpindownable.

She tackled the kitchen last, entering tentatively in case she was disturbing Brandon but he welcomed her in and told her that if he was in the way she should throw him out.

'Is it medical?' he suddenly asked her as she was polishing his kitchen table with wire wool and wax.

Connie looked up. 'Sorry?'

'I've just been thinking about your aversion to chocolate. Is it medical?'

'No,' said Connie.

'Psychological then?'

Yes, chocolate makes me think of my husband bonking every available woman and twenty-four years of lies, she thought, but said instead, 'Probably.'

Brandon opened his mouth to ask another question, then closed it as quickly. 'Forgive me, I'm prying and I have no right to.'

'It's fine,' said Connie, trying to make light of her reaction to chocolate. 'At least you can trust me not to steal your wares.'

'I'm used to everyone raiding my wares,' he laughed. 'When my sisters come over I have to lock up my kitchen and place Rottweilers on the doors. Having said that, my brother is worse than those two put together.'

There was a photograph of three young people at the top of the stairs and Connie wondered if those were his siblings. They were all good-looking with big smiles and kind faces. She always wished she'd had more children, but it wasn't to be. Jimmy said they couldn't afford more than one. She had

274

respected his wishes, but now knowing what she did, she should have come off the pill and let nature take its course. She loved her daughter with her whole heart, but she had always wanted a son, a little boy who wore dungarees and played with cars, who grew up lanky and spotty and then matured into a man like that young estate agent, Tom Stamp. Connie pulled her thoughts away from him and transferred them onto the job in hand and imagined that she was wire-wooling every last vestige of Jimmy Diamond from her life.

Cheryl opened the door to Mr Morgan's music room to find the man himself stark naked and leaning over the stool of his organ, bum upwards. She dropped her cleaning products in shock as she ran out into the hallway and was followed moments later by a bumbling Mr Morgan in a dressing gown, quickly tying the belt around himself.

'What's wrong, Ruth . . . I mean Cheryl? It's why you're here, isn't it?' he snapped impatiently.

His tone of voice was enough to turn Cheryl's upset to infuriation. What the bloody hell did he think was wrong? How did he expect her to react to the sight of a sixty-two-year-old so-called pillar of the community with his substantial naked backside on full view?

'No, it most certainly is *not* why I'm here. I don't know what you were expecting from me, Mr Morgan, but I think you are mistaking the word cleaner for the word scrubber. What on earth do you think you're doing? I'm leaving and I won't be back.'

She grabbed her coat from the stand.

'Wait, please,' Mr Morgan's tone had changed to one of confusion. 'You said you were my new Ruth. I thought you meant . . . I thought . . .'

'I am your "new Ruth" as you choose to put it, Mr Morgan. That doesn't mean I was going to . . . What were you thinking?'

A lightbulb flashed on in her head. Surely not. Surely he didn't mean . . .

'Mr Morgan, what did Ruth do here exactly? Ruth didn't . . . did she?'

Mr Morgan wrapped his arms protectively around his bulk.

'Er . . . yes, she did,' he said.

CHAPTER 44

'Marilyn, do you think you could help me out on a taste test before you go? Have you got time?' asked Brandon, immediately lifting his hands palms out in a gesture of defence. 'Not chocolate. Coffee. Are you okay with coffee?'

'Erm, yes, I'm fine with coffee. And I do have time,' said Connie, from the other side of the kitchen as she was packing her cleaning stuff away.

'I'm testing out some new flavours to use in my mix.' He jerked a chair out from under the newly waxed table and invited Connie to sit down on it. Then he disappeared behind her for a few moments and returned again with six tiny cups full of black coffee with numbers etched onto their fronts.

'Shall I start at one, or is that a daft question?' asked Connie, as Brandon watched her.

'Whatever number takes your fancy,' he replied. 'You can count up, count down or be anarchic and hit number three first.' When he smiled, she noticed he had lines around his eyes which aged him and yet made him seem even more attractive. She transferred her gaze from him onto the cups,

277

reprimanding herself for even entertaining observations like that.

'I'll start at one,' she said, lifting the first cup and sipping, rolling the coffee around in her mouth to touch all her tastebuds, but wishing she hadn't. She had to swallow hard to get it down and if he had not been standing there she would have spat it out.

'Ugh,' she said. 'That was awful.'

'Cheap coffee substitute. A firm sent it to me as a flavouring agent, claiming that it's indistinguishable from a premium-class Columbian roast.'

'I can assure you that it *is* distinguishable from a premium-class Columbian coffee,' coughed Connie. 'And from anything drinkable.'

'I thought the same. Nice to know that my tastebuds are reliable,' said Brandon. 'The others are much better, I can assure you.'

Connie lifted the second one, wishing Brandon wasn't watching her so intently. *There must be voices sounding off in his head about how awful I look*, she thought. *I must be the polar opposite to stuck-up Helena.* Then again, she batted back another thought: *Why should he have any opinion of you at all? You're a cleaner, you're tantamount to invisible.*

'That's nice,' she said, hoping the heat she could feel on her cheeks wasn't manifesting itself as a red blush. 'Vanilla, isn't it?'

'Try number three.'

'Vanilla again, I think, but weaker. With a slightly funny aftertaste.' Connie pursed her lips together and drew in some air above the cup, then took another drink, gulping at it soundlessly.

'You look like a sommelier,' Brandon said, giving her another crinkle-eyed smile.

'I went on a wine-tasting course years ago with my . . . ex-husband,' she replied. It felt strange to lie and call him that, but then again, it wouldn't be long before that's exactly what he would be.

'Oh. Where was that?'

'Wigan,' she answered and he hooted with laughter, immediately apologising for it.

'I'm sorry, I thought you were going to say France or Italy or some place where the grapes were grown.'

'The grapes were grown there,' said Connie. 'Someone Jimmy met at a sales conference invited him to his indoor vineyard . . . don't ask. He was the most pretentious prat I've ever met in my life. His grapes all got foot-rot or whatever the disease is called and "Vin de Vinny" never even made it to the shelves of Costco.'

Brandon was still chuckling.

'I'm not joking,' said Connie, his laughter infecting her. 'He wanted us to come on board and my . . . ex liked the idea of saying that he owned a winery but I've never seen such a sorry load of fruit in my life. I'd seen bigger currants in scones. As for the wine . . . ick!' She shook her head.

'Not good?' Brandon said, wiping his eyes.

'As wine, no. As a chemical weapon, I'm sure it had a great future.'

Brandon released a fresh salvo of laughter.

'Ooh, now number four is very nice,' she said, taking another sip. 'That's my favourite so far. Very strong, very . . . velvety.'

'Okay. That's good.'

'And number five,' Connie sniffed it before trying it, 'is not good. What is it? It tastes like someone has mixed up tea and coffee and then stuck a vanilla pod in it.'

'That's more or less what it is. A hybrid tea and coffee,' explained Brandon.

'You told me the rest of them were much nicer.'

'I lied. Forgive me.'

'Well, whoever thought of that "hybrid" should be shot. Or worse – forced to drink it. Never the twain,' said Connie, standing up and shuddering.

'We're in complete agreement on all five,' Brandon grinned. 'Thank you. You have a good nose.'

Connie's hand shot up to her face. 'No, it's awful. I always wanted a long straight—'

'No, I mean a nose as in a discerning one. For taste,' Brandon interrupted to correct her. 'Not that you don't have a nice nose. On your face.'

'Oh, I see what you mean.' Connie knew she was blushing now. She shrugged her shoulders. 'Comes in very handy in a cleaning job, being able to differentiate between Prosecco and Um Bongo. I get asked a lot.'

'Do you think that there's some connection with your obvious strong sense of taste and your chocolate block, if you'll excuse the pun?' asked Brandon.

'I don't think so,' said Connie. She was aware that she wasn't rushing to leave and wished he had something else for her to test. She would even sample his truffles if it meant she could linger here and enjoy his company for longer. She didn't want to go home. Mentally she had already moved out and found herself a small place with a sunny garden and new windows.

'Well, I hope you have a lovely week,' said Brandon.

'You too.'

'Thanks for helping me with the taste test.'

'Any time.'

'Here, let me help you to your car.' Brandon picked up her bag, ignoring her protests. Connie tried not to look at his bum as she followed him out but it was impossible because it was a very nice one. She hoped to God he didn't look at hers when he was behind.

She popped the lid on her boot and he loaded her bag into it for her. His hand brushed against her and sent a feeling not unlike a rush of bubbles up her arm.

Connie would have to watch herself there, she decided as she turned out of his drive. She had a job to do and a heart fluttering for a man like Brandon Locke was a distraction she could well do without.

'I beg your pardon?' said Cheryl.

Mr Morgan had his head in his hands now and was sobbing. 'Oh please don't tell anyone. My life will be in ruins. I'll not be able to play my organ in church any more.'

'Well, if you don't tell me everything, I shall have to go to the police,' Cheryl bluffed, but the threat worked.

'Mrs Fallis and I had an arrangement,' he began, still shielding his face. 'She did things to my *downstairs* after she'd prepared in the first half hour of our session.'

'Prepared?' Cheryl asked. Despite the fact that Mr Morgan was having difficulty meeting her eyes, she wasn't going to stop interrogating him until the whole story was out.

'Yes, prepared. She got into her dominatrix costume.'

Cheryl swallowed. The idea of Ruth Fallis in shiny black faux leather and fishnets was too much for a Wednesday afternoon.

'. . . and I got into position so she could use her tools on me.'

'Tools?'

'Feather duster, sweeping brush, dust shovel, mini vac.'

Cheryl fought the urge to echo yet another word back at him; but really – mini vac?

'Then after she had administered her attentions to my organ I would service her,' said Mr Morgan, sniffing loudly and wiping his eyes on the sleeve of his robe.

Cheryl was guessing now that he didn't mean Ruth wiped down the keys of his Wurlitzer.

'You had sex with Ruth Fallis?'

Mr Morgan was quick to protest, 'Not penetratively.'

Cheryl didn't know whether to scream, laugh or be sick. So that was why it looked as if the house hadn't been cleaned in ages. Because it hadn't.

'I have to say, she was very good. Well worth the fifty pounds an hour fee. When I heard she had left, I thought she might contact me directly, but no, so that's why I was so very pleased when Diamond Shine told me they were sending me another Ruth who would do exactly what she did to my organ.'

Cheryl wished she could tell Della all this. She could imagine the conversation her frosty-knickered boss must have had with Mr Morgan on the phone, with her talking about his Wurlitzer and him talking about his todger, both of them blissfully unaware they were on different score sheets.

'It was just sex,' he said.

'I'm sure it was,' said Cheryl, although she was pretty sure that Jock Fallis wouldn't quite see it that way. Mr Morgan had just handed her a perfect bullet.

CHAPTER 45

When Cheryl got off the bus and rounded the corner to her house, she could see that more eggs had been thrown at her door and dog muck had been smeared all over her window into the bargain. Calmly, she got out her house key, went inside, deposited her cleaning stuff and then rang for a taxi. Cheryl had a bellyful of guts and a head full of ammunition. Oh boy was she ready to face Ruth Fallis head on.

It felt a little bit stalkerish to look up Brandon Locke on the internet when she got home, but Connie couldn't resist. She found the article in the archives of *Yorkshire Fayre* magazine which was headed 'The Yorkshire Willy Wonka' but there wasn't much personal information about him other than he was married to a physiotherapist wife and, like the real Willy Wonka, had no children. Then she found a mention of Madeleine Locke with her brother Brandon Locke and clicked on it to find a Facebook page and the profile picture was a woman with long hair, wearing a graduation outfit and standing with Brandon. The accompanying top comment read, 'World, let me introduce you to my wonderful brother Brandon. Dad left two months before I was born and I never met him and my mum fell ill when I was a toddler but we managed because we had my amazing big brother to look after us. He helped us with home-work, he ironed our school clothes, he fed us and put up with our cheek and we all turned out pretty okay. I would never have gone to university had it not been for Brandon because I was being stupid and lazy. But I came to my senses because I didn't want to let him down and hey, this is me showing off my master's degree in Economics, Accounting and Finance (I know, so borrrring!) If ever there was a master's degree, nay, doctorate in being the best brother in the universe, then please someone award it to our gorgeous Brandon. (Mark – you're the best little brother in the world, better mention that one.) See you soon, peeps, for celebrations.'

What a man, thought Connie, blowing out her cheeks. She hoped one day she'd find someone just like him, if there were any drop-dead gorgeous, selfless hunks with fantastic bums who had a penchant for middle-aged dumpy women out there. The odds, it had to be said, were against it.

CHAPTER 46

'What do you mean that you do not want new cleaner instead of Astrid? We have other good cleaner for you,' barked Ivanka down the phone.

Oh, she really did have an awful telephone manner, thought Della as Ivanka became more and more annoyed and aggressive.

'But you can't have her, she has left . . . Look, if you want cleaner, then you will have to take another . . . you can't have Astrid . . . yes, I know she has left, that is what I am trying to tell you. But we have better cleaners anyway. Hello . . . hello?'

Ivanka slammed down the phone. 'Stupid thick horse, she has hanged up. That was the last of Astrid's clients. They have all left now.'

'What was that?' Jimmy's head popped around his office door.

'Astrid's clients have all said they don't want another cleaner,' said Ivanka. Della waited for Jimmy to erupt, but he surprised her with a laugh.

'Offer the daft cow her job back,' he said. 'She'll snatch your hand off.'

'I rang already and she told me to piss off and that she has other job. Oh and Gemma has left also.'

Surely that would send Jimmy over the edge, Della thought, but no, he continued to smirk.

'I am very cross for you,' huffed Ivanka, doing her best knotted eyebrows.

'Don't be,' said Jimmy. 'There is no other firm around but Cleancheap. And as we know in this room, but no one else does, I'll soon be head of Cleancheap, so Astrid and anyone else who goes looking for greener grass in a sewerage pipe will be shocked to find themselves back working for me. Then I will sack their sorry arses before the ink on the deal is dried if I feel like it. That's why there's no point in getting myself in a knot about it.'

Ivanka clapped her hands together in admiration.

'If only they knew the truth,' she said.

If only you *knew the truth*, thought Della, as she smiled along with them.

Ruth Fallis's house was easy to find. Just as Hilda had said in the Sunflower Café, it was in the grounds of a scrap yard with a corrugated iron fence. From behind it, two mangy-looking Rottweilers barked at Cheryl, unable to get to her, but she would have taken them on if they had. And, in the mood she was in, she would have obliterated them. There was a 4 × 4 parked at the side of the house and the number plate was F4LL 1S. It was the same vehicle which Cheryl had seen

287

vroom away from her house last Sunday morning. Jock Junior had no doubt been driving it, because neither his mother nor father could have dived into it at such speed when they saw her curtains open.

Cheryl rapped on the door, her mouth juicy with the rush of angry adrenaline which increased when she saw a grubby lace curtain twitch in a downstairs window, but no one came. She hurt her knuckles with the strength of her next knock, then for good measure bent to the letterbox and shouted through it, 'I've got a message for you from Mr Morgan, Ruth. Or would you like me to tell it to Jock instead?'

That did the trick. Within seconds Ruth had thrown open the door, her face a halloween mask of annoyance.

'What're you doing here?'

'I want your son to stop throwing eggs and dog shit at my house or I'll have to tell his dad that his mother has been shoving feather dusters up the local church organist's arse. Is he the only one? Or are there more clients that you call upon with your cleaning kit of perversion?'

'Shhh!' Ruth furiously flapped her hand for Cheryl to lower the volume.

'I had a lovely little chat about what you and Mr Morgan and his organ used to get up to every Wednesday,' said Cheryl, folding her arms and smiling dangerously. 'Fifty pounds an hour, minus what you hand in to the office of course, to cover your tracks – that's a nice little number you've got there. Oh and talking of nice little numbers, that is a bobby dazzler of an outfit you wear, *Madame Ruth*. You did know that Mr Morgan has a CCTV camera in that room, didn't you? Great footage – and so much of it.'

That last bit was a lie, but Ruth swallowed it whole. Her face didn't know whether to go drip-white or bright red and so did a mixture of both, giving it a curious raspberry ripple effect.

'What do you want?' she said, her voice the low growl of a cornered dog.

'I've told you, I want you lot nowhere near my house again or Jock will see what his wife gets up to behind his back. Oh, and I'll have twenty quid for a taxi that's brought me up here and I'll have another twenty quid for all the products I've had to use to clean up the mess your son made. Make that a straight fifty quid for my trouble.'

Ruth's hairy lip curled but she didn't protest as she disappeared back into the house and returned with two creased twenty pound notes and a ten which she held out begrudgingly to Cheryl.

'Here.'

'Ta,' said Cheryl, riding on a rare crest of empowered amusement as she took it from her. 'Pleasure doing business with you. Is that what you used to say to *Mr Morgan*, Ruth?'

Ruth took a step forward. 'You say anything to Jock and I'll . . .'

Cheryl took one forward too so their noses were

almost touching. Cheryl's green eyes were neon with energy and bored into Ruth's. 'You'll do what, Ruth? I'll tell you, you'll do nowt. Because you're not in a position to threaten anyone. Now if any of you lot so much as look down my street in future, I'll make sure that CCTV footage is projected onto the frigging town hall. Do you understand?'

Ruth chewed on her lip, knowing she was stuffed. She edged backwards and gave the briefest of concessionary nods. But it was enough to convince Cheryl that it was over.

She walked towards the waiting taxi, feeling like a victorious warrior, floating above the ground with wings on her heels.

'I'm not surprised you've turned feral,' Ruth called behind her. 'Anyone would who'd been dumped for a Clamp.'

Cheryl spun around. 'What?'

Ruth realised she should have overridden her insistence on always having the last word. Especially as she could tell from the look on Cheryl's face that she hadn't a clue what she'd meant and was marching on her again with a murderous look on her face.

'What do you mean by that, Ruth?'

Ruth lifted her hands defensively.

'I don't know the full story. I just heard that your Gary was seeing one of the Clamps. There was something in the paper.'

'What paper?' Cheryl felt as if some drug had

whooshed through her system that made every nerve she had twang painfully. 'What do you mean "there was something in the paper"?'

'Shhh.'

'Don't you shush me,' Cheryl yelled at her, teeth bared.

Ruth cast a nervous glance back at her house. 'Look, I didn't get the chance to read it all. I was in the doctor's and they called my name out to go in.'

'Tell me or I'll make so much noise that Jock comes out,' growled Cheryl, trying to keep the tremor out of her voice.

'I've told you as much as I know. Honest,' gabbled Ruth. 'There was your Gary and a blonde holding glasses of champagne on the front cover and something about a sausage. I didn't get a chance to read the full story. I swear. That's all I can say.'

They heard a man's voice from inside the house shout Ruth's name.

'Just go, will you,' whimpered Ruth.

'You really had better not be lying to me, Ruth Fallis.'

'I'm not, please.' Ruth was desperate for Cheryl to clear off. She didn't know any more, Cheryl was convinced of it.

Cheryl felt sick as she strolled back to the taxi, no longer feeling as if she was flying, more like she was sinking – and sinking back lower than she could ever remember being before.

CHAPTER 47

Cheryl couldn't remember getting out of the taxi or paying the driver. She'd known that the day would come when she would hear about Gary and another woman but she'd hoped it wouldn't be this soon. She was on automatic pilot as she fired up her ancient laptop and waited minutes until it felt ready to present her with the homepage. She typed Gary Gladstone into Google and the machine whirred and deliberately took its time in presenting her with a list of news items pertaining to a Gary Gladstone who was a serial killer on Death Row in the US, an author, some LinkedIn professionals by that name, various Twitter and Facebook accounts but she knew he didn't have either of those. Adding the word 'Clamp' didn't throw up anything fresh. Neither did 'sausage', though she didn't think it would.

Why were they drinking champagne? Tears jumped to Cheryl's eyes – had he got married after a whirlwind romance? Had he been carrying on with someone behind her back from day one of their split – or even before it – and that's why he hadn't been in contact? What other reason could there be that he and a woman were in the newspaper drinking champagne?

Cheryl typed in 'marriage – Gladstone, Clamp, Barnsley'. No results of weddings, but plenty of snippets about various assorted crimes of the Clamp tribe. It might have helped if she'd known which paper it was and what day. *Think, Cheryl, think.* If he'd got married, it wasn't likely to be in a national paper, so she tried the more local *Northern Star*'s website first. She pulled up all the front covers of the newspapers for the last two weeks but there was no picture of any smiling couple with champagne to be found. Frustratingly, the *Chronicle*'s website was down for essential maintenance so there was just the *Daily Trumpet* to try. The *Daily Trumpet* made the *National Enquirer* look like *The Times*, but she tried anyway. 'Gladstone, Clamp, marriage' – no results. She found a page full of thumbnails of front covers from the past month. There on the Wednesday 12 March issue she saw a couple in the top right-hand corner. Cheryl's heart appeared to be crawling up her throat because there was a lump there that she couldn't shift. She pressed the tiny square to enlarge it and there was Gary, *her Gary*, and a toothy blonde with her hair scraped back so tightly it stretched her eyes into long almond-shaped slits.

'How a Battered Sausage changed my life', see page 5, was the wording at the side of the photo. Cheryl's hands were trembling as she pressed the link saying 'read articles now' then sat back in her

chair with frustration as she was advised that the item was archived and she'd have to pay by credit or debit card to access it. She typed in a million registration details, gave her debit card number and was told that activation might take twenty-four hours. Some bastard in the skies above hated her, it couldn't have been more obvious. She kept pressing the button to 'read this edition now' in the hope that the malignant entity might take a tea-break, and six minutes later it did, because the front page of the *Daily Trumpet* filled her screen with page-numbered tabs at the bottom. She pressed '5' and was greeted by a bigger, more detailed picture of Gary, the blonde, the champagne glasses and them both holding a piece of card between them.

LUCKY BARNSLEY BARRY SCOOPS £50,000 ON SCRATCHCARD

By Beverley Stockwell

Lucky Barry Gladwyn bought a £2 scratchcard yesterday and scooped the jackpot. Barry, 32, was with girlfriend Chartreuse Cramp, 22, in Cod's Gift fish shop, Pennywell Road, but when they were told they would have to wait over five minutes for a battered sausage, they decided to go into Shirt's Newsagents next door and buy a couple of scratchcards to pass the time.

'Chartreuse won a tenner on hers and she said she'd buy the sausage and chips with it, then I scratched mine off and nearly fainted. Mr Shirt had to fetch me a chair,' said Barry. 'We were going to buy some lagers but we said sod it, we'll have champagne, but Mr Shirt only had Cava so we had that instead,' said Chartreuse. So what is Gary going to spend the money on? 'We are going to Meadowhall and I'm going to treat Chartreuse big time,' said Barry. 'We haven't been together long but she's my good luck charm. I think a nice sunny holiday is on the cards for us.'

Bloody *Daily Trumpet*, that's why the search hadn't worked, because it had called him by the wrong name: Barry Gladwyn. He might as well have been Barry Gladwyn, thought Cheryl, because he was a stranger to her. It was as if she had been snatched out of her life for someone else to take her place – sleeping with her man, planning a holiday in the sun with him, going to *their* places. Ridiculous as it might seem to be possessive over a fish and chip shop, why did he have to go to that one with Chartreuse Clamp?

Suddenly, Cheryl's brain was swamped with horrible thoughts. *Is that what Ann Gladstone meant when she said something like 'we know now that you were bad luck for Gary'? Surely she didn't think that's why Cheryl had been asking after him?*

Ann knew her better than that – didn't she? *Maybe she did know that but chose to believe a different truth. One which puts her precious son in the best light,* said a voice in her head.

Gary hadn't been round with the money he owed her, so Cheryl knew that she could wave goodbye to that debt ever being repaid. *If that didn't tell her what sort of man he was, nothing would,* said that gentle, caring voice in her head that was looking out for her. That was the trouble: she did know what sort of a twat he was, but still it was torturing her that he was touching someone else at night, kissing them, eating fish and chips with them.

Cheryl closed down her laptop and went to fill her bucket with soapy water so she could wipe the eggs and the dog crap off the outside of her house. As the dribbling tap made its best effort to fill the bucket, the flow of rain outside increased abruptly, throwing itself against the glass. It was as if the bastard in the sky felt as if he had gone too far recently and decided to help her out for a change.

CHAPTER 48

Jimmy lay in bed, wide awake again. He used to sleep like a log but more and more, since getting engaged to Ivanka, his nights were restless and full of anxiety dreams about feeling trapped. He was on edge more often than not and sleep and consciousness no longer came in clearly defined blocks of time. He'd taken to having the odd cat nap in his office, which he'd never had to resort to before.

He switched on his bedside light and looked over at Connie sleeping beside him. Once upon a time she was the one who was up and down all night, unable to drift off. She'd had so many years of looking after everyone but herself it was a wonder her body hadn't forgotten how to have a solid kip for more than four hours.

She looked different, he thought as he studied her, but couldn't put his finger on how. She was dreaming, because her eyelids were flickering, and he marvelled at how long and thick her lashes still were. Lying there, lit with the soft glow of the lamp, she appeared half her age. Her skin was smooth and so soft for a woman in her forties.

Poor old Ivanka was going to have terrible acne scars, but Connie had skin like cream. His finger came out to touch her cheek; then he pulled back, remembering his promise to Ivanka not to have any sort of intimate relations with Connie.

He tried to imagine life without her and found that it was uncomfortable to do so. They'd been together since she was seventeen and he was two years older; he'd taken her virginity and he knew that she'd stuck to her marriage vows, unlike him. They'd been through the sickness and health and poorer – and he'd been through the richer part alone. He hadn't played fair at all.

He remembered seeing Connie for the first time. He liked tall, slim dark-haired girls and there she was, a blonde on the short side with curves, but her eyes lured him in. Large soft wolf-grey eyes with jet black lashes they were and she had absolutely no idea how pretty she was. She was chatty and funny – a proper prize, though she'd never seen herself as one. Things had moved too fast for them to take a breath, though. They'd planned to travel on the same road through life but he'd used what had happened twenty-four years ago as an excuse to keep disappearing off on a secret path that took him to party-land. They'd both had it rough in the beginning and, though his good times were rolling, she'd continued to have it rough. He'd make it up to her in the divorce settlement. She could have the house and he'd make sure he put new windows in for her.

He hoped Connie would be all right by herself. She was a simple soul, bless her. No harm in her at all, she didn't have any hidden sides to her, no malice, only good. But why was the thought of her moving on to another man and giving him her heart making him feel sick to his stomach?

CHAPTER 49

'Y ou are not very nice lady,' Ivanka said into the phone a second before she crashed it back onto its cradle. 'Bloody bitch.'

'Please tell me that wasn't one of our clients,' Della said, hoping it was.

'Mrs Fretwell. Old bag. She says that we do not treat our staff well and is going to other agency.'

Mrs Fretwell was one of Sandra Batty's clients. That must mean that Sandra was going to jump to Lady Muck, which was marvellous, but they really needed Hilda to defect because she was the main barometer of what the other cleaners should do.

'That's just awful,' said Della, putting on her best cross face. 'But then as Jimmy always says' – she put that in because she knew that Ivanka would take extra notice of it – 'these women have a false sense of their own importance. They think we can't get anyone to take their place if they leave. They don't know that there's a red stripey file there' – and she pointed to the shelf where it sat and watched Ivanka's eyes follow her finger – 'stuffed full of women's names who are ready to work here when we can match them up with clients. They think they're indispensable and they're wrong. People like Hilda and Ava and Cheryl ought to be careful. Jimmy always says that people who give in to any sort of blackmail are first-class idiots.'

Oh *gówno*, thought Ivanka with an inner wince. Hearing Cheryl's name had just reminded her that she had forgotten to pass on a message to her. She would just have to play dumb and pretend she never received it.

As the bus approached Brambles, Cheryl could see that there was a bright yellow skip in the garden and the front door was open. What the heck would Edith want with a skip? she thought.

She got off at the stop and crossed the lane, and as she opened the front gate she noticed the stack of paintings on the grass. The rubbish Van Gogh *Sunflowers* were on top and one side of the frame was broken off. Lance appeared carrying Edith's coffee table out of the house which he then launched into the skip.

'What's going on?' Cheryl called.

Lance tilted his head towards her. 'What are you doing here?'

'It's Thursday,' replied Cheryl, matching his tone for blatant hostility. 'I always come on Thursday.'

He blew out his cheeks with frustration. 'I rang your office and told that daft foreign girl that I didn't need your services any more.'

301

I? That single letter ratcheted Cheryl's anger up by tens of notches.

'I don't work for you. I work for Edith,' she said, hoping her looks really could kill.

He ignored that and disappeared into the house again only to emerge seconds later with Edith's ancient footstool.

'I'm afraid Auntie Edith is no more,' he replied with a put-on smile and threw the stool into the skip, then strode back inside again.

'What do you mean she is no more?'

Out of the corner of her eye, Cheryl saw the Watsons from across the lane come out of their bungalow, no doubt to watch the entertainment.

'Oy, I said what do you mean?' Cheryl didn't care that she was shouting.

Lance emerged with Edith's small drop-leaf dining table this time. He stood it on the grass with its two dining chairs and the stack of Edith's precious paintings.

'She's dead. Dead as a dodo. She is no more, she is a late aunt,' he said in a comedy voice, chuckling, amused by himself.

Cheryl felt numb. Edith gone? She couldn't be. She wasn't aware that the Watsons had walked over until she felt a hand on her arm.

'It's true, love,' Mrs Watson said, her voice heavy with sympathy. 'She passed away a couple of weeks ago. I thought it was strange that you weren't at the funeral. Didn't anyone let you know?'

Cheryl shook her head. This couldn't be

happening. The bastard in the sky had had a good night's sleep and was back in fine malicious fettle.

'Nobody put it in the paper. We were disgusted.'

Lance came out of the house again with what Cheryl thought was a vase.

'She's here if you want to say hello,' he said and bobbed the pot up and down, saying in the voice of a ventriloquist, 'Hello Cheryl. Got a gottle o' geer?'

It wasn't a vase, it was an urn.

Mrs Watson made an appalled 'Oooh' noise. Cheryl's mouth dropped open in horror.

'You cremated her? Why would you do that? She wanted to be buried with Ernest and you knew it.'

'Did I?' said Lance, pretending to think. 'Can't remember that. Catch.'

He threw the urn in the air. Cheryl lunged forwards to grab it and hugged it protectively to her when it was safely in her grasp. She was too shocked to cry or scream at that vile man. Adrenaline was making her heart bang like a bass drum.

'Don't suppose you want all that *original* artwork,' scoffed Lance. 'I can't fit it in the skip. And my aunt would so have wanted to leave you her fortune. There you go, they're all for you. I insist you take them.'

The beneficent tone in his voice totally belied the meaning behind the words. He was taunting her and loving the effect his sadism was having on her.

303

'She loved those paintings,' said Cheryl, hiccupping with emotion.

'Oh yes, she loved them so much she was always shifting them about and that's why she ended up falling off the ladder down the stairs and killing herself. I can't bear to look at them. My poor Aunt Edith. Please take them. They harbour such awful memories for me.' He touched his fingertips to his forehead in ham distress. 'Do let me help you to the bus stop with them. It's the least I can do.'

That amused him because Cheryl couldn't have got on the bus with even one of them, never mind the piled-high load.

'I'll drive you home, love,' said Mr Watson, glaring at Lance. 'You want locking up, you.' He jabbed his finger at Lance. 'I knew you were no good from the off. I said to my wi—'

'Oh piss off, you stupid old fuckwit,' jeered Lance, sauntering back inside and slamming the door to Brambles behind him. The Brambles that Edith said she had bequeathed to Cheryl.

Cheryl had always thought Mr Watson and his wife were a pair of prize busybodies but now they humbled her with their kindness.

'Come on, love. There's nothing you can do for her now,' Mr Watson whispered, casting a hex with his eyes at the present inhabitant of Edith's cottage. 'Sylvia, take her to the car and I'll get these pictures for her.'

Mrs Watson steered Cheryl back across the road.

'I always said to Derek that there was something

304

not right about that nephew of Edith's,' she confided. 'Poor old lass.'

'I can't believe it, I just can't.' Cheryl couldn't take it in. Edith couldn't be gone. It was as if someone had pressed a fast forward button on her life and she couldn't make sense of the speeded-up chunk. She sat in the car with the urn in her lap. The idea that Edith was in that small jar was too weird for her brain to compute.

After four trips across the road, the paintings were loaded up and Mr Watson and Cheryl set off for her home.

'He started stripping her house before the funeral, you know. If that isn't cold-hearted, I don't know what is. He no more cared for his auntie Edith than I cared for Margaret Thatcher.'

'When exactly did she die, Mr Watson?' asked Cheryl, still unable to register that she would never see Edith again, or visit her lovely cottage. She was too full of sadness and shock to consider what Lance might have done; that would come later.

'Let me think,' said Mr Watson, as they pulled up at some traffic lights. 'It was the week before the snow. Yes, definitely, it was early Friday morning that we saw the paramedic car because I'd just been out to the papershop to buy the *Chronicle*. Then we saw the private ambulance mid-morning and I said to my wife, I said, "Sylv, it looks like Edith's gone." He arranged that funeral as fast as you like and didn't tell a soul. It's only because Sylv's niece works at the crematorium that we found out and turned up at the service. Ooh, you could tell he wasn't happy. It was terrible as well, no flowers, no collection, no one else there but us three and the vicar bloke. A disgrace. We were surprised not to see you there, I must say. Sylvia said you couldn't have known but we didn't know how to contact you. I did ask that . . . that thing, but as you can imagine he wasn't helpful. I'm sorry, love. It must be a terrible shock for you. We know how fond you were of each other.'

After Mr Watson had gone home, Cheryl sat on her sofa, the urn at her side, two piles of Edith's paintings on the floor next to her and she felt totally and utterly hollowed out. Dear, dear Edith who had believed that she really did own one of Van Gogh's *Sunflower* paintings. She could see her now, pointing up at her study wall where the painting hung, telling her to remember that it was the most important of all her pieces. Cheryl's eyes brimmed with teardrops. She couldn't bear that she would never see that wonderful, sparky old lady again and that she would never know what happened to her because she certainly didn't believe that she fell off a ladder and down the stairs. Neither would she live in the cottage as Edith had promised her. Another assurance in life, snatched away from her and crushed. Cheryl wouldn't be able to look after Brambles and love it for her. Well, at least she could be the guardian of Edith's paintings and treasure them as she did. She reached over and picked up the painting of the precious *Sunflowers* and one of the remaining three sides of the frame fell off in her hand. The bastard in the sky really was having a field day with her today.

It was only much later that evening when Cheryl's mind at last began to close down through sheer exhaustion and her head started to empty to make way for sleep that meaningful thoughts were able to stretch and breathe. Cheryl was just nodding off when the conversation she'd had with Lance on the Sunday, the day of the snow, drifted back to her. He'd told her not to come on the Thursday of that week because Edith had a hospital appointment, hadn't he? Yet she was already dead by then. He'd been calm as milk when lying to her that his aunt was fine and having a nap. Then, as if they had been suddenly released from a place where they were trapped, a cage full of thoughts rushed at her, bombing her brain. Edith's words on that last meeting: *All my artists upstairs are happy where they are and I think the downstairs lot are too now, so there will be no more changing.* Her insistence that she never took the ladder upstairs any more. Lance snooping on their conversation. Lance hearing that he was going to be disinherited.

Lance Nettleton had killed her lovely Edith.

Cheryl scrambled out of bed to phone the police then thought better of it because it was after midnight and they'd think she was drunk.

Instead she made a list of all the evidence and decided she would ring them at 9 a.m. sharp. Until then she made an attempt to get some sleep and managed it in fits and starts until half past seven.

CHAPTER 50

A watched pot never boils, they say. *Well a watched clock doesn't move either*, thought Cheryl as she sat impatiently staring at its hands crawl round and round until they reached ten to nine, then she couldn't wait any longer. She rang the non-emergency number and told the call centre operative that she wished to speak to a police officer as she believed someone had been murdered, even though it had been registered as an accident. It all sounded very melodramatic and unbelievable in the cold light of day and she was sure the operator was making circles at the side of her head as she transferred her call, indicating she was talking to a loony.

Her nerve began to whittle away with every minute that she was kept on hold. She was contemplating putting down the phone when a burly voice answered, 'DC Oakwell. Can I help you?'

Cheryl took a deep breath. Even though she had practised what to say at this point, the words dried up in her mouth.

'Hello,' she began, 'I'm ringing because I believe that an old lady was murdered by her nephew and it was covered up as an accident because she left me her cottage in her will—'

'Just . . . just hang on there,' the detective sliced off her gabbling. 'Can I start with your name and address and the details of the person you are calling about.'

'My name is Cheryl Parker,' she told him, 'and I live at twelve Joseph Lane. Until recently I was a cleaner for a ninety-three-year-old lady called Edith Gardiner who lives at Brambles, Iris Lane, Hopthorpe. She's supposed to have fallen down the stairs trying to climb a ladder but I know she didn't.'

She gave him time to write that down.

'Now, what makes you think she didn't have an accident?' said DC Oakwell eventually.

'She wouldn't have taken the ladder upstairs. She used to climb it downstairs but . . .' *Damn,* she thought, *too much information.*

'So, this ninety-three-year-old lady used to climb a ladder to do what exactly?'

Cheryl knew she shouldn't have mentioned that Edith climbed ladders on a regular basis but there was no way to undo the damage now.

'She would swap her paintings around on the walls, but the last time I saw her she said she was happy with how they were. I asked her if she ever took the ladder upstairs and she said she didn't.'

'And why did you ask her if she took the ladder upstairs?' posed DC Oakwell.

Oh heck, she was fast making herself number one suspect here.

'I saw that she had moved another picture and I said to her that I hoped she never took the ladder upstairs, and she said she never would again.'

'Again?'

'Er . . . that's right.'

This isn't going well, thought Cheryl. She wasn't casting Edith in a very sane light.

'Okay then. So what do you think . . . happened?'

He didn't believe her, she could tell. DC Oakwell was doing his duty and recording her statement, but it was clear to her that he thought he was wasting his time.

'She has a nephew, Lance Nettleton. He lives in her house now. Until recently her will stated that he would inherit Brambles but Edith changed her mind and left it to me. She showed me the will the last time I saw her, which was the day, or the day before, she died. That's why I'm convinced Lance killed her. She said that her house would fall to hell before she left it to him.'

'You're her cleaner, you say?' asked DC Oakwell.

Cheryl sighed. She could imagine what he was thinking. A ladder-climbing nonagenarian leaves her house to the cleaner not her next of kin and she's not bonkers?

'Yes. I've been her cleaner for years and I loved her. She was a wonderful old lady, bit batty but—'

'Batty? Confused?'

Oh bugger, something else I should have kept my trap shut about, Cheryl thought.

She tried to temper what she meant. 'Not batty, eccentric. But she knew what she was doing where it counted. Lance, her nephew, hadn't been back in her life long and she didn't like him. He was stealing from her. There were cheques missing from her book and I was going to have a go at him about it. The last time I saw her—'

'Do you have a copy of this will?' Was Cheryl imagining it, or was there a note of interest creeping into DC Oakwell's voice.

'No. She never got the chance to take it to a solicitor. I know that Lance overheard us talking about it because I found him eavesdropping on our conversation. I know he killed her. I rang when we had the snow to see if she was okay and he was there and told me that she couldn't come to the phone, but was perfectly fine. Only she was dead by then. He kept the funeral quiet so I didn't know anything about it until she was cremated, and she'd wanted to be buried next to her husband . . .' Cheryl forced herself to stop and take a breath.

'And you say that this man is living in her house now?'

'Yes. He's thrown all her stuff out. She's not even cold in her grave . . . well, she's not even in her grave. He was going to put her ashes in the skip but I brought them home with me.'

'Pardon?'

'He was making fun of the urn. He threw it into the air for me to catch, so that should give you an idea of what an ars— awful person he is.'

'So you have been up to the house, presumably?'

'Yes, yesterday,' said Cheryl. 'I went up to clean for her but I didn't know that he . . . Lance . . . had rung up Diamond Shine, that's the cleaning agency, to cancel me because they never told me. That's when I saw the skip and I knew something was wrong. Please will you go and talk to him? I know what it sounds like but he's murdered my friend. I'm not bothered about the house, but I'm very bothered about what happened to Edith.' She tried to keep a lid on her emotion but it was too hard.

'You're not bothered about the house, you say?'

Oh, how Cheryl wished she could articulate properly what she meant. Like people did on *Question Time*.

'Look, I loved Brambles, and of course I wish I owned it, but I didn't have chance to get used to the idea that it would be mine anyway. And if Edith had changed her mind again and left it to the cats' home I would have thought celery vee, but—'

'Excuse me, can I just interrupt you there: "celery vee"?'

'Erm, you know, when you mean, "oh, well, that's the way things go".'

'Ah, *c'est la vie.*'

Cheryl cringed. He must think she was a real

idiot. 'I know I'm not putting this very well but I know that Lance Nettleton was the last person Edith wanted to inherit her house. She wanted me to have it because she knew I'd love it like she did.'

'But there's no actual evidence for your claims, other than what you've told me?'

She'd hooked his interest but it was slipping away. She needed to lie to make him go around there.

'He admitted it,' she said, crossing her fingers hard to authorise the fib. 'He leaned into me and said, "I stopped you getting Brambles, didn't I?" And he winked. Please, you must go and question him.'

'Is that true?'

Cheryl quickly sat down on the edge of the sofa. 'Yep. Sure as I'm standing here.'

'Well, I've got your number. I'll be in touch Mrs . . . er . . . Parker.'

'Miss Parker. Thank you. Will you let me know? When do you think you'll go?'

'I'm not sure it will be today.'

Jesus, they should be up there with a full forensic team in half an hour and making Lance do a polygraph.

'But you will let me know?'

'I promise you someone from the department will be in touch with you,' said DC Oakwell, not very convincingly.

When Cheryl put the phone down, she thought

that it wouldn't do any harm going back up to Brambles and telling Lance what she knew. If he thought the police were on to him, he just might be scared enough to incriminate himself. It was worth a try, for Edith.

CHAPTER 51

Della was quite impressed with the offices of F. U. J. Financial Holdings/Lady Muck on her first trip there early on Friday evening. It was a much more modern and open space to work in than the Diamond Shine office. And she noticed that the store cupboard was full of good quality cleaning products in case the girls wanted to use them rather than buy their own. Seeing them triggered off an idea in her head which she squirrelled away for later.

'Jimmy thinks I'm shopping in Morrisons,' Connie said. 'Well, I will be after this but I thought we needed to touch base face to face for a catch-up. Plus I thought you'd like to see HQ for the first time.'

Della sat down stiffly on one of the two swivel office chairs. 'Good idea. I like it and it's very well situated. Handy being able to park at the back, too, so that no one will be able to see your car from the front.'

'Yeah, I've been lucky. It's not cheap, though. Especially when I think what our first office cost when we set up Diamond Shine.'

'Where was that?' asked Della.

'Above a laundrette on Ketherwood Road. Godawful place, no heating. But we thought it was fabulous, because it all felt very real and exciting that we were in business.' Connie delved into the bag in her mind which contained the remaining memories of those days. 'We had an old desk that we'd bought from a junk shop, two chairs, shelves made out of bricks and planks of wood. Oh, it was very high tech. Mum and I and Jimmy walked all over Barnsley posting leaflets through letterboxes in all weathers. In those days we worked as a team of equals.' She felt a stab of sadness inside her breastbone. When had it all started to change? And why hadn't she noticed it and done something about it before it was too late? She hopped back into the here and now.

'Can I get you a coffee? Or a tea?'

'Tea would be nice, please. Black, no sugar.'

Connie went off into the kitchen and Della sat waiting. She noticed a photo on Connie's desk of a smiling woman holding a baby and a beautiful blonde at their side. She picked it up and studied it.

'That's my Jane and my mum and my auntie Marilyn,' said Connie, returning with two mugs full of tea.

'Marilyn? So that's where you got the name from?' said Della.

'My auntie Marilyn could have ruled the world if she'd lived longer. Bloody womb cancer,' said

Connie with a sad smile. 'She and my mum were wonderful women, but my aunt Marilyn was the beauty of the family. It helps me to think that I'm her when I'm ringing up trying to find clients.'

'And have you found any more?'

'Well I've got Gemma's clients, of course, and Astrid's, and a couple of enquiries trickled in today for house and office bombs, but they're just one-offs.' Connie looked down at the photograph as Della replaced it on the desk. 'In the old days, me and my mum used to love doing bombs, gave us something to get our teeth into.'

'Oh, your mum worked with you?' Della took a cup from Connie. 'Thank you.'

'She was the most hard-working woman I ever met. Tough as nails and soft as cotton wool at the same time.' She smiled and Della noticed the love in her eyes.

'Is she still around?'

'She died last year. Physically anyway. Mentally, she died long before that. Alzheimers. Bloody awful disease. I looked after her as long as I could but she needed specialist care. It broke my heart having to put her in Oak Lodge. But she was a living shell, a walking coma. I used to wish she'd just slip off during the night and be free. Then one night she did and I thought I was going to die with her.' She coughed hard and turned away blinking.

'My mother has Alzheimers too. She's in Sunset Park,' said Della.

'That's such a beautiful place,' said Connie with a sad smile. 'I would have liked Mum to have gone there.'

Della didn't want to talk about her mother. She didn't want to imagine what it must have been like to have a mum who was also her best friend. She felt the loss of that relationship keenly, even though she'd never had it to lose.

'So, back to business,' she said. 'We have to get Hilda to leave Diamond Shine. She doesn't like change. She'll stick faster than a limpet with a super-glued foot until she's forcibly winkled off her rock.'

'How do we do that, then?'

'I'm not sure yet. But I'll think of something. There has to be way, there is always a way.'

'Oh, before I forget.' Connie opened a drawer in the desk and handed over an envelope. 'It's your wage from Lady Muck,' she explained.

'Thank you,' said Della, taking it, though it gave her no joy to. If she allowed herself to really think about what she was doing she would be disgusted with herself, because it was against all her principles of loyalty and made her feel more than a little grubby.

'How are things in the office? Is he giving any clues to what's happening next between him and . . . her?' Connie asked, after taking a small sip of tea, but it was too hot.

'There was a slip-up last week when Ivanka told Jimmy off for something he'd said and he was clearly afraid that I'd picked up on it. He knew that I was surprised because it all happened too fast for me to stop myself reacting. I suspect there were words said about that between them.'

'Jimmy's been very restless at home,' said Connie. 'Anxious. Like a cat on hot bricks.'

'He's convinced that Roy Frog doctored the website out of some sort of revenge, because he hates Jimmy yet he knows he'll have to sell out to him sooner or later, and that's certainly the theory I'm fuelling. He believes that Astrid and Gemma have gone to work for Cleancheap not knowing that he will likely end up as their boss again in the near future, and that's making him feel very clever and smug. He has plans to grind poor old Roy Frog into the ground when the day of negotiation comes for stooping to the level of taking on his staff and hacking his passwords.'

'Oh dear,' replied Connie. 'He's got that all a bit wrong, hasn't he? Poor Mr Frog.' And she laughed, and Della found herself smiling with her.

'I tried to get him to buy me a new car last weekend,' sighed Connie, 'but he said the business couldn't afford it. That annoyed me.'

'I can imagine.'

'What does she look like? Ivanka?'

'Erm . . .' Della found that she wanted to tilt any description to the unflattering, despite the fact that she didn't want to feel sorry for Connie. She didn't want to feel anything for Connie if she could help it.

'She's tall and long-legged with long dark-blonde hair but they're those extension things and the colour doesn't quite match. She's slimmish but she's put on a fair bit of weight since she started working for us.' She didn't add that she suspected it was through all the fine dining Jimmy had introduced her to.

'Pretty?'

'She's not my idea of pretty,' said Della, which was true. 'She's got full lips and a little nose and wears a lot of make-up, because she's very spotty. I confess I liked her to start with, before I realised what an expert liar she was. She's getting more arrogant with every passing day. I have no doubt she is gearing up for being boss-lady, which is why I shall shortly be going on the sick to let her rule her potential kingdom. She has a lot more faith in her abilities than I do.'

'Do you think he loves her, Della?' Connie asked, trepidation flooding the brave question that Della suspected she really didn't want to know the answer to. She didn't want to know the answer to it herself either. But yes, she did believe Jimmy might be in love; he was certainly going to a lot of trouble for Ivanka.

'I think he's definitely infatuated. I wouldn't be surprised if it's a mid-life crisis thing.'

'Well, if it is, and it fizzles out I shan't be around to pick up the pieces and try and patch my marriage together, just in case that had crossed your mind.' Della noticed how Connie's eyes were locked on the photo on her desk as she spoke. Then she snapped them away and looked straight at Della. 'It's not happening fast enough. What can we do?'

At that moment it came back to Della what she had been thinking when she looked at the stores cabinet.

CHAPTER 52

Cheryl knew that Lance was in because his car was outside and she'd just seen a curtain jerk closed upstairs, but he wasn't answering the door when she hammered on it.

'I want to talk to you, Lance Nettleton,' she shouted through the letterbox, feeling braver as she spotted the Watsons from across the lane step out of their front door; she knew now they were totally on her side. 'You murdered Edith. I know it and you know it.'

The door to Brambles was suddenly ripped open and there stood lanky Lance with his dyed black hair and stupid moustache as if someone had drawn a line on his top lip with a thick Sharpie.

'Piss off or I'll call the police.'

'I've called them myself and they're coming up,' hissed Cheryl and just for a moment, she saw him blanch.

'I've told them all about you stealing cheques from Edith's chequebook and how you heard Edith say that she was leaving her house to me and so you killed her,' she shouted, loud enough for the Watsons to hear because they would spread it around, she was certain of that. 'She would never have gone upstairs with a ladder. You killed her because she had disinherited you, you slimy, vile, creepy—'

Lance stormed forward and grabbed Cheryl's arm, then as quickly released it, when he realised he could be laying himself open to a possible charge of assault.

'I'm going to have you up for slander,' he barked at her.

'You can't, because slander's when you tell lies and I'm not because you really are a murderer. Why did you tell me she was lying down and couldn't come to the phone when she was already dead? Why did you keep the funeral a secret? I'll tell you why: because you wanted her cremated to destroy any evidence . . .'

'There was no evidence because there was no crime, you stupid cow. Now fuck off,' Lance screamed and Cheryl knew he was rattled.

'She wanted to be buried next to her husband and you denied her that. You're scum and the police will find that out.' Oh how she wanted to fly at him and hurt him, like he hurt her lovely old friend.

She turned to the Watsons and called over, 'You tell everyone what he did. He mustn't get away with it.'

When she turned back, Lance had scuttled back into the house, pulling the door shut behind him and locking it. She opened her mouth to shout some more, but she had done what she came for and was spent. Another couple of people across the lane were framed in their doorways observing the drama and Mrs Watson was scurrying over to enlighten them. Cheryl straightened her back and walked over to the bus stop. If only what she had just done had changed anything; but it hadn't. At least the smarmy git hadn't got Edith's money. The original will had bequeathed all her money to the local cats' home. It was just a shame that a much shadier animal got the rest.

CHAPTER 53

The house phone rarely rang for Connie these days, even though there was a time when she never seemed to be off it, talking to doctors, nurses or staff at Oak Lodge; but never a gossipy, swap-news, catch-up conversation and she so wished she had someone that she could talk to now and confide in. Ironically, based on those credentials, the nearest thing she had to a friend was Della. Her enemy was the best friend she never had – what did that tell her about the state of her life?

So when it rang that Sunday morning she expected it to be for Jimmy, but it wasn't.

'Hello, Mum.'

'Jane! How good to hear from you, love. Are you back from your holiday then?'

'Last night. I sent you a postcard, did you get it?'

Connie laughed. 'No, love, but you know what the post is like and I hear that American post is especially bad, isn't it? Did you have a good time? Was the weather nice?'

'Yes, very and no, it was freezing,' Jane laughed. 'Mum, I'm flying over next Sunday. It's just a shortie – I'll be there a few hours. Anders has a meeting in Leeds and I said I'd come with him. Any chance I could take you for lunch?'

'There is every chance, my darling,' said Connie giddily. 'I'll tell your father. He'd love to see you.'

Jane gave a small dry laugh. 'I think we both know he won't give a damn so I'd rather you didn't say anything. I really mean that. Besides, I want to talk to you in private.'

Connie felt a wave of sadness wash over her. She wished she could travel back in time and change so many things, one of the main ones being the relationship between her daughter and her father. He hadn't given her what she had needed most: his time and attention. It was worse than not having a father around at all. Now that Connie knew he didn't have time to take his daughter to the pictures or the zoo because he was supposedly working so hard, yet had enough of it to escort floozies to places of interest, her blood could have boiled until it flew out of her veins. 'Okay love, you just tell me where and when and I'll be there. You are all right, aren't you?' Connie didn't like the sound of that 'want to talk to you in private' line.

'Of course I am,' Jane laughed and her mother's anxiety went back to bed. 'We will have a long natter next week. Antonio's? I'll text you with the time. How are you? Everything okay?'

'Yes, everything's fine.' *Apart from the fact that your dad is a lying tosser with a secret mistress and*

I'm spending your inheritance on Windolene. 'Just fine, love.'

The police hadn't called Cheryl by Sunday morning, which had really annoyed her, though she had sort of expected it; but she had no intention of letting them forget her and was going to ring them again Monday morning. The one good thing was that she was so obsessed with gathering any detail which would constitute a case against Lance that Chartreuse Clamp and Gary and his lucky sausage episode was pushed to the back of her mind. Then, just as she was about to make herself an omelette for lunch, there was a knock on the door.

She looked through the window to see a man in a dark woollen coat standing outside. She put the chain on the door before opening it and felt the hair stand up on the back of her neck because he looked very official.

'Cheryl Parker?' said the man. 'DC Oakwell. We spoke on the phone on Friday. I wonder if I could come in.' He held up a black leather-type wallet holding a warrant card with his photo on it. He'd had his hair cut since the picture was taken, she noticed. It was much shorter now and a touch more grey. She'd imagined DC Oakwell to be older when she'd talked to him on the phone, and slightly built, like Jack Frost. She hadn't expected him to be so tall and smart or attractive. She thought he might have a very nice smile, although he wasn't exhibiting one at the moment because he was wearing a strict face of authority. But a home visit could only be good news, couldn't it? They *were* taking her seriously after all. She was delighted to open the door.

'Come in,' she smiled. 'Can I get you a drink?'

'Er, no thank you,' he said stiffly, taking a small notepad and pen out of his inner coat pocket. A drift of his aftershave tickled her nose and she found herself breathing it in deeply. It was, as Astrid might have put it, a proper man smell.

'So, did you go and see Lance Nettleton?' Cheryl asked him excitedly. 'Did you find out any information?'

'I did go up there, yes,' replied DC Oakwell. 'And I did speak to Mr Nettleton, who denies that he made any admittance to pushing his aunt down the stairs . . .'

Cheryl huffed, before she was cut off, 'Well, he would say that, wouldn't—'

'Look, I have to warn you that Mr Nettleton is considering making a formal complaint against you.'

Cheryl's eyes rounded and she placed her finger on her chest. 'Wha-at? Me? Are you joking?'

'No, Miss Parker, I'm not joking at all,' said DC Oakwell, who certainly didn't look as if he had much humour in him. 'From what he tells me, you went up there throwing stones at his window to alert his attention—'

'I most certainly did not . . .'

'. . . and accusing him of murdering his aunt, deliberately maligning him in front of the neighbours even though there is no evidence to support that. You can't just throw allegations around like that, you know.'

Cheryl shook her head in disbelief. 'Why did he pretend that she wasn't dead when she was, then?'

'He said that he didn't want you at the funeral. He said that his aunt was going to end your employment and he thought you might make trouble for—'

'That is so a lie,' shouted Cheryl, tears rushing to her eyes. 'Edith loved me. And I loved Edith. It was Lance that she didn't want around.'

'Please calm down,' said DC Oakwell, pressing down his hands as if there was a huge volume button underneath them.

'I'm sorry, but I'm telling you the truth. Why would he give me her ashes if that was the case? He was mocking her. The neighbours all saw him.'

'Look, Mrs Gardiner's injuries were consistent with a fall down the stairs whilst she was carrying a ladder. I've checked,' said DC Oakwell, his voice as deep and calm as hers was high and agitated. 'You told me yourself, she was always moving her pictures around.'

'But she wouldn't have gone upstairs to do that.' Aware that she was shouting, Cheryl throttled back on her sound level. 'And I suppose he denied knowing about the new will?'

'There is no evidence of a new will.'

Cheryl threw her hands up in the air. 'So you can't do anything? He's got away with murder, literally, and you can't do anything. I thought you'd come round to tell me you were arresting him.'

DC Oakwell cleared his throat. 'No, I'm here to tell you that if you go around there again, he will make a formal complaint and I'll have to come back and arrest you. I managed to calm him down but he was really angry; so please take my advice and back off, or you'll find yourself in big trouble and he *will* be able to prove your guilt.'

Cheryl opened her mouth to say more, then shut it again. The detective was right. 'Thank you,' said Cheryl. She felt drained.

'Mr Nettleton went to great pains to stress that he made the gesture of giving you some paintings. His aunt was going to give you them when she terminated your employment as a gesture of thanks, he said.'

That flared up Cheryl's temper again. 'That's bollocks. Edith would never have given those paintings away whilst she was still alive. She thought they were original masterpieces . . .' Cheryl knew then that she had put the final nail in the coffin of her argument. As DC Oakwell looked over her shoulder at the crap Van Gogh's *Sunflowers* in their new Bargainbuy frame on her wall, Cheryl knew he was imagining a dotty old lady with delusional tendencies who sounded very much like the sort of person who might go upstairs with a ladder and fall down the stairs. It was over.

Even if he hadn't given her the answer to why Lance would give her Edith's ashes, it was over. Lance had won the jackpot of a beautiful old cottage and a stay-out-of-jail card.

As if DC Oakwell allowed himself a personal moment of sympathy, he put his hand on her shoulder, looked into her furious green eyes and said, 'You're not in any trouble, so let's keep it like that, shall we? Don't go near Mr Nettleton again.'

Cheryl nodded, but she didn't promise in actual words that she wouldn't.

CHAPTER 54

Connie liked Astrid Kirschbaum from the first moment she met her and that was not at all what she had intended. Connie did not want to develop friendships with the women she secretly employed in case this whole exercise ended in disaster. Her primary intention had to be revenge, not setting up a charitable home for cleaners. But it was impossible not to warm to Astrid, unfortunately.

The house they had been booked to clean that Monday morning had been inhabited by students but it looked more as if an army of tramps had lived there.

'How can anyone live like zis?' said Astrid, clicking her tongue against her teeth in disgust. 'They are animals.'

'I don't know any animals who would leave pizza under a sofa to grow mould like that,' Connie grimaced as she snapped on her Marigolds and held up a Frisbee of rock-hard blue crust.

'That is a pizza? O mein Gott,' said Astrid and stuck out her tongue as if she was about to be sick. 'Are we supposed to clean the furniture too?' She gave the stained armchair a glare of horror.

'Nope, the owner is throwing it all out. He asked if we could push as much of it to one side of the room as possible.'

'He's lucky I am so strong,' sniffed Astrid. 'He is getting mixed up with house cleaners and house clearers I think.'

'He said there wasn't that much and none of it was heavy,' said Connie in his defence. The biggest item was the sofa and it was only a skinny-framed two seater.

'Okay then, let's go,' said Astrid. 'Which side of the room do you want? Left or right?'

Connie picked right and wondered how long it would take for the questions about Lady Muck to start. She was glad when they came because she knew that any information she could feed to Astrid would be passed on to her cleaning friends at Diamond Shine.

'So what's this Lady Muck like, then?' asked Astrid, as she scrubbed at the furry skirting boards.

'She's nice, really nice,' said Connie. 'Fair, decent. But she doesn't take any crap.'

'Zat is good to know,' said Astrid. 'Some clients think you are pieces of meat to be manhandled. I vas sacked from my last job for retraining one of them.' Her large blue German eyes glittered with amusement.

'Oh? Do tell,' Connie invited.

'My friend there, Cheryl, vas having some

problems with a touchy-feely man. So I went instead of her to his house and gave his *Nüsse* a gentle death-grip. Ze sound he made nearly shattered the windows. Alas, it cost me my job but it's okay. I would have done the same thing over again if I had to. And I know that she would have done it for me too if she had been big and strong.'

'That's a shame,' said Connie. 'Lady Muck would refuse to send girls to houses like that. She does her best to make sure that it's a good place to work. She knows there are a lot of girls out there who join an agency then leave to set up their own taking all their clients with them, so she makes it attractive to stay with her. She knows that cutting corners is false economy.'

'So she really is a woman then who exists?'

'Oh yes, a real woman.'

'What does she look like?' Astrid stopped rubbing at the dirt on the paint for a moment. 'I imagine someone very regal, beautifully dressed with hair like Marilyn Monroe.'

Astrid might as well have described her darling aunt. She'd paid for private elocution lessons and spoke like a Royal and had perfect blonde hair and a fantastic figure which she liked to show off.

'You're exactly right,' smiled Connie. 'That's just what she is like.'

'I'm very good judge of character,' said Astrid proudly. 'I always have been. For instance, I could see through the woman at my last job in der office. Cold, nasty piece of work.' And she made a spitting action.

'De . . . did you?' Connie puffed out her cheeks. She'd almost dropped herself in it there by saying Della's name. Although she wasn't sure if Astrid was referring to her or Ivanka.

'Yes. She sits very quietly and sweetly in the office but I think she is like the still waters and runs very deep. I would not be surprised if . . .' She stopped herself, aware that she was gossiping with someone whom she didn't know very well.

'If what?'

'Oh nothing. Just my thoughts.'

Connie left it for a few minutes before asking casually, 'Were there many women in the office? Lady Muck runs her business by herself.' She wanted to push Astrid to talk about the cold nasty piece of work woman, who she presumed now was more likely to be Ivanka.

'Two,' said Astrid. 'One was older. She was very stiff. She was no nonsense. I liked her but I also felt sorry for her.'

'Sorry for her? How come?' Della didn't seem the sort of person to her that people felt sorry for.

'I think she was in love with the owner of Diamond Shine,' said Astrid, stage whispering across the room as if they might be overheard. 'He was very charming.'

'Was he?' asked Connie, curious to know more of what his cleaners thought of her husband.

'Oh, very,' said Astrid. 'He was one of those men

who get better looking with age, like George Clooney. Not that I'm saying he looked like him but he was a handsome man. Though he knew it,' she sniffed derisively. 'Funny, gift of the gab, charismatic . . . One of those men who say all the things you want to hear, I call him *Herr Silberzunge* – Mr Silver Tongue.' She laughed. 'You couldn't not like Jimmy Diamond. When he flirted with you he made you feel like a million dollars, and he flirted with everyone. Zat is why I knew there was something going on with the *other* woman in the office.' And she made a *pah* sound. So it *was* Ivanka she didn't like then, not Della.

'What do you mean?'

'He didn't flirt with her. They don't look at each other. It's as if they are trying too hard to look apart. Now why would they do that? But everyone thinks I'm nuts in ze head for thinking that.'

'Really?' Connie's throat felt dry. It still hurt to know that she was one of the last to have heard about what had been going on under her nose.

'I tell you, he must have a really ugly wife if he thinks that a spotty, moody girl is an improvement,' laughed Astrid.

Connie gulped. 'Maybe she just trusts him.'

'I was once a man,' said Astrid. 'I would never trust one of the bastards.'

CHAPTER 55

Della put down the phone and said aloud a very disappointed, 'Oh dear. That's not good.'

Ivanka's interest was sparked. 'What is it, Della? Someone else is leaving?'

'Mmm, yes, though she doesn't know it yet. I've just had a complaint about Cheryl from Mrs Gardiner's nephew. Apparently the old lady died but Cheryl has been up to the house accusing him of murder. All the neighbours heard and he's had to report her to the police.'

'My God,' said Ivanka, drawing in a dramatic breath. 'We can't have people like that working here.'

Nope, you cannot have decent, kind, hard-working girls on your books, agreed Della in her head, but said instead, 'You're right, we can't. It's sad but she will have to go.'

'I don't think it is sad at all,' Ivanka protested. 'She is a disgrace.'

Della didn't feel good about joining in a character assassination of Cheryl. The lass had worked for Mrs Gardiner for years and would be in a state as it was without learning she was going to be fired as well, even if Lady Muck was about to be her fairy godmother. She also knew that Cheryl would feel disgraced to be sacked for such a reason. She dialled Cheryl's number, but there was no answer and she found she was glad she didn't have to speak to her. This whole business with Connie had softened her and she wasn't quite sure what she felt about that. Life was much more straightforward when she could do her job without worrying about upsetting anyone.

She fought against getting involved with people when she didn't have to and could never understand why the girls formed attachments to clients, especially the old ones who were going to die soon and punch a hole in their hearts. But some people just sneaked up on your affections, like Ivanka did. And like Connie was doing, too. Finally admitting to herself how much of a knob Jimmy Diamond was had brought with it a concern for his wife, for his daughter, for the workforce who bankrolled his extra-marital dinners and his trips abroad and the flash secret lifestyle that she had helped to facilitate – and she felt ashamed of her part in it all.

'I'll keep ringing her for you,' volunteered Ivanka with relish. 'I'm quite happy to put these women in their place.'

'Thank you,' said Della, feeling both relieved and uncomfortable at the same time. She hoped all this upset was going to be worth it.

★   ★   ★

Cheryl wasn't in a good place that Monday morning. She had just left her client who was under the impression that cleaners were non-persons. She didn't like him and she didn't enjoy working for him and the events of yesterday with the police were playing in her head on a continuous loop. As she was waiting for the bus, she heard her phone vibrate in her bag. It was Diamond Shine, and she saw that she had missed three calls from them as well. She picked up to hear Ivanka's prickly voice.

'Is that Cheryl?'

'Yes, it is.'

'It's Ivanka. We've had a complaint about you. From a Mr Nettleton,' she said, sounding as if she was really enjoying relaying this information. 'It's a very serious one—'

But today Cheryl was in no mood for Ivanka or Lance Nettleton and cut her off. She knew what was coming so she might as well run to meet it and get it over and done with.

'Are you ringing to sack me?'

That took the wind right out of Ivanka's sails. 'Yes.'

'Don't bother,' said Cheryl, her voice weak but her resolve strong. 'I resign and I won't be working my notice either, so take your shit job and stick it right up your spotty arse.' Then she hit *end call*.

Boy, that felt good. Just for a few minutes she wouldn't think about the fact that she was now unemployed but let herself enjoy the feeling that she had taken a little power back from the bastard in the sky.

Just as Astrid was packing away her cleaning equipment bag her mobile went off.

Connie eavesdropped on her half of the conversation. 'They did what? . . . I hate them for you . . . Yes, I can text you the number . . . Yes, very nice . . . so far so good.

'A friend of mine,' explained Astrid as she put the phone back in her bag. 'She worked for Diamond Shine also and has just told zem to stick their job up their bum. She wanted the number for Lady Muck. I hope she has some vacancies.'

Oh, Connie hoped it was Hilda. 'I think she has. Who's your friend?'

'Cheryl. I love her,' said Astrid. 'She could do with some luck.'

Couldn't we all, thought Connie.

CHAPTER 56

Cheryl found a discarded *Daily Trumpet* on the bus and read it to take her mind off things. The front page featured a fresh call out for help in the cases of local missing people: sadly, too many teenagers, a pensioner who had wandered out of an old people's home a month ago, a very round-faced lady in her twenties missing for almost two years – and a strange case of a woman found washed up on the beach of Robin Hood's Bay over a year ago with no memory of who she was. She wished she were looking at a front page that read, LANCE FRIGGING NETTLETON EXPOSED AS OLD LADY'S MURDERER. COTTAGE HANDED TO LOCAL CLEANER. But even for the *Trumpet*, that was one headline too unbelievable.

As soon as she reached home, she rang Lady Muck and was delighted to be given a job on the spot. *She sounded ever so lovely*, thought Cheryl. She had a beautiful voice, polite but also warm; not at all like that cow Ivanka who was on a mission to shove Della out of the door, so Astrid said. She rang Miss Molloy then to explain why she wouldn't be coming to clean that afternoon, and also her other two favourite clients, Mr Fairbanks and Miss Potter, and was touched to find that they didn't want anyone else but her. They all said that they would transfer their business to the Lady Muck agency if it meant they could keep her. She really did have no intention of working out her notice with Diamond Shine, even if that meant they kept her week-in-hand payment. She'd survive. No, she'd more than survive. She'd seen Ruth Fallis off and now Ivanka. And Ann and Gary Gladstone could sod off as well. And Della and Jimmy and that arsehole Lance Nettleton and the bastard in the sky. She wasn't going to let any of them grind her down any more.

She decided she needed to christen this new improved version of Cheryl, and caught the bus to Pogley Top where she had a slap-up afternoon tea for one at the Sunflower Café.

CHAPTER 57

In Mr Savant's immaculately clean house, that Wednesday, Connie found she had enough spare time to give one of the bedrooms a total bottoming. It was a relief to spend an hour upstairs as the music he was playing was loud and discordant, but at least there was some singing instead of that awful *Pygmalion* and its spoken voices. She presumed this must have been his late wife's room from the soft pink wallpaper and the accoutrements on the dressing table: a large old-fashioned hairbrush and hand mirror, an empty puff-ball perfume bottle, photographs in silver frames.

She couldn't think why Mr Savant needed her at all to work for him, because he must have dusted and cleaned the house himself in between her visits. Maybe he was lonely and liked the company of another presence in the house, even if it was only for a couple of hours per week. She'd had a few old clients like that in the early days of Diamond Shine.

There was a wedding picture in an art deco silver frame, the young couple in a vintage man-standing-behind-seated-bride pose. Mr Savant was instantly recognisable by his long, dour face, although he was skeletally thin back then, with razor sharp cheekbones; but it was Mrs Savant who held Connie's interest. She was absolutely enormous and the voluminous white wedding frock didn't do her any favours at all. There was another picture of an older Mrs Savant in another frame, bloated and even more obese: Mr Savant had his arm as far around her as was possible and they were both smiling. They appeared to be a happy couple despite the huge size difference. Mrs Savant had a fat forehead that seemed to be in danger of falling over her eyes and no neck; her head seemed to be directly connected to her shoulders. *No wonder she had died in her early forties,* thought Connie. She thought she was carrying a few extra stone, but Mrs Savant was something else. It flashed past Connie's mind that Mrs Savant must have eaten a lot of cream buns in her time. Maybe that was why Mr Savant continued to keep them in his fridge, so he could feel as if life had carried on the same after her passing? She dismissed that theory as codswallop as soon as she had thought of it, because that would have indicated the actions of an insane man, surely, to keep buying buns twenty-plus years after his wife had died? Mr Savant was nothing if not compos mentis. Connie put it out of her mind and carried on cleaning. My, though, the Savants were an odd-looking couple. But, it was entirely possible for two people who didn't look at all well-matched to fall in love. Hadn't she and Jimmy proved that all those years ago when he was drop dead gorgeous and she was the plainest girl in the sixth form?

As she drove to Brandon's house later, Connie had a small panic attack. Cheryl was starting to work for her today. A nice woman, by all accounts. A good woman who might be left high and dry if this whole Lady Muck scheme didn't succeed. Connie didn't know if she even wanted it to succeed past the point of damaging Diamond Shine beyond all repair. She had only really planned up to that point. She had visualised herself as a Britannia-type heroine holding a sword aloft and standing victorious over the Diamond Shine office sign, crushed beneath her feet; but beyond that was only opaque fog. Could she really better in a few weeks all that Diamond Shine had achieved in years? *Who are you kidding, love?* She pushed it out of her mind in order to think of something more pleasant – in this case two hours in the presence of the wonderful Brandon Locke.

There was a silver, two-seater convertible in the drive with a personalised number-plate. She'd seen it before. It was Helena's car.

Connie gave a cursory ring on the doorbell and then walked straight in – to find Brandon and his ex-wife embracing in the hallway. They sprang apart as she dipped her head, apologised, dumped her cleaning stuff and strode quickly into the lounge out of the way. She took back everything she thought about him. He'd disappointed her. She heard stifled voices coming from the other side of the door, Helena's slightly raised, then the heavy front door crashed shut and Brandon raced into the lounge as Connie busied herself looking for her duster in her bag.

'I'm sorry about that,' he said.

'None of my business,' replied Connie, snapping more than she intended.

'It wasn't what it looked like.'

'I didn't see anything,' she said, not looking at him.

'I didn't know it was coming.'

Why was he telling her this? It didn't matter what she thought, she was merely the hired help. And he was a man she had just caught in a clinch with another man's wife, even if she'd once been his.

'Marilyn, please listen.' Brandon's hand was in his hair, the palm flat on his head as if pressing down on a pain. 'I am so embarrassed. I was just saying goodbye to her and she put her arms around me and wouldn't let go. Short of throwing her off, I didn't know what to do.' His eyebrows dipped in contemplation. 'I'm even wondering now if she wanted you to see us like that.'

'I can't think why,' said Connie, shrugging her shoulders. She felt inexplicably down, as if a happy little balloon inside her had just been popped. 'Really, you don't have to explain to me. Honestly.'

'I could do with some advice, if you have a few minutes,' he said with a hopeful, if slightly nervous, smile. 'You can take it off your cleaning time.'

Connie knew she should have said, 'No, I'm here to work, nothing else,' but she was too kind, and when he asked if he could put the kettle on for them, she found herself saying yes.

The kitchen was scented with cherries and brandy, and notes of dark chocolate swirled in the aroma. The air was almost edible.

'Sit down, please,' said Brandon. He seemed jittery, upset. He spilt some sugar on the floor and uttered a mild expletive as he wiped it up. He sat down opposite Connie and pushed a dark brown mug in the shape of a chunk of chocolate in front of her.

'I'm not the type of man who oversteps the boundaries,' he said. 'I feel really bad that you might think I am.'

'I'm just the cleaner, Mr Locke; it really isn't any of my business,' said Connie, finding it hard to look at his face, which made it obvious that she did have an opinion and that it wasn't a good one.

'When Helena left me for Dominic, I can't say that a big part of me wasn't relieved,' he began. 'I think I felt guilty about that. She blamed my obsession with work for forcing her to look for affection elsewhere. Maybe if I had loved her enough, I wouldn't have been so obsessed by my work. Some part of me wanted to make amends, which is why I thought it would be a good idea to stay friends. I'm beginning to think it would have been easier in the long run if we hadn't.' And he sighed as if he had the weight of the world and two other planets on his shoulders.

If he's going to this much trouble to explain things, he must be concerned, thought Connie.

'Can I ask you a personal question?' He waited for her to nod before going on. 'Did you stay on a civil footing with your ex-husband? I mean, I don't know your circumstances. It might be essential you do that if you had children.'

Oh heck, thought Connie. She'd dropped herself in it by lying that Jimmy was her ex. Would they end up being friends? Erm . . . she didn't have to think too hard about that one.

'No, there is absolutely no friendship. Yes, we have a daughter but . . . but she's grown up now.'

Brandon moved his chair closer still to the table. 'Did you move into another relationship straight afterwards? God, I'm so sorry if this sounds intrusive. I don't want to talk about it to my sisters, because they'd worry. They never liked Helena; I doubt I'd get an unbiased view.'

'I think that would have been a disaster,' said Connie, wondering if she would have another relationship ever again. Twenty-four years of deceit and lies and disrespect was quite enough for one lifetime.

'I know Helena married Dominic on the rebound. Looking back, it was almost as if she was showing me how easy it was for her to move on. I never minded her popping round for a coffee at first when she married him, because everything was above board. Dominic was okay with it – I was even at their wedding. But recently she's been coming around more than ever, dropping hints that all in their matrimonial garden isn't rosy, making nostalgic references to our own marriage. It's become uncomfortable. I don't know why she grabbed me today because she's never done that before. Just as the door started to open, she flung her arms around me when I wasn't expecting it. Thinking about it now, she knew it was you at the door because I said, "Oh, Marilyn's here." I was grateful for your arrival. I thought it might move her along.'

He looked sincere, thought Connie. But then so had Jimmy when he told her she couldn't have a new car because the business was struggling. Then again, she shouldn't judge all men by one deceiver's actions. Her Auntie Marilyn's partner Steve had been a jewel. He had adored her and would have done anything for her.

'Maybe it's like cat spraying,' said Connie, wishing she had picked a better way of putting it. 'Marking her territory, I mean.' If Brandon's account of things was straight down the line, it was obvious that was the answer. 'Though why she'd want to make a point to your cleaner is a bit beyond me,' she added, in case it looked as if she was intimating that tall, leggy Helena was somehow jealous of short, dumpy Connie.

'She was always jealous,' said Brandon. 'Even of my sisters.'

Miserable sod, thought Connie.

'I don't know what to do. This is a new situation for me, Marilyn, and after what happened today I realise I might have to do something before things get out of hand. What do I do?'

Connie thought for a few moments whilst she drank her coffee. It had a hint of cherry, like the aroma that was filling the room. 'Well, I think a gentle process of distancing yourself might be in order, until your only connection is a card at Christmas, otherwise she'll feel encouraged by your accessibility.'

'Yes, yes, that's good. Aargh,' he slapped his forehead with his hand. 'I'm having a party in a couple of weeks and I've invited both her and Dominic along.'

'Well, that's okay if the two of them will be there. Just make sure that she isn't allowed to hog your attention. But if you're being super nice to her, that's going to make you look extra attractive to her, if she's having problems with hubby.'

Brandon laughed to himself. 'I thought being fair was the less complicated option.'

'Not always,' said Connie. 'Jerking a plaster off your arm might hurt, but it's quick. A slow pull takes ages and is actually more painful in the long run.'

'I like your analogies,' said Brandon.

'I don't think Aesop has much to worry about,' Connie replied, standing up to get back to the lounge, although she could have sat with him for much longer.

By the time that Connie started on Brandon's kitchen, he had moved on to making wild strawberry truffles. The room smelt like a summer garden.

'Want one, Marilyn?' He held out a tray full of plump squares with a splash of red piping on the top as she was packing up to go.

'Thanks, but no,' she said and he chuckled.

'Whatever has put you off chocolate must be serious,' he said.

'Yes,' she said, in such a way that further questions on the subject would not be encouraged, but he wasn't put off.

'Let me hazard a guess that it was something to do with a man.'

'Possibly.'

He knew he'd guessed correctly.

'My chocolate makes no false statements,' smiled Brandon. 'It's just magnificent. Excuse the modesty.'

Connie grinned. 'I'll take your word for it,' she said. 'See you next week, Mr Locke.'

He caught her arm as she passed him.

'Thank you for talking to me, Marilyn.'

She was aware of his fingers touching her.

The warmth of them seemed to sink straight through her skin. 'I'm not a psychologist, though. I'm your cleaner, so my advice might be totally wrong.'

'I don't think you are wrong,' he said and his fingers slipped away, yet she could still feel them there.

Her legs felt as wobbly as a drunk's as she walked to the front door. She wished he hadn't touched her and she wished he were still touching her at the same time. There was a bright red light in her head flashing 'danger' because her heart was as hungry as Helena's was and Brandon Locke was as incredible as his creations and more than capable of turning her to the dark side.

CHAPTER 58

'I'm sorry he's not in at the moment,' lied Della. 'I will tell him you called again. Thank you, goodbye.'

Jimmy popped his head around his office door. 'Who was that?'

'A Supersponges rep,' Della said, poker-faced. 'He's a pest and they're ridiculously expensive anyway.'

Jimmy disappeared back into his office. The word 'expensive' was like garlic to a vampire on him.

Della drummed her fingers on the desk as she considered what to do. They had a problem. Roy Frog had called a couple of times now and she had headed him off at the pass. He had finally decided the time was right to come crawling to Jimmy to see if he wanted to buy Cleancheap from him. Once Jimmy owned that, there was no way that Lady Muck, as it was at present anyway, would be able to bring him down because he'd be too big and powerful.

Della needed to put the plan she had thought of into action sooner rather than later and for that, the timing and set-up had to be perfect. Even Field-Marshal Montgomery would have a problem employing the tactics she had conceived. First of all she needed to stir up some more trouble between Jimmy and Roy Frog. She knew how Jimmy operated better than any woman in his life and how much he relished having control. It was time to set Connie the task of putting in some wifely duties.

Connie and Della arranged to meet after work at Lady Muck HQ in Maltstone. Connie had the kettle on when Della let herself in with her key. *She looks different*, thought Della, *as if she's lost a bit of weight on her face.* Not that what she was wearing gave any clue that she might have lost it elsewhere. One of those hideously loose dresses of which Connie seemed so fond.

'How are things?' Della asked.

'Well, Astrid and Gemma seem happy enough. Cheryl did her first day yesterday and I haven't heard anything, so I'm presuming that no news is good news. I'm doing a house bomb with her tomorrow so I can pick her brains. I learned quite a few things when I worked with Astrid,' Connie called from the kitchen.

'Like what?' asked Della.

Like you're in love with my husband.

'Like she thinks the absence of flirting between Jimmy and Ivanka is very telling.'

'That's interesting,' said Della. 'She's very astute.'

'She isn't so astute that she suspects that I could be casting her and her friends adrift in a couple of weeks if I don't get any more clients and cleaners. What's the news from inside the camp?'

'Ivanka is getting cockier and enjoying every little iota of power that I'm letting her have, Jimmy is walking about as usual like the proverbial dog with two dicks and we have a massive problem.'

Connie, walking in with two mugs, stopped momentarily in her tracks. 'Uh-oh, that doesn't sound good.'

'It isn't. Roy Frog's rung a few times now asking to speak to Jimmy. Luckily it's been I and not Ivanka who has answered the phone, but it's only a matter of time.'

'And Roy is going to beg Jimmy to buy him out?'

'Well, not exactly beg,' said Della, holding out her hand to take the mug from Connie. 'He would try and save face by saying that it was an investment opportunity that Jimmy couldn't afford to miss and he's giving him the chance to buy him out first, even though everyone and his aunt knows that if he doesn't sell up, he'll go bankrupt. Jimmy will want to appear as if he isn't that bothered because Cleancheap aren't up to his standard, and make him wait so Roy will get to desperation point and sell it to him for a song. Games, games, games.'

'How long will all this go on for?' asked Connie,

offering Della a biscuit from a tin, but Della refused it.

'Not as long as I'd like. I was hoping that Roy wouldn't ring for a few more weeks, so things must be getting critical. I need you to work on Jimmy at home. Tell him to avoid Roy Frog and make him sweat. Meanwhile, I'll stir things up in the office.'

'Chocolate pancakes,' announced Connie suddenly. 'Sorry, I'm thinking aloud. I'll cook chocolate pancakes. He loves them. Music might have charms to soothe the savage beast, but in our house chocolate pancakes can soothe the duplicitous git.'

Della laughed and Connie thought that when she laughed she looked like a totally different woman: younger and prettier.

'Can I say something to you without you taking offence?' said Della later when she had finished her tea and had stood to go. She didn't wait for an answer. She would have said it anyway. 'What you wear does nothing for you at all.'

Connie looked down at herself.

'I've always looked like the back end of a bus,' she said.

'That's it, you don't,' replied Della. 'You've got beautiful hair, stunning eyes and an obvious waist, though you can't see it in those swing frocks you wear. They make you look much bigger than you are.'

'Do they? I thought they covered me up,' said Connie.

'They cover you up all right, but not in a good way.'

'Well, thank you, Della. That's kind of you to say,' said Connie, genuinely touched that the older, serious woman had said what she had.

'I hope I didn't offend you.'

'Not at all. I've not had much time for myself over the years.' That was true. Until her mother died last year, Connie had barely time to look up.

'Well, there are a lot of changes in the air,' said Della. 'You should make sure you fly your sail with them.'

'When all this is over and done with, and we're no longer undercover, we should go for afternoon tea at the Sunflower Café, you know, the one you told me about that Hilda's sister runs. Have you ever been?' said Connie.

'No, I haven't,' replied Della. She'd never had a friend to take afternoon tea with, although she didn't say that because it made her sound like one of life's rejects. 'I've driven past it, although I can't say it looks much from the outside.'

'It doesn't, but inside it's very different. I would guess you'd like it.'

'It's obviously influenced your decorating,' said Della, pointing to the only picture on the wall of the office. A sunflower with hand-written words on the huge yellow head. She walked up to it for a closer look.

'I think I remembered all the lines in the right order,' said Connie.

Keep your face to the sun and the shadows will fall behind you. If only, thought Della. She'd always kept her face to the shadows, on full alert for what could – and inevitably did – come out of them to hurt her.

CHAPTER 59

Jimmy walked into a house scented with chocolate and he stood for a few moments before taking his coat off and inhaled deeply. Chocolate pancakes were just what he needed after a pig of a day. Ivanka was still holding firm to her no sex rule and applying pressure on him at every available opportunity. She was nagging and he hoped that wasn't a portent of things to come. Connie had never nagged him; then again she might have done if she'd known what he'd done behind her back. Maybe he should have lied a bit more to Ivanka, but that was a mistake realised too late.

'That smells nice,' he said, walking into the kitchen and seeing his smiling wife stirring chocolate sauce in a pan. 'I hope they're what I think they are.'

'Well you enjoyed them so much on Pancake Day, I thought I'd break with tradition and give you some more. I bought too much chocolate and it could do with using up now that I'm not eating it.'

He looked at Connie's huge dress and thought

that she was wasting her time because she'd never be able to stick to a chocolate ban and even if she did, she wouldn't slim down in forty-odd days, but he didn't say so. He didn't want to get into an altercation with another woman today.

By the time he had changed into a pair of jeans, there was a delicious portion of shepherd's pie set on the table waiting for him.

'Is it our anniversary or something?' he said, pulling the scent of onion-packed gravy into his nostrils.

'I'd be having words if it was and you'd missed it,' trilled Connie. 'No, I just thought I'd cook something you enjoy. It's nice to have you home early for a change so we can eat together.'

'Not much on your plate,' replied Jimmy, pointing to the small portion in front of her.

'I had a cheese sandwich earlier on,' she fibbed. 'Shall I push the boat out and open a bottle of wine?'

'Yes,' he said. 'And don't give me one of those little glasses, I could do with a nice big one today.' He rubbed the back of his neck which was stiff with tension. When he went back to the spa in the gym for another spray-tan, he'd book in for a de-stress massage as well, he decided.

They didn't usually talk much when they ate together, which was rare anyway these days, so it was hard for Connie to make their exchange appear as if it wasn't staged. Jimmy played right into her hands by introducing the subject of Roy

Frog to her just as she was wondering how on earth she could bend the conversation around to where she wanted it to go. A wispy picture of Brandon's smiling face passed through her brain as she poured chocolate sauce over the freshly griddled pancakes she had made for dessert.

'I'm definitely going to buy Cleancheap,' Jimmy said. 'We can't afford it, but I can't afford anyone else to have it either. Not that anyone else would want it.'

'Really?' said Connie.

'I'd have a monopoly if I owned Cleancheap now that Dreamclean's gone down the Swanee.'

'When did it go up for sale?' Connie asked, appearing intensely interested.

'It hasn't yet. Don't you worry, Roy Frog will be ringing me as soon as he's finally decided that he has nowhere else to go. He's been hanging on hoping for a miracle and trying a few dirty tricks, but the clock is ticking and I'm ready and waiting for his call.' Jimmy rubbed his hands together with glee.

'Dirty tricks? What sort of dirty tricks?' Connie topped up Jimmy's glass.

'He got his son to hack into my website and alter all the wording, little twat.'

Connie couldn't resist asking, 'Are you sure it was him?'

'Without a shadow of a doubt. Who else would do that?'

Connie nodded, trying to keep her face straight.

'You're right. Who could be bothered but a competitor. They don't sound very reputable.'

'They're totally shit.' Jimmy spooned in a huge mouthful of pancake and talked through it. 'And he hates me. I can't wait to buy him out and sit in his chair.'

'There's no one else interested, you say?' asked Connie, pretending she was thinking hard on this point.

'Nope. Just me.'

'Didn't you confront him about the website?'

'No . . .'

'So he thinks he's got away with trying to ridicule you. He must be laughing up his sleeve.' Connie humphed.

'Yeah, but as soon as he rings I have every intention of grinding his face in the mud.'

'What, you're going to meet him the moment as he snaps his fingers? Huh. He'll think you're a puppet on a string.' Connie poured more chocolate over the remaining pancakes on Jimmy's plate. 'He's an arrogant git, isn't he? He might as well say, "Okay, I'm ready now for you to buy my business after I've tried and failed to nobble yours."'

'Ah, but I'll negotiate hard.'

'I'd tell Della not to put any of his calls through for at least a month. Make him sweat. Seems to me that you need to give him a clear message who has the power here.'

Power was a magic word to Jimmy. The mention

of power and the taste of chocolate pancakes were a very effective combination.

She knew her message had hit home because he stopped chewing and had a faraway look in his eye as he no doubt imagined Roy Frog grovelling across the office carpet towards his desk, begging for forgiveness.

'You can afford to eke out negotiations if no one else is interested in buying Cleancheap but you. What have you always said when doing business, Jimmy – that you have to be prepared to walk away and convince them you really are walking away? Roy Frog *knows* you'll buy it from him in the end, so you have to try extra hard in making him believe that you won't. Imagine the total panic he'd feel if he thought you weren't playing a game and really did have no interest in Cleancheap. Now that really *is* teaching someone a lesson.'

'God, you're right, Con,' Jimmy said slowly, turning what she had said over in his mind. 'He does know I'm definitely going to buy.'

'And the longer you leave it, the less you'll have to pay him. Can you remember Smartie Hayes trying to sell you that bankrupt stock of mop buckets when we were up Ketherwood Road and making out as if he was doing us the world's biggest favour? I ended up buying those buckets for a quarter of what he was originally asking. If I'd hung on a bit longer, I think he'd have paid me for taking them off his hands.'

Thank God for that memory which had just made a welcome and perfectly timed appearance in her head.

'Yes, yes, I do,' Jimmy said, a smug smile creeping across his lips. He grabbed his phone and made a diary note to tell Della and Ivanka that if Roy Frog rang, to say that he was playing golf. He would decide when to open negotiations, not Roy. As Connie so astutely put it, he'd show Roy Frog who really had the power.

CHAPTER 60

Connie received a text from Della the next morning. There were no words, just a thumbs-up icon. She laughed. This whole situation was far too serious to be described as 'fun' but just for that moment, that's what it felt like.

She arrived at the abandoned office on Lamb Street where she and Cheryl had been booked to do a one-off three-hour bomb. Connie pulled up at the side of the dripping wet young woman with the thin coat on and no hood. Cheryl's blonde hair was dark with rain and she was shivering, but that didn't stop her giving Connie a big warm smile of greeting.

'You must be Cheryl. I'm Marilyn. I'm not late, am I?' Connie said, looking at her watch.

'Hi Marilyn. No, I'm early. The next bus wouldn't have arrived for another twenty minutes and I hate being late. I'll be glad when I can afford a car.' It was madness that she wasn't spending the money Mr Herbert left her on a runaround for work and she wished that annoying voice telling her to keep the money in the bank would shut up.

'Must be hard travelling everywhere on the bus,' said Connie, putting a key in the door lock. 'Come on, let's get inside out of this weather.'

'I've only been doing that for a month,' said Cheryl. 'I used to borrow my partner's car but we split up and he took it.' *Even though I paid half towards it and all of the joint car insurance,* Cheryl added to herself.

'Oh by the way, Lady Muck says welcome to the team and if you've any concerns tell me and I'll pass them on to her,' said Connie.

'She sounded nice on the phone. Well-spoken,' said Cheryl, peeling off her coat. 'And Astrid, that's my friend who told me to ring her, says that she's had a good start and picked up favourable vibes. She prides herself on her vibes.' She chuckled. 'So what's Lady Muck's real name?'

'I don't know, we all just call her Lady Muck,' said Connie, hoping that would stop any further questions on the subject. 'But it doesn't matter; she's good to work for. Fair.'

'Well, I hope I'm as happy working for her as you seem to be.'

'Wouldn't you fancy going it alone?' asked Connie.

'I'd rather not. I like it when I'm paired up with the other girls to do two- and three-person jobs, plus you've got some support from an agency when things go wrong.' Then Cheryl realised what she had said and gave a dry sarcastic laugh.

'Worked as a cleaner long?' asked Connie.

'Ever since I left school. I'm not moaning though.

I love making things sparkle and shine. I just wish I could earn a decent living at it. I'm not greedy; a nice house, a little car less than five years old and a job that lets me pay all my bills and have a bit of spare is all I ask.'

Connie had known the woman for two minutes and already she knew she would grow fond of Cheryl very quickly. She reminded her of Jane; someone who never stood out in a crowd, but should have done. Kind, sweet, not that confident and who deserved more luck than she had in life.

Cheryl looked around her. 'You can really get stuck into somewhere like this. I always enjoy it when I'm sent to do a bomb with someone.'

Connie started picking up some sheets of A4 that were littered over the floor.

'What made you leave your last place?' she asked.

Cheryl shrugged her shoulders. 'I fancied a change.' She didn't want to tell Marilyn the real reason in case she relayed back to Lady Muck that she was a trouble-maker and that would be the end of this job.

'Wasn't anything to do with the touchy-feely man then?' asked Connie. 'Astrid said she'd sorted him out for you.'

'Oh, you heard about him. Astrid lost her job because of it,' said Cheryl. 'I felt awful about that.'

'Lady Muck thought it was hilarious,' smiled Connie. 'She wouldn't stand for any of her girls having to put up with stuff like that. Astrid's account of what she did was very funny though, I have to say.'

'Aw, she's great,' said Cheryl. 'I'm glad she found work straightaway. We were both with Diamond Shine a long time. I know she feels as let down as I did that they weren't more supportive of us when we needed them to be. If I'm honest, Marilyn, I didn't fancy a change at all. The company took the word of someone against me and *poof*, I was gone.'

Oh you are so useless at keeping your mouth shut, she reprimanded herself.

'Have your clients come with you?' asked Connie, though she was just making conversation. She knew the answer to that already, since Cheryl had told her other persona Lady Muck that they had.

'Well, my lovely Miss Molloy, Miss Potter and Mr Fairbanks have. Mrs Hopkinson hasn't, but I'm not that bothered, I couldn't gel with her like I did the others. You get so attached to some people in this job. One of my ladies died recently . . .' She waved her hand frenetically indicating that she couldn't talk about it any more because she was getting upset and so Connie didn't question her. Like Cheryl she got stuck into the job and let her mind empty as she scrubbed.

369

CHAPTER 61

'So what are the advantages for me now that you're working for a new boss then, Cheryl?' asked her Friday morning Mr Fairbanks.

'Absolutely none for you, Mr Fairbanks, but you still get the same sparkling service. The advantages are all mine,' Cheryl smiled, bringing a cup of black coffee over to him. He always had a drink and two dark chocolate Digestives at eleven as he took a break from writing his book, *Yorkshire – Its Influence and Its Artists*, and watched the local news on the TV. She was so glad Mr Fairbanks had insisted that if she was moving to another firm, then he wanted her to continue being his weekly cleaner. He was very clever, very learned and a proper old-fashioned gentleman. He had been widowed ten years previously but kept himself always busy and fit – both in mind and body.

'Well, I hope they treat you well. I certainly wish you all the luck in the world,' Mr Fairbanks nodded.

'I think sometimes if I didn't have bad luck, I'd have no luck at all,' laughed Cheryl. 'How's the book going, Mr F?'

'Slowly,' sighed Mr Fairbanks. 'I wonder if I've been wasting my time, to be honest, Cheryl. You see, I'm not writing anything that anyone hasn't said before. There are a few stories I've been given but can't include because, without backing of proof, they would sound ridiculous.'

'Aw, that's a shame. Shall I change your bed this week, Mr F? I know you look forward to "fresh sheet night".'

But Mr Fairbanks wasn't listening. He was staring at the screen.

'Well, I never,' he was saying over and over. 'Look at that, Cheryl, I knew it. I can't believe it's taken so many years, but my father was proved right in the end.'

Cheryl walked over to the TV where a news report was coming from in front of a half-demolished house which appeared to have sunk into the ground. The newscaster's words and Mr Fairbanks' voice melted into white noise because her brain had no room for anything else but the sight on the screen of Brambles Cottage reduced to a misshapen pile of stone, brick and glass.

'Why won't Jimmy speak to Roy Frog?' asked Ivanka, when Della put down the phone after telling Roy Frog yet again that Jimmy was unavailable as he was playing golf.

'He's making him sweat,' replied Della. 'The longer he avoids him, the more Roy will drop the price.'

Ivanka pulled an emery board out of her pen pot and filed a nail. They were so long she could barely type with them but Della didn't care enough to take her to task about them.

'That is madness,' she sniffed. 'Someone else may come along and buy the company.'

'No one wants it,' said Della. 'Jimmy has no competition.'

Ivanka slowly replaced the file. 'I have been thinking. Why would Roy Frog hack into his website if he wanted Jimmy to buy him out? I am wondering if there is someone else who has not yet made their interest known who is stirring up trouble between them.'

Della swallowed. Ivanka was looking at her with her narrowed sloe eyes as if she could see straight through her skull to all the secrets lurking there. She had forgotten to always keep in her sights how wily Ivanka was. Della gave a knowing little laugh.

'Jimmy and Roy Frog have been in the game a long time, Ivanka. They both know how the other operates. Think of it as two stags preparing to clash. The timing has to be perfect for them to butt heads.'

'Okay,' said Ivanka, and returned her attention to her computer screen. But Della knew she wasn't convinced. And it was Ivanka, not herself, who had 'the King's ear' mostly these days.

Cheryl could not believe the scene of devastation on the TV. Brambles looked as if it had been made of paper and folded in on itself. That gorgeous cottage that should have been hers was no more. All those smiles left behind by visitors destroyed, all the happy memories crushed. All that joy and love that warmed the air inside it gone forever. It was heartbreaking; Cheryl's eyes flooded with water. Brambles was so much more than bricks and mortar, it was as if it had a soul. It was like being told that Edith had died all over again.

Mr Fairbanks' voice cut through the thick fog of her thoughts. 'The owner's got minor injuries, so I suppose that's good news. He is one very lucky man.'

Lance Nettleton wasn't just lucky, he was Teflon if he survived that.

'Of course, that house has been a ticking time bomb since it was built.' Mr Fairbanks' voice was the most animated Cheryl had ever heard it.

'I used to clean there,' said Cheryl.

'Then you're very fortunate that you're not under all that rubble,' said Mr Fairbanks, drawing in a long breath. 'It should never have been built. My father told them. He was an architect. He knew that the land wasn't safe to build on because there was a warren of mine-shafts underneath it. But the land owner, now what was his name again . . .' he pinched the top of his nose as if that would help him remember.

'Gardiner?' Cheryl suggested.

'That was it. Ernest Gardiner. Hot head. Knew

everything. He had too much belief in his own convictions and not enough in the facts. My father designed that house for him, before he discovered the danger posed by the mine works. Gardiner went ahead anyway. Nowadays it would have been laughed out of a planning meeting, but this is now and that was then. In the end Ernest built it himself.' Mr Fairbanks shook his head in disbelief. 'My, I shall have to find out all the details about this. Ernest Gardiner said that my father was ridiculously over-cautious. My father couldn't believe it when all his warnings came to nothing, but he was right after all. Even when the house stayed standing, he knew it wasn't safe. "It must have been held up by the devil", he used to say.'

And Cheryl shivered, remembering some of Edith's very last words to her:

Brambles will fall to hell before I leave it to Lance.

CHAPTER 62

Jimmy was supposedly playing golf with Pookie Barnes on Sunday, although Connie didn't know if that was true or not. He left the house in screamingly loud trousers and carrying his golf bag, but she wouldn't have trusted him to be going on a range as far as she could throw him and she was more than delighted to find that she didn't care. All it meant for her was that she didn't have to make up a lie about where she was going that day because, as far as Jimmy knew, she never went out anywhere but to a supermarket or to town. She was going to Leeds to meet her darling Jane and she couldn't wait.

She hadn't seen her daughter since just before Christmas. Jimmy hadn't seen her for over two years and Jane had left the house saying that she never wanted to see him again. They'd had a row about something so trivial that no one could remember what it was, but it had given Jane a platform to air years' worth of hurt that she was so far down on her father's list of priorities. He'd never been to any of her school plays, he'd never attended any of her parents' evenings or her dancing performances. His own father hadn't invested much time in him and yet Jimmy had done okay, so that was the pattern he followed. He hadn't recognised that Jane needed his emotional investment, more than Jimmy had needed his own father's.

Jane was waiting for her mother in the Italian restaurant Antonio's where they always went for lunch whenever she flew over, because it was ideally positioned next to the train station. Connie was glad to see that her daughter looked well and happy and glowing. She'd let her hair grow and it rested dark and glossy on her shoulders. Jane had inherited her father's tall, slim, good-looking genes, rather than her shorter, rounder ones. She had Jimmy's smile too, wide and cheerful with lovely even teeth behind it. Jane was beautiful, thought Connie as her daughter turned that smile in her direction.

'Hello Mum,' she said as she rose from her chair and stepped towards Connie. She threw her arms around her mother and squeezed tight. 'Hey, you've lost weight.'

'Just a bit,' said Connie.

'I can't remember the last time I saw you in trousers and a shirt. You look great,' Jane said, holding her mother at arm's length to study her.

'It's only from Dorothy Perkins,' laughed Connie. She had taken Della's advice and bought herself something that fitted rather than flowed around her and was surprised to find she was right, it suited her much better. Still she wore her big old dresses around the house though so that Jimmy wouldn't notice any changes in her. Connie Diamond was transforming daily, morphing from a barely visible plant into a bold, bonny flower. She wasn't only losing weight, she was gaining confidence and that made her walk taller. Her skin was fresher, her eyes were brighter. If Jimmy had really looked at his wife the way his daughter was doing, he would have seen all this.

They sat down and Jane reached across the table and gripped her mother's hand.

'I was going to wait to tell you, but I can't. Mum, I'm pregnant.'

Connie heard the words but they didn't sink in immediately. Then, when they did she leapt out of her seat and hugged her daughter with all her might, kissing her cheek madly.

They were both crying and laughing when they sat back down again.

'Oh my goodness, how many months gone are you?'

'Thirteen weeks. I didn't want to say anything to anyone until I was past the twelve-week mark and I didn't want to tell anyone before I told you. Anders told his parents yesterday and they're over the moon. This will be their first grandchild too.'

'And Anders? Is he happy?' Connie had only met Anders once and found him rather serious, but Jane said he was nervous on that occasion.

'Oh Mum, he's like a puppy. He's gone mad. I wouldn't let him start decorating a nursery until last week and he's nearly finished it. I hope this means you'll come over and visit more.'

'I'd love to,' said Connie. The thought of a little baby in the family that she wouldn't see often was awful. 'I'll have to tell your father.'

Jane's smile dried up and she shrugged. 'If you must. I can't think it will make much difference. I've survived without him this long.' She saw a cloud of sadness pass across her mother's features. 'Mum, don't worry. I know you'd like a perfect world where we're all one big happy family but we aren't and we never have been. Just because Dad and I are linked by blood, it doesn't automatically make us care for each other, you know. But I promise you, I am going to make sure my little baby feels treasured. Like you made me feel.'

'Did I? Did I, Jane?'

Jane thought of the joy she used to feel on stage at school, scanning the audience and seeing her mum's lovely golden hair. She wouldn't ever say this to her mother in case it hurt her, but she'd wanted to see her daddy more in the early days, except he never came. Then one day she didn't even try and spot him because she knew he wouldn't be there, though it took her a lot of years before it stopped upsetting her. She always felt her father's duty to her had ended at her conception. She didn't want that for her own child.

'Yes, Mum, you did.'

'A baby,' sighed Connie wistfully. 'Was it a surprise?'

'We've been trying for a year. I was starting to wonder if there was something wrong, then my period was late and I took a test and Bob's your uncle. We're both very happy. Anders says we should get married. I'm in no rush.'

Connie didn't try to persuade her daughter otherwise. How could she when she was no role model for what a happy marriage should entail?

Jane waved her mum off at the train station with a cheerful smile hiding so much behind it. Her dad had a grin and patter for everyone but those closest to him, who were entrenched in a cold moat of invisibility. She knew her dad was a dog. She'd seen him in action, when he thought she was too young to make sense of it. Jane was wise beyond her years and she'd known that her life would be easier for cutting out her father, at least for a while. The fact that he'd made no fuss when she did it told her she'd been right. She loved her mother very much and knew she deserved so much more than the crumbs her father threw her from his table. In short, Jane had been waiting the whole of her young life for her father to grow up.

When Jimmy arrived home that night, looking distinctly dry for someone who had been supposedly golfing on a day with heavy intermittent showers, Connie told him the news about their daughter, although she didn't say they had spent the afternoon together.

'Jane rang. She and Anders are having a baby.'

She didn't expect him to run to the cupboard to hunt for party poppers but his cold reaction stunned even her.

'She's only twenty-two. Hasn't she learned anything?' he said, before walking upstairs to change out of his Rupert Bear trousers.

CHAPTER 63

Frustratingly there was no more news in the local papers over the weekend about the collapse of Brambles as their pages were taken up with bigger, grittier stories: a soldier from Sheffield killed in Syria, a big budget Hollywood blockbuster being filmed in Leeds and yet another politician flashing his bits to an undercover *Daily Trumpet* reporter masquerading as a dolly bird on Skype. Not that there could be much more to the story than the relevant facts: Lance was unscathed and the house was gone. Cheryl wondered if it would still have been standing if the new will had been found and she had moved in. Lance wouldn't be too inconvenienced, she surmised. The insurance would cough up and enable him to build something swanky and renew all his possessions. The devil really did look after his own, she decided.

She had been assigned a Monday morning gentleman who would be out working when she cleaned, and as Miss Molloy was in Harrogate today, it was going to be quite a lonely day. The gentleman lived on the same estate as the Gladstones and Cheryl just hoped and prayed that she wouldn't bump into any of them. She hadn't seen Gary since they split and she had no idea how she would react if she saw him, especially if he was with another woman.

Unless she made a quarter of a mile detour to avoid it, she had to pass Ann Gladstone's house to get to her client's. Cheryl kept her eyes forward and resisted any attempt to look at her old car parked outside or to see if there was anyone in view in the large picture window of Ann's front room. She imagined Ann, Gary and his new bird clustered behind the Venetian blinds pointing and sniggering and her heart began to bounce as if that was reality and not her brain torturing her. It was odd to think that she would never again go up the path to Ann's house, kick off her shoes, put on the kettle and sit and watch the TV with her as if she were part of the family. Now Chartreuse would occupy her regular place on Ann's sofa and they would be all labelling her a jinx. Where did all that love and affection go when relationships were severed? she thought. Or, cut off from its blood supply, did a chemical reaction sour it to hate? *Please let me have some more time to get used to all this, God,* she whispered skywards. *Before I see a baby seat in the back of his car.*

When Ivanka flipped over the page of her desk-top calendar, in readiness for the new month ahead, Della noticed there was a circle around 17 April. And lots of gold stars.

'What's that for?' she asked. 'You've got the seventeenth marked up very heavily.'

Caught on the hop, Ivanka studied the calendar as if to remind herself. 'Oh, it's the end of Lent,' she said, with enforced casualness.

'And did you give anything up for Lent?'

'Alcohol,' Ivanka said quickly.

'I suppose you didn't give anything up for Lent, Jimmy,' Della laughed.

'I gave up Lent for Lent,' he said, not turning round from his position at the photocopier. His back was stiff and his voice was snappy.

'I thought you didn't drink that much anyway, Ivanka,' Della said.

'I don't. That's why it is easy to do,' she said with the sort of smugmess that implied that she was very clever to have pulled that out of the air.

That's a hell of an important red ring around the seventeenth to mark the end of giving something up you don't really like, thought Della, itching to phone Connie and tell her what she thought it all might mean.

Connie had just finished interviewing a potential cleaner, who wasn't suitable at all. She had dirt in her fingernails and teeth that hadn't seen a brush and some Colgate in a long time. If she couldn't keep herself in order, it wasn't the best advertisement for her cleaning skills, she thought. She needed a flood of fabulous women with an established client base to come through her doors, but so far they hadn't.

Her secret mobile rang just after twelve and it was Della who was calling her from her car parked outside a sandwich shop.

'I think we need to get even more of a move on,' she said, diving in without the usual 'hello, how are you's. 'I believe that Mr Excrement may have a date with Miss Fan on the seventeenth.'

'Why, what makes you think that?'

'Something important is happening for Ivanka on the seventeenth, she's circled it on her calendar and drawn little gold stars at the side. I know it sounds weak, but she was lying when I asked her about it. And Jimmy seemed furious that I'd picked up on it. I hate to say this, Connie, but my woman's intuition tells me that . . . oh dear, I hate saying this . . . that . . .'

'That Jimmy is going to walk out on me that day.'

There was a sympathetic pause before Della said, 'Yes.'

'Then I have to move things forward from May Day. The seventeeth, you say?'

Connie sounded super-calm, thought Della. Her admiration for her was growing daily.

'That's right,' she said.

'Hell fire, that's just over two weeks away, Della. How can we bring down his kingdom in a fortnight?'

This was all starting to look even more stupid

than ever. And Connie should have known herself better. There was no way she could have pretended to herself that if this new company folded and she had to let anyone go who had joined her in complete faith, she would be able to do so with a clear conscience and a cold heart.

'I don't know,' said Della, 'but as I've thrown my hand in with you, we're going to have to give it a bloody good try.'

'Are you out of your tiny, frigging, Polish mind?' asked Jimmy, as soon as he saw that Della's Clio was safely out of the car park. 'Why didn't you just write all over the walls and your forehead that I'm going to be leaving Connie in two weeks? Better still, why not take a front page advert out in the *Daily Trumpet*? Or maybe you'd like me to ring up and rent a town crier for you. "*Oyez, oyez,* Jimmy Diamond dumps wife for mistress on the seventeenth of April".'

Ivanka sat stiff-backed and silent in her chair, her mouth a defiant pout of indignation.

'How can a small circle around a number say all that?' she said, as poised as he was manic.

'That is such a girl thing to do.' Jimmy lunged towards the calendar and snatched it up to slap it with the back of his hand. 'How is that a small circle? It's a bloody big, bright red circle with great neon gold stars. It says "This is a day when something fabulous happens." This does not say "Hurrah I can start drinking stuff again that I don't drink anyway." A small black circle might say that, not a fucking super-massive red circle and bastard gold stars.'

Ivanka remained cool. 'It's a mark on a calendar. You're being dramatic.'

'I'd rather be dramatic than stupid,' Jimmy barked.

'You are being stupid by not ringing Mr Frog and ensuring that you buy his company whilst it is on the market,' Ivanka humphed.

'Well, I'm not. I'm smoking him out. Even Connie thinks I should.'

Ivanka's eyes narrowed nastily. 'Oh, you listen to your wife but not me?'

'Connie knows what she's talking about. She set this company up with me, don't forget.'

Ivanka curled up her surgically inflated top lip. 'Connie Connie Connie. Maybe you should stay with your fat little wife then if she is so important.'

'Maybe I fucking well should!' Jimmy bellowed.

'Don't swear at me, Jimmy,' she said. 'I hate swearing and shouting and you do it a lot.'

'Is there any fucking wonder,' he replied, deliberately using a fierce expletive. 'Our horse is nearly home and dry. It's galloped, nay flown, safely, clearly over hundreds of fences and it's as if you're the jockey who's just pulled it up yards before the finish line, stood on top of your saddle and announced to the world that we've bloody given it amphetamines.'

Ivanka's face was creased in confusion. She

hadn't a clue what Jimmy was talking about, but what she did know was that he was shouting and talking to her disrespectfully and she could stop that in an instant with her trump card.

'Don't forget, Jimmy, that I have a one-way ticket to Krakow and I will use it,' she said with a triumphant sneer.

Jimmy, who'd had time to think about this threat since she used it on him before, stabbed his finger at her, 'And don't you forget, Ivanka, that however much you flap that ticket at me, I know you won't be able to go back to a life with no money in it. Even if you went, it would only cost you twenty bloody quid to get back here again with EasyJet.'

He threw his hands up in the air and laughed. 'Actually, go back if you want then, and marry a cabbage farmer. If you don't keep your gob shut and Connie finds out and plays really hard ball, he'll be richer than me anyway.'

Ivanka shut up.

CHAPTER 64

Mr Savant was in an odd mood on Wednesday morning, thought Connie. He'd greeted her at the door with an effusiveness that was totally out of character from what she had seen and heard from him so far. At least he wasn't flirting with her. Then again, no man alive would flirt with her in what she had on: one of her shapeless dresses, which was now looser than ever and only fit for cleaning in.

She wished he would turn his music down. Today it was all crash-bang cymbals and horns and very heavy on the ear. But he didn't. He went into the sitting room, sat in his chair and, eyes closed, appeared to be conducting an imaginary orchestra with his index fingers whilst Connie cleaned. It was giving her a headache and she took two paracetamol out of her handbag.

'Please feel free to make yourself a hot drink,' said Mr Savant, appearing suddenly behind her as she turned on the sink tap to fill up a glass with water. 'Sorry, Marilyn, did I startle you?'

'I didn't hear you come in,' said Connie, patting her chest in an attempt to still her shocked heartbeat. He must have teleported from the sitting room, she thought.

'I insist you take a break. And have something from the refrigerator.' He walked over to the fridge and opened the door to show her what was there, and once again it was crammed with cakes. 'They'll only go to waste if you don't.'

They'll go to my waist if I do, thought Connie and she didn't want that. She liked the feeling of being lighter and having more energy.

'Come and have a look, Marilyn.' He beckoned her over and she stood awkwardly between him and the fridge, staring at the gateaux and pastries taking up every shelf. She could smell brandy on his breath which wafted over her from behind.

'My, you always have so many cakes,' said Connie, feeling uncomfortable.

'My niece works in a bakery,' Mr Savant replied. 'At the end of each day, they give her all the leftover cakes which were made that morning so they're still very fresh. And she brings them to me for any visitors I might have.'

'Well, you're very lucky, Mr Savant,' said Connie, thinking that it was a bit odd. They must end up in the bin anyway. He couldn't possibly eat them all and she doubted he had that many visitors. 'Which bakery does she work at?'

'I forget the name,' he said. 'It's somewhere near Wakefield.'

'And she comes every day?'

Surely not. Which niece came every night after

work to drop off a sackful of cream cakes for her uncle?

'Most days,' he said. He seemed even closer behind her now. 'It's on her way home.'

'That's very sweet of her,' said Connie, turning suddenly after feeling the heat of his breath on the back of her head. She hoped she wouldn't have to employ the nut-crushing services of Astrid on him. 'Anyway, I appreciate the offer, but I had a big breakfast this morning, thank you.'

'Well, if you change your mind, don't bother asking, please help yourself,' he said, walking across to the door, where he turned, smiled gently and said, 'You're very comely, Marilyn,' before going back to the lounge.

Poor old soul, thought Connie, feeling slightly foolish that she'd thought he might be trying it on with her. He was lonely and, from the look of his wife, she obviously enjoyed a cream bun or two: perhaps he missed nourishing someone, that was all. She wondered if she would feel lonely when her marriage formally ended. Then again, hadn't she always?

CHAPTER 65

The air in Brandon's hallway was filled with the smells of rum and pineapple which battled to take precedence.

'In here,' called Brandon, urgently. 'Quick, Marilyn.'

She dropped her bags and rushed in, still wearing her coat, expecting to see him lying on the floor with a broken leg, but he was perfectly well and adding chocolate chips to the tempering machine.

'Lord above, I thought something was wrong,' Connie gasped. 'You sounded desperate.'

'I am desperate. Throw me some glamorous Hollywood actress names,' he demanded.

'Er . . . Halle Berry . . . Demi Moore . . . Sigourney Wea—' Connie reeled off.

'No, older. The black and white years.'

'Okay, okay . . . erm, Loretta Young . . . Betty Grable, Greta Garbo, Sophia Loren, Greer Garson . . . Jean Harlow . . . Marilyn Monroe.'

He looked over his shoulder and grinned at her, before switching his attention back to the machine. 'You kept the greatest till last.'

Connie felt a flush of heat rush to her cheeks.

'I've had a brainwave,' he said. 'I've been working on a range and I needed a name for it, then I heard the doorbell and thought, *That must be Marilyn* and it came to me in a flash, the concept, packaging, everything: *Goddess*. Each flavour named after a glamorous movie star. I just wanted to make sure there were enough names to go with.' He ripped off a square of kitchen roll from the holder on the wall and wiped his hands on it as he turned around to face her, his eyes shining with enthusiasm.

'That's a smashing idea,' said Connie. 'Betty Grable was my mum's favourite. That's why she gave me Elizabeth as a middle name. "Connie," she said, "I've given you the middle name of the woman with the best pins in the world in the hope that you'll have them too." It didn't work though.' She laughed. 'I was actually born on the same day that Betty Grable died.'

'It must be a sign,' Brandon grinned. 'I can't tell you how thrilled I am. My head has just produced a year's worth of ideas in two minutes, thanks to you. Okay, here's a question: I know you don't eat chocolates, but if you had to choose a flavour for Marilyn Monroe, what would it be?'

Connie tilted her head in thought. Her aunt Marilyn made the most fabulous homemade summer pudding, crammed with tart berries which she offset with a huge spoonful of sugar-crusted clotted cream.

'Summer pudding,' she said without hesitation.

'Oh yes, very good. Summer pudding it is then,' nodded Brandon, his mouth spreading into a mischievous smile. 'But you have to be the taste-tester for it because it has to be irresistible.'

'We'll see,' said Connie, unbuttoning her coat and dropping her eyes from his because they were just too brown and warm to hold for too long.

As Connie cleaned upstairs, she found herself humming 'Betty Grable' by Neil Sedaka. Her mum really had given her the middle name 'Elizabeth' in her honour. She smiled at the thought that she had inspired Brandon. It had been a long time since anyone had made her feel useful.

The flavour drifting from the kitchen had changed to a heady rich vanilla. When she carried the vacuum cleaner downstairs, it was like walking into a giant ice-cream.

Brandon was still in an extremely good mood.

'Throw me some more names, Marilyn. You're my good luck charm.'

Connie reeled off a list. 'Hedy Lamarr, Audrey Hepburn, Grace Kelly. Brigitte Bardot, Rita Hayworth . . .'

'Not so fast, I can't write them all down. You've been thinking about these, haven't you?'

'Yes, as I was busy upstairs,' said Connie.

Brandon stopped writing for a moment. 'That reminds me, Marilyn. If I wanted to book you for some extra time on Friday, do I have to ring your boss or can I arrange it directly with you?'

'You can just tell me and I'll let them know in the office,' she said.

'I've had some curtains made and they're arriving tomorrow. Any chance you could sort them out for me if I leave you a list of what goes where? I'm not useless, I could do it myself but there are a lot of them and I haven't really got the time, nor the patience. Plus you'd do it so much better.'

Connie thought for a moment. She had no cleaning jobs on Friday, so yes, she could do that.

'Brilliant. I'm going to a chocolate-tasting conference and driving back Friday morning,' Brandon said with a grin. 'It's a hard life.'

'Oh, it must be,' Connie smiled. The smell of vanilla was intoxicatingly beautiful. She could have happily drowned in it. 'The house smells gorgeous today.'

'The best vanilla pods are from India. I've just had a consignment delivered,' said Brandon. 'They're so soft and lush, not like those dried-up sticks you buy in supermarkets.'

'Not as good as that vanilla essence my mum used to buy from the Co-op, I bet,' Connie half-laughed, half-grimaced. 'When I was at primary school we once made truffles for pensioners. Our uniform was light green and when my mum picked me up from school, she said that I had so much chocolate on my clothes, she thought I was in camouflage gear.'

Brandon laughed. 'Did the pensioners enjoy them?'

'I don't think they were fit for human consumption,' smiled Connie. 'The hygiene standards were sadly lacking. It's hard to stop young confectioners licking their fingers when they're creating, even that awful cheap cooking chocolate which we used.'

'You'd be surprised at the different grades of chocolate,' said Brandon. 'A lot of firms use cheaper palm oil instead of cocoa butter these days but I don't. You will never achieve the same gloss and snap by compromising.'

'It sounds like a science,' said Connie.

'It is a science,' replied Brandon with no joke in his tone now. 'And you can throw in hard politics and a lot of environmental concerns as well. It's a very serious business.' He clicked his fingers, having just remembered something. 'Talking of serious business, I've been screening my calls so I didn't get trapped in a conversation with Helena and by not answering, I think I've very much annoyed her. I had to eventually pick up and got a proper earful for not being available.'

Connie winced. 'All the more reason for distancing yourself. She thinks you are still her property. She should be talking to her husband about her matrimonial problems, not her ex. That's straying into the danger zone.'

'Which is what I told her.'

'And?'

'She cried. Helena was always very good at backing off and coming in at another angle.'

'Women can be very manipulative,' nodded Connie. As she knew only too well. She could have given Helena lessons in manipulation at present.

'Luckily I have been very busy since last week, in fact, this has been the only day I've actually worked in the house.'

Then I'm very lucky to have seen you, thought Connie, then batted that thought away. She didn't like that on Tuesday nights she was starting to get rather giddy about the prospect of Wednesday afternoons.

'Which has been a blessing as Helena is her own boss, so she could call round at any time,' he went on.

'Oh, what does she do?' That information had been in the Yorkshire Willy Wonka article, but she couldn't admit that she knew. He'd think, quite rightly, that she'd been spying on him.

'She's a physiotherapist,' he said. 'She has her own treatment centre. She's done very well for herself. Dominic is an investment banker. She's much better off financially with him than she ever was with me.'

'Money isn't everything,' said Connie.

'I wouldn't know. I haven't had any until recently and I'm too busy to spend it. Would you like to try a pineapple and coconut liqueur bite?'

He smiled because he already knew the answer.

'Thanks, but no,' she said.

'I will convince you to like chocolate again one day, Marilyn,' grinned Brandon. 'I shall make something you won't be able to resist.'

Connie didn't argue but she very much doubted even the lovely Brandon Locke could persuade her to eat chocolate without thinking about a marriage that was flavoured with twenty-four years' worth of deception.

CHAPTER 66

'Con, have you seen my white Ralph Lauren shirt?' Jimmy shouted impatiently after he had searched his wardrobe and the dirty washing basket. 'I need it for tonight.'

It was the annual Mop and Bucket Award ceremony in Leeds and, though Jimmy wasn't nominated for one himself, he enjoyed going to it every year. He had never taken Connie with him. Connie wouldn't have enjoyed that sort of posh do anyway, he convinced himself. It would be much better next year when he could take Ivanka and enjoy the jealous stares of his peers that he had a young, tall blonde stunner on his arm.

'Where the bloody hell is it?' he growled.

'No idea, I'll have a look for it,' Connie replied.

'Oh bollocks. I need it.'

'I'll give you a ring when I find it and you can pick it up on the way.'

'I wasn't planning on coming back here though,' he sulked. 'I was going to drive straight to Leeds from work. I'm giving Pookie Barnes a lift. I can't understand it, I could have sworn it was hanging up in the wardrobe.'

'You've got other white shirts, haven't you?'

'Yes, but I wanted to wear that one. It's my favourite. I feel good in it.'

Jimmy had always been very particular over his clothes. He could justify spending two hundred pounds on a shirt because he said that the better the shirt, the better he felt and so the better impression he made and the easier business flowed. The most expensive item in Connie's wardrobe was her swing coat which had been forty pounds in the winter sale. But that was going to change. She had dropped one and a half dress sizes since Lent had begun and decided that as soon as she was a size fourteen, she would drive to Meadowhall and go mad in House of Fraser.

Jimmy lifted up his small case and his suit protector and passed his wife going down the stairs.

'Okay, well, I'll take a substitute but I'll come back for it if you find it. I'm out all morning at the bank, so, if it turns up, ring the office and leave a message for me, will you?'

'Have a good day and enjoy yourself tonight if I don't see you.'

She waved him off and then went upstairs to the carrier bag under the bed which contained a pressed, pristine Ralph Lauren shirt.

'What's this pencilled in the diary?' Della tapped her finger on the page. 'Meeting with Roy Frog on Monday?'

'It's a meeting with Roy Frog on Monday,' Ivanka replied dryly.

Della pressed down on the annoyance rising within her; it was becoming harder and harder to appear equable.

'Jimmy doesn't want to meet with Roy Frog yet. He wants to keep him waiting.'

'It's madness,' said Ivanka. 'So I have arranged conference with Roy myself.'

Well, you'd better arrange to *un*conference him, Ivanka, Della was about to say, but stopped herself. This could be the breakthrough she was waiting for. A plan dropped into her head as beautifully and completely as if a god had dropped it from the sky. It was a risk, but the deadline was nearly up and this was the time for risks.

'Yes, maybe you're right.'

Ivanka turned back to her screen wearing an ultra-smug smile.

Della could have kissed Ivanka for her interference, if that wouldn't have been too ironic.

Della read the text in the toilet on her secret phone: WILL BE IN OFFICE IN 10 MINS. WANTED TO SEE 2ND MRS DIAMOND FOR MYSELF.

She'd felt the phone vibrate in her bag a good five minutes ago when the message came through, so Connie's arrival was imminent. Della felt slightly apprehensive and hoped Connie wouldn't give herself away. And strangely, too, she felt protective towards her. She didn't want the sight of the pouty, leggy and much younger blonde to hurt her.

Two minutes later there was a knock on the door and, without waiting to be answered, it opened and there stood Connie. Della had expected her to be dressed up to the nines wearing power-red lipstick, but she'd gone for the opposite effect: one of those awful big dresses, this time in drab grey, under an equally massive dowdy coat, flat shoes, light-flesh coloured tights and no make-up. *Why has she dressed like that?* was Della's overriding thought.

'Excuse me, who are you?' said Ivanka, rising to her feet.

'This is Jimmy's wife,' said Della, with carefully acted coldness. 'Mrs Diamond. We haven't seen you in here for a long time, are you well?' Her manner towards Connie was polite, but chilly. An onlooker would have picked up immediately that there was no love lost between the two women.

'I'm fine thank you, Della.' Connie turned to Ivanka. She stretched out her hand towards her and said, 'How do you do. So nice to meet you at last.' She had been prepared to pretend to be nervous, but found she really was. Ivanka was tall and pretty and young and sleeping with her husband. Connie hadn't anticipated that she might want to scream and claw at Ivanka's face with her nails, but she did. She wanted to see the girl for whom Jimmy had bought a ritzy car when he'd said that he couldn't afford to buy one for his own daughter. She had to put a face to the name of the woman who was hoping to fill her marital shoes, because she had strong black moments of doubt that her plan was probably going to fail and she needed to find some strength to overcome them if she was to carry on.

Ivanka reached over and they performed a stiff handshake.

'I'm afraid Jimmy isn't here,' said Della.

'Oh, it's fine,' said Connie, aware that Ivanka's eyes were glued on her, analysing her clothes, her face, her body. 'I'm dropping this shirt off for him, if you could let him know. He couldn't find it this morning.' She smiled and licked her lips nervously. 'Do . . . do you happen to know who . . . who he's going with this evening?'

'Pookie Barnes,' said Della. Ah, she suspected now where Connie was going with this.

'A . . . anyone else?'

'I imagine there will be the usual crowd. I don't have a list of names, I'm afraid.'

'Ah. Oh well. I expect he'll tell me all about it when he gets back,' she gushed. 'Don't you ever go to these functions, Della?'

'No,' said Della.

'Oh. Well, it's been nice seeing you again. Has Jimmy told you he's going to be a granddad? Jane is pregnant. Jimmy as a granddad? Can you imagine?'

'Congratulations,' said Della, aware that Ivanka was now watching her as well. Analysing her exchange with Connie. The girl didn't miss a trick.

'Well, goodbye then. Nice to meet you, Ivanka.'

'Likewise,' replied Ivanka, competing with Della for frostiness.

Connie seemed to shuffle out like a woman much older than her years. When the door shut behind her, she knew that Ivanka would be sneering and she was right.

'That is Jimmy's wife?' asked Ivanka. 'My God, no wonder . . .' She stopped herself, but Della was straight on it.

'No wonder what?'

'No wonder that . . . Jimmy spends so much time in the office. She's a dog.'

'Ivanka.' Della forced herself to cough. 'Excuse me. That's not very nice,' but she made sure that Ivanka saw she was trying to cover up a smile of amusement.

'What was she wearing? My God, it was awful. Like a circus tent.'

Ivanka was laughing hard now. She'd wondered what Jimmy's wife would look like in the flesh and now she knew. She'd been jealous of Connie until a few moments ago but that had all disappeared now. And she had picked up immediately that Della didn't like her either. And was she imagining things, or could Connie have thought that there was something going on between Della and Jimmy? Ha – if she only knew. Well, she would, very shortly.

Della's voice cut into her thoughts. 'Would you put the kettle on for me, Ivanka. My throat is absolutely killing me. I hope I'm not coming down with something.'

Ivanka swaggered into the kitchen singing 'Who let the dogs out' under her breath.

Oh but what sort of dog do you think she is, dear, thought Della, knowing that neither Jimmy nor Ivanka had any idea they were soon to be savaged by a Pitbull.

CHAPTER 67

Jimmy sat staring at the carrier bag on his desk with the pristine white shirt in it. Connie's purpose in bringing it over may have been to see Ivanka, but she would never have guessed the impact it would have on her husband. For the first time in years, the sight of that shirt forced him to think with his brain instead of his dick and he didn't like that because thinking with his dick was easier. His dick had no conscience or interest in the consequences of his actions, but his brain tethered him to emotions and responsibilities.

He knew that Connie must love him very much. He really had been a shit husband, and yet she had stuck by him and twenty-four years on she was still putting herself out for him. He pictured her scouring the whole house for that shirt then giving it a wash to freshen it, pressing it to his exacting standards and then racing over so he had it for the evening. Then he tried to imagine Ivanka doing the same and he couldn't.

He'd never seen a prettier woman than Connie at seventeen, with her curves, her soft dove-grey eyes and her hair like sunshine. She made Ivanka look like King Kong by comparison. He'd thought with his dick back then as well, too busy enjoying the here and now and presuming things would always be as good and uncomplicated. But Time was evil, it liked to alter things, stretch and distort, strengthen, weaken, destroy at its whim. His affair with Ivanka would recalibrate as soon as he left Connie, because doing it behind Connie's back was what kept it illegal and exciting. His wife's love for and trust in him kept real life at the door but it was waiting to rush in and engulf him when she had gone. Pookie's mistress was up the duff and he was panicking because she wanted to keep the baby. What if Ivanka wanted kids? They hadn't talked about it because that was brain stuff, not dick stuff. Being married to Connie, oddly, he was as free as he was ever going to be – he could come and go as he pleased, do what he wanted behind her back, but once he was Ivanka's she would screw him to a track and ride with him to make sure he stayed on it. He'd had three dreams in the past week alone about being suffocated.

He could hear Della coughing in the main office. The sound of anyone coughing always annoyed him.

'For God's sake, Del, get a glass of water,' he called through the door.

'I've already got one. I think I'm coming down with something,' she said. 'My throat is on fire.'

Jimmy came out of his office and over to her.

'Isn't she back yet?' He thumbed towards Ivanka's desk.

'Ivanka never hurries if you send her on an errand,' said Della, looking at the clock. She would be at least another twenty minutes coming from the post office.

'Here,' he said, and produced a packet of mints from his pocket.

'Thank you,' Della said. He surprised her then by dropping heavily onto the chair opposite.

'Del, do you ever think, "What the fuck am I doing?"' he said, with a loaded sigh.

'In what way?' asked Della, noticing the dark circles under Jimmy's eyes.

'Is the grass greener on the other side, do you think?'

'Sometimes it is, yes,' said Della. She watched him scratch his head as he stared into space. He seemed weighed down with whatever was occupying his thoughts. 'And sometimes it isn't.'

'Cheers for that,' he said with amused sarcasm and she laughed.

'What's up, Jimmy? You look down.'

Down was an understatement, depression was leaking out of every one of his pores.

'Oh I don't know, Del. Maybe I'm having a mid-life crisis,' he said.

'You've been having one of those since I started working for you, Jimmy Diamond.'

He didn't laugh then. Della studied him as he stared blankly at the stapler on her desk. He was so handsome, even more so now that he had acquired a few lines around his eyes and some stray white hairs at his temple. She had to stop herself reaching out and stroking his head. A vulnerable Jimmy Diamond would be dangerous for her will.

'Ever wish you could go back and start again?' Jimmy said, raising his big blue eyes to hers.

'Doesn't everyone,' Della replied softly.

He reached out his hand and closed his fingers around her wrist and despite everything that she was planning against him, her heart began to race.

'I don't know what I'd do without you, Del. You're my best girl, do you know that?'

Della's throat was bone dry. She could have been his best girl if he'd only asked. Even now, if he leant across to her and kissed her she would respond and kiss him back with fervour. She wouldn't be able to stop herself.

'In another lifetime, you and me might have made a go of things,' he said. A small groan escaped Della's throat. His eyes were soft and shining and his voice smoky with emotion. She might hate him but she had never stopped loving him either.

'I've done some rotten stuff and you've seen loads of it yet you've never judged me, Del. I've never trusted anyone as much as I trust you.'

Oh Jimmy, Jimmy my darling. Please, just kiss me once. Just once.

Della gulped. She had to do this. She didn't want to, it didn't feel right but she had to.

'Jimmy, there's something I need to tell you about your wife. And you're not going to like it,' she said.

CHAPTER 68

Through the window Connie saw Jimmy's car pull up outside so she got into position. She propped open her handbag on the kitchen table with her purse then picked up a cloth. She was wiping down the work surface with it when Jimmy came in.

'Oh hello, Jim,' she said with a small startled gasp. 'I thought you were going straight to Leeds.'

'I forgot to pack something,' said Jimmy. He was lying as usual. She knew he'd come home to suss her out.

'Do you want a cuppa before you go, or something to eat?'

'No, I'm okay,' said Jimmy. 'Thanks for bringing me the shirt, Con. You should have rung, I'd have called back for it.'

'Well, I'm at a bit of a loose end these days,' Connie smiled. 'I've been thinking about getting myself a part-time job or something. Have you any vacancies for cleaners?'

Jimmy looked momentarily horrified by that suggestion.

'It was . . . nice to see Della after so many years,'

said Connie, leaving a significant pause. 'She hasn't changed much.'

'Naw, she never changes,' smiled Jimmy. 'She was a dried-up stick when she came and she's still a dried-up stick now.'

'That's not very nice, Jim.'

'Well, at least I'm honest,' he chuckled. 'She does a good job, but then so does my desk and my chair.'

Connie looked up at him with confusion forming her features. 'Why would you say that, Jimmy? She's the best worker you'll ever have.'

'You're not going to believe this, right,' he gave a forced laugh. 'Della actually told me that she thinks you came to deliver that shirt to check her out because you think there's something going on between us.'

'Wha-at?'

Jimmy slapped his hand on his thigh like Dandini in *Cinderella* might have. 'I know. I sat and listened to her saying it, in all seriousness, and I don't know how I kept a straight face.' He formed his fingers into round glasses and lifted them to his eyes. '"You're not going to like this, Jimmy, but I think your wife might suspect we are having an affair",' he said, parodying Della's voice.

'Why would she think that?' asked Connie.

'Christ knows. She's been reading too many Mills and Boons,' said Jimmy. 'The thought of it!' He shuddered and made an exaggerated 'brrr' sound. 'I mean, you wouldn't, would you?'

'Jimmy, give up,' said Connie.

'I bet she's full of cobwebs,' Jimmy sniggered. 'You don't think that, do you, Con?'

Connie threw her cloth at him. 'Course not. Now, Jimmy Diamond, go and get whatever you've forgotten and bugger off out of here.'

'I'm going, I'm going,' he said, laughing, and was straight up the stairs and back down them again. He called 'See you tomorrow,' and left.

Connie picked her phone out of her handbag and brought it to her ear. Della had been on the other end of it listening to the whole conversation.

'Della, are you still there? Are you all right?'

'Yes, I'm here.'

'How did you know he'd come here?'

'Because he will have panicked that you suspect he's up to something. I don't think he's one hundred per cent made up his mind what he wants to do yet, if I'm honest.' Della recalled the conversation about grass being greener. 'I think the nearer it gets to the end of Lent, the more he is doubting his plans.' Her voice croaked on the last word and Connie could have wept for her.

'Oh, why did you ask me to do that?'

'I wanted to hear what he said.'

'You know Jimmy's a bare-faced liar though, Della. If I'd have asked about Ivanka, he would probably have called her an acne-faced trog. Plus if he was trying to persuade me that you and he . . .'

'It's okay, Connie, I know. Thank you.' Della's voice was tight, controlled, but there was a motherlode of tears waiting behind it.

'Please don't thank me for doing that. It was awful.'

'I needed to hear it,' said Della.

'You loved him, didn't you, Della?' Connie asked gently.

'I'll be in touch next week,' replied Della, not answering the question. 'I'm going on the sick but with any luck everything will be in place by close of business tomorrow night.'

'Take care,' said Connie, but Della had already hung up.

CHAPTER 69

Della was in work very early the next morning with a carrier bag full of goodies. She snapped on a pair of rubber gloves, went into the supply cupboard and twisted the tops off the bottles of carpet and upholstery cleaner before pouring extra strong bleach in. Next she poured red and blue dye into various containers. She mixed up potions like Severus Snape and hoped that she would knacker carpets, washing, upholstery and furniture all over Barnsley. Della had cried for hours but through the night her sadness had crystallised into a sharp, destructive hate. Today was D-Day and she was going to give it everything she had got.

Cheryl was in a light and happy mood when she set off for Mr Fairbanks' house. She'd just received her first payment from Lady Muck deposited in her bank account and, true to her word, she'd made up Cheryl's wage to the full sixteen hours, and given her travelling expenses. And the sun was shining high and bright in the sky and trying to push out some warmth to offer assurances that spring was finally on its way.

'Morning, Mr F,' she called in the direction of the lounge.

'Morning, Cheryl,' he replied. 'Isn't it a grand day.'

'Lovely,' said Cheryl. She felt better this morning than she had for a long time. She had slept well, not had any sad dreams about Gary and she'd won a tenner on a scratchcard. She'd buy herself a bottle of wine tonight and a chicken fried rice supper from China Moon around the corner. Sometimes the simple pleasures lifted people the most.

'What's on the news today?' Cheryl said as she gave Mr Fairbanks his coffee and chocolate biscuits at eleven. 'Anything exciting?'

'Not unless you count a lot of old women doing pole-dancing for charity,' shuddered Mr Fairbanks. 'I only wish I could remove that sight from my memory with one of your scrubbing brushes.'

Cheryl laughed. 'How's the book coming on?' she asked, as always. She knew he appreciated that she was interested in its progress.

'Not very well,' he said. 'I think I am going to abandon it as a bad job.'

'Aw, that's a shame,' said Cheryl, lifting his saucer to dust the table underneath it.

'Mmm . . .' Mid-mouthful of biscuit, Mr Fairbanks suddenly recalled something he had to mention and hurriedly chomped whilst waving his hand.

'Steady on, Mr F, don't choke,' Cheryl chuckled.

'Cheryl, I knew there was something I needed to tell you. That house that collapsed last week, do you remember?'

Will I ever forget? thought Cheryl.

'The man who lived there escaped with a few cuts and bruises only,' he went on.

'Yeah, I know.' *Lucky swine.*

'Well, I didn't realise that he was the nephew of Ernest Gardiner who built the house.'

'That's right, but by marriage,' said Cheryl. 'I used to clean for Edith, Ernest's widow, who was the blood relation of Lance Nettleton, that's the' – *twat* – 'guy you're talking about.'

'Ridiculous chap,' said Mr Fairbanks, taking off his glasses and giving one of the arms a chew. 'Wasn't insured, apparently.'

Cheryl's head snapped up. 'What do you mean?'

'Moved all his possessions from his old house into Brambles but didn't switch his cover policy over. And there's no buildings insurance on Brambles, of course. No bank on this earth would have underwritten that.'

'Really?' Cheryl's eyes were glittering with disbelief. What was that German word her English teacher used to use all the time that would sum all this up for her if it was true. Ah yes, *Schadenfreude.* 'How do you know all this, Mr Fairbanks?'

'Old boys' network,' said Mr Fairbanks. 'Bad lot, I heard, Nettleton. Refused to pay Mrs Gardiner's gardener and wouldn't let him have his tools back either.'

'I know this is awful, Mr F, but I hope it is true that he's had rotten luck for a change,' said Cheryl, letting loose a hysterical giggle. 'Oh I'm sorry, this isn't like me at all to gloat.'

'Cheryl, please sit down,' said Mr Fairbanks, full of concern. 'Are you all right?'

'I don't think I've been this overjoyed in a long time,' laughed Cheryl, wiping the tears that were dropping out of her eyes. Tears for Edith, tears for justice. 'I think Lance Nettleton murdered Edith Gardiner, Mr F.'

'My goodness, what do you mean?' Mr Fairbanks' huge hairy eyebrows rippled in shock.

'I had the misfortune to come across Lance Nettleton when I was cleaning for Edith. She had decided to change an earlier will she'd made in his favour and disinherit him. Edith died within twenty-four hours of him finding that out. No one will ever convince me he didn't murder her. But there's no proof.'

'Oh my goodness. That's terrible, terrible. Poor Edith. Darling old girl. Batty as they come, but then all the Lakes were. Match made in heaven with the Gardiner family.'

'Yes, she was quietly nuts,' smiled Cheryl. 'I loved being with her.'

'Batty, but not nuts, Cheryl,' Mr Fairbanks

corrected her. He tapped his skull where the frontal lobe lay. 'The Lake family had it all in perfect working order up here.'

Cheryl begged to differ. 'I think Edith lost it a bit, Mr F. She was convinced that all the paintings she had around the house were original master-pieces. The *Mona Lisa*, Van Gogh's *Sunflowers* . . .'

'Did she ever tell you that her grandfather was a painter? Percy Lake.'

'She did. I can't say I ever heard of him though.' It was hardly a name up there with Monet, thought Cheryl.

'Oh, you won't have done, no. But he was a fascinating man all the same. I talked at length to Edith about him years ago. I was going to feature him in my book but she said that she'd rather I didn't. He was a bit of a crook, you see. Are there any more biscuits, Cheryl? I'm in the mood for a third today.'

'Yes, I'll go and get them, Mr F.'

Cheryl hurried back with the rest of the packet.

'Were you aware that Percy Lake was reputed to be a friend of Van Gogh?'

Cheryl burst out laughing. 'Yes, she told me that one.'

'Oh, don't laugh, Cheryl, it could be true. Obviously I only have Edith's word for it all but the dates she told me tie up with established facts.'

Cheryl's laugh dried up. 'When you say Van Gogh, you do mean Vincent Van Gogh? The *Sunflower* bloke?'

Mr Fairbanks smiled. 'The *Sunflower* bloke indeed.' He put his glasses back on. 'Let me find my notes.' He disappeared into his study and came back with a file which he proceeded to rifle through. 'Yes, here we are. Percy Lake. One of the most incredibly talented artists the world has seen and yet no one has ever heard of him – now what do you think about that, Cheryl?'

Cheryl shook her head. 'I'm lost,' she said. 'Surely if he was that much of a talent, everyone would know about him.'

'Let me go back to the beginning, as Edith told me.' He referred to his notes to refresh his memory. 'In 1873 a young Percy Lake ran away from the north and his destiny, to be a miner like his father before him, because he had a natural talent for art. He somehow managed to worm his way into a job with an international art dealer in Covent Garden at the same time as a young Dutchman, who suggested they share lodgings in Brixton.'

'Who was that then?' Cheryl spluttered in amusement. 'Vincent Van Gogh?'

'Yes,' said Mr Fairbanks. 'The man himself.'

Even though he was not at home on Friday, the house still greeted Connie with a chocolately aroma, this time heavily scented with mint. There was a stack of parcels in the hallway and a hand-written note on top.

Dear Marilyn,

These are for the lounge. I've put the rest at the side of the appropriate windows (study, bedroom 1, bedroom 2, bedroom 3). Just let me know what I owe you.

*Cheers – Brandon *

She noticed there was a small mark after his name and wondered if he had been about to draw a kiss, then thought better of it. So, he stopped a natural reaction to put a kiss, why was that then? *Oh for God's sake Marilyn . . . Connie, whatever your name is . . . just put the bloody curtains up!* She laughed at herself and lifted the stepladder which was propped up against the wall and carried it into the lounge.

The blue brocade curtains added a softness to the room. If he had chosen the material himself, then he had excellent taste, but she knew that already. The house was grand without being pretentious; its primary aim was comfort and easy living whilst being pleasurable to the eye. She imagined Brandon slobbing on the huge sofa at night, a glass of red wine and a dish of Doritos on a small table at the side of him. He liked to read, she knew, because there were books parked all over the house – a thriller by his bed, a biography of a wild rugby player here on the coffee table, shelves full of them in his study on all subjects from cartoons to car manuals. Connie had always loved books. In the house she lived in next, she would have a huge antique bookcase full of them.

It was strange to think that she had this secret life setting up a rival business behind her husband's back, cleaning for clients whilst he thought she was at home polishing the microwave for the umpteenth time and washing his socks. He hadn't a clue that she was aware of nearly everything he was doing and planning. She wouldn't have been surprised if he had already written his leaving speech to her about how he hoped they could stay friends and would be more than financially generous with her and would sign over the house to her. Well, she didn't want it and couldn't wait to say so now. He was going to get a bigger shock on the seventeenth of April than she was.

Surprisingly she wouldn't be upset to leave her marital home with all its many memories. A fresh new space for one person would be good for her. And she would make sure that her divorce settlement afforded her that – she had copies of Jimmy's secret bank accounts hidden in her wardrobe as insurance.

Connie had just started on the upstairs curtains when there was a ring on the doorbell. She climbed down the steps and had only reached the top of the stairs when it rang again, impatiently, and whoever was outside was trying the handle. 'Give me a chance,' she grumbled as she hurried to the front door and opened it. There stood Helena, still with that supercilious look on her face. Her eyes flicked over Connie from head to toe and back again with open disapproval.

'I'd like to see Brandon, please,' she said, clearly not happy at having to explain her purpose in visiting to a lowly domestic.

'He's not in,' clipped Connie, riled by her attitude.

'Really?' Her tone suggested she didn't believe that.

'Well, his car isn't on the drive.' Did Helena think he'd concealed it under a plant pot?

'I'll wait.' Helena attempted to side-step past her, but Connie barred her entrance.

'I'm afraid you can't come in.'

Helena gave a small dry laugh of disbelief. 'I beg your pardon?'

But Connie wasn't fazed by her. Over the years she'd had to battle belligerent cleaning staff, doctors, councils and hospitals for her mother and Jimmy's aged parents, and a jumped up swishy-haired snob was no match for her.

'I told you, Brandon isn't here,' she said firmly. 'So no, you can't come in.'

Helena tried to look around Connie as if expecting to see Brandon hiding there but she had more chance of getting past Cerberus into the underworld than she did getting past Connie into Brandon's house.

'Brandon, is it now?' she said pointedly, as if

referring to his first name was proof that Connie was sleeping with him.

'I'll tell him you called,' said Connie, shutting the door in her face. She had curtains to hang and no time to fight on any more fronts with anyone else at the moment, thank you.

'You're joking, right?' Cheryl laughed with a snort of disbelief.

'I'm not joking at all. They shared much in common, walking, talking, nature, reading. Interestingly, though Van Gogh liked to sketch, he had not yet decided that he wanted to become an artist, unlike young Percy who knew he was not fit for anything else. You see, Vincent was fascinated by Percy's great natural talent. Painting came effortlessly to him but Vincent had to study and work at it. Now,' said Mr Fairbanks with relish, 'this is where things get very exciting. Or at least they would do if I had proof of it. Art historians place a huge value on Van Gogh's seeing John Constable's *Cornfield* in the National Gallery and being highly influenced by it, but before he had laid eyes on that, Percy Lake had brought Vincent Van Gogh to Yorkshire. Vincent had rather an obsessive love for a young lady, unrequited, I hasten to add, which made him quite depressed. So Percy thought he would whisk his new young friend up to the cheerful north with all its dramatic scenery, including a certain Farmer Barraclough's wheat field near Woolley. According to what

Edith's grandfather told her, young Vincent was reduced to tears by the beauty of it. They sat there sketching with charcoals until there was no light and Vincent was so desperate for his drawing to be coloured that he scribbled over his work a guide to the various shades of what he could see so he could recreate it later in paint. This, remember, was before he was supposed to have been influenced by Constable.'

Mr Fairbanks rubbed his forehead. 'Is it a true story or an elaborate lie woven by Percy Lake to add interest to himself? But if it is a lie, it's an extremely well-researched one. What we do know for definite is that Van Gogh drew a lot of fields after his supposed trip up north; he finally made up his mind to become an artist; he was influenced by someone or something to stop sketching, stop using monochrome and start using colour, pastels, oils as Percy Lake did. And, what we also do know for a fact is that Farmer Barraclough kept a field in which he grew only sunflowers in remembrance of his late wife. Incidentally, Percy Lake was to return to Barnsley and marry Barraclough's daughter Lily ten years later and have a daughter with her – Anna Cornelia – Edith's mother. Also incidentally, Anna Cornelia was the name of Van Gogh's sister, of whom Percy was very fond.'

'This just can't be true,' said Cheryl, shaking her head. Van Gogh hanging around fields in Barnsley wasn't at all credible. 'Did Van Gogh really live in England then?'

'Yes, for about two years.'

'It . . . it just . . .' Cheryl laughed in disbelief again. 'It can't be true, can it?'

Mr Fairbanks threw up his hands. 'Will we ever know? Van Gogh was a prolific letter-writer yet there is no mention of Percy Lake in the surviving correspondences. Or maybe he was mentioned in a letter which was lost or destroyed? We have no proof that Percy Lake ever met Van Gogh in London. But then he did name his daughter after his so-called friend's sister who lived in London at the same time. Percy may have made the whole thing up. He was a shady man. But then he would have to be in his chosen profession.'

'Burglar?'

'Art forger. Percy and Vincent returned to London but it seemed that Vincent was becoming more unstable. The following year Percy stepped in to protect their landlady's daughter from Vincent's unwanted amorous advances and Vincent was thrown out of their lodgings. And, sadly, Vincent, so Edith's story goes, tossed Percy aside as he so often did with people who were close to him. He went his way and Percy went his, but their crossed paths served to ignite the genius in both of them. The rest is history as far as Van Gogh goes, but as for Percy, well he was a master of his craft but his concepts for original work were poor. He was commissioned to make a copy of a painting which was damaged, and that's how he found his true vocation. His talents lay in copying the works of others, mixing the paints as the great artists did, using aged canvases . . . oh yes, there are works of art all over the world which have passed the critical eye of experts and are accepted as originals. Slippery as an eel he was, fox-wily. As skilled in being a ghost as he was in being an artist. If Edith still had any paintings of his, I expect they are underneath the rubble now.' And he gave a long, pained sigh. 'What a tragedy.'

'Well, I have all Edith's paintings at home,' said Cheryl. 'Bloody Lance Nettleton was about to throw them in the skip.'

'*All*?' asked Mr Fairbanks, snapping to attention. 'How many did she have? And you say that you have them?'

'Yes, there are quite a few of them. And I found a couple of sketches behind the Sunflowers when I reframed it.'

'God be praised.' Mr Fairbanks stood up so fast the blood rushed to his head and he had to sit down again. 'Cheryl, can you take me to your house immediately, please. I have to see them.'

CHAPTER 70

Brandon's bedroom looked transformed when Connie hung his curtains up. Duck-egg blue, heavy drapes, a perfect complement to the pale grey walls. The two large picture windows afforded views of the garden, which badly needed some attention, but she imagined it would be stunning when it was knocked into shape. According to the position of the sun, it must have been east-facing, so it channelled all the morning sunshine, the perfect place to build a terrace for having breakfast outside in the summer. Hot strong fresh coffee and croissants with salt-crusted butter and apricot jam, and conversation, both parties still in dressing gowns . . . She imagined it would be bliss to share a breakfast like that with a man like Brandon Locke.

The front door opening pulled her out of her daydream. Brandon was back. She didn't like the way her insides appeared to cheer at the news.

'Hi,' he called. 'How are you getting on?'

'Just finished and admiring my handiwork,' Connie shouted back.

She heard him take the stairs quickly, more than

one at a time, she guessed. He appeared at the bedroom door smiling, unshaven and all the more handsome for being a little rough around the edges.

'Wow,' he said. 'They look pretty good. I can't say that I'm the type to get excited about curtains, but I'm impressed.'

'They must have been expensive,' said Connie, folding up the ladder.

'Here, let me do that. I don't know the going rate for custom-made curtains but my hand was shaking when I typed my pin number into the machine,' he laughed. It was a great sound, she thought. Genuine and deep as if it came from a happy place within him.

'Your ex-wife called round,' said Connie.

'I gathered,' said Brandon, wincing as he trapped his finger shutting the ladder. 'I had a text from her.' He started to walk down the stairs.

'Ah.' *I bet there were a few expletives in that*, added Connie inwardly, as she followed him.

'I'm sorry you had to deal with her. She can be very . . .' He struggled with saying the word and she could tell he was trying to be a gentleman, which was why he had found himself in this position.

'I can be very . . . too,' replied Connie, with a smile, which made him chuckle.

'I had a text message from her earlier asking if she could come around and talk and I said I wasn't at home. Evidently she didn't believe me.'

'Well, it's not my house. It's not up to me who comes in so I couldn't really do anything else,' said Connie.

'Thank you,' said Brandon. 'Now I'm going to make you a coffee and won't take no for an answer.'

'I wasn't going to say no,' laughed Connie. She was parched after all that climbing up and down and stretching. *Be careful* said that annoying voice inside her. *Sod off voice* she answered it back.

'I've got another favour to ask,' said Brandon, resting the ladder, on the wall at the bottom of the stairs. 'A week on Tuesday, I'm having what a pretentious git might call a soirée. Sort of cheese and wine party but instead of wine we're having chocolate.'

Connie looked confused. 'A cheese and chocolate party?'

'Sorry, it's been a long drive.' He scratched his head, mussing up his mad, variegated black, grey and white hair. 'I mean chocolate and wine. No cheese. Could I hire you for the evening to help out, circulate with chocolates? Do you do that sort of thing? I was going to ask my sisters but then I remembered the last time I did that, they both got paralytic and ate half my stock.'

Connie grinned. 'Yes, I can do that.' A week on Tuesday was two days before Lent, two days before the end of her marriage because, even if Jimmy was considering changing his mind about throwing her out on the scrap heap, she hadn't changed hers about throwing him on it.

* * *

429

Mr Fairbanks stood squarely in front of the painting of a man wearing a hat and carrying art canvases and he sighed with true, unadulterated pleasure.

'Do you know what this is, Cheryl?'

'Nope,' she said. Nor did she, other than being a nice predominantly yellow picture that sat well in her sunshiney kitchen.

'This is *Painter on the Road to Tarascon*. During the war the Nazis declared Van Gogh a degenerate and burned his original. This, I guarantee you, is a copy by Percy Lake and as near as dammit to the original as you will ever find.' He moved to the next. 'And this is Chagall.'

'I didn't think it was that clever myself,' said Cheryl. 'But I wouldn't throw—'

'You misunderstand me, I mean Marc Chagall,' Mr Fairbanks interrupted. 'My God, I need to sit down, Cheryl.'

She quickly brought him a chair before he fell. He was breathless but laughing. 'This is the most exciting morning I've ever had.'

'They're just fakes though, surely they're worth nothing.'

'They aren't fakes, Cheryl. They are *genuine forgeries*. There is a difference. Hans van Meegeren, Tom Keating, Eric Hebborn fooled experts all over the world but the skills of Percy Lake outshine even them. Genuine forgeries of this standard fetch tens of thousands of pounds.'

Cheryl pulled another chair over before she fell down.

'The *Sunflowers* isn't a genuine fake though, is it?'

'Sadly not,' smiled Mr Fairbanks. 'If only. I think Edith must have picked that up at a car boot sale. Oh, that reminds me, did you say you found some sketches when you reframed it?'

'Oh, yes, I forgot about those. Nearly chucked them away,' said Cheryl, fetching them from a cupboard in the kitchen. 'The frame on the *Sunflowers* fell off and that's when I found them tucked between the painting and the backing board. I thought they were just padding until I turned them over.'

Mr Fairbanks' hands were shaking as he reached inside the manila envelope in which Cheryl had stored them. Cheryl had never seen him so agitated and as he pulled out the three sketches, he made a strange gurgling noise in his throat. The first was of a man sitting in a field, heads of wheat high behind him, and he was drawing – and scrawled across the top left corner was the name Percy. The second was drawn by a different hand, again a young man drawing, sitting in a field, 'Vincent' written in the identical place across the top left; the third sketch a field of sunflower heads, covered in scribbles.

'Jesus Christ,' said Mr Fairbanks, which made Cheryl's eyes pop open. She didn't think Mr Fairbanks was capable of such a blasphemy.

'Unless I am very much mistaken, my dear lady, this is Barraclough's farm and this is Vincent Van Gogh as drawn by his friend Percy Lake. So this

431

is Percy Lake as drawn by . . .' He couldn't say it, his words collapsed into a breathy whisper. 'My goodness, I could be holding his genuine work. And this is Van Gogh's first step into the world of colour, the five shades of paint he intended to use for the flower field. Now, is it the real article? If only we knew. Any criteria for establishing originality was known by the master forgers, of course.'

'Surely he wouldn't have just signed it Vincent though?' Cheryl wasn't convinced by the cursive single name.

'Yes, Cheryl, that's exactly what he did. He deplored how his surname was so mispronounced so he used his first name. Many of his works aren't signed, he saved his signature for the pieces of which he was particularly proud.' Mr Fairbanks was gasping with joy.

'But . . . surely . . . not?' Cheryl couldn't believe that someone as learned as Mr Fairbanks could take this all so seriously. *It couldn't be, could it?*

Mr Fairbanks rested his hand on Cheryl's arm.

'I think you'd better go and find me the number of Christie's in London, my dear Cheryl. We need to get the experts to look at this haul.'

Della coughed until her throat became hoarse in reality.

'Don't you dare be ill,' said Jimmy. 'The place will fall to bits without you.' He knew without even glancing at Ivanka that he would get grief for that later. 'Why did you say that about Della?'

she would pout. 'The place will be *better* without her because I will be running it.'

He was beginning to really dislike the sight of her lips puckering up into that pinch of annoyance.

Della watched the clock nudge towards home time. She felt evil and disloyal and crazed and didn't give a flying fart. The chances were that what she had planned to happen next week wouldn't. Her perfidy would be exposed and Jimmy would sack her on the spot but she didn't care any more. She would rather have walked out than be thrown out, but if her scheme failed, well, at least she had given it her best shot. Jimmy rode on the tide of the 'here and now' and maybe she should take a leaf out of his book and employ those tactics for once.

'Della, you don't look very well,' said Ivanka, with a concern that sounded too excessive to be genuine. 'You should take some time off.'

'If I feel as bad on Monday as I do now, I can assure you I will be. But you know what to do, don't you? Jimmy prides himself on making visitors feel welcome so sit them down with a tea or coff—'

'I know,' cut in Ivanka, with a smile that barely covered her irritation.

'I'm going to get off early tonight,' said Della, groaning as she got to her feet as if every muscle ached. 'You have a good weekend. Are you doing anything nice?'

'I am going for a meal with my cousin,' said Ivanka.

'Well, you enjoy yourself. In fact, the chances are that I won't be in on Monday, I'll warn you now. I really need to recharge my batteries.'

'Aw, well you take good care, Della. The office will be in good hands.'

No it won't, thought Della. Good.

CHAPTER 71

Della and Connie met at Lady Muck head-quarters in Wheatfield Lane at ten-thirty the following Monday.

'So how are you?' asked Connie from the kitchen as she stood waiting for the kettle to boil.

'Terrible. I am so ill,' replied Della dryly. 'I've always been very good at mimicking voices so when I rang Ivanka this morning and told her that I had flu, she was more than convinced.'

'You mimic voices?' asked Connie.

'*Ivanka, I am so sorry, but I won't be able to make it in for a few days,*' said Della, in her best flu accent.

Connie was impressed.

'You'll like this one too. *Hello, I'd like to make an appointment to see a Mr James Diamond. My name is Diana and I'm the assistant for Mr Kersov, head of cleaning services at Manchester airport.*' Della's voice was pure smoke and sex.

'That is amazing,' laughed Connie. 'You didn't really ring up and make a false appointment though, did you?'

'Oh you have no idea how many hand grenades

I've pulled the pins out of which are set to go off this week, Connie,' said Della, noticing Connie's sunflower picture on the wall out of the corner of her eye. *Be like the Sunflower* . . . She could give those giant plants lessons in bravery and boldness with what she'd implemented since Friday.

Ivanka sat at Della's desk trying it for size and finding that it fitted her very well. She was alone in the office and imagining what life would be like in just over two weeks' time, when she could finally call this her kingdom, when she was free to announce to the world that Diamond Shine was a company run by herself and her fiancé. They didn't need two women in the office anyway, as she would prove beyond all doubt this week. She introduced a reception area to the office by placing two chairs and a small occasional table by the door and nudged the desks into a slightly different formation to mark her stamp on the space. Then she pulled a *Women by Women* magazine out of her bag along with a bottle of spring water and a sugar and cinnamon pretzel. There was no point in looking industrious when there was no one else in the office to impress, so she busied herself reading about reality star Kasey Queen and her fourth renewal of her wedding vows in two years of marriage. Ivanka couldn't decide whether she and Jimmy should get married in Las Vegas, the Bahamas or Venice, but she could have a new wedding gown and a different destination every year if Jimmy agreed to an annual renewal of their nuptials.

There was a knock on the door at eleven precisely. Ivanka grudgingly put the magazine away and opened the door to a small man with thinning hair wearing a trenchcoat and carrying an old battered briefcase with a noticeably wide gusset. If there was a room full of people and one had to guess which man was Roy Frog, he would have been picked out immediately. Roy Frog had large bulging eyes and a thin straight line of mouth which looked long enough to post a letter through.

'Roy Frog, here for a meeting with Jimmy Diamond at eleven,' he said, in a voice gruff from years of cigarette smoking.

'Oh, come in, Mr Frog,' said Ivanka politely. *Mój Boże*, was it that time already? So where was Jimmy then? 'Please take a seat here. Can I please get you some refreshment?'

'I'll have a tea, very strong, milk and two sugars please,' he replied, sitting down in 'reception' and picking up the *Daily Trumpet* from the table.

'I will make you tea whilst you wait,' said Ivanka. 'I am sure that Jimmy is on his way.'

Ivanka went into the kitchen area and switched on the kettle. The teabag tin was empty and strangely there was no jar of coffee either. Nor was there any milk in the fridge. She would have to go to the shop at the entrance of the estate, which was a nuisance.

'Please wait here, Mr Frog. I am just going out to get some tea,' she said.

'I'll have a coffee instead.'

Ivanka gave him a painful smile. 'I need to buy coffee too.'

'Oh.' Roy Frog wasn't very impressed. Not only was there no Jimmy Diamond, but there wasn't even a cuppa to be had whilst he waited. It gave him too clear an indication of how he was regarded.

'Are you good to stay here alone?' Ivanka asked.

'Yes, I suppose I'll be all right,' he said flatly.

Ivanka chuntered to herself all the way to the shop. How come there was no coffee or tea in the cupboard? There was always a plentiful supply of it. She bought a box of teabags, a jar of coffee, a two pint container of milk, a packet of biscuits and asked for a receipt so she could claim the money back. She walked into the office to find Roy Frog passing time by examining the cleaning supplies on the shelves.

'Let me guess, Des's Discount Warehouse?' he said to Ivanka with a smirk. 'Not even I use that crap. You never know what's in it.'

If Della had been there she would have been cheering because she would never have been able to plan this better.

'We like it,' said Ivanka firmly but with a smile, closing the cabinet doors. 'Please take a seat and I will refresh you.'

Nosey *sukinsyn*, thought a narked Ivanka as she

438

prodded a teabag in a mug so that Roy Frog could have the strong brew he had asked for. She heard the door open and let loose a sigh of relief. Jimmy had arrived for his meeting, thank goodness. But when she walked through with the drink and a plate of biscuits, it was to find Meg, Ava, Wenda and Val carrying empty supermarket bags-for-life.

'We've come for supplies,' said Ava, bristling at the sight of Ivanka. The feeling of dislike between Ivanka and the girls was mutual. The girls thought Ivanka was up her own arse, Ivanka thought that they belonged to an underclass.

'Okay,' said Ivanka. 'But please be quiet, there is a visitor waiting to see Jimmy.'

Ava pretended to zip up her mouth.

'Maybe you would prefer to wait in Jimmy's office,' said Ivanka, hoping to spare Roy Frog the sight of Meg's enormous backside poking out of the store cupboard. She led him through and set the mug and biscuits in front of him, closing the door behind him so she could ring Jimmy and find out where the hell he was. Except that she couldn't ring Jimmy whilst the girls were in the office because everyone knew he didn't have a mobile phone. There was nothing for it but to try and ring him on his secret mobile from outside, so she slipped out of the door and down the stairs. Her call went straight through to voicemail. She tried again and the same thing happened. Ivanka left a message. 'Jimmy, where are you? Roy Frog has an eleven o'clock meeting with you and you are not here. Please ring the office.'

She met the girls with their bags full on her way back up.

'Should you be leaving the office unattended with a stranger in?' Meg asked her.

'You just clean and leave the office to me,' snapped Ivanka, striding past them and ignoring the amused '*oooh*'s behind her. They needed some more staff, she decided. Women who respected her and knew their place. She would make sure she set some on this week.

'What sort of hand grenades?' asked Connie.

'Well,' Della began with relish, 'Ivanka had pencilled Roy Frog in for an eleven o'clock meeting. I might have accidentally erased a digit so it reads as if Roy Frog is actually arriving at one. And then I might have booked a meeting at eleven thirty with a firm in Worksop. I know that whenever Jimmy has to go to that area, he likes me to ensure it's in the late morning so he can go straight from home to Sizzles, which is a café on the edge of the town, where he likes to read the newspaper at leisure and have a grill special with a full cafetiere of coffee before he engages in any business talk.'

'Blimey, you do know him well,' said Connie.

'I gave him a typed-up list of this week's appointments on Friday, as I always do. His face lit up with joy when he saw that he had a Monday

440

morning meeting in Worksop. "I suppose you'll be going to Sizzles," I said. "That will fortify you for your afternoon meeting with Roy Frog."' Della grinned. 'I only wish that I could do something to stop Ivanka phoning him on that mobile that no one is supposed to know he has, and telling him that Roy Frog is in his office at eleven. The chances are that they'll just reschedule the meeting and no harm will be done. But as a contingency plan I did throw all the tea and coffee away.'

Connie tilted her head in a puzzled way. 'I don't understand what you mean.'

'Well, Ivanka only drinks water. I'm hoping that she didn't realise there was no tea or coffee until she came to make one for Roy Frog. So she will have had to go to the shop to buy some, leaving Roy Frog alone in the office.'

Connie was still not with her.

'And what would he do in the office?'

'I don't know,' smiled Della, throwing up her hands. 'But maybe somebody else did something in the office and he gets the blame for it.'

'Like what?' Connie stifled a giggle.

'Put dye and bleach in bottles of products, for instance . . .'

'Oh Della, you didn't.'

'Of course not,' said Della, sipping from her mug. 'As if I would do anything as destructive as that.'

CHAPTER 72

After his second cup of strong tea, numerous glances at his watch and a lot of heavy sighs, Roy Frog got up from the chair in Jimmy's office and marched through to Ivanka.

'Where is he?' he said. 'I've been waiting over forty minutes now.'

'Mr Frog, I have been trying to get hold of Jimmy, but I can't. Please let me make you another tea,' said Ivanka, attempting to smooth things over. She was furious with Jimmy for not picking up his phone. She had engineered this meeting with Roy Frog herself after persuading Jimmy that the time was now ripe for negotiation, so she couldn't work out what had gone wrong.

'I don't want another tea, thank you,' said Roy Frog, unable to keep the growl out of his voice.

'I don't understand what has happened,' said Ivanka.

'I do. He's taking the mick,' said Roy Frog. 'First he won't take my calls, then he summons me here but doesn't bother turning up himself. He's on a bloody power-trip, isn't he?'

'I assure you, Mr Fr—'

Roy Frog buttoned up his coat with angry fingers.

'I'm off. And you can tell Jimmy Diamond that he'll come crawling to me over hot coals before I'll agree to another meeting with him.'

'Please, I can try and ring again . . .'

'Sorry, Miss, I've had enough of being treated like a pillock for one day.' Roy Frog charged past Ivanka.

The office phone rang.

Ivanka brightened. 'Please wait. That will be him now.' She dived to the phone and pressed the speakerphone button gambling that it would be Jimmy, just in time to rescue the situation. 'Hello, Jimmy.'

'Hello, this is Harris Marketing Research, could we have a few moments of your time to answer some questions which may benefit your business.'

Ivanka snatched the phone up and shouted impatiently into it. 'Go away, you stupid people.' She turned back to Roy Frog. 'Let us reschedule a meeting at your convenience, Mr Harris, I mean Mr Frog. What do you think?'

'I think you should shove your rescheduled meeting up your Harris,' he said and slammed the door behind him.

Within five minutes of Roy Frog's bat-out-of-hell exit from the car park, Jimmy rang the office.

'Where have you been?' screamed Ivanka down the mouthpiece. 'You've missed your appointment with Roy Frog.'

'Where I've been is on a sodding wild-goose chase,' barked Jimmy. 'Who the hell took the fucking booking for Mr Kersov in Worksop?'

'I don't know. It does not ring any bells with me. It must have been Della,' fibbed Ivanka.

'A Mr Nick Kersov. A joke name for a frigging joke company. I've been driving around Worksop for far longer than I care to imagine. In fact I never want to see the sodding place again for as long as I live. And what are you talking about? Roy Frog isn't booked in until this afternoon.'

'You should have been here at eleven for a meeting with him,' Ivanka matched him for volume.

'Della's list says one. She wouldn't have got it wrong.'

'And I would?' Ivanka was incensed. She stomped through to his office and threw open his desk diary. 'I am looking at your diary now and it says meeting with Roy Frog at . . . wait a minute, how could this have happened?'

'It says one, doesn't it? You've written it down wrong, haven't you?' Jimmy grumbled something nasty and dark under his breath.

'Why didn't you pick up your mobile?' Ivanka yelled. 'Then you might have known he was here.'

'I don't go into Sizzles with a mobile. I go into Sizzles to have peace and quiet.' Even from you, said Jimmy to himself. In fact especially from you at the moment with your nagging about Connie and Della and flaming wedding talk.

'What is Sizzles? What are you talking about?'

'Look, I'm driving back. I'll see you in about an hour.'

'I will . . .' But she was talking to thin air because Jimmy had put his mobile down and, as she found when she tried to ring it back, had switched it off.

'Nick Kersov? Knickers off?' Connie wiped the tears of laughter away from her eyes.

'Oh, there's more to come. I had a very very enjoyable time thinking of potential clients. I will be ringing Ivanka later to book meetings with other people for Jimmy.' And she treated Connie to her best Fenella Fielding silky-voiced PA.

'That is amazing. It doesn't sound anything like you.'

Della was grinning and Connie thought what a very different face she had when she smiled. Della had lovely brown eyes and her lips, in laughter, looked plumper than when they were set in her usual slightly ruched line.

'You should get some of those rimless glasses, Della,' said Connie. 'You need to show your eyes off.'

'They're expensive though, aren't they?' said Della. 'You have to buy toughened glass.'

'When was the last time you spent anything on yourself? You're like me, I reckon, we don't think we're worth it. Well we are, and we should realise that.'

Della took the glasses off her head to inspect

them. She'd had them for so long, she never noticed them any more and she didn't tend to look in a lot of mirrors. They were pure Olive from *On the Buses* frames.

'I'm hardly a style queen. You can tell me to sod off,' said Connie, watching Della scrutinise them.

Della didn't answer for a few moments, then gave Connie a soft smile and said, 'Thank you.'

'What for?' said Connie.

'For trusting me. And for not judging me too harshly.'

It was irony heaped on irony that Della felt that the wife of the man she was in love with would be the first person not to let her down.

CHAPTER 73

Jimmy didn't so much walk into the office as barge into it like a human battering ram and, not realising they had a new 'reception area', nearly went flying over the coffee table. They'd only been without Della for one morning and the place was in chaos.

'Get Roy Frog on the line,' roared Jimmy, kicking the table against the wall. 'And who put this bloody furniture here?' Ivanka jumped to the phone. She was feeling uncharacteristically cowed after finding the mistake in the diary. She couldn't believe she had written it down incorrectly and was really annoyed with herself. It wasn't on her radar that there had been skulduggery afoot from her office manageress.

'His secretary says he is playing golf and will pass on the message,' said Ivanka, putting the phone back down and wincing at having to deliver that news.

Jimmy tightened his lips. Roy was no more at golf than he was presently driving a tractor through a field of turnips. Frog was teaching him a lesson and Jimmy was furious that he had been handed the ammunition gift-wrapped in order to do that.

'You did look after him all right when he was here?' he asked Ivanka.

'Yes, of course. Although Della did not tell me that we had no tea or coffee so when I came to make him refreshment I had to go to the shop and buy some. But I also buy nice biscuits whilst I am there.' She allowed herself a self-satisfied smile knowing she had won some brownie points there. And plunged perfect Della right in the crap.

'Okay,' Jimmy conceded and stepped into his office, then as quickly, he was back out of it again. He circled his finger in the air. 'Rewind that conversation, will you? Just for my own peace of mind, tell me that you meant you went to the shop before Roy Frog arrived.'

'No,' Ivanka tutted. 'How could I have seen that there was no tea or coffee in the cupboard until I come to make it for him? I don't drink it so how would I know?'

Jimmy cleared his throat. 'So, let me get this right, you left him here whilst you went off to the shop, did you?' His voice was deceptively calm and at total odds with the rage building inside him.

'Of course. I could not exactly ask him to go with me, could I?'

Jimmy rubbed his forehead and laughed, not a pleasant laugh, but one of total exasperation.

'You left my major business rival in my office alone with access to all my files, my diary, my contacts, everything? Is that what you're saying?'

Ivanka was now realising what she had done. And she had dropped herself in it too deep to get out of it. But still she tried.

'For five minutes only. At most.'

'Usain Bolt couldn't have got to the shop and back in five minutes, Ivanka. And you certainly couldn't because you take half an hour to walk to the bloody bog and back.'

Ivanka's mouth puckered into a tight furious pout. 'What do you mean? Are you calling me fat?'

'Fat?' exclaimed Jimmy. 'When did I say you were fat?'

'You want me to be fat like your wife – is that it, Jimmy?' shouted Ivanka.

Jimmy spun. 'Oy, don't you dare bring Connie into this. She's a good woman.'

Ivanka's mouth fell open into a long, indignant oval and her black, stencilled eyebrows rose so high, they almost touched her hairline. 'You say to me that your wife is a good woman? And yet you have cheated on her all your marriage and you are leaving her next week for me?'

Jimmy shook his finger at her as he attempted to answer, but all the words he wanted to say crowded together in his mouth and wouldn't come out because deep down he knew that Ivanka was right and he would have been a first-class hypocrite to argue with her. Which, though it had never stopped him in the past, was doing so now.

'Just put the bloody kettle on,' he said, went into his office and shut the door emphatically behind him.

CHAPTER 74

It was a new day. Jimmy had to write off the fiasco of yesterday or he would have gone insane. He walked into his office, late morning, determined that today would be better. Della wasn't back, but he supposed he'd have to treat her absence as a trial run because in nine days' time, she wouldn't be working there at all. What madness had made him agree to Ivanka's terms? Della's non-attendance was just wrong, and made him feel as if he was about to climb the north face of the Eiger without a safety rope.

Jimmy opened up his diary whilst sipping the very good coffee which Ivanka had just made for him. He was quietly impressed by the number of appointments which she had booked in this week. Tomorrow morning he was seeing a Mrs Blige at the other side of Sheffield. Apparently, Ivanka told him, Mrs Blige had heard a lot about Diamond Shine's reputation and that is why she wanted Jimmy's girls to work in the offices she owned. Then in the afternoon, he had a meeting with a Major who was enquiring about contracting a team to clean ten British Legion clubs in the county. The day after that, Thursday afternoon, he was to hook up with the head of maintenance in Asda HQ in Leeds and Friday was equally full with another two clients who wanted to talk shop with him. He hadn't been this busy ever. He had to hand it to Ivanka, today she was shining in her position as office manageress. Yesterday's debacle with Roy Frog, who still hadn't rung back, was obviously just a rogue blip. Plus they'd just had a snog and a bit of a grope in the new reception area which made everything seem a little better.

He was just calculating how much richer he could be every month if he were to successfully secure all the business possibilities that Ivanka had sourced for him when his ear picked up on a conversation happening between his lover and someone on the phone.

'It's gone green? What do you mean it's gone green? . . . Oh, red. Well, why has it gone red then? . . . She isn't here, you will have to deal with me.'

'What's going on?' Jimmy shouted through.

'It's Wenda. She has ruined Mr Red's carpet with some gree . . . I mean she has ruined Mr Green's carpet with some red dye.'

Wenda's voice squealed out of the earpiece, giving the impression that the phone was possessed.

'Put her on speaker,' said Jimmy.

Ivanka pressed the appropriate button.

'Wenda, it's Jimmy, what's up?'

'Where's Della?' asked Wenda.

'She isn't here,' snapped Ivanka. 'I have told you.'

'I've just washed Mr Green's white Tibetan lamb rug with red dye,' said Wenda in a clipped tone.

'What the fuck did you do that for?' groaned Jimmy.

'I didn't bloody mean to,' screeched Wenda. 'The bloody carpet cleaner had green . . . I mean red dye in it.'

'Why aren't you using the company products?' Ivanka said.

'I was. That Des's Discount stuff. I picked it up yesterday, you saw me load it into my bag. He's gone, as the ancient Greeks used to say, frigging apeshit. He was bloody purple when I left.'

'Who? Mr White?' asked Ivanka.

'There isn't a sodding Mr White.' Wenda was screaming now. 'The rug was white until it went red. Mr Green is purple.'

'Oh for fuck's sake,' said Jimmy, pushing his hand through his hair.

'I will ring Des's Discount Stores and complain,' said Ivanka, making a solid executive decision. 'Mr Green wants a new white rug.'

'How much is that going to cost?' asked Jimmy, chewing on his lip as he calculated which would be best – forking out for a new rug or claiming on his insurance and seeing his premium rise at renewal time.

'He said it was five hundred and odd quid. He's getting hold of the receipt for me to give to you.'

'How much?' Jimmy yelled. 'What sort of prat spends that on a rug?'

'It's only small an' all,' said Wenda, which didn't help Jimmy's mood one bit.

'Oh Della, how dare you pick this week to be ill,' Jimmy raged into the air, and then wished he hadn't because he knew that would send Ivanka into a massive sulk. 'Okay, Wenda,' he said with a resigned sigh. 'Just tell him to send in the receipt. We'll get it back from Des or I'll be making his rug red when I cut his balls off.'

No sooner had that call ended than Ava rang.

'Where's Della?' she asked, sending Ivanka's pout into spasm. 'That bloody stain remover I picked up yesterday has bleached Mrs Mularkey's handcrafted curtains. She's gone mental.'

'Am I really hearing this?' cried Jimmy, throwing his hands up to the heavens. 'Or did I eat too much cheese last night and I'm having a nightmare?'

Jimmy left Ivanka on the pretext of needing to see Pookie Barnes, but in reality, he wanted to sit in a pub in nearby Elsecar, have a toasted sandwich, half a Guinness, read the paper and get away from the office and from bleach, Ivanka's sulky face and anything to do with the colours green, red, white and purple.

You won't be able to do this after next week, Jimbo, said a snidey little voice in his head. *You'll have to be totally accountable for your whereabouts and won't be able to sneak off ANYWHERE.*

A woman walked past him on the way to the toilet and smiled politely at him. She had long shiny brown hair, a waist he could have circled with his hands and lips as red as the suit she wore. This time last year he would have been in there like Flynn. He'd always had the gift of the gab, without appearing slimy like some men did. The secret was in not trying too hard, in being friendly rather than flirty. He was so tempted to see if the old magic was there and talk to the woman as she was returning to the table full of friends with whom she was sitting, but he kept his eyes on his newspaper instead.

'Oops, nearly tripped there. That would have been embarrassing.'

He raised his head to find the woman had been speaking to him. She'd opened up the flirting lines of engagement. So, there was life in the old – well not really even middle-aged actually – dog yet but he'd had his wings clipped and was no longer allowed to fly. He had to remain in a coop of his making, with his young, fresh chick. But how green those fields in the distance were starting to look.

'Where have you been, Jimmy?' Ivanka greeted him with furious aggression when he returned to the office. 'I can smell beer. You have been drinking whilst I have been running around like a fly with a blue-coloured arse.'

'I had a half with Pookie Barnes. He's a drinker,

he likes to do business in an alehouse,' returned Jimmy, wishing he'd stayed out.

'Why didn't you answer your mobile? Della is not here, there is no reason to hide it.'

'I forgot to bring it,' he lied. In truth it was in his pocket but switched off. 'Anyway, what's up now?'

'Another carpet has been dyed. Clothes have been washed with bleach and oil. I have rung Des and he said that no one else has complained and so it is our problem. He says that our stock has been timpered with . . . is that a word – *timpered*?'

'Tampered,' Jimmy corrected her. 'That's bollocks, give me the phone. Who the hell would tamper with our stock? Why would they tamper with our . . .'

Jimmy, who had been about to start pressing numbers on the keypad, put down the phone slowly and then he looked straight at Ivanka.

'Did Roy Frog go anywhere near the stock cupboard yesterday?'

Ivanka weighed up the pros and cons of admitting that Roy Frog had been snooping around. It didn't look good for her to admit that she had left him alone long enough to doctor their bottles. She might as well have answered him truthfully though because the long pause before she opened her mouth told Jimmy all he needed to know.

'Jesus Christ,' he said. 'Ivankaaa!'

'I didn't know that he would do this,' bawled

Ivanka. 'I only left him alone for fifteen minutes maximum . . .'

'You said five yesterday.'

'He was only looking in the cupboard. I stopped him. I closed it . . .' She remembered the size of his briefcase. It could easily have carried lots of contaminating liquids.

'What are you thinking?'

Ivanka winced. 'He had a huge bag with him.'

'Jesus, Mary, Joseph, Jason and the Argonauts! And was this before or after Wenda and that lot came in?'

'Before. It was before.'

Jimmy's eyes shuttered down and that small action communicated a huge amount of despair.

'Roy frigging Frog,' he said in a quiet, nasty whisper, then he opened up his eyes and turned to Ivanka. 'If that wanker returns my call, tell him I'm playing golf. Connie was right. I should have played much harder to get. You' – and he jabbed his finger furiously in Ivanka's direction – 'were totally wrong.'

Then Jimmy went into his office, not caring if Ivanka got the hump that he'd mentioned his far wiser wife. He calmed his nerves down with a few quid on the nags via the BET-YER-ASS internet site. He lost seventy pounds and, not for the first time recently, concluded that he was an expert at backing the wrong horses.

CHAPTER 75

Della's house was exactly how Connie had imagined it: a neat little house on a neat little estate, snow-white lace curtains at the downstairs windows, neutral beigey-mushroom ones upstairs. They were meeting here today to bring each other up to speed. There were only nine days now until Lent ended and so much to do before then. And each had something important they wanted to say to the other.

'Come in,' said Della, who answered the ding-dong doorbell chime almost immediately. She had her hair loose from its usual tight bun: it hung thick and shiny down her back and she was wearing trousers and a bright coloured top rather than her customary dark two-piece suits. She looked years younger at leisure than she did in the office.

Connie stepped into a super-clean hallway with a polished wooden parquet floor. There were photos of a black pug all over the walls.

'How are you feeling? Is your bug any better?' she asked, with a grin.

'Alas no,' replied Della. 'I rang into work this

morning with a very raspy throat. Come through. Kettle's on.' She beckoned Connie forwards into the kitchen.

'Have you got a dog then?' Connie thumbed back at the pictures.

'Not any more. When Bobby died eight years ago, I didn't think I could go through losing another one. It broke my heart.'

'I've never had a dog,' Connie said. 'I'd like a cat. I shall have one when I move.'

'So you won't stay in the house?' Della invited Connie to sit down at her kitchen table. There were two chairs and Connie wondered if anyone else had ever eaten at it with Della.

'No. I want a totally fresh start. Somewhere that Jane and the baby will stay sometimes, I hope.'

'What did Jimmy say about the prospect of being a granddad?'

'Not a lot,' huffed Connie. 'He thinks she's too young. Jane and he don't speak, did you know that?'

'He didn't talk about you or Jane much at all,' replied Della. And she would have been the first to admit that she hadn't wanted to hear anything about them, either.

'He was never there for her. If only I'd known that he was absent from her life so much because . . .' Connie puffed out her cheeks to calm herself.

'It was very mischievous of you coming into the office to drop the granddad news to Ivanka,' said Della, putting a mug of tea down in front of Connie.

'I had no idea how I'd feel when I saw her,' said Connie. 'I didn't know what I'd say. The only thing I did plan in advance was how I'd appear to her, at my drabbest. Because the next time she sees me, I'll look very different, I can assure you.'

'I did wonder if that was the case,' smiled Della, suddenly flooded with admiration for the little woman. 'So how *did* you feel when you met her?'

'Angry, really angry,' replied Connie. 'At least at first. I had to take a moment and remind myself though who I really should have been saving my anger for. It wasn't Ivanka who was an emotionally unavailable father to my daughter, who left me alone when I needed him most in my life . . .'

'You're being very strong, Connie,' said Della. 'I don't know how you're managing it.'

'I have my moments,' said Connie, noticing the sunflower pattern on the cup. It was as if they were everywhere, reminding her of what she had to become. 'Sometimes, from nowhere, it's as if a wave of sadness overtakes me and I have to fight it off. Luckily I have so many things I can focus on to make me feel angry and up rather than depressed and down.'

'I think you're marvellous, Connie,' said Della, surprising herself as much as Connie, because she hadn't been aware she was going to say that. 'I'm sorry. I hope you don't think I'm being patronising. It wasn't meant that way.'

Connie laughed a little. 'I don't feel marvellous, Della. I feel scared and out of my depth. But I also know that I have to see this through. I won't let him throw me away like a piece of rubbish.'

'You must have had good times,' Della said softly, sipping from one of the two new mugs she had bought at the weekend. She liked the sunflower emblem, it reminded her of the poem on the wall of the Lady Muck office.

'I fell in love with Jimmy Diamond on the spot,' said Connie, staring beyond Della, seeing the young Jimmy standing there for a moment. We were young and he was a dish. I couldn't believe my luck that he even looked in my direction. We were married within months, it was all too fast.' Connie looked straight into Della's eyes. 'I was pregnant.'

'Pregnant?' Della did her maths. She knew that Connie and Jimmy had been married for twenty-four years, but Jane was only twenty-two.

'Max. He was still-born. He was perfect, beautiful. He had wisps of white-blond hair and long black eyelashes but his little lungs didn't draw one single breath.'

'Oh Connie, I'm so sorry.' Della's fingers came out and rested on Connie's hand.

'He had an affair in the madness of the months that followed. I was mad with grief, I didn't want to live. It was all such a mess. I forgave him and he swore that he would never do anything like that again. I believed him, of course, because I

461

desperately wanted to. Then Jane came along. She was the baby that healed us, or so I thought. I was his "best girl" again.'

Della thought of Jimmy grinning at her, calling her his best girl and she felt a stirring of nausea in her stomach. She wanted to grind his smiling, handsome face into the dirt as much for this gentle woman sitting at her kitchen table as she did for herself.

'Can I be honest with you, Della? When we first started all this, my only thought was to crush Diamond Shine using anyone and anything I could and then walk away from it all, but that isn't the case any more,' said Connie, with real determination in her voice. 'I want to make Lady Muck a success.'

'And can *I* be honest with *you*? I wanted you to crush Diamond Shine, put Jimmy in the gutter and then I'd walk away from both him and you. Now, well . . . I want to put some money into the business,' said Della. 'How do you feel about having a partner? If Hilda and the rest don't come after all I've done now, they never will, but I'm prepared to risk that they'll be joining us very shortly.'

Connie's head snapped up. 'Really?'

Della smiled. 'Really. Jimmy has been too reliant on me for too long and he's become lazy. And I've fed Ivanka too much duff information. I know her, she will want to make a major impact this week whilst I'm away, which will include setting on

462

cleaners who don't know she's my office junior and so will accept her as the boss. I can bet you she has commandeered my desk, made physical changes to the office to put her imprint on it and I can guarantee there will be absolute chaos in my absence.'

'And what about Cleancheap?'

'That's the one huge fat fly in the ointment. We've delayed the union of Cleancheap and Diamond Shine as long as we can but it's bound to happen. I can't see Roy Frog choosing insolvency over selling even to his worst enemy. He'll have to swallow his pride in the end and pick the devil rather than the deep blue sea.' Della lifted her shoulders and dropped them again. 'But I have to believe that we could survive the competition when that day happens, which we could do if the present Diamond Shine girls defect because they've got brilliant reputations.'

'Does Roy Frog want a lot of money for Cleancheap?' asked Connie.

'Don't even start thinking about it,' Della replied, holding up her hand to warn against venturing down that road. 'Yes he does, a ridiculous amount, which I most certainly don't have and I'm guessing you don't have much left of your mother's inheritance from what you've said in the past. Time wouldn't be on our side anyway for building up a business case and applying for a bank loan. I've already considered it. No, the only option we have is to secure ourselves to the mast of Lady Muck and hope she survives the force twelve gale which is currently featuring on the horizon. I have no other place to go.'

'Neither do I,' laughed Connie.

'So – partners then?'

'I think I'd better agree,' said Connie. 'After all you've told me about your dirty tricks, I daren't be on the wrong side of you.'

They clinked their mugs together. 'So, here's to us then, partner,' said Della. She suspected that Jimmy Diamond had had too much luck in life to go down because of the plotting of two women whom he had managed to really piss off; but there was no other way for either of them except to head towards that scary horizon and hope that Jimmy wouldn't crush them with his new super-massive company, even though they knew the likelihood was that he would try – and enjoy doing it.

Cheryl wasn't working that afternoon because she had an appointment with Mr Fairbanks and two gentlemen from Christie's auction house who were coming up to see her from London. The meeting was going to be held in Mr Fairbanks' house; he had been storing Edith's pictures in his private vault.

'I'm nervous,' said Cheryl, bringing in two cups of tea which rattled in their saucers.

'I think we all are,' said Mr Fairbanks. 'Is that a car I hear?'

Cheryl shot to the window and saw a swanky black Mercedes pull into the drive.

'Oh God, they're here,' she said, wiping her hands down her best skirt.

'I'll answer the door, Cheryl. Take a seat, dear, before you fall,' said Mr Fairbanks.

Cheryl sat down only to have to get up again moments later to shake the hands of Mr Elton and Mr Vamplew, two gentlemen who looked as if they came from a different world, one where nothing in it cost less than a million pounds.

Cheryl poured them a cup of tea each and handed it over, hoping she wouldn't spill it over their expensive-looking suit trousers.

'What an amazing story,' said Mr Elton, in very rounded vowels. 'I nearly dropped the phone when I heard what you might have in your possession.'

'I still can't believe any of it,' said Cheryl, hoping she didn't sound too common to them.

'I want to believe it all,' said Mr Vamplew, who was the elder of the two. 'Lovely tea, thank you, Miss Parker. Yorkshire Tea, I hope.' And he smiled at Cheryl and she knew he was trying to put her at ease.

'Yes, it's Yorkshire Tea,' she smiled back. 'So you've heard of Percy Lake, then?'

'Oh yes.' The two Christie's gentlemen shared a knowing glance. 'He belongs to the art under-world. It's amazing how someone of his skill has never come to public attention. Then again, one might argue that part of his talent was the ability to remain invisible.'

Still Cheryl couldn't believe that she might own an original piece of Van Gogh's work. Even sitting with two men who had driven up from London especially to view it. Part of her was expecting a *Candid Camera* crew to appear from behind the curtain.

'May we see the pieces?' asked Mr Vamplew.

'Of course, of course.' Mr Fairbanks got up from the chair. 'Gentlemen, follow me.'

He had a secure room next to his study with a digital eight-figure combination lock on it.

Both gentlemen took gloves out of their pockets as Mr Fairbanks pointed them in the direction of the paintings and sketches. Mr Elton made straight for the *Painter on the Road to Tarascon*. He picked it up and stared hard at it with eyes that didn't want to blink.

'It's amazing,' he said.

'I don't understand though,' said Cheryl. 'How could Percy have got near to the original for long enough to copy it?'

'Percy Lake had a perfect photographic memory,' explained Mr Elton.

'Edith, his granddaughter, told me that too,' agreed Mr Fairbanks. 'She said he only had to look at a painting once and could recreate it perfectly.'

'Never,' said Cheryl. 'Surely not?'

'Here, you are dealing with genius,' Mr Elton kindly clarified. 'Even he wouldn't have understood how he did what he did. It was effortless, inherent, natural to his make-up. It's unbelievable.'

'And these are the sketches?' Mr Vamplew lifted the one signed 'Vincent' from its place on a shelf and he sighed.

'It is signed,' he said quietly to Mr Elton. He took a small gold loupe from his pocket and lifted it to his eye, then he handed both the sketch and the loupe to Mr Vamplew. Then they both turned their heads towards each other and smiled.

CHAPTER 76

As Connie drove up to Crow Edge, she thought – and not for the first time – that there was something *wrong* with the house, but she couldn't fathom out what it was. Something on the outside didn't fit with the inside. She stared at the frontage through her car windscreen but couldn't work it out, then she gave herself a mental slap for being as bad as everyone else in trying to invent a mystery about the place. Yes, it was old-fashioned and Mr Savant was slightly eccentric, but that was all that was amiss. She took her cleaning stuff out of the car and rang the bell. Mr Savant greeted her warmly at the door and she could once again smell alcoholic fumes on his breath, as she had done the previous week. He didn't look like a drinker, but then again, he didn't look like a man who ate a fridge full of cream buns every week. Connie got on with her job and tried not to a) let that awful *Pygmalion* music annoy her and b) think too much. She had forgotten how easy it could be to get sucked into the lives of clients.

★   ★   ★

'Hello, are you nipple clamp?'

That was what Jimmy heard through the door of his office. What the bloody hell was Ivanka ordering? He'd noticed she had a copy of *Fifty Shades of Grey* in her flat. He didn't mind a bit of playing but anything that involved the word 'clamp' sounded too painful.

'Yes, let us say eleven o'clock then, nipple. I look forward to it.' Then the phone went down.

Jimmy came out of his office, shaking an empty coffee cup. He didn't have to remind Della when to put the kettle on.

'What was all that about?' he asked.

'I am interviewing some potential cleaners,' she replied.

'A woman called nipple?' asked Jimmy incredulously.

'Nepal,' corrected Ivanka.

'Nepal Clamp? Jesus, don't people think when they name kids these days? Don't tell me she's got a brother called Ball.'

'I don't know,' said Ivanka, the joke flying over her head. She didn't really do jokes, though. Jimmy realised he had never seen Ivanka have a good old belly-laugh in all the time he'd known her.

'Don't you think you should wait until Della comes back before you set anyone . . .' Jimmy's voice dried up and he winced in anticipation of Ivanka's scowl.

'No, I don't think at all,' said Ivanka, eyes

narrowed, teeth drawn back over her lip, voice full of gravel. 'And you can make your own bloody tea.'

Connie walked from the kitchen into the sitting room and back again. Whatever was bugging her about the house was in this area, she was sure of it, but she could barely think above the racket of that music. Mr Savant was playing it louder than usual. Connie approached the chair where he sat looking out onto the garden to ask if she could turn it down a little but found him asleep. She called his name softly, but he was deep in slumber and an empty glass of brandy was set on the table at his side where the gramophone was. She wondered if she dare lift the needle off the record and give her ears some respite, because she couldn't see a volume button, but she would have to lean right over him to do it.

Mr Savant gave a snuffle which made her jump but he didn't awaken. Connie thought she would chance it. She leaned over as slowly as she could, raising up her arm so it didn't touch Mr Savant's shoulder and lifted off the bobbing needle. The silence was golden. For a few wonderful moments, the only sounds were the strong tick tick of the mantel clock and Mr Savant's gentle snoring. Then, she heard it.

'Hello . . .' tap-tap-tap.

Mr Savant snorted loudly and woke himself up. His eyes opened and settled on Connie standing

470

in the room, listening, trying to trace where the sound was coming from.

'Get out,' he said, throwing himself out of the chair. 'Get out. I want to be by myself.' He almost fell backwards when he turned to set the needle on the record again and performed the manoeuvre so roughly that an ear-splitting scratch ensued.

'Mr Sav—'

'Please just go,' he said, palm flat on his forehead as if drawing comfort from it. 'I don't want anyone in the house today. Not today.' He sank to the chair again, head in his hands, obviously distressed. Connie fought her natural reaction to go over to him. She didn't know him well enough to judge what he might do when upset and drunk.

Connie gathered her cleaning equipment together. She hadn't imagined that voice, she knew she hadn't. But it was no ghost.

Connie left the kitchen and went back into the sitting room and the answer to what was wrong with the house whispered against her brain but zoomed off before she could process it. Mr Savant was sitting in his chair, music blaring.

'I'm going, Mr Savant. I'll see you next week,' she called. He didn't answer. She noticed the brandy glass at the side of him had been refilled.

Connie went back to her car and stared at the house through her front window. *What is it that I'm missing?* she asked herself. She drew her eyes across from left to right, top to bottom: the two small attic windows with bars on them, the first-floor window standing proud on the corner, the etched window where the bathroom was, the two huge windows in Mr Savant's bedroom. Downstairs, the large bay window of the sitting room, the long window of the kitchen, a peep of the cellar windows below. Something was wrong but she still couldn't see it.

Nepal and Alaska Clamp had been born identical twins, although that would have been difficult to believe. Nepal was super-slim and pretty with long faded purple dreadlocks and piercings in her lips, eyebrows, ears and nose. She had streetwise wisdom in her huge blue eyes. Alaska had the same bright eyes, although hers seemed much smaller because they were in a much chubbier setting. She had a round body, round face with a frill of double chins, cropped short blonde hair and a set of teeth that wouldn't have looked out of place on a knacker-man's horse.

'So have you worked as cleaner before?' asked Ivanka, trying not to look as unnerved as she felt in the presence of these two young women. She couldn't believe that Della had considered them of a suitable standard to put at the top of the red stripey 'Priority list of potential cleaners' file.

'Oh yes,' said Nepal, with put-on politeness, an effect which might have been more convincing had she not been chewing gum quite so energetic-ally. 'We've always worked cash in hand before though.'

'Quite,' said Alaska, in a voice that suggested she gargled twice daily with grit.

Then the office door swung open, much to Ivanka's annoyance because whoever was opening it hadn't knocked. It was Hilda and Sandra with their Asda bags-for-life each full of cleaning products. Hilda's eyes landed on Nepal Clamp sitting in front of Ivanka's desk and her expression became instantly murderous.

'Well, well, well, look what the cat dragged in. If it isn't Nepal Clamp,' said Hilda. She turned to Ivanka and snapped, 'What the fuck are these two doing here?'

Even Sandra was taken back at Hilda using the f-word. She'd worked with her for eleven years and never heard the woman say anything more serious than a 'bugger'.

'Hello, Hilda. How's it going?' Nepal was smirking as her eyes returned the older woman's stare.

'None of your business how I am, you skanky little tart.'

Ivanka, who did not appreciate Queen Hilda storming into the office and undermining her, jumped right up onto her high horse.

'Excuse me, please, but do not interrupt my meeting. You can go and sit in reception until I am ready to speak to you.'

Hilda, who judged Ivanka to be a jumped-up little nobody, wasn't going to take that lying down.

'Where the hell is reception? Do you mean those two chairs by the door?' She gave a derisive laugh.

'And where's Della? I want to speak to the organ grinder, not the monkey.'

Ivanka could see Nepal's and Alaska's heads swinging between her and Hilda as if watching a grand slam at Wimbledon.

'Della is ill,' snarled Ivanka. 'So you can talk to me or nobody.'

Hilda lifted up the carrier bag of products, turned it upside down and tipped everything out on the floor.

'Okay then. Miss Pettigrew has now got red dye all over her beige Wilton, the Forresters' bedding has all been bleached and Mrs East-Sinclair has an indelibly stained Villeroy and Boch bog bowl.'

Sandra followed suit and tipped the products in her bag on top of Hilda's.

'Two sets of purple curtains and a green poodle that should be snow-white. Mrs McIlvenny is suing. Foofoo was supposed to be doing a dog show on Friday. I'm surprised she hasn't rung you.'

Ivanka kept a stony expression because she had turned the phone ringer volume to silent and at last count she had sixteen voice-mail messages to catch up with.

'And I don't know what you two are frigging laughing about,' spat Hilda at the Clamp sisters, who were as purple as Mrs McIlvenny's curtains with laughter.

'Hilda, how's your Anthony?' asked Nepal, impish glint in her innocent blue eyes.

'You evil little cow! He's all right, you'll be gutted to hear.' Hilda made a grab for the girl who had broken her grandson's heart so hard that it led him to take an overdose. And if that wasn't enough, Nepal also happened to be the granddaughter of the man who had been the partner of her sister for many abusive years. The Clamps were all scum in Hilda's eyes and there were years of pent-up buried rage waiting in her curled fists for any of them that crossed her path.

Sandra flung herself between Hilda and the still giggling Nepal. Ivanka stood and pointed to the door like Gloria Gaynor singing 'I Will Survive'.

'Get out,' she screamed at Hilda.

'Oy, don't you shout at her, you jumped-up little nowt,' yelled Sandra.

Ivanka had lost control, so there was only one way to save face now in front of the interviewees. 'You're sacked, both of you,' she said.

'Don't you worry yourself,' said Hilda, thumbing at the Clamps. 'I wouldn't work for anyone who employed shit like them. You wait until Della comes back. She'll have your arse on a spit.' She cast a last hateful glare at Nepal and picked up her plastic bag-for-life, which had cost 10p so she wasn't going to leave it.

Sandra followed Hilda out like her lady in waiting.

'And that goes for me an' all.' And she closed the door brutally behind them.

Ivanka sat down as gracefully as she could.

'Now, where were we?' she said, smiling sweetly. It was time for some new blood in Diamond Shine. Out with the old bags like Hilda and Sandra, and in with the new – like Nepal, Alaska and Lesley Clamp. And a welcome back to Mrs Ruth Fallis who, according to the notes in the red stripey file, had been unjustly sacked.

CHAPTER 77

The morning at Mr Savant's was still very much on Connie's mind as she turned into the drive of Box House. She was over an hour early, seeing as Mr Savant had asked her to leave, and she hoped Brandon wouldn't mind. If he did, she would get back in the car and have a sandwich in the Dick Turpin's Arms.

Connie rang the bell and was just about to push the key into the lock when Brandon opened the door. His eyes dropped to his watch.

'I'm early. Is that okay?' Connie asked. 'I can go if—'

'Not at all, come in, Marilyn,' said Brandon, inviting her in to a hallway that smelled of salty caramel. He noticed how she raised her nose and drew in the smell.

'I'm experimenting with birch sap syrup,' he said. 'It takes a hundred litres of sap to make one litre of syrup. But oh – the taste,' and he kissed the O that his finger and thumb formed. 'Come through, come through. I've got something to show you.'

She followed him into his kitchen.

'I was going to clean up a little before you came,' he said. 'Honest.'

Connie smiled. 'Don't you worry about it.'

'Here, here, look at this.' Brandon stood aside so she should see a tray of heart-shaped chocolates. 'Marilyn Smith, meet my Marilyn Monroes,' he said as proudly as a little boy showing his mother a pasta painting. 'And if I say so myself, they are flaming perfect. Greta Garbo is going to be birch sap syrup with a hint of salt, but Marilyn's summer pudding is the star of the box.'

Connie expected him to offer her a sample, and was surprised when he replaced the tray on the work surface.

'How come you're so early then?'

'Oh, one of my clients . . .' *How could she put it?* 'One of my clients . . . erm . . . didn't need me for . . . for the full . . . time.'

'Come on, what's the real story?' He tilted his head at her. 'You're a shockingly bad liar, Marilyn.'

Is that so, thought Connie.

'Okay, the gentleman I see before you is erm . . . a retired widower. He lives in a house that the other cleaners don't like to go to. They think it's haunted,' Connie began to explain, aware that she had Brandon's total attention. 'He's harmless, but a little odd.'

'In what way odd?'

Connie didn't feel comfortable going into too much detail. She had to value her client's privacy after all, but Brandon Locke was so easy to talk to and she really did wonder what his perspective on Mr Savant would be.

'He has a lot of cream buns in the fridge.'

Brandon burst out laughing and then immediately apologised.

'I'm so sorry, Marilyn. Do forgive me.'

'It's not just that,' went on Connie. 'He plays awful gramophone music very loudly and the last couple of times I've been he's obviously had several brandies.' She could tell that Brandon was trying his best not to look amused. She couldn't blame him. She was aware she was making Mr Savant sound like a Reeves and Mortimer sketch.

'He lives in what used to be an undertaker's house. The other cleaners have said they've heard a woman's voice in the wall. Today, I heard it for myself.'

'Really?'

'Yes. I turned the music off when he was asleep because it was driving me daft and that's when I heard a woman calling hello. It was very odd. Mr S . . . my client woke up and er . . . went a bit crazy. He asked me to leave, so I did and I was glad to because I was just a little bit wary of him today, which I never have been before. He might be a pensioner, but he's very fit and strong for his age. I can't help thinking about it though. There's something not right about . . .' She was saying too much and should stop.

'Where's the house?'

'On the back road from here to Penistone. It's called Crow Edge.'

'Not the creepy-looking house set back from the road, by any chance?'

'That's the one.'

'So you now think it's haunted too?'

'I don't know what to think,' said Connie, shaking her head. 'But I'm not scoffing so hard at the other women who thought they heard something – or someone – embedded in the wall now.'

Ivanka was looking very pleased with herself when Jimmy returned from his afternoon meeting. She had set on some new cleaners, sacked those old bags Hilda and Sandra and rung back all the people who had left messages complaining that their furnishings had been ruined. Rather cleverly, she thought, she had pretended to be ringing from the insurance department of Diamond Shine and advised them to claim on their household policies. A couple of doddery old farts had gone away to follow her advice, and the rest were going to check with their solicitors. But, for now, at least the problem had gone away.

Then Jimmy came in with a face like a beetroot with a blood pressure problem.

'Mrs Blige,' he spat. 'Sheila Blige. Another bloody person from another bloody company that doesn't exist.'

'What?' said Ivanka.

'Who spoke to "Mrs Blige" and made that appointment?' he asked as he threw his briefcase angrily onto a chair. It fell off, opened up and the contents spilled out which did nothing at all to help his mood.

'I did. Why, what is wrong?'

Jimmy swallowed down his temper and tried to keep calm.

'Did you check to make sure that she really did exist after the hassle I had with Mr Nick Kersov?'

Ivanka's brow creased in confusion. 'Why should I? Blige is not comedy name?'

'Sheila Blige? Are you kidding me?'

'The address was correct.'

'Yes, the address does exist, but there's no Sheila Blige working at Blige Office Spaces because two hundred and thirty-four Standmain Road is a derelict meat-canning factory.' Jimmy stormed into his office and grabbed his diary. 'And in an hour I'm supposed to be seeing, let me see now . . . oh yes, Major Robert Soul, aka *Major R. Soul*. Now what's the betting that he's a fake name as well?'

Ivanka turned the name over in her brain until she understood what he meant.

'And what's this?' Jimmy slapped his diary. 'Tomorrow meet with Asda – Mr Hunt. First name Mike by any chance?'

'No,' said Ivanka, affronted. 'Eric.'

Jimmy laughed, a dry, disbelieving rasp of a noise. 'Eric Hunt. Oh well, that's okay then. Jesus

Christ, just look at this – Miss Ann Jobb and Mrs Norma Zars on Friday. How can this happen? Who the frigging hell is ringing up and making these bookings?'

'Personal Assistants.'

'Male or female?'

'Both,' Ivanka lied. She didn't want Jimmy to think that she had been stupidly duped by one person making all the same calls.

'So you haven't rung any of these people up to make appointments, they've all contacted us?'

Ivanka sighed an affirmative. Now Jimmy would know that she hadn't worked half as hard as she had tried to convince him she had.

'Roy bloody Frog and his family again,' snarled Jimmy, kicking his briefcase so that it flew across the room; then he swung his arm around in a smooth arc and pointed at Ivanka. 'Don't dare ask me to fix up another meeting with him.' He raised his fists to the ceiling and cried out, 'Come back, Della, for pete's sake,' not caring that it would piss off Ivanka. He was looking forward to her sulking all afternoon and staying out of his way.

'Cheryl, are you all right?' asked Astrid, as they cleaned the empty offices of Dartley Carpets. 'You are so quiet today.'

Astrid's soft concerned voice was all it took for Cheryl to burst into tears. Astrid bounced over to her friend and pulled her into her silicone bosom.

'What on earth is wrong, little friend? Is something else putting his hands where he shouldn't?'

'No, no nothing like that,' said Cheryl, digging deep in her pocket for a tissue. 'It's good news for once. But my body hasn't a clue how to cope with it.'

'You sit down there,' Astrid commanded, pushing Cheryl onto a chair. 'I am making some tea and we will have five minutes rest and you can tell me vat is up.'

Cheryl did as she was told as Astrid busied behind her, humming to herself.

'There, now you tell Auntie Astrid vat is going on,' she said, depositing a mug into Cheryl's hands.

'I think I'm rich,' said Cheryl, tears from her leaf-green eyes running down her cheeks. 'Remember Edith who left me those paintings?' And Cheryl told her the whole story, about Brambles, Lance, Mr Fairbanks, the gentlemen from Christie's and Astrid listened patiently to every word. And when she had finished, Astrid leaned over and gave her a rib-crushing hug.

'There is no one in zis world that I would wish for luck more than you, Cheryl. What a wonderful story. Edith would be so happy for you.' Then Astrid had a moment of sudden realisation. 'What are you doing cleaning an empty office when you could be a millionaire?'

'I don't know anything else, Astrid.' said Cheryl. 'I have nowhere else to go.'

CHAPTER 78

'Are you still okay for next Tuesday?' asked Brandon as Connie put on her coat to go. 'The cheese and chocolate evening?' His eyes twinkled impishly.

'I am. What time would you like me here?' Connie grinned back.

'Seven. P.M. that is, not the morning. My family are coming and a few old friends, business contacts, the press. Helena and Dominic, of course. Possibly Helena's sister who tends to trail along to events with her – Tana.'

Oh God, not another pair of belligerent eyes burning into the back of her neck, thought Connie.

'I was hoping Helena had forgotten but she rang on Sunday asking for a reminder of the time. She'd withheld her number and I was expecting a call so I risked picking up. She knows I'm avoiding her and she's put two and two together and presumes I'm doing that because there's a woman on the scene. It's all getting a bit out of control, to be honest. Sorry, I'm burdening you with detail.' Brandon held up his hands. 'You're too easy to talk to, Marilyn.'

'Well, that's a nice compliment,' Connie said shyly, trying not to look up into his big brown eyes.

Brandon picked up the tray from behind him. 'Please try a Marilyn, Marilyn. They're for you. Think of something nice when you eat it. Think of a humble chocolatier who has spent days trying to make it perfect.'

Connie gulped down the immediate no which rose within her. It would be ridiculous of her to refuse.

'Okay.'

'Close your eyes and open your mouth.'

She shuttered down her eyelids and parted her lips. Moments later she felt a block bump gently against her teeth. *Here goes.* Oh, she hoped she didn't vomit all over Brandon's freshly mopped tiles. She fought back visions of Jimmy with huge beribboned boxes as her tongue brushed against the chocolate and alerted her brain to its presence in her mouth. She bit down, through the outer chocolate coat, and the inner shell which broke beautifully against her teeth and she thought of Brandon telling her how cocoa butter gave the chocolate gloss and snap. She thought of her Auntie Marilyn with her huge red-slicked smile and her homemade summer puddings and as her taste-buds met the sweet centre, she thought of a chocolatier called Brandon Locke with shades of grey and black hair. As the flavours of berries and cream and rich chocolate melded and melted in her mouth, she didn't think of Jimmy Diamond at all.

'Well?' Brandon was waiting for her verdict.

This lovely old house. Marilyn showing her how to do a bum-wiggle walk with a book balanced on her head. Brandon Locke's kind, dark eyes.

'It *is* perfect,' she said, not wanting to swallow the last of it. 'My aunt's summer pudding. Such wonderful memories.'

'Thank you,' said Brandon and he gave Connie a grin that made her heart bump fast in her chest and she was both glad and gutted that it was time to leave him and go home.

She had fourteen missed calls when she checked her secret mobile phone. She dialled voicemail to hear Hilda Curry asking Lady Muck if she had any vacancies. The other messages were the remaining Diamond Shine girls, requesting the same.

CHAPTER 79

Connie pulled in to a layby around the corner from Brandon's house to ring Della because there was no way she could wait until she got home.

'Guess what,' she giggled. 'I've had *the* call from Hilda.'

'You're joking,' said Della.

'I'm not. And I've had a call from Meg. And Sandra and Wenda and—'

Della screamed with joy on the other end of the phone.

'And there's more,' grinned Connie. 'Hilda said that she found it untenable to stay at her last place because they were setting on undesirables. She said she couldn't mention any names, but asked if I had anyone called Clamp on the books because she wouldn't work with them.'

'That's about as discreet as Hilda gets,' laughed Della. 'So Ivanka's recruited some Clamps? That means she's recruiting from the file I planted. My God, I don't believe it. I just don't believe it. I was beginning to think that Hilda would never shift. If only I'd known she was dead set against the Clamps, I would have given them all jobs before.' Della's face was starting to hurt from grinning. 'Is she working her notice period?'

'No.'

'Marvellous. Fantastic. If she isn't, then the others won't be either.'

'Oh, and she asked me if we used Des's Discount Warehouse for our supplies. I told her that no, we only use branded goods, or she was welcome to use her own and claim the cost.'

'I feel very bad for all the furnishings I've ruined,' said Della, with giggly regret.

'There are always casualties in war,' laughed Connie.

Cheryl was still in a daze as she wandered around Morrison's that evening. She wasn't thinking speedboats or fancy holidays, she could barely get her head around the fact that she would be able to put all her bills on a direct debit rather than pay them on a red notification. She put a tube of Colgate into her trolley and then took it out again because she only ever bought the supermarket's own brands and her brain couldn't sanction such a rebellious act.

She walked to the top of the aisle, her brain crowded with questions. Should she sell the paintings after Edith had left them to her? It didn't feel right. Then again, she couldn't keep them in her tatty little house because she'd never afford the insurance. What would Lance say? He might try and have her arrested for stealing them.

'Excuse me, Miss Parker.'

Cheryl turned around to see the tall, imposing, unsmiling figure of DC Oakwell in his serious black coat and for the second time in one day, she broke down into tears.

'Whoa, whoa, there,' said DC Oakwell, resisting a natural off-duty urge to comfort the distressed woman by placing an arm around her shoulder. 'I didn't mean to frighten you. I just spotted you and thought I'd say hello.'

'You're not arresting me, then?' sniffed Cheryl, frantically drying her cheeks on the backs of her hands, hoping that no shoppers could see her. She could have quite happily let the ground open and swallow her whole. As it had Brambles.

'What for?' asked DC Oakwell.

'I thought that . . . Lance . . . Nettleton had put in another complaint.'

'No, not that I know of. I'm here for some apples and Weetabix. I've just finished work. Look.' He raised the basket containing a bag of Granny Smiths. 'You okay? I am so sorry if I upset you.'

Cheryl wished the blasted tears would stop leaking out of her eyeballs. 'I'm fine,' she said, not convincing him at all.

'Please, let me take you for a coffee in the café. You can save your trolley in one of those bay things.

You don't look as if you've got anything that will defrost in it.'

He didn't wait for Cheryl to agree, but removed the trolley from her hands and started wheeling it towards the café. He lodged it in one of the holding bays along with his basket and she followed him, swiping her fingers under her eyes and hoping she hadn't bled any mascara.

'Sit down, I'll grab us a couple of coffees,' he said, pointing to a table for two by the window. He was back with her in a few minutes with two mugs of coffee, plastic pots of milk, packets of sugar, spoons and two Danish pastries.

If the café hadn't been so open and Cheryl thought she could have got away with it, she would have sneaked off, left her trolley and run to the bus station. She felt so embarrassed. It was bad enough DC Oakwell thought she was a trouble-maker and a liar, now he could add to the list 'mentally unhinged'. Breaking down by the cooked chickens in a supermarket wasn't exactly normal behaviour.

'I thought you might like a pastry to dip into your coffee, or is it just me who does things like that?' said DC Oakwell. His off-duty face was kind and smilier, thought Cheryl.

'Thank you,' she said, though she doubted she would eat anything. She hadn't felt properly hungry since she and Gary split up.

'I feel really awful that I frightened you,' DC Oakwell said. 'Miss Parker. Or can I call you Cheryl?'

It was bad news that he remembered her name, Cheryl thought. She toyed with the idea that he was lying about being off duty and was trying to trap her. Were the police allowed to do that though?

'Cheryl's fine, DC Oakwell.'

'John's permissible in a Morrison's café,' he returned. 'And less of a mouthful.'

'You're really not here to ask me about Lance Nettleton then?'

John Oakwell shook his head. 'Not unless it was you who sank the house into the ground. It wasn't, was it?' His eyebrows made a serious dip downwards but she knew he was joking and it coaxed a smile from her.

'You heard about that, did you?'

'Oh yes, I heard. He was a very lucky man to survive that. I bet you're glad that you didn't end up living in the house now.'

Cheryl bristled. 'I wasn't lying, you know. Edith was going to leave the cottage to—'

'I never thought you were lying,' John interrupted her.

Cheryl tilted her head at him. 'You didn't?'

'Nope. Unfortunately we have to work on evidence, not instinct. And trust me, you get very strong hunches about things. For instance, I'm willing to bet that Lance Nettleton didn't admit to you that he killed his aunt but you told me that so I'd go up and question him, am I right?'

'Oh heck.'

Cheryl's eyes darted towards his and found them

waiting for her. They were autumn-hazel and narrowed in amusement and his lips were wearing a smile which totally softened his fierce DC Oakwell persona.

'Between you and me,' John leaned towards her in a conspiratorial manner, 'I found Mr Nettleton a very odious man. But if that ever gets out, I know where you live.' Then he saw Cheryl's eyes grow round with alarm. 'I'm kidding,' he said. 'I mean I do know where you live, but . . .' He picked up a pastry and bit off a chunk, then spoke with his mouth full. 'Okay, I've put a plug in it to shut me up.'

It forced Cheryl to laugh. John offered her the other pastry but she refused it. She wasn't hungry; and she couldn't eat pastries without making the most godawful mess and she'd made enough of a chump of herself in front of DC John Oakwell without letting him see her covered in pastry flakes as well.

He told her over that Morrison's coffee that he loved being a detective and Cheryl told him she loved being a cleaner. John told her that his mum was a retired dinnerlady and his dad had been a policeman too. She told him that she'd never seen her dad and didn't have much to do with her family. She didn't tell him that she owned an original Van Gogh because Mr Fairbanks had warned her that as soon as that fact was common knowledge, she'd discover a lot more 'friends' than she ever knew she had. For now, John Oakwell was having a coffee with Miss Cheryl Parker, a cleaner who lived in a tatty little terrace house but had once been heiress to a house that had recently sunk into the ground.

They finished their drinks and then John asked her if she would like a lift home.

'Thanks, but I'd rather not turn up in a police car,' she said. 'The neighbours' curtains will be twitching again.'

'It's my own personal car,' said John. 'A Renault Megane. No blue lights, no siren, but I do have a roof rack.'

'I have to finish off my shopping,' Cheryl said.

'I'll wait for you. By the celery vee,' and he winked.

Cheryl found that she zipped around the aisles faster than Red Rum in the last furlong of the Grand National. True to his word, John was waiting for her, not in the veg department though, but by the exit.

'I didn't ask if you were single,' said John, pulling his car up outside her house and turning to face her.

'I am single, yes,' said Cheryl. Her heart was making very pleasurable 'ooh' sounds.

'I am as well,' said John. 'Do you like going to the pictures?'

'I do,' said Cheryl. The *ooh* sounds were making her whole chest vibrate.

'Well, if you're free Saturday, we could have a spot of dinner somewhere and then go and watch something . . . whatever you fancy. There's a new Nicholas Cage film or a Bill Nighy romantic comedy thing or that horror everyone is talking about . . .' Then he threw back his head and laughed. 'I've just remembered, it's called *Underneath the House.*'

CHAPTER 80

By Thursday Jimmy had to get out of the office before he exploded. Whilst Ivanka was dilly-dallying in the post office he was forced to take call after call from furious customers threatening legal action, thanks to modified Des's Discount products. Then some daft bint rang asking for a company name so she could set up a direct debit for work undertaken by Hilda.

'Diamond Shine, Mrs Cotton, of course. As usual,' replied Jimmy, trying to keep his impatience in check as the second phone line flashed, indicating that he had more incoming crap to deal with, most probably.

'No, I mean her new place of work.'

'Her new place of work?' What the bloody hell was the old bird going on about?

Ivanka picked that moment to walk in. Jimmy mouthed, 'Where the hell have you been?' at her.

'I'll come back to you, Mrs Cotton,' said Jimmy and smashed the phone down on the cradle.

'What the fuckery has been going on?' yelled Jimmy, spinning round to his sulky-faced lover. 'I'm being sued left, right and centre for ruined carpets and cushions and please, please, please don't tell me that Hilda has left.'

'Many cleaners used the materials in the cupboard so there is much damage,' said Ivanka, swinging her bag onto her desk. 'It's okay, I dealt with it. I told them to go to their own insurers. Some will not be bothered to do that. I thought I would try and save the company some monies.'

'Are you frigging daft?' Jimmy threw up his hands. 'Once you get solicitors involved, that's when things get expensive. The damages were no fault of mine, but now you've made them mine. Bloody hell, Ivanka, what were you thinking?' He addressed the wall nearest to him. 'I've never sworn as much in my life, did you know that? People with Tourette's haven't used half as many "f" words as I have this past week. No wonder that Shirley Valentine talked to you, it's the only thing she could get any bleeding sense out of.' He switched his attention back to Ivanka. 'And why has Hilda left?'

'She was disrespectful to me, Jimmy.' Ivanka was as calm as he was animated. 'She thought she had the power over me.'

'Disrespectful? *Disrespectful?* Ha,' he half-laughed, half-cried. 'Hilda does have power over you. She has it over me as well. Where Hilda goes, the others will follow. You better get her on the phone now and apologise to her before we lose all our pissing workforce.'

'I will do no such thing,' said Ivanka. 'I have set

on new girls. Meet with Roy Frog and buy the company and Hilda and everyone else will be working for you again. But I warn you, Jimmy, they accept me as the boss, or I will sack them again. Hilda called me a monkey. I will not stand for that, as her superior and your wife and you must stand by me on this.'

Jimmy slumped down on Della's chair. He supposed Ivanka was right, of course and he knew she wanted to make an impact so he shouldn't be too harsh on her. It would all be different when it was common knowledge that she was the boss's bird.

There was no one else the cleaners could have gone to but Roy Frog, but it wouldn't do him any good. However many of Jimmy's best workers the boggle-eyed git lured over, they wouldn't save Cleancheap from going down. What was Roy Frog playing at though? He was going to an awful lot of trouble to cause shit for the only person who could save him from insolvency. Why would Roy Frog, on a sinking rubber dinghy, fire rockets at the big safe ship which had come to save him? It didn't make any sense to Jimmy at all. His rival's purpose couldn't have just been to score some scrappy points of revenge.

'Okay, sweetheart,' he said, sighing hard and holding out his hand for Ivanka to take. 'Everything will be okay and of course I'll stand by you.'

Jimmy didn't know if this week was a true indication of whether they could cope without Della in the office, but it was looking as if he would have to anyway. The train he had set in motion with that engagement ring was approaching its terminus. Then he thought what a horrible word 'terminus' was. It didn't have good connotations at all.

CHAPTER 81

The Sunflower Café was full that Friday meeting. Even girls who didn't usually turn out for the monthly cleaning get-together were present. There was a happy buzz in the place, especially as the gossip had reached most of them about Cheryl's turn of fortune. Connie had been invited along by both Cheryl and Astrid and sat with them in the sunny little room, feeling that she had 'Jimmy Diamond's Wife' written across her forehead in fluorescent lettering. At some point they'd have to know that Marilyn Smith was actually Connie Diamond. She hoped they'd understand. She hoped that working happily for Lady Muck would make them forgive her everything.

The three-tiered plates crowded with finger sandwiches, tartlets, pastries and Patricia's clotted cream scones were set on the tables, the teapots were being tipped and the cluck of chatter filled the room, then Hilda rapped the table with the salt pot to start off the proceedings.

'Hello everyone,' she said. 'Thanks for coming. I know you'll have a few questions and things to talk about so let's get cracking. Is there anyone here present who is still working for Diamond Shine?'

A hand was raised at the back.

'Shirley,' said Hilda. 'Are you staying with them?'

'Am I 'eck as like, I'm handing my notice in tomorrow,' Shirley replied. 'I just wanted to make sure we were all in it together.'

'Yes we are,' came a general mumble in response.

'And no one should work a notice period either,' said Hilda. 'Any payments you get from now on should be given to Lady Muck, that's right, isn't it Astrid?'

'Ja. Zat is reight,' Astrid replied in her usual half-German, half-Tyke.

'We have a new member with us that I'd like to introduce you all to,' said Hilda. Connie felt her cheeks starting to glow as a sea of eyes turned in her direction. 'Marilyn Smith. It's because of Marilyn that I learned about Lady Muck so we have her to thank. Or to curse if owt goes wrong.' There was a ripple of amusement but Connie wasn't laughing. She felt sick with the weight of responsibility she had brought on herself.

'So? Any questions?'

'Is there any more egg mayonnaise?' asked Meg Thompson.

'Not that sort of question, you greedy bugger,' snapped Hilda. 'Be serious.'

'Can I open a window?' Sandra fanned her face. 'I'm having a flush.'

'I'll open it for you,' Patricia called.

'I've got a question. What about Della? Will she be all right?' asked young Gemma, which brought another mumble of agreement from everyone. Connie smiled inside that Della was held in such affection by the women.

'I don't know,' said Hilda. 'I hope so. I'd like to put a good word in for her with Lady Muck if I ever get to meet her. I must admit it's a bit of a funny carry on, not knowing what the boss looks like.'

'Well, you don't in a lot of companies, Hilda,' said Ava. 'Our Leonie works for Marks and Spencer and she's never met the big boss.'

'This isn't exactly Marks and Spencer though, Ava,' said Hilda.

'Astrid, is there any more egg mayonnaise on your table?' Meg was still chasing her choice of sandwich. Hilda cast her an impatient glance.

'It's just the way Lady Muck does business for now,' put in Connie to stop the speculation. 'I heard she was setting on an office manageress to take some of the pressure off her. She wants to be more accessible to you all, I know that.'

Understanding 'ah's followed.

'I hear Norma Know-it-All has been set back on,' announced Hilda.

'And her Grumbleweed lover?' sniggered Sandra, still fanning her face but looking shades less scarlet than earlier.

'And Lesley Clamp, Alaska Clamp and Nepal

501

Clamp. I hear that Ruth Fallis's sister will be joining them as well.'

'I thought she was in the clink,' said Ava.

'She's out. But it won't be long before she's back in. She'd nick a cat turd out of a litter tray if it wasn't nailed down, that one. So is everyone clear what they're doing?' Hilda waited for a nod or a shake of the head and got both. 'You need to chuck any Des's Discount supplies in the bin. Don't use them. They're contaminated. You buy your own products, save the receipts and accounts of your car mileage or bus tickets and send them in to Lady Muck with any payments. Don't take the mick, girls. We're on to a good number here, so if anyone feels they want to spoil it for the rest of us, you'll have me to answer to, all right?'

'Okay, if there aren't any more egg mayos, I'll have a cheese savoury if there are any spare.'

Patricia arrived behind Meg with a plate of personal egg mayo sandwiches and said, 'Here, Meg. Before you wither away.'

Meg was overjoyed and began to tuck straight in.

'There's more chance of Ivanka winning Miss Universe than there is of Meg withering away,' laughed Hilda. 'Now, let's raise our cups and toast Lady Muck, whoever the bloody hell she is.'

'To Lady Muck.'

The Sunflower Café was filled with the united voices of the toast. Connie tried not to grin proudly. She thought she could fall in love with Hilda Curry. The woman was a brilliant leader and Jimmy had been a fool not to treasure his workforce more. She would make sure that Lady Muck gave them the value they deserved.

'And now some happy news for those of you who don't know. Our own little Cheryl has had some luck for a change. She was left some paintings by a client and they're worth a few bob.'

A round of applause broke out and Cheryl smiled shyly. Wenda patted her on the shoulder and whispered through a honeyed ham and mustard finger sandwich, 'About time, lass.'

'To Cheryl.' There was another toast of raised tea-cups and Connie felt that every woman present, without exception, was rejoicing for Cheryl. The affection in the room was almost touchable. Those afternoon teas in the café, she knew, were a precious bubble filled with sisterhood and support as well as scones and sunflowers.

'Next meeting is in three weeks, back to the usual pattern of first Friday of the month,' said Hilda, then she called over to her sister. 'For God's sake, Pat, get Meg a goody bag before she cries.'

Connie liked the women so much. This time next week, Lent would be over and her new life would have begun. She supposed that she should call a meeting and enlighten everyone about what was really happening. She wondered if she should do that before or after Jimmy made his grand announcement to her that their marriage was over and would be shocked to find that he was delivering old news. She decided that everything might as well happen on the same day. Lady Muck therefore had six days left of anonymity.

Hilda caught up with Cheryl just as she was about to get a lift home with Astrid.

'Can I have a word, love?'

'Course,' said Cheryl, letting Hilda pull her into a quiet corner.

'It's about Gary,' Hilda said.

The name made Cheryl's insides stand to attention.

'I thought I'd better let you know what I heard.'

'What, Hilda?'

'He's spent all that money he won. Went mad shopping with that . . . that tramp and blew the rest on scratchcards hoping to repeat his luck. *She* isn't with him any more, obviously. But watch it if he comes crawling back to you now. It won't be long before the papers get hold of your news. He might even have heard already about your turn of fortune.'

'Thank you, Hilda,' said Cheryl.

'Mind how you go, lass.'

Cheryl didn't know what she thought about that news as she walked out to Astrid's car. She couldn't foresee how she would react if Gary did turn up at the door. Would it definitely be because she had the prospect of some money? Could Hilda have got it wrong, and things had ended with Chartreuse Clamp because he was missing her? After all, Hilda

504

was known to be biased against the Clamp family. She hadn't a clue; but what was clear was that she should cancel her date with John Oakwell, because it wasn't fair to go out with him when another man was still on her mind.

CHAPTER 82

Connie went into Meadowhall the next day to buy herself a new dress for Brandon's Tuesday soirée. Just a plain black one that would look like a hired-help uniform, she decided. She bumped into Cheryl in Debenhams.

'I've been shouting over at you for ages,' said Cheryl. 'Didn't you hear me?'

Connie had heard someone saying 'Marilyn' behind her but hadn't thought any more about it.

'Er, no. I'm usually in a world of my own,' Connie excused herself. 'So what have you bought then, anything nice? Some new clothes? I expect the newspapers will want to take some photos of you soon.'

'I hope not.' Cheryl grimaced. 'That's really not my thing at all. I've bought some books and a couple of tops but I'm not used to spending, if I'm honest. I keep thinking someone is going to jump out and tell me it's all a big joke and Edith's pictures aren't worth the canvas they're painted on.' She didn't say that she needed to get out of the house in case Gary called round. She wanted more time to think about what to do. 'What about you?'

'Black dress,' said Connie. 'Nothing special. Client is having a party on Tuesday and wants me to distribute chocolates.'

'That doesn't sound bad,' said Cheryl with a whistle. 'Have you got time for a coffee? I'll pay.'

'Get out of the habit of saying that to people,' Connie admonished. 'You'll find too many of them will let you.'

They went downstairs on the escalator to the store café and had a coffee and a fat slice of Victoria sponge each. Connie insisted on paying and won the battle only because she promised that Cheryl could treat her next time.

'Lady Muck is going to be busy next week,' said Cheryl. 'What with all the new cleaners on board.'

'I hope so,' said Connie, lifting a forkful of sponge to her lips. 'She's worked hard. She deserves some success. So, will you carry on cleaning now you're rich or . . . no, daft question. Of course you won't . . .'

Cheryl cut her off. 'Yes, yes I will. You hear about lottery winners who turn all miserable because they're bored, don't you? They buy a speedboat and a Rolls Royce and lose all their friends. Well, I want things to carry on as normally as they can. Mr Fairbanks – that's my art-expert gentleman – he can't believe I'm still cleaning his house for him. I said "You didn't think I'd just leave you, did you?" I'm very fond of Mr Fairbanks and Miss Molloy and Miss Potter.' In fact, Cheryl had had a very interesting afternoon with Miss Potter yesterday.

'I think it's going to be hard to keep to your normal life when you own a Van Gogh, love,' Connie smiled. 'You're going to have to be very careful about any new friends you make.'

'I've made a new friend,' Cheryl blurted out, looking at Connie with troubled green eyes. 'And I don't know what to do about it.'

'Go on,' Connie encouraged her.

'It's a policeman,' Cheryl said. 'I thought – I still think – that the lady who left me the pictures was murdered by her nephew. So I rang the police and I spoke to this detective John Oakwell. Then the nephew reported me for harassing him, so this policeman came to the house to warn me off. Then I bumped into the . . . John on Thursday in Morrisons and we got talking. We went for a coffee and I'm supposed to be going with him to the cinema tonight.'

Connie waited for her to go on and when she didn't, she said, 'And the problem is . . .?'

'I'm still thinking about my ex. Who is a dick.'

'Ah.'

'John's really nice. He's got really nice smiley eyes and he's handsome and he's big and smart and—'

'How do you fancy giving me his address and I'll go out with him instead.' Connie smiled.

'I was with Gary for ten years. He lied to me so much and gambled all our money away and I know we've split up and he's a total knob but . . . but . . . Oh I'm so confused. You know when people have rotten limbs cut off and they say they still feel them . . . Do you know what I mean, Marilyn? Why is my head saying different stuff to this?' She touched her fingers to her chest where the heart was.

Connie pulled a tissue out of her handbag and passed it to Cheryl just in time as a fat teardrop rolled down her cheek.

'Sometimes you have to listen to your head, sweetheart, because hearts can be very stupid. Sometimes you just have to let go of that limb because the body is playing every trick it can to make you re-attach it, but it's past the point of saving and would poison you if you did.'

'Do you think?'

'Ten years is a long time to be with someone, Cheryl. Eventually the heart will catch up with the brain, but it's a bit slower on the uptake.'

Cheryl nodded. 'You been through this, Marilyn?'

No, but I will be soon, said Connie to herself. *And I'll have to remember that it's a damned sight harder to take the advice that you give so easily out to others.* She nodded without giving any detail.

'Got any more shopping to do when we've finished this? I could give you a lift back to Barnsley if you haven't,' she said.

'Ooh, that would be handy, if that's okay with you,' said Cheryl. She was glad she had bumped into Marilyn and had a talk. She felt better for sharing it and hearing someone else's perspective on it. Especially someone like Marilyn who radiated kindness like sun-rays. She only hoped that if Gary was going to try and worm his way back into her life, he'd do it now, whilst she was full of Victoria sponge and courage.

CHAPTER 83

Not only did Gary come around when Cheryl was still full of sponge and courage, but he called on her when she had just put on her new dress, her new shoes and her new red lipstick. She'd never worn such a brave, bold shade before, but she and Connie had gone for a wander around the make-up and perfumes in Debenhams before they drove home and Cheryl had heard the slick red lippy call to her all the way from the Mac counter.

Cheryl heard their old car first, then saw it pull up outside the house through the window and immediately her whole body started to shake. Her idiot heart was thumping like a horse's legs against a stable wall. It missed a great long beat when Gary knocked on the front door and when her hand reached out to open it, she saw how much it was trembling.

There he was on her doorstep, with his grin and his handsome boyish face and a large bunch of pink flowers wrapped in cellophane. There was a 'thirty per cent extra free' sticker on it.

'Hi Cheryl,' he said and she saw his Adam's

apple make a pronounced nervous rise and fall in his throat. 'Can I come in for a moment? These are for you.'

She took the flowers from him because he was holding them out to her and she was too polite to leave him stuck in that position.

'Yes, come in then,' she said whilst her head screamed at her, *Don't let him in, for God's sake.*

Gary stood in front of the fireplace and turned a full circle. 'It's funny to be back here. I'd forgotten how cosy it is. I've missed the old place.'

Don't ask him if he wants a drink, warned her head. Courtesy, however, won the day.

'Can I get you a coffee or something?'

'Only if you're having one. I'm not disturbing you, am I? You going out?'

'No, you're not disturbing me,' she said, partly answering his volley of questions.

Yes he is frigging disturbing you, said her head.

Cheryl put the kettle on, which didn't take long to boil as she'd only just had a cup of tea herself.

'You've got a new picture up,' said Gary pointing at the *Sunflowers* before following her into the kitchen. She could smell his aftershave, she'd always liked it. When he had first left, she would go into Boots, spray some into the air from the sample bottle and let the cloud of scent settle on her. He'd felt hers again just for a moment or two.

'Yes I have,' she said, aware that he was close behind her, within touching distance. She didn't know what she would do if his fingers made

512

contact with her. She poured coffee and milk into two mugs and handed him one. It was his old mug, she'd bought it for him for Christmas. It said 'You are my cup of tea' on it. She thought she'd taken it to his mum's house with his other stuff. She hoped he wouldn't think she'd deliberately kept it, but chances are he would, she thought with a flinch of embarrassment.

He sat down at the small kitchen table.

He's sitting. You'll never get rid of him now, said her head.

'You look lovely, Cheryl. That red lipstick really suits you.'

'Oh, it's er . . . I'm just trying it out.'

You never could accept a compliment, could you? That's going to change, girl.

'It's nice. Really nice.' Gary drank some coffee and his eyes didn't leave her. 'My mum says hi. She's sorry about, you know, being a bit off with you. It upset her seeing you and she didn't know what to do for the best. She said she really wanted to give you a big hug.'

Yeah, course she did, and I'm Celine Dion.

Gary gave her his best pair of big round apologetic eyes. 'I'm sorry, I've been a bit of a tosser, haven't I, Cheryl?'

You're telling me.

Cheryl shrugged. 'I don't know what you want me to say, Gary.'

'We've been through a lot together you and I, haven't we?'

Well, you've been through my bank account.

'Well, we were together for ten years, Gary. A lot happens in that time.'

'Do you remember that holiday we had in Kos?' he grinned.

She remembered it too well. The weather had been perfect, they found a small café where the food was great and the lagers ice-cold and delicious. The sea was clear and blue. They made love on crisp white sheets as a gorgeously refreshing breeze blew through the green slices of shutters at the window.

'Yes, I remember.'

Gary coughed. 'I've been thinking . . . Say no, but what if we went back there. Started again. Did it properly this time?'

No.

Cheryl smiled. That phantom limb of her relationship was starting to throb. It was a trick of the mind, though, according to what Marilyn had taught her. The limb was gone for a reason. 'Did it properly this time?' she echoed.

'Yes.'

'Started again, you say?'

'Yes.' Hope was shining in his eyes.

'It was so lovely in Kos. I felt truly happy that week.'

'Me too.' He reached for her hand. Cheryl stared at it, but her own stayed curled around her mug.

'The thing is, Gary, I thought I did it properly last time. I didn't cheat on you, I didn't deceive

514

you, I loved you, I respected you, I supported you, I gave our relationship my all. You, however, lied through your back teeth, ravaged my savings over and over again, broke my heart, won a fortune thanks to a battered sausage, shagged a teenager and now you're back here for what reason?'

Oh my God, did you really just say that. Did you REALLY say that, girlfriend?

'Cheryl, I knew you'd think that I came back because I heard . . . because . . .'

'Because you heard that I inherited some money. Let's be honest. Well, you're right, I did. Loads of it. Enough to set you and me up for life, and to have as much IVF as my body could take. Enough to let me buy Kos, never mind holiday on it. Enough to give you a battered sausage every day for the rest of your life. Oh Gary, I loved you so much.'

She realised she had used the past tense. The shaking in her hands had stopped. She could see the phantom limb sitting across the table, but the ache was quickly fading to nothing.

'I *still* love you, Cheryl.' Gary reached further forward with his hand, almost demanding by the gesture that she hold it. Cheryl studied his slim fingers and thought of John Oakwell's hand which was large and square and would have dwarfed Gary's.

'No, you don't. You killed us. And now I'd like you to leave, because I've got a date with an absolute hunk of a man and I need to finish getting ready.'

He thought she was joking. It was only when she swiped away his mug, poured the contents down the sink and opened the front door wide for him to leave that he realised she wasn't.

Gary looked winded.

'You've changed, Cheryl,' he said as a parting shot.

'I know. And isn't it bloody marvellous,' she replied, hearing the voice in her head cheer as she closed the door on him. Boy, she was so glad she hadn't texted John Oakwell to cancel their date to go and see a film about devilish activities which happened underneath a house.

CHAPTER 84

As Jimmy tucked into his Sunday morning fry-up, he wondered where he would be this time next week and what he would be feeling. He looked across as Connie whilst he chewed a mushroom, and his heart gave a heavy thud as if it had just fallen off its perch. She didn't know he was studying her; her hair had an angelic halo of brightness, courtesy of the strong sunlight in the window behind her, and her eyes were large and grey and amused at something she was reading in the newspaper. She looked lovely and it wasn't just her thinned-down cheeks that made him think that she had a spark in her that hadn't been there for years. As if she were lit up from the inside, like she used to be in the early days.

He put down his knife and fork; he didn't want the breakfast. 'Shall we go out for lunch?' he asked on a whim.

Connie's eyes snapped up from the newspaper. 'Lunch? You and me?'

It shouldn't have been such a shock to her, he thought. He couldn't remember when the last time they'd gone out together had been.

'Yes.'

'Oh, that would be nice,' said Connie. She had agreed to it before she had chance to think about it.

'The Boat?' It was up on the moor and tucked out of the way.

'Okay. I'll go and wash my hair,' said Connie. They were having their last supper early, it seemed.

Cheryl woke up in bed and stretched and smiled like a contented cat. What a lovely evening she'd had with John Oakwell. He'd picked her up in his car, getting out of it to open the door for her like a proper gentleman. They'd driven to Sheffield, eaten Chinese food and seen the film. He'd reached for her hand in the dark and gently tickled her arm and she thought her head was going to blow off with pleasure. They'd had a drink in the cinema bar afterwards and talked some more and she learned that he hadn't had a relationship for five years, had no children, owned a Burmese cat called Pong that he adored, lived in a mortgage-free house in Maltstone, played rugby for the police team and would be forty next Christmas Day. She hadn't thought about Gary Gladstone once all evening. Or battered sausages. She also learned that he did a fantastic goodnight kiss on the doorstep and that her insides turned to liquid when he playfully pinched her nose and said that he'd ring her tomorrow. If Van Gogh could have painted the colours of her spirit now, he would have had to load his brushes with his best bright golds and bold sunshiney yellows.

The Boat wasn't half as nice as Jimmy remembered it from the last time he had been, with a rep from a bleach factory. The cheeky cow had ordered lobster and champagne. Now the sticky menus featured pies, burgers and typical microwave fare.

'Do you want to go somewhere else?' he asked Connie.

'No, it's fine,' she said. 'It's a treat for me not to cook anything.'

He ordered a red wine for her and a white wine for himself. It was piss-water and he asked for his money back and told the barman that they wouldn't be dining there after all.

'Come on,' he told Connie, and steered her outside and back to the car. 'We're not eating in that shithole.'

Jimmy drove on towards Holmfirth where he knew of a gastropub called the Slaughterman. Despite the name, it had a five-star reputation for food. Today Jimmy didn't want to think about Ivanka and a new life, he had gone into full-throttle reverse thrust. He wanted to pretend that he and Connie's paths hadn't split all those years ago – that they were the couple they should have been.

'So, what's the occasion?' asked Connie with a put-on smile when they were seated at a window table facing out onto a dramatic landscape of the moody moors. Jimmy had a crisp glass of white Mouton Cadet, Connie a robust Pinotage. The Slaughterman was stylish and clean and everything the Boat hadn't been.

Jimmy shrugged. 'I honestly don't know. I just felt like it. I really enjoyed that chat we had about Roy Frog the other week . . . well, I didn't enjoy talking about him, but I did enjoy talking to you. You know, when you made me those chocolate pancakes.'

And, for once, Connie knew he was telling the truth. These were their dying days and things felt so much more intense near the end. She so very much wanted to take with her a souvenir from them. She wanted to enjoy a little window through to another world of what might have been. Suspend all plans and hostilities, just for an hour or two and have lunch with her husband, the father of her daughter – and her son. She wanted to have lunch with the man that the boy she had loved so much had grown into.

'Very hard man to deal with is Roy Frog,' said Jimmy, absently breaking a toothpick in half.

'So you're still negotiating the deal, are you? Employing your delaying tactics?'

'Yeah. Anyway, I shouldn't talk about work.' He closed off that world from his head and all it entailed, and that included Ivanka.

'Isn't the scenery beautiful, Jim?'

He watched Connie sipping a glass of wine from a bottle which probably cost more than the crappy frock she had on. She had never asked for much in their marriage, and the little she had asked for, he hadn't given her. She didn't even give herself anything.

Feeling him staring at her, she turned away from the window and towards him again. 'You look tired, Jim. You should give yourself a break at Easter,' said Connie, meaning it. She'd never seen him with fluidy bags under his eyes before. His cheeks looked pinched and pale.

'A bit of proper sun would be nice,' he said. 'We haven't had a holiday for . . . God, how long, Con?'

'We couldn't have left your mum in the state she was in,' returned Connie. 'And when she passed away, I wouldn't have left mine. I couldn't have sprawled out on a sunbed knowing either of them would be panicking.'

'God bless them both, wherever they are.' Jimmy raised his glass in the direction of heaven. He didn't doubt that if there was such a place, they'd both be there. He wasn't sure he would be headed for the same destination, though.

'They've got chocolate waffles on for dessert,' said Jimmy, catching sight of their listing on the splayed pages of the menu underneath the glass surface of the table.

'Lent isn't over until Thursday,' replied Connie.

Lent. Jimmy was really starting to hate that word. 'Still holding fast?'

Connie thought of Brandon placing the chocolate between her lips.

521

'Still holding fast,' she fibbed.

'I'm glad I'm not a sheep,' said Jimmy, looking across at the white balls of fluff on the hillside.

In the window, Connie could see Jimmy's faint reflection, washed of lines and stress and he looked like the boy again, the boy whom she had fallen in love with in a matter of seconds and who had made her insides feel as if someone were stirring them up with a huge whisk. He'd set off fireworks in her head when he asked her to go for a walk with him and she thought she would die from happiness when he kissed her under the big oak tree in the park.

Their meals arrived – they had gone straight to mains. Fillet steak for Jimmy, halibut for Connie. He noticed that Connie looked at the platter as if it were a rare piece of artwork. She should have been used to dining like this, he thought, it shouldn't have been a novelty for her.

'Looks lovely,' said Connie. She was glad it was nouvelle cuisine tiny portions because she wasn't all that hungry. She tried not to think that this would be the last time she and Jimmy would ever go out together because she would cry. Despite all the crap, she would sob for what could have been.

'I fancy buying a villa in Spain,' said Jimmy. 'Wouldn't it be nice to have a home from home in the sun?'

'One day, when the money comes rolling in, eh?' said Connie.

'Oh yeah, yeah of course. I meant that.' Connie saw him puff out his cheeks as if he'd swerved his foot away from his mouth just in time.

'How's your steak?' she asked.

'Really good,' he said, and held a forkful out for her. 'Here. Try a bit.'

She looked at it without moving.

'Come on, there's no chocolate on it, Con.'

Connie leaned forward and took the chunk of meat with her teeth. It was uncomfortably intimate to eat from her husband's fork.

'They've cooked it nice for you.'

'Sorry, I forgot you don't like it rare. Fish good?'

'Beautiful.'

A couple came to sit at the next table, about the same age as them. He reached for her hand across the table and absently played with her fingers as they read the menu. He ordered champagne, telling the waiter that it was their twentieth wedding anniversary.

It would have been our silver wedding anniversary in July, thought Connie. Twenty-five years and yet they were strangers, plotting against each other.

Jimmy dipped into the conversation taking place on the next table. The couple were happily conversing as if they talked a lot to each other. Ivanka wasn't a chatty person although she was obsessed by studying people in restaurants: the quality of their clothes, the cost of the wine they ordered, the excellence of their plastic surgery.

She never made Jimmy laugh like Connie used to with her incessant banter. He suddenly wanted to hear her cheery voice, filling him in on details of her day and what she'd heard on the news or read in the *Daily Trumpet*. But he knew he never would again.

He put his knife and fork down on his plate, swallowing the emotion which was filling his throat.

'You've not finished, have you?' asked Connie, looking at the half-steak he'd left.

'Yes,' he said. 'I'm full.'

'Me too,' said Connie, grateful for an excuse to stop pretending to enjoy the meal.

'Do you want a pudding or a coffee?'

The couple next to them were clinking glasses.

'No, thank you.'

On a parallel planet, it was Connie who was cherished and loved and married to a man who put shine in her eyes and champagne in her glass, thought Jimmy. He didn't want it to be too late to do that. They were only in their early forties, he could turn their ship around and set it on another course. One with soft winds and sunshine.

Jimmy paid the bill, then helped Connie on with her coat.

'Thanks, Jimmy, that was a nice treat,' she said.

'We'll do it again.' He meant it as he said it.

Oh Christ, what a mess.

CHAPTER 85

When Della walked back into the office after her week off 'ill', the first thing she couldn't help but notice and be amused by was the appearance of the two 'reception area' chairs, the small coffee table between them and the cactus in a pot stood on it. The cactus had two long prickly stems which appeared to be flipping the bird. Della grinned. This was Ivanka's stamp, a hint of the new regime. She also knew that her chair had been used because it was lowered. Well, Ivanka would be welcome to it very shortly because this time next week, Della would be sitting on a chair in a small office in Maltstone working her magic for Lady Muck. The King was dead for her. Long live the Queen.

When Jimmy arrived, he appeared genuinely pleased to see her.

'My best girl is back,' he cheered. But her heart didn't lose a beat as it had done before whenever he had called her that.

'I see there are some changes,' Della remarked, looking at the paperwork scattered untidily over her desk.

'Oh . . . er . . . yeah . . . the furniture . . . and I think Ivanka had to sack someone . . . gross misconduct. She'll fill you in, whenever she decides to show up.'

Well, Jimmy had been in for five minutes, so Ivanka was due, thought Della, casting her eyes on her watch. As the big hand swept to the o'clock position, in came the girl herself. She wasn't happy that Della was back at the boss's desk. Less than ten minutes ago she had warned Jimmy to instruct Della that there had been an adjustment of seating arrangements.

'Hello Ivanka,' said Della. 'My, you have been busy.'

'It was difficult week,' came the reply. 'I had to make some tough decisions.'

'So I see.'

Out of the corner of her eye, Della could see that Ivanka was communicating some kind of message to Jimmy with her eyebrows. It didn't look a very friendly one.

'I was . . . er . . . thinking of giving Ivanka some extra duties,' said Jimmy, nervously. 'Just in case you are ever away again. I thought . . . maybe . . . you could exchange desks and she . . . she could practise being office manager for this week. Maybe?' He winced then, as if he expected Della to throw the long-armed stapler at him by way of response.

But his jaw nearly hit the floor when Della said, 'Very sensible idea. Let's do it. It will be nice to ease myself back into work gently. I have to say that I don't exactly feel one hundred per cent.'

She picked up her filing tray and pen pot and placed them on Ivanka's desk.

'I'll make some coffee,' she said. 'It'll be a change to play the office junior for a few days.' She turned to Ivanka and tried not to let the tongue in her cheek get in the way of her words. 'Judging by how much you achieved last week, I think you'll bring the house down as an office manageress, Ivanka.'

And Della grinned for the full duration of the kettle-boil.

The *Daily Trumpet* was first to cover the story of local woman Cheryl Parker who had inherited some very valuable paintings, including a sketch by Van Eyck. They reported that the paintings were presently with the art agent Christie's. It wasn't a very large article and it was tucked away on the left-hand side of page six, presumably because not even the sensationalist *Trumpet* believed that a great master's work of that magnitude could turn up in Barnsley.

John rang Cheryl just as she got off at her bus-stop.

'I've been reading about you in the paper,' he said. 'Is it true?'

'No,' she replied.

'I thought as much.' He laughed.

'It's a Van Gogh, not a Van Eyck.'

527

'Ha.'

'No, I really mean it.'

There was silence on the phone then.

'John? Are you still there?'

'Er, yes. Wow. That's, er . . . wow.' He sounded as if he had just been pinged with a stun gun. 'It's not one of those pictures that Lance Nettleton told me his aunt wanted you to have, is it?'

'Yes,' said Cheryl. 'I imagine he's rather regretting that now. I think I'm probably going to get a solicitor's letter demanding them back.'

'Well, considering there are witnesses and an official police statement pertaining to the fact that his aunt insisted they were yours, and there was obviously such a bond of affection between you and the old lady that he also gave you her ashes, I think that he might be thwarted at the first hurdle if he tried that one.'

Cheryl breathed a big fat sigh of relief. 'Thank God. I was worried that when the story broke, he'd come after me.'

'Are you still coming out to dinner with me tonight, or do you have press calls to make?'

Cheryl smiled. 'I'd love to. It's my turn to pay.'

'If I ask you out to dinner, lady, I'm paying,' said John sternly. 'Whether you own a Vincent Van Gogh or a Dick Van Dyke. Is that understood?'

It was beautifully understood.

According to the dated *Yellow Pages* in the office, there was a bridal shop in Maltstone: White

Wedding. Ivanka thought that she would take a look there after work. After all, she needed to seriously start planning for her own white wedding now.

She was therefore deeply disappointed to find, when she drove over there, that the shop was no more. The large bay window was empty and all that remained was the sign over the door which had been painted over with a weak white solution so that the dark lettering of the former shop name underneath it could still be seen.

She was checking her make-up in the flop-down vanity mirror in her car when she saw a woman emerge from behind the building, carrying some letters. She crossed the road and put them in the postbox there, then walked back. It took Ivanka a few moments to fathom where she knew the woman from because she looked quite different from the last time she had seen her: smarter and much slimmer. It was Jimmy's wife.

CHAPTER 86

Tuesday started off beautifully for Della, abysmally for Ivanka, in the offices of Diamond Shine. A client phoned to complain about Alaska Clamp, calling her dirty and lazy and refused to pay for a ridiculously lax clean. Della tried not to crow as the conversation between Ivanka and the client escalated to a high pitch, which resulted in the client telling Ivanka to shove her cleaners and that she would go elsewhere.

'Stupid woman,' said Ivanka. 'Alaska brought with her many good references for work. We do not need clients like her who do not appreciate the jam on their teacakes.'

'Did you check that the references weren't fake?' asked Della.

'Of course,' Ivanka replied. It was more than obvious from her prickly, irritated tone that she hadn't. Della tutted.

'You get a feel for the awkward customers, don't you?'

'Precisely.'

'It's like Jimmy always says, there are some customers who just aren't worth the hassle.'

'I know.'

No, you don't know, thought Della, *because I just made that up.*

Jimmy had been shut away in his office for most of the day. His head was having a tug-of-war with itself. After a night of insomnia, he had spent a large chunk of the early hours of the morning in the bath trying to map out his life. Should he stay with lovely, steady, loyal Connie or carry on with his plans to move permanently into the arms of Ivanka. Although 'permanently' was a word he used with slight caution as he was aware that Ivanka was over twenty years his junior. Connie was a 'forever' person; he couldn't say the same about Ivanka with as much conviction.

Since Sunday, he had been desperately trying to formulate a plan that would give him extra time to think, but so far he had come up with nothing that would make Ivanka agree to that. Then in the car that morning she had slipped her hand down his trousers and all his plans had gone to cock. Literally. The balance had tipped back towards a life with Ivanka. Now he had a migraine and wanted peace and quiet in his office with the blinds down and the PC turned off.

'Do you know Jimmy's wife well?' Ivanka asked Della.

Wonder what is making her ask that, thought Della. 'Hardly at all,' she answered, appearing uninterested by the subject matter.

531

'I would not have thought they were a couple,' sniffed Ivanka. 'She is very fat and ugly.'

Della found that she had to bite her lip to stop herself jumping to Connie's defence. *She's not fat, she's definitely not ugly and she's a damned sight more decent than you are, you horrible girl tart*, she wished she could have yelled at Ivanka. Instead she said, 'I can't say I've ever taken much notice of her. Why do you ask?'

'No reason,' said Ivanka. 'I thought I saw her yesterday.'

'Oh. Where was that then?' Della made herself appear more interested in the stamp she was sticking on an envelope than the conversation.

'In town centre. Maybe it wasn't her.'

Ivanka wasn't sure why she had lied to Della. Her instinct had made her do it and she had to ask herself why that was.

Della had volunteered to go to the post office later that afternoon, the office junior duty. Whilst she was out, dotty Mrs Cotton rang again and Ivanka took the call.

'Oh hello, can I speak to Hilda please. It's Ida Cotton.'

'I'm sorry, Hilda does not work for us any longer,' said Ivanka.

'Can I speak to Lady Muck then?'

'Lady Muck?' repeated Ivanka. 'What is Lady Muck?'

Jimmy, who was just coming round after his

second dose of Nurofen, listened in on Ivanka's half of the conversation.

'Are you Lady Muck?' asked Mrs Cotton.

'No, I am not Lady Muck.' Ivanka was affronted.

'I forgot to leave Hilda's payment out for her. I must set up this direct debit. What's Lady Muck's account number?'

'I don't know what you are talking about. Hilda has left us so how can I help you?'

'Have I got the wrong number?'

'Obviously you have got the wrong number.'

Jimmy decided that he really would have to put Ivanka on a customer service course. She had the telephone manner of the Gestapo.

'Oh I'm sorry. Goodbye then,' said Mrs Cotton.

'Silly old witch,' said Ivanka, after putting down the phone.

'Who was that?' asked Jimmy, popping his head out of the door.

'Mrs Cotton. She was one of Hilda's clients.' Ivanka drew a circle in the air next to her head. 'She is ninety-nine pences short of a pound.'

'What was that bit about Lady Muck?' asked Jimmy, his interest sparked.

'She wanted the account number of Lady Muck so she could set up a direct debit.'

'What or who the hell is Lady Muck?'

'Jimmy, I have no clue and I don't care. I am busy trying to find cleaners to replace your idiot work force.'

Jimmy slunk back in his office, switched on his

PC and looked for Lady Muck on the internet. He couldn't find anything local or relevant. He might, though, after some further digging, he decided. He'd ask Della to do some detective work when she came back.

CHAPTER 87

Something had been niggling Jimmy since Mrs Cotton's phone call earlier that day. It wasn't his imagination either that Della had reacted strangely when he asked her if she could find anything out about someone called Lady Muck.

'Lady Muck?' she said, running the name through her brain. 'Never heard of them.'

Just for a moment then she had looked jumpy, nervous and then overcome it as fast, but it was enough of a reaction to flag up an alert in Jimmy's head.

Ordinarily, Della could find needles in haystacks blindfolded with big padded gloves on, but she couldn't discover a single thing about Lady Muck. She said that she had rung Hilda to ask who she was, but her call wasn't answered. And another thing, why had Della said that she had never heard of *them*, before Jimmy had clarified that they were a cleaning firm?

'Ring Wenda then, she and Hilda are as thick as thieves,' Jimmy told her.

Apparently Wenda hadn't picked up either, nor Sandra nor Ava.

'This is all a bit odd,' said Jimmy, starting to smell something in the air which was rat-scented.

'I don't see what's odd about a group of women not wanting to talk to someone after they were thrown out of their jobs,' humphed Della.

'They walked,' corrected Jimmy.

'They had their reasons for going,' re-corrected Della.

'Well a couple might have; the others followed like bloody sheep. Oh, I know what I meant to ask, how come Ruth Fallis is back working with us?'

'I set her on,' said Ivanka, proudly.

'Why?' asked Jimmy.

'What do you mean why? She is good worker.'

'Ruth Fallis?' Jimmy laughed, noting that Della hadn't jumped in to offer her opinion. It was not like Della to hold back.

'Yes, her name was in the file of people who were recommended.'

Della realised she ought to react hard and immediately to that. She had the most awful tingly feeling that Jimmy might be onto her.

'What file? There's no file recommending her. She's a trouble-making thief. When did she get a job back here?'

'Last week.' Ivanka threw open her desk drawer, pulled out the red stripey file and threw it on her desk. Della picked it up and flicked through it.

'No, no, no, this is all wrong,' she said. 'These are the names of people who should, under no circumstances, be employed. The Clamps? What on earth . . . Where's the reject file?'

'On the shelf,' Ivanka pointed. Della pulled it out and opened it.

'These are the girls who are recommended and waiting,' she said, knowing that quite a few of them were now employed by Lady Muck. 'Someone has switched them.'

'My God, Roy Frog,' gasped Ivanka. 'The bloody bastard.'

'Bloody bastard indeed,' said Jimmy. 'Wait till I see him.'

Roy Frog seems to have caused an awful lot of damage in the short time he was in my office, thought Jimmy. Or maybe this Frog was more of a convenient red herring.

CHAPTER 88

John Oakwell was on duty so he couldn't stay for a coffee, he told Cheryl when he made an impromptu visit to her house that evening. He merely wanted to drop a present off for her. He handed over a plastic bag, apologised for the lack of gift-wrapping, kissed her and left her in a whirl of smiles and quivering nerve-endings. She couldn't remember Gary ever making her feel like that when he kissed her. She could have quite happily glued her lips to John Oakwell's and snogged him for ever.

He had bought her a book, that was obvious from the shape and size of the gift. She pulled it out of the carrier and found a large coffee-table volume of *The Life and Works of Vincent van Gogh*. She flicked through to find there were as many glossy pictures as there were words. Her heart sighed at his thoughtfulness. He had written on the title page:

To Cheryl, who should be as proud of owning a VVG as the VVG should be proud of being owned by Cheryl – John XXX

God, he is fantastic, she thought to herself, wondering how plain old Cheryl Parker had managed to hook a beefcake like John Oakwell. Owning a Van Gogh was something else, but it didn't make her insides soup like the thought of the big, strong detective did.

Cheryl turned to the first page; there was a quotation from the great man himself.

What would life be if we had no courage to attempt anything?

It was as if he had spoken directly to her and she knew it was a sign that she'd done the right thing.

Thankfully Jimmy wasn't back from the office – or wherever – when Connie set off for Brandon's house that evening. If he had been, she would have put her old coat on over her smart black dress and told him she was going shopping, but it removed the complication now that there was no need to lie to his face. She had left him a cottage pie on a low heat in the oven and wondered what she would do with all her spare time when she didn't have his meals to make or his shirts to iron.

Brandon greeted her effusively at the door.

'Come in, come in. I'm so glad you could make it, Marilyn.'

Box House was thickly scented with chocolate. In the doorway, a hint of citrus featured which was traded for buttery caramel at the bottom of the stairs.

'Very glam,' he said, indicating her black dress when she had taken off her coat.

'Yeah, right.'

'I mean it.'

'It wasn't my intention,' laughed Connie. 'I was trying to appear a bit of a servant and blend into the background.'

'Well, you failed,' smiled Brandon. 'You look great.'

So do you, thought Connie. He was wearing dark grey trousers and a pale blue shirt: casual but smart. He'd had a recent hair trim, and a close shave, but still managed to appear more slightly rough artisan than the smooth corporate man look that Jimmy achieved so effortlessly.

Connie followed him first into the dining room where a towering chocolate fountain on the table was the focus of attention and then into the kitchen where platters of chocolate filled every available surface amid trays set with empty wine glasses.

'I'll be circulating as well,' he said. 'But another pair of hands would be good and no doubt my sisters will dive in if they have to. You'll easily spot them, they'll have their mouths full,' he chuckled. 'Louisa has been chief tester for the Goddess range. Her favourite by far is the Marilyn. Madeleine has a penchant for anything with salt and caramel. My brother, alas, won't be here. That means there will be some wine left for other people.'

Connie noticed little cards on the trays – 'Greta

Garbo', 'Lana Turner' – and 'Marilyn Monroe' sat in the middle of the quirky hearts.

'Help yourself to anything,' said Brandon, throwing his arms wide.

'Wonderful. I have my eye on that lovely writing desk in your study,' smiled Connie.

Brandon wagged his finger at her. 'Cheeky,' he said and winked at her and Connie's insides turned as runny as the soft toffee in the Greer Garsons.

The press arrived with the first few guests to take pictures of Brandon in various poses: holding a tray of chocolates, standing by the chocolate fountain, looking wistfully out of the window, which was by far the most awkward of the poses he had to make. He pulled a face at Connie when the photographer asked if he would mind standing at the bottom of the stairs with his elbow resting on the newel post, staring pensively up at the ceiling. He breathed a very large sigh of relief when that part of the evening was over.

As the photographer left, two women gushed into the house and towards Brandon. They had to be his sisters, thought Connie, watching them embrace and smile and chat. Then in strutted the horribly familiar figure of Helena, followed by an even slimmer blonde with similar features and a portly man in a very loud knitted jumper. Connie watched as Helena made a bee-line for Brandon, proffering both cheeks to him and pulling over the woman who must be the sister Brandon had told her about, but he bobbed his head at her without kissing her, then shook Helena's husband's hand politely but briefly. He made his excuses and went off to greet more new arrivals.

Connie headed towards them with a tray of wine. Helena swept up a glass of red without any acknowledgement or thanks. As she moved off, Connie heard Helena say in a loud voice, 'That's the one I was telling you about.' Connie swapped her tray of drinks for one of chocolates. She tried to appear as invisible as possible as she wove between the people but it was with more than a little dread that she approached the part of the room where Helena's party posed.

'Here, let me help you,' said a voice behind her in the kitchen. It was Brandon's sister. 'Bran tells me you're his inspiration for the Marilyns. They are my absolute fave. Nice to meet you, by the way, Connie. I'm Louisa.' The pretty, smiling woman held out her hand to Connie. 'I'll send Mad over to say hello to you when she stops flirting with the reporter from the *Express*.'

'Thank you, that's very kind of you.'

'I've promised Bran I won't eat everything, but I had my fingers crossed when I said it,' she grinned, picking up a tray of honey and apple truffles and gliding off into the dining room with them.

Connie poured some more wine into glasses. She noticed that Brandon's other sister Madeleine was carrying a tray of empties towards the dishwasher.

'You all right?' asked Brandon, suddenly appearing at her side. 'I didn't expect everyone that I invited to turn up, but it appears they have.'

'I'm fine, you go and do your thing,' said Connie.

'You're a diamond,' he said. She would have laughed at that, if she hadn't been so busy.

Connie picked up a tray of Marilyn Monroes and circulated. They seemed to be very popular. Brandon was talking to a woman who was taking notes. Everyone looked as if they were having a great time. Connie could barely keep up with the wine distribution and was happy to have the help of his sisters, and a male friend of Brandon's stepped in to remove all the empty bottles to the recycling bin outside.

'Over here, wine woman,' called Dominic above the tops of the guests' heads. He was swaying as if he was standing on the deck of an unsteady ship. Connie could feel Helena's unrelenting stare on her profile as she replaced yet another of Dominic's empty glasses with a full one.

'Chocolate?' Madeleine held a tray of Marilyns out towards the party.

'Don't like those ones,' Helena said to her sister. 'Disgusting.'

'I do,' said Dominic and grabbed a handful, sending a few cascading onto the floor.

As Connie walked back into the kitchen for another tray of wine, she heard Brandon calling her. His shirt had a chocolate smear on it and he had a red imprint of lipstick on his cheek.

'You okay?' he asked.

'Totally okay,' she smiled.

'I am so sorry; I didn't think it would be this mad.'

'It's great. Everyone seems to be loving it.'

'Some are enjoying themselves too much,' said Brandon, casting his eyes over to his ex-wife's new husband who had just staggered into a group of women and caused one of them to spill red wine all over her – luckily – black dress.

'You always get one at the best parties,' said Connie. Her eyes drifted up to his and neither of them seemed to want to break the contact.

'I just wanted to check that you were all right. Thank you.'

And to her shock and delight, he bent towards her and kissed her softly on the cheek. The effect on Connie was ridiculous. It sent shockwaves through her whole body. No, no, this couldn't be happening. The last thing she needed was to start falling for Brandon Locke. Her body was overreacting, she tried to tell herself. She had been starved of affection for so long it was merely responding to a friendly peck from a nice, kind man the way that a ravenous dog would to a scrap of meat. She was glad Brandon moved away then because she knew she was blushing hard.

'Well, if it isn't Brandon's little bouncer,' said a nasty, slurred voice in Connie's ear.

Helena.

'Excuse me,' said Connie, trying to edge past

her, but Helena pushed Connie with everything she had, sending her careering into the table to the side of her. Chocolates jumped into the air and landed all over the floor and the full wine glasses on Connie's tray splashed all over her. She banged her hip hard on the corner of the table as she went down and there were multiple cries of horror before a couple of people flew quickly over to help her up from the mess of liquid, glass and chocolate.

Connie's side was throbbing but that was nothing compared to the pain of embarrassment that she was suffering, knowing that everyone's eyes were upon her. Concerned people were picking up the debris around her and fetching over kitchen roll and tissues for the bleeding wounds on her hands and arms which compounded her humiliation. Through the huddle of kind people around her, Connie spotted Brandon speaking angrily to Dominic. Then Helena butted between them and Brandon held up his hand to cut off whatever she was saying.

'Oh Marilyn, are you okay?' Louisa rushed at her. 'Come on, let me get you out of here,' she said. 'Brandon's throwing that bloody awful woman out. I haven't a clue why he invited her. Are you hurt? Oh my, you're bleeding.'

They walked out of the kitchen towards the staircase, the stares of sympathetic people following her. Connie was trying to walk as normally as possible but her hip was killing her. She didn't want

545

to draw more attention to herself, she didn't want Brandon's evening ruined.

'I hope I haven't spoilt things,' Connie said, trying unsuccessfully to stop tears from constricting her throat.

'You haven't, *she* has,' hissed Louisa. 'It's his ex-wife. She's an absolute cow.'

Brandon took the stairs quickly to catch up to them.

'Marilyn, I am so sorry. Are you okay?'

'No, she isn't,' Louisa answered for her. 'What the hell did you invite that lot for, Bran?'

'I'm perfectly fine,' said Connie, not wanting an argument between brother and sister to ensue on top of everything else. 'Please just leave me for five minutes and I'll be right as rain. Both of you.'

Someone was calling Brandon downstairs.

'Really. I'll just dry myself off. I don't want a fuss.'

'You take your time,' said Brandon. 'People are starting to leave anyway.'

'Go on, you help your brother,' urged Connie as Louisa was reluctant to leave her.

'Are you sure?'

'Yes.'

Connie locked the bathroom door, sat on the edge of the bath and looked at herself in the full length mirror. Her hair was wet, her tights were ripped, there were pulls in her new dress and her mascara had run. She turned her face away not wanting to see more. Her hands were throbbing with cuts; there was still a piece of glass in the base of her thumb which she wriggled out with her fingernails. Her whole right side hurt. Her brain hurt. God, what a mess she was in, inside and out. She could die at the thought that Brandon had seen her sprawled all over the floor covered in wine. Everyone in the room must have been glad that it hadn't happened to them. People would remember the woman on the floor and laugh more than they'd remember Brandon's magnificent chocolates and his hospitality. She wished she could have teleported out of there and back home without anyone noticing her.

She opened the door and saw that the hallway was empty now. The few remaining guests seemed to have gathered in the dining room. Holding her hip, Connie walked as quickly and quietly as she could down the staircase and into the kitchen to get her bag and her coat. Madeleine was in there and came over, brow furrowed in genuine concern.

'Marilyn, are you all right? You look shocked. Can I get you a taxi home?'

'No really, I'm fine. I can drive. But if you'd tell your brother that I've gone home, that would be very kind of you.'

'I'll go and get him,' Madeleine said.

'No, please, I just want to leave quietly.'

'I understand,' replied Madeleine, sympathy heavy in her kind, brown eyes. She gave Connie a tight hug.

'You take good care. Brandon is absolutely

furious. I told him that Helena was not someone you kept as a friend after a disaster of a marriage. He can be ridiculously nice, my big brother.'

'Will you tell him I'll see him tomorrow, as normal,' said Connie and slipped out of the back door. She wanted to get home, and to bed as quickly as possible in the hope that sleep stopped the images bombarding her brain of what had happened tonight.

She had just opened her car door when she heard Brandon's voice calling her.

'Wait, wait,' he was saying. 'Please don't go.'

She tried to pretend that she hadn't heard him, but he was with her in seconds and she couldn't very well carry on ignoring him when he was standing next to her.

'Please come inside, I want to talk to you when everyone has gone,' he said.

'I need to get home,' she replied.

'I know who you are, Connie,' he said.

CHAPTER 89

Connie froze.

'Please come back inside.' Brandon took her elbow and guided her carefully into the house and pulled out a chair at the kitchen table for her to sit on. 'Give me five minutes. I need to say goodbye to a couple of people and then I want to talk to you. Is that okay?' he asked.

Connie nodded, her brain whirring with questions. How did he know? What did he know? Did he know she was a married liar? One of those bitter women who wanted revenge on their ex-husbands? She couldn't bear it if he thought ill of her.

Connie didn't know how long she sat there, feeling like a naughty kid parked outside a headmaster's office waiting her turn for a showdown. It was only five minutes in reality, but it felt like much longer with the thoughts that were torturing her. Eventually Brandon appeared, shut the door behind him and pulled out the seat next to her.

'My sisters are seeing off the last stragglers. We won't be disturbed.' She felt the heat of his big brown eyes on her face.

'Connie . . .' he said eventually.

She couldn't look at him. 'How do you know my name?'

'Because you're a terrible liar,' he said, with an amused smile. 'I picked up on a few things you said that you probably didn't mean to. And you told me that you were born on the day that Betty Grable died, so I knew exactly how old you were. And that your primary school had a green uniform. Ours was the only one in the area that had a green uniform, did you know that?'

'Ours?'

'You went to the same school as me. I'm a couple of years above you and you wouldn't remember me, probably. Hardly anyone called me Brandon, most people called me Chubb.'

Connie understood the reference straight away. 'Chubb – Locke, I get it.'

'No, they called me Chubb because I was fat. Fat with those awful blue standard issue glasses on. I was your prototype typical school nerd.'

'You?' Connie couldn't help the exclamation. There was no way on earth that someone like Brandon Locke could ever have been an ugly duckling.

'Yep. Imagine the stick I got at school because I, the fat kid, wanted to work with food for a living. And I never lost sight of that dream, because I saw this little girl trying to do a handstand in the playground, but she couldn't. And then she did.'

Connie was the fat, clumsy kid of her year. The one who couldn't do the handstands that the other girls did. Then her mother put a package in her hand. 'These are magic,' she had said. 'You can do anything when you wear these.' Bright pink pants, magic pants. And Connie had worn them and managed the handstand.

'I never forgot her,' said Brandon. 'Over the years she became the one person I used to recall whenever I thought I was punching above my weight. When teachers said I couldn't go into cookery because I was a boy, I thought of her steely determination. Whenever anyone said that a tiny backstreet chocolatier couldn't compete with the big boys in the industry, I thought of her, never giving up. And here she is again, inspiring a range of chocolates that I am convinced will lift my company into a different league. That little girl was you. It was, wasn't it? She had bright pink frilly pants on.'

Connie lifted her head. That detail was the proof. She was the actual girl he remembered. Connie didn't know what to say. Her first thought was that the fact that the sight of her young gauche, ridiculous self – and those nuclear magical pants – had made enough impact on Brandon to stay with him for over thirty years was hardly flattering. Then again, hadn't he just said that she had motivated him to succeed? And kept on motivating him through his career?

'It wasn't hard to piece things together,' he went on. 'There was only one Constance in the school records at the time I was there. I traced where she went and what she did. I know your married name is Diamond and that your husband runs a cleaning firm which isn't Lady Muck. So . . . do you want to fill in the missing bits for me?'

Connie rubbed her forehead with her fingertips. She felt as if she had just been arrested and was being urged to tell all and incriminate herself.

'You're Lady Muck, I presume?' asked Brandon. His voice was calm, he wasn't cross with her.

'My marriage is going to end in the next couple of days.' Connie plunged in with the facts, hoping she wasn't going to sound like a total bitch. 'I recently found out that Jimmy – my husband – has been unfaithful to me for the whole of our twenty-four-year marriage and he was planning to dump me after Lent. So, I decided to fight back. I set up a rival company, stole his workforce and am gearing myself up for the moment when he tells me that he is moving in with the nineteen-year-old fiancée he recently became engaged to and I tell him that I know and that's why I'm divorcing him and have tried to smash his business to smithereens.'

She stood to go. Hearing that was enough to make him never want to speak to her again. She made bitter Helena look like Pollyanna. She hadn't expected Brandon to leap up and push down on her shoulders so that she was sitting again.

'You must be very hurt,' he said.

'Hurt, angry . . . oh God I'm so angry. More than anything else I'm that.'

552

'It can't be easy, knowing he deceived you so much.'

'He did worse to other people in my life.'

Brandon was waiting for her to go on. And she wanted to go on, so she did.

'All the time I was telling our daughter that Daddy wasn't around because he was working so hard, he wasn't there because he was with other women. He said we couldn't afford to buy her a car when she passed her test and yet he bought his . . . mistress a top of the range sports model. Jane's grown up in a traditional family unit, yet I might as well have been a single parent. My mother worked her fingers off for us, setting up the business, cleaning, even when she was riddled with arthritis. But when she became ill and I could have put her in the best place for her, Jimmy said we couldn't afford it. She went in an inferior nursing home because Jimmy was too busy squirrelling his money away and spending it on his harem. I can live with the fact that our house is draughty and rotten because he's got better uses for his cash, but I can't forgive him for what he denied my mother and his own child. Even his own parents. We could have had hired nurses, someone to help me deal with three sick old people over the years; we had enough in the bank, but he kept it secret from me and let me bear so much more than I needed to. He stole time from me, which is so much more precious than his stupid money.'

Hot angry tears were dropping from Connie's

eyes, leaving a burning trail down her cheeks. She noticed that Brandon was holding her hands, though she couldn't remember him taking them. Both of his were closed around hers. She could feel his warmth travelling up her arms and reaching her heart.

'I trusted him. He bought me chocolates whenever he went away "on business" and I took that as a sure sign that he loved me. But he didn't buy them, ever. His office manageress did. He didn't care enough to do even that for me. So that's why I'm taking his business from him.'

'Ah.' Brandon's one-word reply carried with it total understanding. What she had told him explained her aversion to chocolate perfectly. His finger rose to touch her cheek and carried one of her teardrops away. 'It would have been far easier to cut holes in his trouser crotches,' he said and she laughed, without meaning to. She lifted her eyes and found his waiting for her, intense in their gaze, which might have been rather nice had she been confident and beautiful and not plain, plump Connie who was covered in wine and squashed truffles. She felt herself starting to blush.

'I'd better go home,' she said, pulling her hands from his.

'No, you'll stay here for a few more minutes until you're fit to drive. You don't want to have an accident on the way home, do you?'

I'm more likely to crash if you don't let me go,

thought Connie. Her nerves were twanging like overwound harp strings in such close proximity to Brandon Locke. This man was too kind, too considerate, too handsome, too sexy to be a calming influence. He was making her insides sing, just like Jimmy did all those years ago when she was seventeen and she had a momentary marvel at how that heady feeling of fancying someone didn't lessen with the years.

'You deserve better, Connie,' he said.

'Yes, I do. And I'm going to have it,' replied Connie with steel in her voice, if not in her quivering limbs. 'I'm going to make sure my business is a success. I've got a lot of women working for me now. I have to carry on and do right by them.'

'Oh, I have every belief you will,' he said. His hand came out to cup her damp cheek and the palm was soft as cocoa-butter, gentle on her skin. She hadn't been touched so tenderly for years and it made her gasp. Her eyelids dropped as she savoured the contact and when they opened again it was to find him so close to her that his breath was melding with hers. She stiffened in shock when she felt his lips against her own, soft and searching, and a mingle of scents and tastes assailed her: the foresty zing of his aftershave, wine and chocolate. Surely he wasn't going to kiss her, was he? Oh my GOD he was.

Then the kitchen door opened, crashed immediately shut again and a female voice cried, 'Oh whoops, I'm so sorry.' The moment had been broken and they moved apart, laughing at Louisa's ill-timed interruption.

'Dear Connie,' Brandon said. 'My little girl in the pink knickers. Why didn't you say it was you when I first started telling you this story?'

'Oh come on, what were the chances that I was the same kid you saw? Besides I was plump with no front teeth and scabby knees from all that falling over. It's not the first impression that I'd want anyone to remember,' laughed Connie softly.

'I've never forgotten her. I've carried her in my heart for years,' said Brandon.

Connie stood up. Her head felt like a loaded party popper and if Brandon Locke touched her again tonight, it would blow off her neck in a shower of confetti.

'Come tomorrow, Connie,' he said. 'As usual. But we'll talk. No work.' He picked up her bag for her. 'Are you all right to drive?'

'Yes,' she said.

'Promise you'll come.'

'I promise. I'll be here after I've finished at Mr Savant's house. Twelve latest.'

He kissed her on the cheek and she wanted to breathe in his chocolatey scent until he filled up her lungs to the very top.

'Good night, Connie,' he said.

'Good night, Brandon.'

She tried not to limp to the car, aware that he was watching her from the window. Oh God, as if life wasn't complicated enough, she was going to be hobbling in the morning. And she was in love with Brandon Locke.

When Connie pulled up in car, Jimmy was in the bath.

'Con, is that you?' he called from the midst of suds. 'Where the hell have you been? I've rung your mobile loads of times.'

'I didn't have it with me,' she replied, glad that she could get out of her wine-sodden clothes before he saw them and the questions started. 'I went late-night shopping in Meadowhall. Waste of time though. And I fell over in the car park. Tripped over a pot hole.'

When Lent was over, she would never lie again. It was too much hassle, there were too many 'truths' to remember, and she hated it.

'Couldn't do me a favour could you tomorrow? Have a trawl on the internet and see if you can find anything about someone called Lady Muck.'

There was a long pause before Connie repeated the name, 'Lady Muck?'

'Yep.'

'Never heard of them.'

'Me neither, but have a look for me, will you?'

'Okay.'

Jimmy settled back into the suds. It was only later that he would remember how similarly Della and his wife had reacted to the name Lady Muck.

CHAPTER 90

Connie didn't have the best sleep that night because she spent a great chunk of it replaying Brandon's kiss over and over like a favourite part of a film. She didn't think about being pushed over by Helena. Maybe if his ex hadn't attacked her, she and Brandon wouldn't have talked and kissed. She'd love to tell Helena that one day. But the harsh light of day brought with it the realisation that it was going to be awkward seeing him again. He'd be embarrassed, she knew. The best thing to do was pretend it never happened. Men like Brandon Locke didn't kiss women like Connie Diamond unless it was in a moment of misdirected sympathy. They'd both had their guards down, but today was another day and drawbridges had been lifted, portcullises dropped.

Minutes before she set off to Mr Savant's house, Connie switched on her secret mobile and found a message that Della had sent her yesterday.

JIMMY ASKED ME IF I'D HEARD OF LADY MUCK

SORRY, JUST SEEN MSG. JIMMY ASKED ME ABOUT LADY MUCK AS WELL. WANTS ME TO DO A SEARCH

Connie replied.

CAN YOU MEET ME AFTER WORK? AT HQ. 5.30PM?
Della answered almost straight away.

YES. SEE YOU THEN, Connie sent.

Connie bent over to pick up her bucket and winced. She felt as if she had been rammed by a rhino and her fingers were cut and sore too. She was so physically low that she felt her spirits being dragged down and knew it would take all she had to stay strong. Lent was over tomorrow. The thought of Jimmy's face when she told him that she was Lady Muck had kept her going through all this; she didn't want to be denied that sublime moment yards before the finish line.

Connie rang four times on Mr Savant's doorbell but there was no response. She stood back and looked up at the frontage to see if she could see anyone at any of the windows, and it was then that she realised why the house looked 'wrong'. Inside, the huge bay window of the sitting room was about two foot away from the wall which separated it from the kitchen. In the kitchen, the window was about two or three foot away from the adjoining wall yet the distance between them on the outside was much wider. It would suggest there was an extra room between them, but there wasn't. There was no door in the hallway between the one that led to the sitting room and the one that led to the kitchen. She was trying to visualise it when Mr Savant opened the front door.

'Marilyn,' he said. 'Do come in, come in,' and he beckoned her forwards with such an excessive circle of the arm that she instantly knew he was drunk again. This was confirmed when he nearly fell over her in the hall. That godawful soundtrack to *Pygmalion* was playing again.

'Marilyn. I believe we didn't part on the best of terms last week,' Mr Savant was slurring. 'I do apologise. Please, please, please.'

'It's okay, Mr Savant. Look, let me make you a cup of tea' said Connie gently.

Mr Savant brightened instantly, as if someone had triggered a change of mood by flicking a switch in his back. 'Yes, let's have tea and cake, lots of cake, Marilyn. I have lots of cake.'

'Well, you sit down in your chair and I'll bring you a drink and a bun,' said Connie, motioning him forward.

'Yes, yes I will do that,' he said and saluted, then walked falteringly into the sitting room, with Connie close behind ready to make an attempt at catching him if he fell. Mr Savant made it safely to his chair and closed his eyes. Connie made him a cup of tea, and took one of the many usual fat fresh cream buns out of the fridge for him, but it was obvious from his snoring that Mr Savant was fast asleep when she put the tray down on the table at his side. She didn't wake him; it would be better if he slept off the alcohol, she decided.

With Mr Savant unconscious, Connie was able to check out the strange anomaly with the rooms. There was definitely a section of house that was unaccounted for by the layout of the inside, but she presumed that it was a dead space. It couldn't have been anything else with no door or even a window serving it.

So Connie got on with cleaning the house and found, to her surprise, that there was more to do today. Mr Savant hadn't done so much tidying up this week as he usually did. He hadn't made his bed either, which was a first and he had evidently been sleeping in Mrs Savant's room on top of the covers as well, as they were in disarray too.

Downstairs the record came to an end and there was blessed silence. Connie hoped he wouldn't wake up and put it back on again. She brushed the stairs and swept the hallway and that's when she heard the tapping again. It was coming from the space between the doors of the sitting room and the kitchen.

Connie pressed her ear to the wall. It didn't sound like water and air rushing through pipes, as she had concluded last time. It sounded like someone hitting the wall with a shoe.

'Hello, hello, please.'

She heard the voice clearly and jumped back. *The ghost.* Bang bang, 'Hello, hello. Please, are you there? Help me.'

Connie rested her ear to the wall again and listened hard. There was someone behind it thumping it to raise attention.

'Hello,' Connie called.

'Hello. Please get me out of here.'

Mr Savant gave a large sleepy snore. He was very much in the land of Nod.

'How . . . how do I do that?'

'There's a switch on the wall in the lounge. It's wooden. It blends in with the panelling. It's five squares up, ten squares in from the window.'

'Okay, I'll go in there now.'

Connie trod as quietly as she could into the sitting room and counted up and across. Sure enough, there was an almost invisible wooden lever, which appeared at first glance like a split in the panel. Connie jerked it upwards and a door popped open. Connie pushed it to find a room in semi-darkness and a bed and on the bed, swathed in a sheet, was the largest woman that Connie had ever seen in her life.

'Oh thank God,' said the woman. 'Can you get me out of here?'

'Hang on, I'll ring the police.'

Connie started to shake with panic. She turned and screamed as she collided with Mr Savant, who pushed her backwards into the room and the panel was pulled shut behind her.

Jimmy's brain was sparking with theories, some impossible, some bordering on lunacy, but he wrote down on a pad everything that crossed his mind. When Della nipped out for a sandwich at lunchtime, Jimmy made sure she had driven off before he went into the main office to speak to Ivanka.

'Get Wenda on the phone,' he said. 'And put the speaker on.'

'But she will see the number and not answer. Della left lots of messages for her to ring back yesterday.'

'You try,' said Jimmy.

Ivanka huffed, found the number in Della's desk diary and rang. It was picked up after three rings. Ivanka raised her eyebrow at Jimmy.

'What's up?' said Wenda in her rough, scratchy voice.

'Why didn't you return the voicemails Della left you, Wenda?' asked Jimmy.

'What bleeding voicemails?' replied Wenda. 'If you're ringing about my notice period then you can sod off, Jimmy Diamond. None of us will work with thieves and tramps and—'

'I'm not. I've got to tell the tax people where you're working for . . . erm . . . tax reasons. P45s and P60s and all that stuff,' Jimmy said, hoping she'd swallow it.

'Uh,' said Wenda.

'We don't want you to get in trouble with that lot,' said Jimmy. 'They'll fine you if they don't know what you're up to and where you're up to it at.'

'S'pose.'

'So, do I tell them you're at Cleancheap now?'

'Cleancheap?' Wenda laughed. 'Why the bloody hell would any of us have gone to Cleancheap?

Talk about jumping out of a frying pan and into a towering inferno.'

Ivanka's jaw dropped open.

'Where are you then?' asked Jimmy. His adrenaline levels were spiking.

'You can tell them I'm with Lady Muck.'

That name again.

'Who else is there? I might as well tell the tax people for them as well.' Jimmy pushed down hard on his building fury.

'Well, Hilda Curry, Sandra, Gemma Robinson, Cheryl, Marilyn Smith – oh hang on, not her. She never worked for you, did she . . .' Wenda reeled off more names of his mutinous workforce.

'And where are they based?'

'Oh 'eck, I haven't got the address on me. I've got the phone number though.'

'Okay, can I have it?'

'Well, you can't have it now because I'm talking on my phone. I'll have to ring off and write it down and ring you back,' said Wenda.

'I'll call you in five minutes,' said Jimmy. 'If you could do that, Wenda, it'll save you a lot of hassle in the long run.'

'Aye, okay. If I must.'

He put the phone down. Jimmy slumped to the chair and shushed Ivanka when she started to drown him with questions. He needed to think and he couldn't do that with her prattling on in the background. He had to herd all the facts into order in his head. The sabotage of the supplies, the doctoring of the website – what if that wasn't all down to Roy Frog? But why would anyone else do that? Who might want to?

Jimmy gave it five minutes then called Wenda so that she could dictate the number of Lady Muck, a mobile number. It wasn't Della's mobile number, he noted. He had been half-expecting that it might be. He rang it immediately but it went through to voicemail. A woman's silky voice purred that Lady Muck was away from her desk at the moment and to leave a message and contact details. He didn't.

Jimmy noticed Della's car pulling back into the car park.

'Don't say any of this to Della,' Jimmy warned Ivanka. 'Don't mention Lady Muck.'

'Why is—'

'Just do it,' snapped Jimmy, brooking no further discussion. 'The fewer people who know about this the better, okay?'

Della going off sick, Della handing over the reins of the company she had more or less run single-handed for fifteen years to a young upstart pup of a teenager without so much as a humph . . . it was as fishy as a four-week-old kipper. But why would Della do that to him? She wouldn't. It couldn't be her. But just to be on the safe side, he'd make sure that any investigative work he did on Lady Muck, would only be between himself, Ivanka – and Connie, of course.

CHAPTER 91

Brandon was making a huge chocolate statue of Marilyn Monroe in his hallway for an event happening within the hour and he was really stretching the deadline. It was almost finished, then he realised that he had forgotten to fill it with all the trays of strawberries banked behind him. Someone rang the doorbell – his guests were arriving and he was thrown into panic. He started to stick strawberries all over the chocolate Marilyn, but she looked ridiculous. More ringing and now hammering at the door too, his guests were starting to become impatient. He could see the door juddering in its frame and his eyes shot open.

He was on the sofa in his lounge where he had dropped off in the wee small hours. He and his sisters had stayed up talking and shared a bottle of wine before they had caught their taxis home. Helena's ears would have been burning. So would Connie's, but in quite a different way. His sisters agreed that Connie looked like a total sweetheart and they were giddy that their brother had been caught *in flagrante delicto* with her. He was looking forward to seeing her again today. He had fallen asleep thinking about her: her smell, her gentleness, her soft grey eyes, her surprising core of steel.

But there really was someone insistently ringing the doorbell, that was what had dragged him from his dream back into consciousness. He sprang to his feet and hoped it wasn't Helena because it smacked of her impatience.

But when he unlocked it, it was to find an elderly woman in a dark coat holding the hand of a small, blonde-haired toddler with huge, bright eyes.

'I'm sorry to disturb you,' she said, 'but do you have the time please?'

'Oh, er, yes.' He absently tilted his wrist to look at his watch but he must have taken it off before he had fallen asleep. 'Just bear with me one minute,' he said and darted into the kitchen to refer to the clock on the wall.

'It's half past one,' he said, returning to the old lady.

'Thank you, so much,' she said, tugging at the little boy's hand as he seemed reluctant to leave. 'Come on, love. Let's go home.'

That was quite odd, thought Brandon, but then his thoughts were hijacked by the realisation that if it was half-past one, why hadn't Connie arrived yet? She'd promised she would be here by twelve and they'd talk. Was she embarrassed about last night? Did she think she had told him too much?

He had the number for Lady Muck's office stored in his mobile phone so he rang it, but it went through to voicemail. He left a message asking Connie to contact him because he very much wanted to see her, then went to make himself a cup of restorative coffee and waited impatiently for her to return his call. Fifteen minutes passed and he rang again, hoping that nothing was wrong. When he'd seen her after Helena had assaulted her, he'd wanted to scoop her up in his arms and carry her away. The sight of her so vulnerable, her grey eyes bright with tears, had been the moment that fanned the flame of his growing affection for her into something much more raging. He had felt in her kiss that his feelings weren't running just one way. *So where was she?*

He recalled a previous conversation he'd had about the client Connie visited on Wednesday mornings who lived in the spooky undertaker's house. He knew he was being ridiculously dramatic for even thinking about driving past the house to see if she was running late, but still, he snatched up his car keys from the work surface.

Connie hammered on the door with her fists, which were now sore from the repeated action.

'Mr Savant, you let me out now before you get into trouble.'

'He won't,' said the woman on the bed. 'He's frightened.'

'Frightened? Maybe he wants to try being locked

up in a room that no one knows about,' yelled Connie. 'Is he keeping you prisoner? How long have you been in here?'

'Oh, I'm not in here all the time. At least I wasn't until a couple of weeks ago, but I can't walk any more. I'm too big and too sore.' The woman had a high, young voice. 'You're Marilyn, aren't you? He talks about you.'

'Yes, yes I am,' Connie replied. This wasn't the time to complicate things by explaining who she really was. 'Who are you? Why are you here?' She was annoyed with herself for not acting when she heard the voice through the wall the first time. She'd tried to rationalise it away and look at the mess she was in now. Connie sank down on the bed.

'I'm Isabel. Isabel Harper.'

The name hit a nerve in Connie's brain. Where did she know it from?

'He's not well,' said Isabel. 'I've begged him to stop this now, but he won't.'

'Stop what?' Connie's throat felt constricted with anxiety. 'Why does your name sound familiar?'

'I'm a missing person,' Isabel enlightened her. 'I was a voluntary missing person for over a year and a half, but then it all started to go wrong.'

'Voluntary missing person? What do you mean?' asked Connie, scanning the room for anything she could use to get out of here. She'd smash up the couch if she had to, there would be wood inside it and possibly some metal.

'I met Julian . . . Mr Savant in a café in Sheffield. I was crying. He bought me a coffee and a bun. He was kind.'

'How old are you?'

'Twenty-two,' said Isabel. 'I don't want to be here when I'm twenty-three next week.' Isabel wiped her eyes on her fleshy hand. 'He's lonely and I know he cares very deeply for me. I feel so guilty for leaving him, but a few weeks ago I told him that I wanted to go home now.'

'Were you . . . were you like that . . .? Er . . .'

Connie realised she should never have started that question. There was no polite way to ask if Isabel had been that size when she met Mr Savant. She couldn't have been, really. She couldn't move.

'I've always been big,' said Isabel. 'I like food. I take comfort in it. I know you shouldn't, but I do. My parents aren't like me at all. We used to argue a lot. One day, we had a huge row. I left home, I wanted to eat and eat until I was sick, eat the pain away. You won't know what I mean . . .'

Connie reached over for Isabel's plump hand, a gesture of sympathy, empathy, total understanding. She did know what she meant. She'd had years of attaching emotion to food, confusing love and chocolate.

'Julian said he needed a housekeeper. I had nowhere else to go so I came to live here. I didn't tell anyone where I'd gone; I wanted them all to worry. Julian did all the housework though, he just wanted to sit and talk and drink tea and he brought me buns and milk shakes and he loved to see me eat. He enjoyed taking care of me. He treated me like a princess.'

Nausea rocked Connie's stomach. 'Were you lovers then?' She tried not to think about the visuals of that.

'No, no,' said Isabel. 'He *tended* me. I'd never had anyone who thought I was beautiful before. The more I ate, the more he adored me. It was wonderful, for a while.'

'Then you changed your mind. You wanted out?'

'There's only so long you can pretend the rest of the world doesn't exist, even protected as I am in this house. It was wrong of me to just disappear. The police have spent so much money trying to find me, my family think I'm dead and I need to try and make amends for that. So, I told Julian I wanted to leave and he said that was impossible. He couldn't live without me. He loves me. He wouldn't hurt me . . .'

'He is hurting you, love,' said Connie. 'He's killing you.' Now she knew where all the cakes came into the equation.

'I don't want him to go to prison. He's a very sad man. He said he'd find me some company. He said he'd find me a friend.'

Jesus, he was trying to fatten me *up,* thought Connie. He was mad. She launched herself against the wall and screamed.

571

'It won't do you any good,' said Isabel. 'There was another cleaner who came before you but she didn't take any notice. I kept knocking but she never answered.'

'I'm afraid that I shall be getting out of here somehow,' said Connie. The man was bonkers if he thought she was going to stay at Crow Edge just to keep this poor woman company. It was like being in a Stephen King horror story. *Misery*. Although, in this instance, Mr Savant did his hobbling with meringues, eclairs and Devil's food cake.

Brandon drove slowly past the old house so that he could see down the drive and was at first totally relieved to see that Connie's car was still there. But his second thought squashed any delight he might have felt because it was now nearly three hours since she should have left Crow Edge. So what was she still doing in there? Connie would have let him know if she was going to be late, he felt sure of it. Brandon could not shake off the suspicion that something wasn't quite right. In fact that's exactly what Connie had said about the place when they had been talking about it the previous week. She also told him that she'd been wary of her client, and that he'd been drunk. Brandon decided that he'd call into Crow Edge and find out what had happened to her; he'd rather Connie was avoiding him than be in any danger. He turned his car around at the first available opportunity and pulled into Mr Savant's drive. A chill wriggled down his spine as he rang the doorbell. He'd always thought this a strange-looking house whenever he passed it. No one answered so he rang and rang again repeatedly. Someone was in, though, because there was music playing loudly enough to hear from outside and the curtain in the large front window had just moved.

Brandon had been about to try the handle when the door opened a few inches and part of a man's face appeared in the space.

'What do you want?' he said.

'I'm looking for C . . . Marilyn Smith. Your cleaner. I need to speak to her urgently.'

'I don't know anyone by that name,' said Mr Savant and made to shut the door. Brandon, knowing that was a lie, rammed his shoulder against it, hard enough to force his way in.

'I need to know where she is – and now,' he said, charging past Mr Savant into the large square hallway. 'Connie,' he called. 'Connie, where are you?' But he couldn't hear anything for the music. Followed at a close distance by Mr Savant, Brandon strode towards the huge gramophone and lifted the needle off the record. The silence made his ears ring.

'What do you think you're doing?' Mr Savant made a grab for Brandon's arm, but he was no match for the younger man's strength.

'Connie, where are you?'

In the secret room, Connie heard that blessed voice and her whole body flooded with joy.

'Brandon! In here, in here. Behind the wall.' Brandon heard Connie's muted voice.

He felt along the wooden panels. 'Where? I can't get in.' Brandon cried out as something solid and heavy hit him in the shoulder. He spun round and raised his fist, but he couldn't hit the elderly man square in the jaw, which is where his punch would have landed, so he pushed him backwards with all his strength instead and Mr Savant toppled but, at least, had a soft landing on his sofa.

In the hidden room, Connie was manic with relief. 'There's a lever, Brandon. It's . . .' She turned to Isabel to be reminded.

'Five panels up, ten in from the window,' said Isabel. She was huddled in the sheet, shaking and frightened. There was silence as Brandon searched, then there was a crunch, a creak, a sliver of light, and Connie and Brandon threw themselves at each other and he held her so tightly against him that he squeezed all the air from her. Then he pulled her away from him to study her face as he stroked her hair back from it.

'Are you all right? Did he harm you?'

'I'm fine,' replied Connie. *Now that you're here.*

'I was so worried.' He crushed her to him again. She could feel his breath on her neck.

'Please don't get the police,' cried Isabel. She could hear Mr Savant sobbing hard.

Brandon looked beyond Connie into the room at the gargantuan woman on a sofa scattered with throws and cushions.

'We're going to have to, love,' said Connie, not wanting Brandon Locke to ever let her go.

CHAPTER 92

Four police cars, a fire engine and two ambulances were there within fifteen minutes. The fireman had to break down the wall to release Isabel as she was too large to fit through the panelled door. She was very distressed at the sight of Mr Savant being read his rights; he looked shrunken and confused. Connie wasn't so forgiving.

'That poor girl,' she said, watching the ambulance men trying to manoeuvre her out. Delayed panic crashed into Connie's head about what might have been if Brandon hadn't arrived to save her and she started shaking. She felt Brandon's arm slip around her, rubbing warmth back into her and just for a moment, she let herself believe that this was her husband. Being Mrs Brandon Locke would be such a different life from being Mrs Jimmy Diamond.

There were policemen everywhere, more had arrived. Brandon sat with Connie whilst one of them took notes from her. Then one of the paramedics asked to check her over. He was urging her to go to hospital.

'He didn't touch me,' said Connie. 'I'm all right.'

'Can she leave?' asked Brandon.

'We've got your contact details. We'll obviously need to be in touch,' said a policewoman with a kind face and voice to match.

Outside, Isabel was at last being lifted into the ambulance. She called over desperately. She was in pain from being jolted and lifted and moved. 'Marilyn, are you okay?' Her hand came out from under the thick blanket which had been wrapped around her.

'I'm fine. Are you?' replied Connie, gripping it tightly.

'My family are coming.' Isabel was crying softly.

'You let everyone look after you,' said Connie. 'I'll come and see you.'

'Thank you, thank you.' Isabel was holding her hand even harder. 'What will happen to Julian?'

Connie was sure that some part of her would consider feeling sorry for Julian Savant in the future, but not at the moment.

'You just concentrate on yourself. Let the doctors see to you and let another set of people see to him.'

'Come on, let me take you to my house for a while,' said Brandon, leading Connie off. 'We can collect your car later.'

There were three cars and a van parked nearby on the main road. A photographer with a long-range camera was being herded back from the drive entrance by a policeman. Brandon opened his car door for Connie and shielded her from the searching lens with the bulk of his body. Then he got into the driver's seat and set off quickly for the safety of lovely Box House.

'My God, you will never guess,' said Ivanka, reading from the new *Daily Trumpet* local news page on the internet. 'Remember that Mr Savant who lives in the haunted house? He has been arrested. He had two sex slaves in his house.'

'Don't be daft,' scoffed Della. 'He was nearly seventy.'

'Is true. Look.'

Della and Jimmy came to read over Ivanka's shoulder. The news report didn't contain much detail, but the comments underneath from neighbours and gossipy sensationalists provided substantial padding.

'You can't rely on what's written there for facts. Look, someone has said there was a man carried out on a trolley who looked dead because he was completely covered in a blanket, someone else has said that a man and a woman came out of the house and drove off together,' said Jimmy. 'Sex slaves my arse.'

'This is the *Daily Trumpet* after all,' said Della. 'They reported yesterday that a vet had to tranquillise the mayor for running amok in the park when it was *a mare*. When I come back from the loo, I'll put the kettle on.'

She found she was shaking when she locked

herself in the toilet to ring Connie and make sure she was all right because she knew she cleaned for Mr Savant on Wednesdays. Della laughed with relief when Connie picked up, said she was fine and, though she might be there slightly later than planned, she'd fill her in with the details at Lady Muck HQ.

Brandon made Connie a hot chocolate.

'I don't care if you hate chocolate, you're having this,' he said, stirring it as he brought it over to the kitchen table, where she was sitting. 'It's warm, it's sweet and it's nourishing.'

Connie had no intention of protesting. She lifted the mug to her mouth and inhaled the rich scent of raspberries swirled up in the creamy chocolate. It tasted as good as it smelled, like a liquid summer pudding.

'How did you know where I'd be?' asked Connie.

'I remembered us talking about the house you went to before me. I only wish I hadn't left it so long before I drove out there. I dread to think what would have happened if that woman hadn't come to the door.' He blew out his cheeks and raised his eyebrows as he sat down on the chair next to her.

'What woman?'

'I fell asleep on the sofa. Someone woke me up at half-past one ringing the bell. A woman with a little boy, her grandchild I presume from their ages. She said she was sorry for disturbing me, but did I have the time. It was then that I realised you were late. I rang the Lady Muck number but it went straight to voicemail so I thought I'd better check things out.' He nodded as if thinking to himself. 'It was all a bit weird when I think about it. I'd never seen her before, and there's a pub in sight, so why wouldn't you go there to ask?'

The hairs stood up on the back of Connie's neck.

'What did she look like?'

'Erm . . . dark grey hair, loose curls to the shoulder. Slim, about five foot seven. She had a navy-blue coat on, buttoned right up to the top.'

'And the little boy?' Connie's throat was dry, constricted.

'Very blond, large eyes . . .' Brandon stopped. The kid's eyes had reminded him of Connie's, but he thought it might freak her out to say that. 'Can't think of anything else, just a small kid, holding her hand. Why?'

She didn't say that she thought it might be her mother and her son come to help her. He'd think she was mad. *It's a coincidence, Connie,* said her head. *Don't be hysterical. It's not your mum. She didn't come back to save you. It was a woman out walking who wanted to know what the time was.*

'Just curious.'

'Drink,' said Brandon, pushing the mug in her hands upwards. Connie obeyed, gulping down a mouthful. That woman, whoever she was, might have indirectly saved her life. It had to be her mum. And she was with Max. Connie's eyes glittered with tears. She made a small noise in her throat that was half laughter, half sob.

'You all right?' Brandon asked, his hand touching her shoulder in concern.

Connie nodded and smiled. 'Yes, yes, I really am.'

'Boy, what a couple of days,' said Brandon. 'Could we fit any more drama into it?'

'Tell me about it.'

'I thought that maybe you'd decided not to come to the house today.'

'I said I would and I would have,' replied Connie. 'Had I not been thrown into a secret room as a companion to a fellow prisoner.'

Brandon reached for her hand; it was small and soft in his own much larger one.

'Will you still go ahead with your plan to leave your husband?'

He was stroking her fingers and making her brain fuzzy and not wanting to concentrate on anything but the sensation.

'If you mean: did the events of today make me realise that I should try to pull out all the stops and rescue my marriage, then you are way off target with your thinking.'

She wasn't imagining that she saw Brandon's shoulders sag a little with relief.

'By the end of tomorrow I'll be single again,' she went on, 'and I'll have to work my backside off to make sure that both myself and my company survive. I imagine that Jimmy will play dirty when he realises what I've done.'

'You'll survive whatever rockets he launches at you, I have no doubt,' Brandon said, his brown eyes glossy with admiration and something else that she daren't acknowledge. This was the wrong time for them to fall in love.

'I don't want you to be my cleaner any more,' said Brandon.

'I understand,' nodded Connie. As hard as it was to hear, he was right and she had been about to say the same.

'No, you don't. I want you . . . us . . . to be . . . more. I love being with you, Connie. I can't stop thinking about you.'

Oh, these were words which she shouldn't take to heart and yet she very much wanted to seize them and hold them to her like a warm, soft cushion.

Connie put her hand gently on his face.

'You and I both know what happens when you rush into rebound relationships.'

'You're not Helena,' said Brandon, taking her hand from his cheek and kissing the palm.

'Thank God you noticed,' smiled Connie. Oh, she wanted to lean forwards and feel those lips on her own. But her head was bursting at the seams. She had a band of wonderful women who must take priority for the foreseeable future. She was primed to fight now, not to love. This was the worst timing ever.

'I'm falling for you, Miss Pink Knickers,' said Brandon. 'But I know you need time. Don't forget me, will you. You came back into my life when I needed some more inspiration. I think that means we are kind of spiritually tied, so I know our paths will cross again. They have to. It's written in the stars.'

He's so absolutely gorgeous, thought Connie, but too many people were relying on her not to let her ship capsize. She had used the women for her own ends, now she owed them security.

'Drive me back for my car, please,' said Connie.

'Only if you kiss me. Just once more. So I have a memory of you every time I work with chocolate and raspberries.'

Connie leaned forward and savoured Brandon's arms closing around her, his lips on hers, his fingers in her hair. Her gallant chocolatier, who would make her think of kisses and brown eyes and strong square hands, cherries, Indian vanilla pods and summer pudding-filled hearts whenever there was a whisper of chocolate in the air.

CHAPTER 93

Della had finished her third coffee when Connie arrived in Lady Muck HQ. To Connie's surprise, Della threw her arms around her as soon as she reached the top of the stairs; then, as if remembering that she didn't do that sort of thing, she took a step backwards.

'I was so worried about you, Connie,' she said.

'Oh Della, I'm sorry I'm so late . . .' Connie began, but Della wouldn't hear the apology.

'It doesn't matter. I don't have much else to do in the evenings. Are you all right? I only wish I'd listened when the girls said they'd heard strange voices in Mr Savant's house.'

'To be fair, anyone would be more inclined to believe there was a ghost in an ex-undertaker's house than a forty-stone woman locked up in a secret room.'

'Forty stone?'

'I'm guessing. She was very large.'

'The poor girl,' said Della.

'I rang the hospital but they won't tell me a thing. I imagine there are a lot of reporters chasing a story.'

'You're lucky they haven't come after you,' said Della.

'Isabel – that's the girl – thinks my name is Marilyn Smith. If any reporters speak to her and she gives them that name, I'm hoping that'll hold them off from tracing me. At least until tomorrow is over. Coffee?'

'Yes, please.' Della didn't say she was all coffee-ed out.

'Oh, and Jimmy has found the number out for Lady Muck. I found four missed calls on my mobile from his office number. He didn't leave any message,' Connie revealed. 'I'm guessing he didn't recognise my voice from the recorded message though.'

'It was only a matter of time before he—'

In her bag, Connie's Lady Muck mobile phone rumbled loudly. She pulled it out quickly and flashed a panicked look at Della.

'It's him again.' *Talk of the devil and he's sure to appear.* One of her mum's classic sayings.

'Keep calm,' Della said. 'Speak to him.'

Connie took a deep breath and conjured up her inner Marilyn. She remained on her feet to take the call. Power phone calls were better taken when standing, she'd read. Della stood close so she could listen in.

'Lady Muck Cleaning Services, how may I help you?'

Jimmy hadn't been expecting quite so satiny a voice. It had crossed his mind that when he rang the number, Della would have picked up. He now realised that was nonsense. Lady Muck sounded glamorous and cultured. He imagined that she was wearing a powder blue Jaeger suit and toying with a string of pearls at her neck.

'Jimmy Diamond, Diamond Shine Cleaning Services. I believe you're my rival,' he said in a voice packed full of bolshieness.

'I believe I am, yes. So what can I do for you, Mr Diamond?' trilled the voice at the other end.

'Can we cut the crap, Lady,' he said, the title irreverent in tone rather than respectful. 'I want to know how you've ended up with most of my workforce.'

'Oh, I don't know,' replied Lady Muck. 'Maybe it's something to do with the benefits we offer our ladies and that we value their work.' She was privately educated, Jimmy could tell. She was exuding superiority and confidence – and she was as cool as a glacier with Ray-Bans on. He was really having to bite his tongue.

'That's corporate bullshit and you know it.'

'Maybe it would help if we had a meeting. We could talk over all your concerns.'

Blimey – Jimmy hadn't been expecting that so easily.

'Yes, the sooner the better,' he said.

'Tomorrow. Let's say five o'clock.'

'Where are you based?'

'Penistone, but we'll aim for neutral territory. F.U.J. Holdings in Maltstone. It's above the old

White Wedding bridal shop opposite to the Garden Centre, do you know it?'

'I'll find it.'

'It's presently vacant but I have the keys. I won't be there before exactly five so if you arrive early, you'll only have to wait in your car.'

She was enjoying calling the shots, he could tell. Well, they would be the last shots she called so she might as well enjoy them.

'I'll be there on the dot.'

'Very much looking forward to it, Johnny.'

'It's Jimmy,' he said, his tone glass-brittle. 'Have we ever met? Do I know you?'

'No, you don't know me at all,' said Lady Muck, and put the phone down.

Connie felt her spine collapse. She was shaking.

'Well done,' said Della, patting her on the shoulder. 'You handled that perfectly. We will be ready for him.'

'Do you think he knew it was me?'

'No. You're nearly as good at voices as I am.' Della smiled.

'I only have one in my repertoire. My auntie Marilyn used to speak like that, really lovely. Like a princess.' Connie held her hand straight out and it was still trembling. 'If I'm like this now, God knows what I'll be like tomorrow.'

'You weren't prepared for that phone call – you will be ready for five o'clock tomorrow.'

'I've enjoyed being Lady Muck and Marilyn

Smith,' sighed Connie, walking into the kitchen to make the coffees. 'Back to being bog-standard Connie tomorrow.'

Della didn't think there was anything bog standard about Connie at all. She used to, but then she'd had her wrong from day one.

'Will you keep the name Diamond when you leave Jimmy?'

'No, I'll be Miss Clarke again tomorrow, as soon as I've said my piece,' replied Connie. 'I dread to think how many documents I'll have to change back into my maiden name.'

'I'll help you if you like,' offered Della. 'Which brings me around to why I wanted to meet with you. Well, one of the reasons. Connie, I have two spare bedrooms in my house. You are very welcome to move in with me until you get on your feet.'

Connie, who was spooning coffee granules into the cups, fell into momentary shock, humbled by Della's kindness.

'Thank you, but I was going to book a Premier Inn for a while. I don't want to—'

'Oh for goodness sake,' snapped Della. 'You can't live in a flaming Premier Inn. You need a washing machine, you need storage, you need some home comforts to help get you through all the crap that is going to come. You need a fr—' Della bit off the word, in case it sounded too presumptuous.

Connie lifted her head and smiled, before returning to her coffee-making. 'I do, Della. I do need a friend. And a washing machine. I accept. Thank you.'

It was an acquired art, accepting help when it was offered. She was more used to giving it. That was something else she should change.

'Good, that's settled then,' sniffed Della. 'I've got a double garage. Plenty of room to store furniture in.'

'I shan't be bringing much. I want to start afresh. I'd rather have a coffee table from a charity shop that hasn't got any memories for me than bring stuff out of the house.'

'You haven't started packing then?'

'No. I'll do it in the morning. It won't take me long.'

'Tomorrow is going to be hard, Connie.'

'My whole life has been hard, Della.'

And Della, who thought for many years that Connie Diamond lived a charmed existence of luxury, knew that she'd had it far more difficult than she could have imagined.

'I think Jimmy's starting to put two and two together. It won't be long before he arrives at four,' said Della. 'I went out for a sandwich today and when I came back, I knew something had happened. The atmosphere in the office was . . . tense. They're keeping things from me.'

'Just one more day to go,' said Connie.

'Are the girls coming here tomorrow?'

'Yes, they'll all be here at four o'clock on the dot, "Lady Muck" told them. They'll turn up. No one would refuse three hours' pay for an hour's meeting.' Connie pulled out a small ballotin of chocolates. 'These are Marilyns. Try one. A client gave them to me.'

'I thought you had stopped eating chocolate,' said Della, reaching in and lifting one to her lips.

'These don't make any false statements,' replied Connie. 'They're just magnificent.'

Ivanka sat in her car, yawned from boredom and checked her watch yet again. She had parked behind a van so she couldn't be seen in her distinctive sporty number. She'd followed Della from work as discreetly as was possible, but had lost her on the outskirts of Maltstone. On a whim, she'd driven to the building which she had seen Connie leave the previous week, the old White Wedding bridal shop. And bingo – there she had seen Della's car parked in front. Della had been in the building for over an hour and a half before Connie Diamond arrived. And now, three-quarters of an hour later, there was finally some more movement: Della and Connie Diamond were both standing at the corner of the building, hugging goodbye before they both got back in their vehicles and drove off in different directions. Ivanka's bottom was numb from having to sit and wait for them but that sight was worth everything.

Sure that the coast was clear, Ivanka drove around to the side of White Wedding. She got out of the car and walked to the back of the building.

There was a sign for F.U.J. Holdings at the side of a door. *Fuck U Jimmy? Is that what that stands for?*

Oh, the pair of bitches if it was. Jimmy was being cheated by his own wife and his soon-to-be ex-office manageress. It was all starting to make sense now, but Ivanka would spend the night picking through the bones of the information she had, ready for a spectacular presentation tomorrow. She couldn't wait: Lent was going to end with the biggest explosion in history.

CHAPTER 94

Jimmy had been sick through the night. He had sat on the toilet in the wee small hours, rehearing his speech to Connie about leaving her, but everything made him sound like a selfish twat. He didn't want to accept that it sounded like that because he *was* a selfish twat.

He got up at six. Connie was still sleeping like a baby. She had nothing on her mind, bless her, that was evident. She had no idea what ton of cement was going to fall on her later today, he thought, studying her gentle face. His heart felt as heavy as a house-brick with guilt. He blew her a kiss from the door and whispered, 'Bye, Connie. I'll miss you,' and he meant it. He had wondered for a long time if he still loved Connie, but now in the last hours of his marriage he knew he must have because his eyes were full of tears at the thought of never waking up beside her again.

He didn't go straight to work, but off for a breakfast to Big June's portakabin parked at the side of the Dearne Valley Parkway, a trucker's heaven. He bought a bacon sandwich but it was rubbery and greasy and he abandoned all but that first revolting mouthful. He couldn't even stomach the coffee because it was cheap-quality and weak as witch-piss. It would all be worth it, he promised himself. When he was in Ivanka's bed on the first night of his new life with the mess behind him, it would all be worth it.

Ivanka swaggered into work. She hadn't met Jimmy for their usual secret assignation around the corner that morning because after tonight they wouldn't have to sneak around any more. They would be free to canoodle in public. At last. She arrived early, ten minutes after Jimmy had opened up the office. They were both in before Della, which was rare.

'What's up with you?' asked Jimmy, moving in for a sneaky kiss. 'You look like you've lost a pound and found a tenner.'

Oh, she was desperate to tell him what she had learned, but more than that, she wanted to play with Della like a cat with a mouse. She couldn't wait to see the duplicitous old cow squirm.

'I am celebrating that soon I will have lots of jam on my teacakes,' she smiled.

'Put the kettle on for me, love,' said Jimmy, smacking her bottom.

'I think we will have an office junior to do this duty,' said Ivanka. 'Talking of this, what time are you going to sack Della?'

'Oh . . . er . . . I thought you might like to,' said

Jimmy. He'd come up with that idea at three a.m, this morning.

Ivanka clapped her hands together. 'Oh yes, I would like that very much. I will do it at lunch-time. You can go and leave me to it.'

Oh deep joy, thought Jimmy. He had to admire her sauce. 'Della won't take being made redundant very well,' he warned. 'She'll be asking for a generous payout. Try and beat her down a bit.'

'Don't you worry, darlink,' crooned Ivanka. Beat her down a bit? Ivanka intended to grind her so far into the floor that only the top of her greying bun would be visible. Jimmy had better be prepared to be impressed about what a truly clever girl she was, and he'd never doubt her abilities again when he discovered that they wouldn't have to give Della a single penny. She would be leaving with her tail between her skinny legs under a black cloud of gross misconduct. That would teach her for trying to take the buttered, jammy teacake from Ivanka's mouth.

Connie pulled the suitcases down from the top of the wardrobe and blew off the dust and cobwebs. Not many of her clothes fitted her now, they were all too big and baggy. She was looking forward to buying a fresh new wardrobe for her fresh new life. She threw the largest dresses in black bags and took them outside to the bins. She collected her passport, bank books, address book, shoes, make-up, toiletries, her treasure box which was full of cards that Jane, her mother and Jimmy had sent to her over the years. She combed through them quickly and pulled out those from her husband. *To my beautiful wife on our tenth anniversary. My love always. To my best girl.* She tore them in half and threw them on his side of the bed. Then she twisted off her wedding ring and tossed it in the box for safe-keeping until she had time to sell it. She packed her photo album and some books and pens and bits and bobs. She filled a cardboard box with a few pans and plates and kitchen things and carried it to her car. Then she took it out again. She didn't even want to eat off the plates in this house. She'd take the bare essentials to tide her over but nothing else.

Her new life fitted easily in the back of her small car and she didn't mind that it did. She'd buy things as she needed them. She went back into the house, had a bath, changed into her nice new skirt and blouse – and a brand new pair of bright pink Marks and Spencer knickers. She was more nervous about revealing herself to the girls than she was about leaving her husband. But then she cared more about them now than she did her husband.

Jimmy scuttled out of the office at half past ten. He didn't like the atmosphere, it was almost sparking from the vibes of Ivanka's intentions. He bought a couple of newspapers and drove off to Sizzles for a proper breakfast and some respite from the mess his life had become. It was a long way to drive for some bacon, but he craved the magic soothing effect the place had on his nerves.

In the office there were more phone calls from disgruntled customers. Fussy Mrs Hopkinson was convinced that her new cleaner, Ruth, had taken some money from her change jar and didn't want her back in her house. Ivanka spent half an hour ringing people who were on the genuine 'passed muster' file, only to find that all of them had jobs now – some in the cleaning trade, some out of it.

Della wasn't fooled by Jimmy's lightning exit from the office. He'd been a bag of nerves that morning whereas Ivanka was a glacial walking smirk. Della read from that that they had worked out that she was responsible for most things, if not everything, for which they had blamed Roy Frog, and that her dismissal – at the hands of Ivanka – was imminent. But she played along with their charade of a normal day in the office – for now.

'I think this is all very odd,' said Ivanka, feigning confusion. 'So much has gone wrong in such a short time. How can this be?'

'I have no idea,' Della said, returning Ivanka's sloe-eyed stare with a mirrored amount of barely covered hostility. 'Maybe it's what you call *hubris*.'

'Oobis? What is that?' asked Ivanka. 'Fat people?'

'Not obese, *hubris*,' replied Della. 'You should look it up.'

Ivanka didn't like the knowing tone in Della's voice, but it didn't matter because Ivanka was a wrecking ball and for the duration of the morning she had been pulling herself back to the optimum angle to cause most damage. Now, she was only a few delicious seconds away from smashing into Della and witnessing all that self-importance, superiority and condescension gush out of her like blood.

Ivanka smiled sweetly. 'There's something I have to tell you, Della. I hope you don't mind but I'm making you redundant.'

Della's head swung around in a smooth cool arc of perfect composure.

'Are you now?' she said.

Damn. The wrecking ball missed the target. She pulled it back again and prepared to let it swing at her a second time.

'It is okay though because you will get a nice payout for working here so long.' She lifted her finger thoughtfully to her lip. 'Actually, no, you won't, because I think it was you who put dye in the supplies, it was you who left a false trail of everything that went wrong directly to Roy Frog, so you will be sacked for gross misconduct and you won't get a penny. Oh what a shame. I am so upset.'

Della smiled calmly and saw the annoyance register on Ivanka's face that she was taking this all so impassively. She picked up her bag and her coat and stood to go.

'You are a very stupid little girl,' she said as Ivanka leapt to the door and opened it widely to shoo her out. 'No doubt Jimmy uses his money to keep you interested and you use sex to keep him interested. That isn't love, it's power. I wish you luck at the helm of a ship which is manned by a crew of degenerates.'

'When we buy out Cleancheap you will be laughing at the other side of your face, Lady Muck,' smirked Ivanka.

Della stood squarely in front of Ivanka, matching her for malice, but far surpassing her in poise.

'One, I'm not Lady Muck,' said Della. 'Two, when Jimmy calls you "his best girl" just bear in mind that he's called every woman that from here to Kingdom Come. I'm his best girl and his wife is also his best girl. Oh, and talking of Connie, this is for her.'

'What is?' said Ivanka.

Della drew back her hand and slapped Ivanka as hard as she could and her palm cracked on target against her spotty cheek.

'That is,' she said, then walked out through the door of Diamond Shine for the very last time.

CHAPTER 95

Jimmy relaxed into his corner seat in Sizzles. He felt all his cares slide off his shoulders as a proper filter coffee hit the taste receptors in his throat. He ordered back bacon, poached eggs and mushrooms and knew it would be as superb as always. He checked his watch and reckoned that Ivanka would be getting ready to do the dirty deed by now. He hoped that she had managed to strike a deal with Della that wouldn't cost him too much. She seemed very confident that she would be able to handle it adequately.

He tried not to think how much of a mess Diamond Shine was in at the moment because as soon as he acquired Cleancheap, everything would even out again. He had to stop fannying about on the golf course for a bit though and make sure the only ball his eye was on was in the office. He'd suss out Lady Muck later on; maybe there was a chance of a possible merger. If not, he'd flatten her – he had no choice. He wanted no more rivals on the scene.

His breakfast arrived and he sighed with joy. A Sizzles grill, a cup of dark roast and a couple of newspapers and all was good. At least it was until he picked up the local rag and saw the picture on page three of a very large woman on a stretcher being carried into an ambulance, holding the hand of his wife Connie and a caption underneath which read: *Savant's prisoner Isabel Harper being comforted by fellow victim Marilyn Smith.*

Ivanka was in tears. The slap stung but it wasn't that which was causing her the most pain, it was that Jimmy called other women 'his best girl'. That was *their* special phrase but if he'd used it for that old bat Della – and anyone else with a cleavage – then he'd ruined it for ever. He could go to hell, she was going out shopping to spend some money and take the hurt away. She would lock up the office and buy things and for good measure she would turn off her mobile so he wouldn't know where she was, what she was doing or who with if he tried to ring her. That would teach him. *The bastard.*

In Lady Muck's office, Connie reached into the ballotin which Brandon had insisted she take yesterday and lifted out the last chocolate. He'd made them with real affection, she knew. The piped M on the top looked like a heart. She put it whole into her mouth and heard the soft crack of the inner dark chocolate shell break against her teeth, allowing the creamy, berry flavours to rush towards her taste buds. It was as yummy as he was.

She thought that Cheryl might like the job of cleaning for him. And he'd like her too. She would miss him, but it was best to cut off contact now before she became any more involved with him. She had no choice – she must blinker herself and concentrate on her business because there were rough times ahead and she'd need to give Della and the girls all that she had. Maybe life would be kind to her and guide Brandon back onto her path when the timing was better – she could but hope. The summer pudding chocolate conjured him up in her head like a magic picture. She closed her eyes and thought of his lovely house, his gorgeous sisters, his smile, his eyes, his crazy-mix-of-grey hair, his fingers against her cheek. As she swallowed the last of it, she placed all her memories of him into a box in her head, closed the lid and tied a ribbon around it. A rich dark brown one, the colour of Brandon Locke's chocolate eyes.

The sound of a key turning in the lock downstairs jolted her back into the real world.

'Only me,' called Della, treading up the stairs. 'I've been sacked.'

'Ah.'

'So I brought a celebratory lunch. Think you could handle a small glass of Prosecco with a Ploughman's bap?'

'I think I might manage that quite well,' replied Connie with a grin.

*   *   *

'Ivanka, will you ring me back urgently,' barked Jimmy into his mobile. 'My battery is nearly dead and it doesn't help that you have your phone switched off so I have to leave a succession of bloody voicemails.'

Jimmy threw the mobile down on the passenger seat and tore away into the stream of traffic.

Where the hell had he heard that name Marilyn Smith recently and why was there a picture of his wife up at Savant's house in the newspaper? Why did they think her name was Marilyn Smith? And where the hell was Connie, because she wasn't picking the house phone up. He rang her mobile – not caring now if she realised he had one of his own – but she didn't answer that either. What the fuckery duckery dock was going on?

He tried to think. He was associating Marilyn Smith with Lady Muck for some reason. The answer drifted tantalisingly past him and every time he made a grab for it, it shot off and flipped him the bird.

'Oh Jesus, this is all I need.'

Jimmy was half-way down the M1 slip road when he saw the gridlocked traffic clogging up every lane.

Wenda. It was part of that conversation with Wenda.

Then he remembered. Marilyn Smith worked for Lady Muck, Wenda had said. But the woman in the paper was definitely Connie and she didn't work for Lady Muck, that would be unthinkable. So why had that mistake been made? This was a box full of jigsaw pieces from at least three pictures. None of it made any sense at all.

CHAPTER 96

Connie reapplied her make-up and studied the result in her small handbag mirror.

'I'm nervous,' she said.

'Just be yourself,' said Della. 'Literally.'

'I can't remember who I am any more,' smiled Connie. 'It'll be a relief to stop lying. I'm sorry you missed out on a redundancy package, Della.'

Della flapped her hand dismissively.

'Don't you worry. Jimmy would have managed to wriggle out of paying me somehow. Plus, I don't deserve one after all the damage I've done to the company.'

'Because I dragged you into my mess,' said Connie.

'I have my own mind. It was my decision to join you.' Della picked up the two empty mugs from which they had drunk their tepid Prosecco. Despite that, it had been delicious. It tasted of victory and new starts – and an unexpected friendship that was growing like a hardy flower from the tilled, turned soil of their lives.

'I can see Hilda's car pulling up,' said Della, nudging the window blind to one side. 'The rest of the convoy can't be far behind. Are you ready?'

Connie stood up and smoothed the wrinkles out of her skirt. 'As I'll ever be.'

Jimmy's phone battery was now completely dead. His temper, however, was thriving. He had been trapped on the motorway for over two hours and to add to all of his troubles his bladder was bursting. At last the traffic started to move and he was furious to find that there was no over-turned lorry, no pile-up, no car on fire to explain why he had been stuck in a car, desperate for a wee and prohibited from discovering why his wife was being called one of two 'sex-slaves' in the *Daily Trumpet*.

When he reached Diamond Shine, he couldn't spot Ivanka's Audi in the car park, but he didn't care about anything but peeing. He jerked his zip down so fast that it stuck, but his bladder had already commenced releasing and was past the point of no return.

'Jesus Christ,' Jimmy screamed at his penis. 'Are you revolting as well?'

That was certainly Ivanka's opinion when she deigned to make an appearance fifteen minutes later with two armfuls of shopping bags.

'Where the hell have you been?' Jimmy screamed at her.

Ivanka wrinkled up her nose in disgust. 'Why have you peed yourself?'

He didn't answer that. 'I've been ringing you. And you've been shopping. I don't pay you to shop. I pay you to work, and if you haven't noticed, the company is on its arse.'

'You are a bastard, Jimmy Diamond,' said Ivanka, stabbing him in the chest. 'I am your best girl, am I?'

'Of course you are. What are you talking about?'

'So how come your wife is your best girl and Della is your best girl.' *Stab, stab, stab.*

'Ow. You're the only one I say it to and mean it.'

Ivanka folded her arms across her chest, a gesture that managed to look both aggressive and defensive at the same time. 'I have been busy investigating for you and then I find out that in your heart you have no more affection for me than a fat woman and a dried twig.'

Jimmy opened his arms up. 'Don't be silly, love,' he forced himself to say because he really wanted to yell, *oh shut up being dramatic you daft cow and tell me what you're on about.*

Ivanka moved into Jimmy's embrace, almost tripping over her bottom lip.

'You would be so proud of me, Jimmy.'

'What for? What have you done?'

Ivanka pushed him backwards. 'You stink of pee.'

Jimmy raised his hands like an American TV evangelist and implored her, 'Please, Ivanka, just tell me for fuck's sake, love. I'm not only at the end of my tether, I'm five miles past it.'

Ivanka gave a theatrical pause before her big reveal. 'Della and Connie are friends.'

Jimmy waited for more and when none came he laughed.

'That's it?'

'Well . . .'

'It's bollocks. They hardly know each other.'

'I saw them hugging. In Maltstone. They are friends, I could tell from watching them. They spent an hour and a half together.'

Ivanka had his interest now.

'Where?'

'Outside the old bridal shop on the main road. Jimmy, Della was the person who put the dye in the bottles. It wasn't Roy Frog. She says she isn't Lady Muck, but she is working with her, I know.'

Jimmy's eyebrows rippled in bafflement. 'How do you know all this?'

'I followed Della yesterday. Then I sat and worked everything out last night. Except for who this Lady Muck is. She is the missing piece.'

'Who could she be?'

A face took over his whole brain. *Surely not. No, that couldn't happen . . . Jesus, no.*

'Get your coat, Ivanka, we're going to Maltstone.'

Ivanka's eyes glittered with delight. 'I'll tell you everything I know on the way there, Jimmy. You will see I'm yur best girl.'

There was nearly an hour until Lady Muck said she'd be at the office, but he bet she'd lied and would be there early. He changed into the spare suit trousers and underwear he kept in the office. His intentions were brave enough, but he was shaking when he palmed his car keys and his charging phone.

Della opened the door and invited the women in. Every one of them rounded her eyes at the sight of their old office manageress and asked, 'What's going on?' to each other in various formats.

'All will be revealed in the meeting,' replied Della, shepherding them up the stairs, They twittered questions at each other until Della called for order.

'Good afternoon, ladies, we won't keep you long,' she said. 'We don't have many chairs, but there are a couple for anyone who might need them more than others.' She noticed that Hilda had taken up residency on one already.

'I'd like to introduce you to Lady Muck,' she said. 'I know you've all been curious about her. Well, here she is.' Della's hand gestured towards the small kitchen at the back from where the woman they all knew as Marilyn Smith emerged, except this version was preened, perfumed and much more petite than the Marilyn they were used to seeing in her voluminous frocks. Utter confusion was etched on their faces.

'Please, let me explain,' said Connie, her voice vibrating with anxiety in the sudden charged stillness that filled the room. 'My real name is Connie. I am Mrs Jimmy Diamond.'

Connie allowed the subsequent uproar to air for a few seconds before calling for hush. 'Please, hear me out. I've been married to Jimmy for twenty-four years. And for twenty-four years he's screwed around behind my back, spent all our money on other women, and today he's going to leave me for Ivanka.'

'I told you,' said Astrid, throwing out her arms as if she had just sung an opera and was waiting for the applause to commence.

'And he had planned to get rid of Della so that Ivanka could take her place.'

'Yes, yes, I knew zis too. I said, did I not? Woman's intuition. I have more oestrogen than all of you put together.' Astrid was jubilant beyond measure, until everyone starting shushing at her.

'So, at the end of February, we decided to set up in opposition to him,' Connie went on.

'Is it a fake firm?' cried Wenda with panic in her voice.

'No, no, it's a proper, legitimate firm. You'll all have jobs with us as long as we can keep going. But we've got storms ahead. We can't stop Jimmy buying Cleancheap, we've delayed it all we can but when he does he will undercut prices ridiculously to drive us out of business. I promise you though, we will do everything in our power to survive.'

'But you'll sink like the boat-load of sewer rats you are,' said a male voice thrown across the room from behind them. They turned to see Jimmy Diamond at the top of the stairs, Ivanka in his wake.

CHAPTER 97

'*Et tu, Brute?*' Jimmy levelled at Della, staring her hard and straight in the eyes as he passed her, then his head swung forwards to his wife. At least he realised it was his wife after he had done a double-take, because Connie looked as if she'd had intensive plastic surgery since he last saw her that morning. She had eyes that shone with life and energy and a waist and a face that didn't look twenty-four years older than the one he had fallen in love with in RumBaba's nightclub. She was straight-backed and poised and elegant in a way that *his* Connie never had been. It was as if she'd been replaced by one of those aliens that grew in pods in that film, what was it called again? He did a quick rifle through his brain – *Invasion of the Body Snatchers*, that was it. It was slightly easier to think of her as a monster considering what he would have to say to her, because it didn't have anything to do with spousal affection.

'Well, I wouldn't have believed it of you. Either of you. How long have you been planning all this then? When did you set this global enterprise up?'

610

He swept his arm around the spartan office with the single solitary picture of a flower on the wall and gave a sarcastic snort.

'Since your wife found out you'd got engaged to Ivanka behind her back,' quipped Della, which resulted in a ripple of disgusted female expletives.

'You were going to throw Della and me out with the rubbish. Your best girl and your best girl,' said Connie and pointed to Ivanka. 'I suppose she's your best girl as well.'

Ivanka's lip started wobbling and she moved possessively closer to Jimmy.

Jimmy shook his head slowly, disbelievingly. 'You did all those things to damage me? Roy Frog was totally innocent?'

'Yup,' said Connie.

Jimmy couldn't believe she'd admitted it so easily. He'd thought it was more likely that Ivanka had got the wrong end of the stick. He'd hoped she had.

'Do you really hate me that much, Con?' He held up his hands as if ready to catch the answer when it was issued from her lips.

Under normal circumstances Connie wouldn't have washed her dirty linen in public, but here, today, she was past caring what details anyone heard about the rag that her marriage had been reduced to.

'I hate how you've acted, Jimmy. Do you remember how many times your daughter cried because you weren't there at her school plays or her dancing concerts?' Connie began, her voice stronger than she could have imagined considering the weight of emotion attached to her words. 'And do you remember saying that we couldn't afford to buy a car for our nineteen-year-old daughter, and yet you bought your nineteen-year-old "fiancée" a brand new Audi? How do you get engaged when you're married to someone else, Jimmy?'

'Tart,' Wenda shouted.

'And do you remember my mother, who worked way past the point when she should have done, when her arthritis was killing her, to help set up your business. What did you do with the money that we could have spent to make her more comfortable? How many of your "best girls" did you spend it on?'

'Oh come on, Con. Your mum was too far gone to know where she was. Oak Lodge was a nice place. We did all right by her.'

'*Nice* wasn't good enough for my mum. It should have been the *best* place we could afford after all she did for us.' Connie reined in the scream that threatened to hijack her control because she wanted to make every word clear so that every word counted. 'We could have had help with your own mum and dad but you left it all to me, Jim. You didn't want to waste cash on paying someone to give me a break when you had hotels and fancy dinners to pay for, did you?'

'I . . .' Jimmy noticed that every woman in the room had eyes narrowed into slits trained on him.

He wouldn't have fancied his chances if Connie had commanded them to 'Kill'. His instinct was to balance this up.

'Come on, Con, think back. We didn't have an easy start. I worked all hours God sent me whilst you . . .' He stopped. Oh, *no,* what had he nearly said then?

Connie felt the punch of his intended words. She wanted to crumble to the floor in tears; then she spotted that silly little picture on the wall out of the corner of her eye and it was as if it was sending her strength.

Be Like the Sunflower. She was Connie Clarke, daughter of the formidable flower that was Janet and niece of the beautiful, sunshiney Marilyn. She had strong roots and her head should always be held high. Connie finished the sentence off for him and shamed him.

'. . . Grieved, Jim. Say it: whilst I *grieved* for our baby son. You left me to cry alone in our bed whilst you crawled between the sheets of my best friend.'

'Vanker,' shouted Astrid.

'I was in pain as well,' Jimmy appealed to the audience. 'I couldn't think straight. We were just kids, love. One minute I was Jack the Lad, the next I was being pushed down the aisle because you were up the duff. If we'd known . . . I mean . . . Oh hell, I don't know what I mean.'

'Oh I do,' spat Connie. 'If only we'd known our baby would be born dead we wouldn't have had to bother.' She wasn't sobbing but tears were sliding down her face, scalding her cheeks.

He *had* meant to say that, and he would have hated himself for it if he hadn't had twenty-four years' practice of pushing that realisation down. He would never let himself picture his young, broken wife lost in her heartbreak whilst he was between the legs of her perfidious friend Jesse. He'd told himself, and Connie, that he was confused and suffering, and he was, but he had been lucid enough to take what Jesse Mountjoy was offering on a plate to him.

Jimmy's line of defence was always to attack; after all, that's what strong people did: turn some-one's weapon back on themselves. He needed to save face, he couldn't afford for the industry to learn that his own wife and his right-hand woman had trounced him – he'd be a laughing stock. Jimmy Diamond had to be seen to be a man that you didn't piss off. The bottom line was that he was at war with a rival firm here and so he would fight them as he would fight anyone – dirty and relentlessly and he would win. He began to applaud slowly and walked forwards, to the beat, towards Connie.

'Oh, you think you're so clever, don't you? But do you really believe that I am going to let you destroy in a couple of months what it's taken me nearly a quarter of a century to achieve, *ladies*?' He smirked nastily, like a shark circling a pair of injured seals as he took his phone out of his pocket.

'I'd like you to observe your own death. I'm going to make the call that will blow your stupid little company out of the water because, as soon as I take over Cleancheap, you are right – I will stand *any* losses I have to make to drive you out of business, and unlike you, I can afford to do that for ever if needs be.' He swept his extended arm across the cleaners, like Elvis live in concert. 'And the same goes for you lot. You won't find any work in this town and you can trust me on that. All those years I gave you a wage and you do this to me. Well, you'll see how I repay loyalty like that. Watch and learn.'

Jimmy sniggered to himself at the chorus of indrawn breaths. He pressed contacts: FROG and then speakerphone.

Burr burr. 'Good afternoon, Cleancheap.'

'Good afternoon, can you get me Roy Frog, please. Tell him it's Jimmy Diamond and I want to make him an offer for his company. Now.' Jimmy's voice was hard, firm and uncompromising.

'One moment, please.'

Della looked at Connie. They both knew that Jimmy would do what he had to do to salvage his pride. Sunflowers didn't stand a chance against a combine harvester.

'Mr Diamond?' The receptionist's tinkly voice cancelled the equally tinkly hold music.

'Yes.'

'Mr Frog can't come to the phone at the moment because he said he is playing golf in his office but

615

to tell you to, quote: "piss off because he's sold it already".'

There was a blast of gasps and giggles as Jimmy hurriedly pressed the speakerphone button off.

'He's done what? Who to? Put me through to him now. Who'd buy his shit company but me?'

'One moment please, I'll ask for you,' said the receptionist.

'I did.'

There was a pin-drop silence as everyone turned to look at who had just spoken.

Cheryl.

'Eh?' Jimmy exclaimed.

Cheryl gulped. Her green eyes were wide as dinner plates. 'It was me. I bought it from Mr Frog.'

'You?' Jimmy laughed hard. 'Yes, love, course you did . . .'

'Mr Frog said it was a Miss Cheryl Parker,' said the receptionist into his ear. 'Goodbye.'

Jimmy took the phone away from his ear and put it away in his pocket in slow motion. His eyes travelled back to young Cheryl, wringing her hands, then they drifted across to Della, standing with her arms resting defiantly on her slim hips, then to his wife. Triumph was radiating from Connie as she stared at him with unblinking wolf-grey eyes. She looked as if she should have been standing on a chariot rather than on an office carpet.

'Say something, Jimmy.' Ivanka nudged him hard with a surprisingly bony elbow.

'What is there to say?' said Jimmy. 'I've been done up like a kipper.' He laughed at the absurdity of it all. 'Who'd have believed it. Not me. Not in a million years.' Then he turned and walked, with his shredded ego and his spotty girlfriend, down the stairs and out of the building, silently and crushed.

Silence was also reigning in the office space but it was a very different sort of quiet, one crackling with the electricity of joyous bewilderment. Cheryl blushed, hating that everyone was staring at her.

'Come on then, Cheryl. Don't just stand there, lass,' said Hilda eventually. 'Did you really buy out Roy Frog?'

'Yes,' said Cheryl, her throat blocked with trepidation because she wasn't quite sure her actions were approved of. 'I had a word with my Friday afternoon lady, Miss Potter, who was once a business manager in the bank, to see if it was a good idea. I wanted to make sure that the money Mr Herbert left me was put to good use, you see. So I went to see Mr Frog and he accepted the five thousand as a downpayment. I didn't think he would but he nearly bit my hand off. He said it would have killed him to sell to Jimmy, and he'd heard about my paintings, so he knew I'd be good for the rest.' She shrugged, mortally embarrassed to be the centre of such intense attention. 'I wanted to make sure that all your jobs were safe, 'cos I knew they wouldn't be if Jimmy bought out Cleancheap. I was hoping to get a meeting with Lady Muck after I met her today. Maybe . . . maybe, join up together.'

She looked hopefully towards Connie, then Della, but they were both numb with astonishment. 'I hope that's okay with everyone. I did do the right thing, didn't I? You're my friends. It felt right to spend Mr Herbert's money like that. He didn't have any friends to care for, or to care for him. I'm lucky that I have.' She looked around for approval, but couldn't read any expressions on their faces except blank shock.

'Right then, can we have a show of hands from all those who think Cheryl did good?' asked Hilda.

Slowly hands started to raise like plant stalks breaking through the earth, then the spell of quiet smashed, joy burst like a fireball into the room and Cheryl, Della and Connie were suddenly engulfed in embraces and kisses and laughter and the affection of friendship.

618

CHAPTER 98

Jimmy was waiting for Connie when she came out of Lady Muck HQ half an hour later with Della. He called to her from where his car was parked across the street.

'Connie, please, can I have a word?'

'Go on, you go, I'll talk to him,' Connie said to Della. 'I'll be okay.'

'I'll have the kettle on at home,' said Della and got into her car as Jimmy crossed the road. Connie could see that Ivanka was in the passenger seat of Jimmy's car, not looking too happy.

'Can we go and sit on that bench for two minutes,' said Jimmy, pointing further down the street to the seat near the bus stop.

Neither of them said a word as they walked; Jimmy was first to speak when they sat.

'I'm sorry,' he said. 'For everything.' His head was bowed and he was staring at his hands clenching and unclenching between his knees. 'I'm getting out of the game and leaving the way open for you. You deserve it.'

'When did you decide all this?' asked Connie,

not believing him. It wasn't as if he didn't have past form for deception.

'Just now, in the car, sitting, waiting. Well, I set off home but then I turned round. I guess you're not going back to the house again, are you? I saw the boxes in your car.' His voice was quiet, loaded with emotion.

'No, Jimmy. I've taken what I need.'

He nodded resignedly and gave a little laugh. 'I thought so. Ten out of ten for planning.'

Connie made to stand but he held out a prohibiting hand. 'Connie, just a couple more minutes. I want to say to you that I hope you make a success of the business.' He coughed away the croak in his throat and Connie could see that his eyes were glassy.

'What will you do, Jimmy?'

'I'm going to bugger off to Portugal for a bit. I'll dissolve the company, sell the office, get rid of the house if you don't want it and give you your share in the divorce. I'll split everything down the middle, Con. I won't cheat you any more.'

'Thank you.'

A tear dropped from Jimmy's eye onto the ground, making a small dark circle on the pavement. For once it was he who was crumbling and Connie who was strong.

'Good luck, love. I hope you're happy. I hope you find someone who deserves you more than I did. I will miss you, you know.'

He looked up at her and just for a moment, she

620

was back in RumBabas, sneaking peeks at each other with quickening hearts. Two kids with their lives ahead of them who took things too fast and got out of sync and never got back into it again. And never would.

'Goodbye, Connie Diamond. You're a lovely woman. Really lovely. I never gave you credit for how strong you've been. I wish I could wind the clock back twenty-five years.'

'You'd have still done the same, Jim.'

He let that sink in and nodded. Yep, knowing himself, he probably would.

'Goodbye, Jimmy. Take care of yourself.'

She walked away from him and to her car, spine ramrod straight, stride measured and confident, the outside at odds from the inside which felt sore and ravaged, but she knew the pain of that separation was temporary and necessary – and understandable. She was shedding a twenty-four-year old tight skin, so that the new Connie had room to breathe and grow. Connie lifted her face to the spring sun and left the shadow of her old life behind her.

EPILOGUE

*Ten months later – The Yorkshire Annual
Industry Awards*

Connie had smiled when she saw Brandon's name on the official nomination notification because Chox chocolates were pitted against Lady Muck, and others, for the prestigious Yorkshire Annual Industry Awards. And now they were here in the grand banqueting hall of the King's Hotel in York and he must be somewhere in this huge crowded room because proceedings were going to start in five minutes.

Connie looked over at Della, sitting stiffly at the table and looking totally out of her comfort zone by being in a gorgeous black sequinned gown which looked beautiful on her tall, slim frame. Connie and Cheryl had had to press-gang, plead, beg and blackmail her to come here and, in the end, she had given up resisting. Connie chuckled to herself as Della picked up her glass of champagne and sipped on it, then licked her lips approvingly and went straight back for another mouthful.

Della was the kingpin of Lady Muck, organising everyone, dealing with non-paying clients and cleaners' gripes; not that they had that many of either these days. The office was an especially happy place, thanks to the presence of a Pug pup called Edgar who accompanied Della everywhere. She had met a fellow Pug owner in the park where she walked Edgar every evening, a rather dashing plumber called Steven, and though Della fobbed off any suggestion of a fledgling romance, Connie teased her that it was strange she flushed every time his name was mentioned. And that she'd started wearing rimless glasses and having her roots done.

Cheryl was loving the pomp and ceremony of the evening, though. She was in a long green dress, which matched both her shining eyes and the emerald in her week-old engagement ring. She was a rich woman now, but could have been an *extremely* rich woman had she not decided to hang on to her trio of *Artists in a Cornfield* sketches. They were hanging in a gallery in London, but remained her property until such time as she felt that she wanted to sell them; and that time wasn't yet.

Mr Fairbanks completed his book which had a fascinating insight to the work of Percy Lake, his friendship with his famous Dutch flatmate and the very probable influence of a field of South Yorkshire sunflowers upon the modern art world.

Percy's paintings were sold; and with the staggering

proceeds Cheryl had bought a modest cottage, but one with a beautiful garden, just like the one at Brambles – after a detailed structural survey, of course. Lance Nettleton had, inevitably, tried to pressure her to return the paintings but he had blotted his copybook there after telling too many people that he had given them up to Cheryl, as per his aunt's wishes. He hadn't stood a chance and the solicitors' fees had crippled him even more than the bitterness of his own stupidity and greed had done.

They'd been through so much in the past year, all of them. Their lives had been turned upside down and inside out and all for the better. Connie kept in touch with Isabel who was now ten stone lighter and back in the bosom of her family. Her feelings towards Mr Savant had softened too. The court had considered Isabel's plea of mitigation and he was doing well under psychiatric care, though he wasn't ever going to feature on Connie's Christmas card list.

'Hello, Marilyn,' said a wonderfully familiar voice behind her. Connie turned and there he was, mad grey striped hair, gorgeous grin, looking utterly snoggable in a black tuxedo. His pupils were dilated so much she couldn't see any brown parts to them, only deep velvet black.

'Hello, Brandon,' she said, her throat catching on his name.

'I was hoping we would bump into each other,' he said. 'You look beautiful.'

Connie felt beautiful too. She'd had her hair cut short and wore it like her retro Auntie Marilyn used to style hers, and was in the sort of dress that she would have braved too – red and glittery, which suited her now small-waisted, curvy frame. She felt confident and competent, brave and bold. She walked with poise and purpose and a tiny bit of Marilyn's swagger. Her mum and her aunt would have approved.

'Thank you. And so do you. Well, handsome, I mean.' Oh boy did he look handsome. Just being near him again was setting off all sorts of strange fizzes in her nerve endings.

'Congratulations on your nomination,' he said, immediately apologising. 'God, that sounded so stuffy and corporate, didn't it?'

Connie chuckled. 'You've been doing well too.'

'Yeah, but yours is like a fairy story. I've been following your progress.'

Connie wanted to leap on him and kiss him. But she'd had her chance to be his ten months ago and turned him down. Brandon Locke wouldn't be single now. She tried to sneak a look at the third finger of his left hand to see if it was ringless. Any woman he chose would want to rush him towards that altar with their heels on fire. She couldn't be that lucky to find he was free.

'Well, we've all worked hard. The profit margins are smaller than they were at Diamond Shine, but we're doing good. Everyone seems happy.'

Connie smiled at him and wondered how the hell she'd had the balls to walk out of his life. It had been the right thing to do then but she'd thought about him so many times and wondered where he was, what he was doing . . . who he was kissing.

'Where's Jimmy these days?' Brandon took a step closer to her to let someone behind him past and she caught that dear familiar scent of him.

'Portugal. He and Ivanka split up, but from what our daughter tells me, he's enjoying the free spirit life. He's really trying hard to build some bridges with Jane. He's been over to Holland to stay with her and her husband and our granddaughter Maryse, who is absolutely gorgeous. That's as much as I know. Our divorce featured a full and final, financial and emotional settlement. It's great that he's in Jane's life, but he's not in mine.' Brandon was so close to her now. His hand brushed against hers and sent tingles zooming up to her shoulder.

'Sometimes it's best to cut the ties totally. I learned that one the hard way,' Brandon said.

'Yes.' Her brain was mush. She couldn't think what to say to him. She felt his thumb stroke her knuckle, then his fingers close around her hand.

'I've missed you, Connie,' he said. 'I've never stopped thinking about you.'

'Ladies and gentlemen, the fiftieth Yorkshire Annual Industry Award ceremony will commence in two minutes,' came a booming announcement.

Brandon looked into her gentle face and her cloud-soft eyes. 'Do you think we could catch up over dinner. Soon? Now? . . . okay then, tomorrow?'

'I would like that very much.' She smiled serenely but her legs were like jelly. Her knees were vibrating under her posh frock. 'You've never left my thoughts either,' she managed to say.

'I knew you'd come back into my life. I never doubted it. If not, I was going to give it a year and then force fate's hand.'

Connie wanted to cry with delight. Her stomach felt as if a thousand butterflies had just cracked out of their chrysalises and were excitedly trying out their new wings.

'I have to ask,' Brandon said. 'How's the aversion to chocolate?'

'I don't have it any more,' said Connie. How could she have an aversion to chocolate when the man she loved had eyes like melted Bournville? 'Although I never did quite recover my taste for rose creams.'

'Ah, that's great, then, because I've got a new range of chocolates in development and I need some inspiration. And a chief taster. *Songbirds.* There isn't a rose cream in sight.' His large square hand was cupping her cheek now. She turned into it and savoured its warmth and she knew that she'd had all the time away from him that she ever wanted to have. It was her turn to stand with him in the sunshine.

'Sounds good. I'd be happy to help.'

His finger gently tilted up her chin. 'There's a Connie chocolate.'

'How does she taste?' asked Connie.

Brandon's lips made a delicious descent and came to rest on hers. 'Magnificent,' he said.